SILESIAN STATION

In July 1939 John Russell returns to Berlin as the newly-appointed Central European correspondent of an American newspaper. With his communist past, German son and English-American parentage he's the perfect catch for any of Europe's warring espionage services. Through the long Berlin summer, through trips to Prague, Warsaw and Moscow, Russell seeks to satisfy his secret masters, protect his girlfriend Effi and his son Paul, and retain some fragile sense of personal integrity. As if this wasn't difficult enough, a friend needs his help in finding the missing Jewish niece of an employee. Surely saving just one person shouldn't be so difficult...

SILESIAN STATION

Silesian Station

by

David Downing

Magna Large Print Books
Long Preston, North Yorkshire,
BD23 4ND, England.

British Library Cataloguing in Publication Data.

Downing, David
    Silesian Station.

    A catalogue record of this book is
    available from the British Library

    ISBN   978-0-7505-3047-7

First published in Great Britain in 2008 by Old Street Publishing Ltd.

Copyright © David Downing 2008

Cover illustration © Roberto Pastrovicchio by arrangement with Arcangel Images

Published in Large Print 2009 by arrangement with
Old Street Publishing

Magna Large Print is an imprint of Library Magna Books Ltd.

Printed and bound in Great Britain by
T.J. (International) Ltd., Cornwall, PL28 8RW

For Nancy

A safer life

Miriam Rosenfeld placed the family suitcase on the overhead rack, lowered the carriage window and leaned out. Her mother's feelings were, as ever, under control, but her father was visibly close to tears.

'I'll visit as soon as I can,' she reassured him, drawing a rueful smile.

'Just take care of yourself,' he said. 'And listen to your uncle.'

'Of course I will,' she said, as the train jerked into motion. Her mother raised a hand in farewell and turned away; her father stood gazing after her, a shrinking figure beneath the station's wooden canopy. She kept looking until the station had been dwarfed by the distant mountains and the wide blue sky.

Her great-grandfather had come to this part of Silesia almost sixty years earlier, driven west by pogroms in his native Ukraine. He had been a successful carpenter in a small steppe town, and his savings had bought the farm which her parents still owned and worked. Seduced by the vista of looming mountains, his had been the first Jewish family to settle within ten miles of Wartha. Mountains, he'd told his son, offered hope of escape. The Cossacks didn't like mountains.

Miriam dried her eyes with the lace handkerchief her mother had insisted she take, and

9

imagined her parents riding back to the farm, old Bruno hauling the cart down the long straight track between the poplars, the dust rising behind them all in the balmy air. It had been a wonderful summer so far, the crops ripening at an amazing speed.

Her father would need extra help now that she was gone, but where would they get it? Other westward-bound Jews had been less obsessed by memories of the Cossacks, more interested in the joys of city life. The Rosenfelds were still the only Jewish family in the area, and hiring non-Jewish help was no longer allowed.

Her father's younger brother Benjamin had hated life in the countryside from an early age. He had left for Breslau when he was fifteen, but even Silesia's capital had proved insufficiently exciting, and after two years in the trenches Benjamin had settled in Berlin. During the 1920s he'd had a bewildering variety of jobs, but for the last six years he had worked in a printing factory, earning enough money to buy smart clothes and the exciting presents which distinguished his yearly visits. He had seemed less self-satisfied on his last visit, though. His own job was secure enough, he said, but many other Berlin Jews – most of them, in fact – were not so fortunate.

For those whose world barely stretched as far as Breslau, some of Uncle Benjamin's stories were hard to take in. The Rosenfelds had never married non-Jews, but they were not particularly religious, and kept the Jewish traditions that they followed very much to themselves. Miriam's father had always been well-liked by neighbouring farmers and the merchants he did business with, and it had come as something of a shock the previous year when the local government inspector, an old friend of the family, told them about new regulations which only applied to Jewish-owned farms. On a later visit he had given them a blow-by-blow account of events in Breslau during the first week of November – two synagogues burned, seven Jews killed. He wanted them to know that he was talking as a friend, but perhaps they should think about emigration.

They thanked him for his concern, but the idea seemed preposterous. A depressing letter from Benjamin detailing similar events in Berlin gave them momentary cause for concern, but no more than that. Benjamin wasn't talking about emigrating, after all. And how could they sell the farm? Where would they go?

Life on the farm went on in the usual way, up with the light, at the mercy of the seasons. But beyond its boundaries, in the village and in Wartha, it was slowly becoming clearer that something important had changed. The younger men – boys, really – not only lacked the civility of their parents, but seemed to delight in rudeness for rudeness's sake. They were only children, Miriam's father claimed; they would surely grow up. Her mother doubted it.

Then a group of boys on their way back from a Hitler Youth meeting intercepted Miriam on her way home from the village shop. She wasn't frightened at first – she'd been at school with most of them – but the mockery soon turned to filth, their eyes grew hungry and their hands started tugging at her hair and her sleeves and her skirt. It was only the sudden appearance of one boy's father that broke the spell and sent them laughing on their way. She hadn't wanted to tell her parents, but one sleeve was torn and she'd burst into tears and her mother had dragged the story out of her. Her father had wanted to confront the boys' parents, but her mother had talked him out of it. Miriam heard them arguing late into the night, and the following day they announced that they were writing to ask Uncle Benjamin about finding her a job in Berlin. Things might be bad there, but at least she'd be with other Jews. There was always strength in numbers.

She hated the idea of leaving, but no amount of pleading would change their minds. And as the days went by she noticed, almost reluctantly, the depth of her own curiosity. She had never been further than Breslau in her seventeen years, and had only been there on the one occasion. The massive square and the beautiful town hall, the masses of people, had left her gasping with astonishment. And Berlin, of course, was much, much bigger. When Torsten had taken her to the cinema in Glatz she'd seen glimpses of the capital in a newsreel, the huge stone buildings, the fields for just walking in, the swerving automobiles and gliding trams.

Uncle Benjamin eventually replied, sounding doubtful but promising work at the printing factory. The date was set. Today's date.

Away to the south, the line of mountains was growing dimmer in the heat-haze. She took a deep gulp of the familiar air, as if it were possible to take it with her. A new life, she told herself. A safer life.

The train clattered purposefully on. The fields grew larger as the land flattened out, lone trees and small copses stationed among them. Red-roofed villages with solitary church spires appeared at regular intervals. A black and white cat padded along between rows of cabbages.

It was really hot now, the sun pulsing down from a cloudless sky. The platform at Münsterberg seemed almost crowded, and two middle-aged women took the corridor seats in Miriam's compartment, acknowledging her greeting but ignoring her thereafter. At Strehien the sounds of a distant marching band could be heard, and the station seemed full of uniformed young men. Several took up position in the corridor of her coach, smoking, laughing and talking at the top of their voices, as if the world deserved to hear what they were saying. Two older men – businessmen by the look of them – took the seats opposite and next to Miriam. They raised their hats to her and the other women before they sat down. The one at her side had eaten onions for lunch.

Half an hour later they were rolling into Breslau, dirt tracks giving way to metalled roads, small houses to factories. Other railway lines slid alongside, like braids intertwining on a thickening rope, until the train rattled its way into the vast shed of glass and steel which she remembered from her first visit. The onion-eater insisted on getting her suitcase down, joked that his wife's was always a great deal heavier, and tipped his hat in farewell.

Torsten's face appeared in the window, with its usual nervous smile. She hadn't seen him since he'd taken the job in Breslau but he looked much the same – unruly hair, crumpled clothes and apologetic air. The sole children of neighbouring farms, they had known each other since infancy without ever being close friends. Their two fathers had arranged for Torsten to ensure that no harm befell her between trains.

He insisted on taking her suitcase. 'Your train's in an hour,' he said. 'Platform 4, but we can go outside and get some lunch and talk.'

'I need the ladies' room,' she told him.

'Ah.' He led her down steps and along the tunnel to the glass-canopied concourse. 'Over there,' he said, pointing. 'I'll look after your suitcase.'

A woman at one of the wash-basins gave her a strange look, but said nothing. Outside again, she noticed a nice-looking café and decided to spend some of her money on buying Torsten coffee and cake.

'No, we must go outside,' he said, looking more than usually embarrassed. It was then that she noticed the 'Jews not welcome' sign by the door. Had there been one by the ladies' room, she wondered.

They walked back down the tunnel and out into the sunshine. Several stalls by the entrance were selling snacks and drinks, and across the road, in front of a large and very impressive stone building, there was an open space with trees and seats. As Torsten bought them sandwiches and drinks she watched a couple of automobiles go by, marvelling at the expressions of ease on the drivers' faces.

'It's better outside,' she said, once they'd chosen a seat in the shade. The large stone building had *Reichsbahn Direktion* engraved in its stone façade. High above the colonnaded entrance a line of six statues stared out across the city. How had they gotten them up there, she wondered.

'Is it all right?' Torsten asked, meaning the sandwich.

'Lovely.' She turned towards him. 'How are you? How's your new job?'

He told her about the store he worked in, his boss, the long hours, his prospects. 'Of course, if there's a war everything will have to wait. If I survive, that is.'

'There won't be a war, will there?'

'Maybe not. My floor boss thinks there will. But that may be wishful thinking – he comes from Kattowitz, and he's hoping we can get it back from the Poles. I don't know.' He smiled at her. 'But you'll be safe in Berlin, I should think. How long will you be there for?'

She shrugged. 'I don't know.' She considered telling him about the incident with the boys, but decided she didn't want to.

'Could I write to you?' he asked.

'If you want to,' she said, somewhat surprised. 'You'll have to send me your address.'

'I'll need yours then.'

'Oh. I don't have a pencil. Just send it to the farm. They can send it on.'

'All right,' she said. He was a sweet boy, really. It was a pity he wasn't Jewish.

'It's nearly time,' he said. 'Have you got food for

15

the journey? It's seven hours, you know.'

'Bread and cheese. I won't starve. And my father said I could get something to drink in the restaurant car.'

'I'll get you another lemonade,' he said. 'Just in case there's nothing on the train.'

They reached the platform just as the empty train pulled in. 'I'll get you a seat,' Torsten shouted over his shoulder as he joined the scrum by the end doors. She followed him aboard, and found he'd secured her a window seat in a no smoking compartment. Other passengers already occupied the other three corner-seats. 'I'd better get off,' he said, and a sudden pang of fear assaulted her. This was it. Now she really was heading into the unknown.

He took her hand briefly in his, uncertain whether to shake or simply hold it. 'Your uncle is meeting you?' he asked, catching her moment of doubt.

'Oh yes.'

'Then you'll be fine.' He grinned. 'Maybe I'll see you in Berlin sometime.'

The thought of the two of them together in the big city made her laugh. 'Maybe,' she said.

'I'd better get off,' he said again.

'Yes. Thanks for meeting me.' She watched him disappear down the corridor, reappear on the platform. The train began to move. She stretched her neck for a last look and wave, then sat back to watch Breslau go by. The rope of tracks unwound until only theirs was left, and the buildings abruptly gave way to open fields. Farms dotted the plain, so many of them, so big a world.

A few minutes later the iron lattice of a girder bridge suddenly filled the window, making her jump, and the train rumbled across the biggest river she had ever seen. A line of soldiers were trotting two-by-two along the far bank, packs on their backs.

Cinders were drifting in through the toplight, and the man opposite reached up to close it, cutting off the breeze. She felt like protesting but didn't dare. The compartment seemed to grow more stifling by the minute, and she found her eyes were closing with tiredness – anxiety and excitement had kept her awake for most of the previous night.

She woke with a start as the train eased out of Liegnitz Station, and checked the time on her father's fob watch. It was still only three o'clock. She'd tried to refuse the loan of the watch, but he had insisted that the sun and the parlour clock were all he really needed. And she could always send the watch back when she'd bought herself one of those smart new ones that people wore on their wrists.

Fields and farms still filled the windows. Two of her fellow passengers were asleep, one with his mouth wide open. He suddenly snorted himself awake, eyes opening with annoyance, then closing again.

Feeling thirsty, she reached for the bottle Torsten had bought her. She felt stiff after her sleep, and the sight of a man walking past the compartment encouraged her. She would look for the restaurant car, and buy herself a cup of tea.

A young soldier standing in the corridor told

her the restaurant car was three carriages ahead. The train seemed to be going faster now, and as she walked along the swaying corridors she felt a wonderful sense of exhilaration.

The restaurant car had seats either side of a central gangway, booths for two on the right, booths for four on the left. She took the first empty two-seater and examined the menu. Tea was thirty pfennigs, which seemed expensive, but a cup of coffee was fifty.

'A cup of tea, please,' she told the young man who came to take her order.

'No cake, then?' he asked with a grin.

'No thank you,' she said, smiling back.

As he walked away she noticed a woman in one of the four-seaters staring at her. She said something to the man facing her, and he turned to stare at Miriam. The woman said something else and the man got up and walked off in the direction her waiter had taken. A minute or so later he returned with a different waiter, a much older man with a bald head and bristling moustaches. The set of his mouth suggested an unwelcome task.

He came over to Miriam's table and lowered his head to talk to her. 'Excuse me, miss,' he said, 'but I need to see your identity papers.'

'Of course,' she said. She pulled them out of her shoulder bag and handed them over.

He scanned them and sighed. 'I'm sorry, miss, but we're not allowed to serve Jewish people. A law was passed last year. I'm sorry,' he said again, his voice dropping still further. 'Normally, I wouldn't give a damn, but the gentleman back there has complained, so I have no choice.' He shrugged. 'So there it is.'

'It's all right,' she said, getting up. 'I understand,' she added, as if it was him that needed reassurance.

'Thank you,' he said.

As he turned away, the woman's face came into view, a picture of grim satisfaction. Why? Miriam wanted to ask. What possible difference could it make to you?

Another passenger looked up as she left the car, an older woman with neatly-braided grey hair. Was that helplessness in her eyes?

Miriam walked back down the train, grasping the corridor rail for balance. Was this what life in Berlin would be like? She couldn't believe it – Uncle Benjamin would have moved somewhere else. In Berlin Jews would live with other Jews, have their own world, their own places to drink tea.

Back in her seat, the glances of her fellow-passengers seemed almost sinister. She took a sip from her bottle, conscious that now she would have to ration her consumption. Torsten had known, she thought, or at least guessed. Why hadn't he warned her? Embarrassment or shame, she wondered. She hoped it was shame.

She resumed her watch at the window. Silesian fields, meandering rivers, village stations that the train ignored. It stopped at a large town – Sagan, according to the station sign. She had never heard of it, nor of Guben an hour later. Frankfurt, which she remembered from a school geography lesson, was the first thing that day to be smaller than expected.

The last hour seemed quicker, as if the train was eager to get home. By the time the first out-skirts of Berlin appeared, the sun was sinking to-wards the horizon, flashing between silhouetted buildings and chimneys, reflecting off sudden stretches of river. Roads and railways ran in all directions.

Her train ran under a bridge as another train thundered over it, and began to lose speed. A wide street lay below her window, lined with elegant houses, full of automobiles. Moments later a soot-stained glass roof loomed to swallow the train, which smoothly slowed to a halt on one of the central platforms. *'Schiesicher Bahnhof!'* a voice shouted. Silesian Station.

She pulled down her suitcase, queued in the corridor to leave the coach, and finally stepped down onto the platform. The glass roof was higher, grander, than the one at Breslau, and for several moments she just stood there, looking up, marvelling at the sheer size of it all, as passengers brushed by her en route to the exit stairs. She waited while the crowd eased, watching a strange locomotive-less train leave from another plat-form, and then started down. A large concourse came into view, milling with people, surrounded with all sorts of stalls and shops and offices. She stopped at the bottom, uncertain what to do. Where was Uncle Benjamin?

A man was looking at her, a questioning ex-pression on his face. He was wearing a uniform, but not, she thought, a military one. He seemed too old to be a soldier.

He came towards her, smiling and raising his

20

peaked cap. 'I'm here to collect you,' he said.

'My uncle sent you?' she asked.

'That's right.'

'Is he all right?'

'He's fine. Nothing to worry about. Some urgent business came up, that's all.' He reached out a hand for her suitcase. 'The car's outside.'

Into the cage

John Russell lifted his glass, reluctantly tipped the last drops of malt down his throat, and placed it ever so gently down on the polished wooden bar. He could have another, he supposed, but only if he woke the barman. Twisting on his stool, he found an almost depopulated ballroom. A threesome at a distant table was all that remained – the blonde torch singer who had been making everyone nostalgic for Dietrich and her two uniformed admirers. She was looking from one to the other as if she was trying to decide between them. Which she probably was.

It was gone three o'clock. His twelve-year-old son Paul had been asleep in their cabin for almost five hours, but Russell still felt too restless for bed. A turn round the deck, he told himself, a phrase which suggested ease of movement, not the obstacle course of couples in thrall to passion which usually presented itself at this hour. Why didn't they use their cabins, for God's sake? Because their wives and husbands were sleeping in them?

He was getting obsessive, he thought, as he took the lift up to the boat deck. Four weeks away from his girlfriend Effi and all he could think of was sex. He smiled to himself at the thought. Thirty more hours at sea, five from Hamburg to Berlin.

It was a beautiful night – still warm, the slightest of breezes, a sky overflowing with stars. He started towards the bow, staring out across the darkly rolling sea, wondering when the French and British coastlines would become visible. Soon, he guessed – they were due to make their stop at Southampton before midday.

He stopped and leant his back against the railings, gazing up at the smoke from the twin funnels as it drifted across the Milky Way. He hoped Effi would like her presents, the red dress in particular. He had gifts for Paul's mother Ilse and her brother Thomas, things that could no longer be found in Hitler's never-ending Reich, things – as the popular phrase had it – from 'outside the cage'.

He sighed. Nazi Germany was everything its enemies said it was, and often worse, but he would still be glad to be back. America had been wonderful, and he had finally managed to swap his British passport for an American one, but Berlin was his home. Their home.

He turned to face the sea. Away on the distant horizon a tiny light was flashing at regular intervals. A lighthouse, presumably. An extremity of France. Of Europe.

It really was time for bed. He walked back down the starboard side and slowly descended seven decks' worth of stairs. As he let himself into their cabin he noticed the folded sheet of paper which had been pushed under the door. He picked it up, backed out into the corridor, and studied it under the nearest light. It was a four-word telegram from Effi's sister Zarah: 'Effi arrested by Gestapo'.

Light was edging round the porthole curtain when he finally got to sleep, and two hours later he was woken, accidentally-on-purpose, by his son. 'It's England,' Paul said excitedly, wiping his breath from the glass. The Dorset coast, Russell guessed, or maybe Hampshire. The town they were passing looked large enough for Bournemouth.

Sat in the bathroom, he wondered whether it would be quicker to leave the ship at Southampton. One train to London, another to Dover, a boat to Ostend, more trains across Belgium and Germany. It might save a couple of hours, but seemed just as likely to add a few. And he very much doubted whether the *Europa* carried copies of the relevant timetables. He would just have to cope with twenty-four hours of inaction.

At breakfast the elderly couple who had shared their table since New York seemed even more cheerful than usual. 'Another beautiful day,' Herr Faeder announced, unaware that his upraised fork was dripping egg yolk onto the tablecloth. 'We've been really lucky on this voyage. Last year we were trapped in our cabins for most of the trip,' he added for about the fourth time. Russell grunted his agreement, and received a reproachful look from Paul.

23

'I can't wait to get home, though,' Frau Faeder said. 'I have a feeling this is going to be a beautiful summer.'

'I hope you're right,' Russell said amicably. The Faeders probably came from another planet, but they'd been pleasant enough company.

Once they'd hurried off to claim their favourite deck chairs, he poured himself another coffee and considered what to tell Paul. The truth, he Supposed. 'A telegram came for me last night,' he began. 'After you were asleep.'

His son, engrossed in chasing the record for the largest amount of jam ever loaded onto a single piece of toast, looked up in alarm.

'Effi's been arrested,' Russell told him.

Paul's jaw dropped open. 'What for?' he eventually asked.

'I don't know. The telegram just said she'd been arrested.'

'That's...' He searched for an adequate word. 'That's terrible.'

'I hope not.'

'I expect she said something,' Paul volunteered after a few moments' thought. 'That's not very serious. Not like murder or treason.'

Russell couldn't help smiling. 'You're probably right.'

'What are you going to do?'

'I can't do anything until we get back. And then ... I don't know.' Kick up a fuss, he thought, but better not to tell Paul that.

'I'm sorry, Dad.'

'Me too. Well, there's nothing we can do now. Let's get up on deck and watch the world go by.'

24

As Herr Faeder had said, it was a beautiful day. The *Europa*, as they discovered on reaching the bow, was in mid-Solent. 'That's Lymington,' Paul said, after consulting his carefully-copied version of the large chart below decks, 'and that's Cowes,' he added, pointing off to the right. Many small boats were in view, a couple of yachts to the south, white sails vivid against the darker island, a flurry of fishing craft to the north, sunlight flashing off their cabin windows. Only the squawking gulls disturbed the peace.

'I had a wonderful time,' Paul said suddenly. 'The whole trip, I mean.'

'So did I,' Russell told him. He smiled at his son, but his heart ached. He knew why Paul had chosen this moment to say what he had, and what he might have added had he been a few years older. His son was a German boy in a German family, with an English father and an American grandmother, and he was growing up in a Germany that seemed bound for war with one or both of those countries. For four happy weeks the boy had been able to step outside the competing inheritances which defined his life, but now he was going home, to where they mattered most.

And though Paul would never say so, Effi's arrest could only make things worse.

They spent most of the day outside, watching the to-ings and fro-ings at Southampton, the warships anchored in The Nore roadstead off Portsmouth, the freighters in the Channel. The setting sun was colouring the white cliffs gold as they passed through the Straits of Dover, the lights brightening on the Belgian coast as darkness fin-

25

ally fell. They went to bed earlier than usual, but despite hardly sleeping the previous night Russell was still wide awake. He lay there in the dark, wondering what had happened, where Effi was. Maybe she'd already been released. Maybe she was en route to the new women's concentration camp at Ravensbrück. The thought brought him close to panic.

The *Europa* docked at Hamburg soon after ten the following morning. It seemed an eternity before disembarkation was underway, but the queue at passport control moved quickly enough. Russell was expecting a few questions about his passport – he'd left the Reich four weeks earlier as a UK citizen and was now returning as an American – but the German Consulate in New York had assured him that his resident status would be unaffected.

The officer took one look at Russell's passport and one at his face before calling over his supervisor, an overweight man with a large boil above one eye. He too examined the passport. 'You are travelling directly to Berlin?' he asked.

'Yes.'

'The Berlin Gestapo wish to interview you. About a relative who has been arrested, I believe. You know about this?'

'Yes.'

'You must report to Hauptsturmführer Ritschel at the Prinz Albrecht-Strasse offices. You must go straight there. Understood?'

'I need to take my son home first.'

The man hesitated, caught in the familiar Nazi

dilemma – human decency or personal safety. 'That would be inadvisable,' he said, reaching for the best of both worlds.

'I'm back,' Russell thought.

There were no questions about his passport, no search through their American purchases at customs. The taxi-ride to the station reminded Russell of his last visit to the city, when he'd been reporting on the launching of the battleship *Bismarck*, and the wonderful sight of Hitler struggling to contain himself as the ship refused to move.

Arriving at the station, he bought what seemed the most likely newspaper, but could find no reference to Effi's arrest. He didn't know, of course, how long ago she had been in custody. There were forty minutes until the next D-Zug express left for Berlin, so he parked Paul and the bags at a concourse café table and found a public telephone. Without a full address he had to almost beg the operator for Zarah's number, and the telephone rang about a dozen times before she answered.

'Zarah, it's John.'

'You're back? Thank God.'

'I'm in Hamburg. I'll be in Berlin this afternoon. Is Effi all right?'

'I don't know,' Zarah almost wailed. 'They won't let me see her. I've tried. Jens has tried.'

That was bad news – Zarah's husband Jens was a ranking bureaucrat and ardent Nazi, with all the influence that combination implied. 'What has she been arrested for?'

'They won't tell me. Two men from the Gestapo came to the house, told us that she had been arrested, and that I was to let you know by

27

telegram – they even told me what ship you were on. They said not to tell anyone else.'

'Has there been anything in the newspapers?' Russell asked, suspicion growing.

'Nothing. I don't understand it. Do you?' she asked, more than a hint of accusation in her voice.

'No,' Russell said, though he probably did. 'I'll be back in Berlin about four,' he told her. 'The Gestapo want to see me the moment I arrive. I'll call you after I've seen them.'

He hung up and rang a more familiar number, that of Paul's mother and stepfather. Ilse picked up. Russell briefly explained what had happened, and asked if she could meet the train at Lehrter Station. She said she would.

He walked back across the busy concourse, feeling both relieved and depressed. The whole thing was a set-up, aimed at him. Why else keep it quiet? Effi might have said something out of turn and been reported – it was hardly out of character – but when it came down to it the Gestapo were more than capable of simply making something up. Whichever it was, they had their leverage against him. Which was good news and bad news. Good because it almost certainly meant that he could secure Effi's release, bad because of what they would want in return.

Paul was looking at the newspaper. 'The Führer revealed that the new Chancery would have another purpose from 1950,' he read aloud, 'but declined to say what that would be.'

A lunatic asylum, Russell guessed, but he didn't think his son would appreciate the joke.

'Can we go up to the platform?' Paul asked.

'Why not.'

The D-Zug was already standing there, a long red bullet of a train. Paul placed a palm on its shiny side, and Russell could almost hear him thinking: 'This is what Germans can do.'

They finished lunch an hour into the journey, and Russell slept fitfully for most of the rest. Ilse and her husband Matthias were waiting on the Lehrter Station concourse, and both seemed really pleased to see Paul. Russell thanked them for coming.

'Do you want a lift?' Matthias asked.

'No thanks.' The idea of them all drawing up outside the Gestapo's Prinz Albrecht-Strasse HQ for a family visit seemed almost surreal, not to mention unwise.

'I hope it's all right,' Paul said. 'Send Effi ... tell her I want us to visit the Aquarium again.'

'Yes, call us,' Ilse insisted.

'I will. But don't tell anyone else about her arrest. The Gestapo don't want any publicity.'

'But...' Ilse began.

'I know,' Russell interrupted her. 'But we can always make a stink later, if we need to.'

Goodbyes said, Russell deposited his suitcases in the station left luggage and hailed a cab. 'Prinz Albrecht-Strasse,' he said, 'the Gestapo building.' The cabbie grimaced in sympathy.

It was usually a ten minute ride, but the evening rush hour was underway and the bridges across the Spree were choked with traffic. The eastern end of the Tiergarten was crowded with walkers enjoying the late afternoon sunshine.

29

'The summer before the war,' Russell murmured to himself. Or maybe not.

The traffic thinned after the Potsdamer Platz traffic lights, and disappeared altogether as they swung into Prinz Albrecht-Strasse. The cabbie took Russell's money, joked that he wouldn't wait, and drove off towards the Wilhelmstrasse. Staring up at the grey, five-storey megalith, Russell could see his point.

He'd been in worse places, he told himself, and even managed to think of a couple. Pushing his way through the heavy front doors, he found himself surrounded by the usual high columns and curtains. A great slab of a desk stood in front of a flag which could have clothed half of Africa, always assuming the locals liked red, white and black. Behind the desk, looking suitably dwarfed by his surroundings, a man in official Gestapo uniform – not the beloved leather coat – was reading what looked like a technical manual of some sort. He ignored Russell's presence for several seconds, then gestured him forward with an impatient flick of a finger.

'My name is John Russell, and I have an appointment with a Hauptsturmführer Ritschel,' Russell told him.

'For what time?'

'I was asked to come here as soon as I reached Berlin.'

'Ah.' The receptionist picked up the telephone, dialled a three-figure number, and asked if Hauptsturmführer Ritschel was expecting a John Russell. He was. Another call produced a uniformed Rottenführer to escort Herr Russell upstairs. He followed the shiny boots up, wondering why the Gestapo rarely wore their uniforms out of doors. A need for anonymity, he supposed. And Heydrich probably liked to economize on laundry bills.

The stone corridors were infinitely depressing. So many offices, so many thugs behind desks.

Hauptsturmführer Ritschel looked the part. A shortish man with thinning fair hair, a face full of ruptured blood vessels and eyes the colour of canal water. There were beads of sweat on his brow, despite the wide open window and a shirt open at the collar. His leather coat was hanging on the door. 'Herr John Russell?' he said. 'How would you like to see Fraulein Koenen?'

'Very much.'

'You may have five minutes. No physical contact.' He turned to the Rottenführer. 'Take him down and bring him back.'

This time they took a lift. The floors were numbered in the usual way, which seemed somewhat incongruous in the circumstances; basement, in particular, seemed a less than adequate description of the cell-lined corridor which awaited them. The silence of the grave was Russell's first impression, but this was soon superseded. A woman sobbing behind one door, a restless shuffle of feet behind another. A man's voice intoning 'shut up, shut up, shut up' as if he'd forgotten he was still speaking.

Oh my God, Russell thought. What had they done to her?

The Rottenführer stopped outside the penultimate door on the right, pulled back the sliding panel for a brief glimpse inside, and drew back

31

the two massive bolts. The door opened inwards, revealing Effi in the act of getting to her feet. As she spotted Russell behind the Rottenführer her face lit up, and she almost jumped towards him.

'No physical contact,' the Gestapo man said, spreading his arms to keep them apart.

They stood facing each other. She was wearing grey overalls that lapped around her wrists and ankles, making her look more waif-like than ever. Her black hair looked tousled and unusually dull. She tucked one strand behind an ear. 'I never liked grey,' she said.

'How long have you been here?' Russell asked.

'Three nights and three days.'

'Have they hurt you?'

She shook her head. 'Not my body, anyway. But this is not a nice place.'

'Have they told you why you've been arrested?'

Effi smiled ruefully. 'Oh yes. That bitch Marianne Schöner informed on me. You know she never forgave me for getting the part in *Mother*. According to her, I said that Hitler had achieved the impossible – he'd surrounded himself with midgets yet still managed to look small.'

'But you didn't say it?'

'I probably did. It's not bad, is it? No, don't answer that – they'll have you in here too.'

It was his turn to smile. She was scared and she was angry, but there was still fire in her eyes. 'They've only given us five minutes. I'll get you out of here, I promise.'

'That would be good.'

'I love you.'

'And I you. I had much better plans for your

homecoming than this.'

'They'll keep. Paul sends his love, wants to go to the Aquarium with you again.'

'Send him mine. Have you seen Zarah? Does she know I'm in here?'

'She's frantic with worry. They wouldn't let her see you.'

'Why not, for God's sake?

'I think this is aimed at me.'

She gave him a surprised look.

'There's nothing in the papers, nothing to stop them simply letting you go if they get something in return.'

She rubbed the side of her face. 'Why didn't I think of that? Oh I'm sorry, John. I should learn to keep my mouth shut.'

'I wouldn't want that.'

'What do they want from you?'

'I don't know yet. Just some favourable press, perhaps.' He glanced at the Rottenführer, as if inviting him to join the conversation.

'That's five minutes,' the man said.

She reached out a hand, but before he could respond the Rottenführer was between them, hustling him out of the cell. 'Try not to worry,' Russell shouted over his shoulder, conscious of how fatuous it sounded.

Back upstairs, Hauptsturmführer Ritschel looked, if possible, even more pleased with himself. Russell took the proffered seat and implored himself to remain calm.

'Your passport,' Ritschel demanded, holding out a peremptory hand.

Russell passed it across. 'Has Fraulein Koenen

been formally charged?' he asked.

'Not yet. Soon, perhaps. We are still taking witness statements. Any trial will not be for several weeks.'

'And until that time?'

'She will remain here. Space permitting, of course. It may be necessary to move her to *Columbiahaus*.'

Russell's heart sank, as it was supposed to.

'After sentencing it will be Ravensbrück, of course,' Ritschel added, as if determined to give a thorough account of Effi's future. 'And the sentence – unfairly perhaps – is bound to reflect Fraulein Koenen's celebrity status. A National Socialist court cannot be seen to favour the rich and famous. On the contrary...'

'Effi is hardly rich.'

'No? I understand that her father gave her an apartment on her twenty-fifth birthday. Do many Germans receive that sort of financial help? I did not. And neither, as far as I know, did anyone in this building.'

It was a hard point to argue without free access to all Gestapo bank accounts, which Russell was unlikely to be granted. 'The court may not share your presumption of guilt,' he said mildly.

'You know what she said?'

Russell took a deep breath. 'Yes, I do. But people have always made jokes about their political leaders. A pretty harmless way of expressing disagreement in my opinion.'

'Perhaps. But against the law, nevertheless.' He picked up the passport. 'Let's talk about you for a moment. Why have you become an American

34

citizen, Herr Russell?'

'Because I'm afraid that England and Germany will soon be at war, and I do not wish to be separated from my son. Or from Fraulein Koenen.'

'Do you feel emotionally attached to America?'

'Not in the slightest,' Russell said firmly. 'It's a wholly vulgar country run by Jewish financiers,' he added, hoping he was not overdoing it.

Ritschel looked pleasantly surprised. 'Then why not become a German citizen?'

'My newspaper employs me as a foreign correspondent – if I ceased to be foreign I would no longer be seen as a neutral observer. And my mother would see it as a betrayal,' he added, egging the pudding somewhat. It seemed unwise to mention the real reason, that being a foreigner gave him a degree of immunity, and some hope of getting Paul and Effi out of the country should one or both of them ever decide they wanted to leave.

'I understand that you wish to keep your job, Herr Russell. But just between ourselves, let's recognize this "neutral observer" nonsense for what it is. The Reich has friends and enemies, and you would be wise – both for your own sake and that of your lady friend – to make it clear which side of that fence you are on.' His hand shot out with the passport. 'Hauptsturmführer Hirth of the *Sicherheitsdienst* wishes to see you at 11am on Wednesday. Room 47, 102 Wilhelmstrasse.'

Russell took the passport and stood up. 'When can I see Fraulein Koenen again?'

'That will depend on the outcome of your meeting with Hauptsturmführer Hirth.'

Standing on the pavement outside, Russell could still feel the movement of the *Europa* inside him. A black-uniformed sentry was eyeing him coldly, but he felt an enormous reluctance to leave, as if his being only a hundred metres away might somehow help to protect her.

He dragged himself away, and started up the wide Wilhelmstrasse. The government buildings on the eastern side – the Finance, Propaganda and Justice ministries – were all bathed in sunlight, the Führer's digs on the western side cloaked, rather more suitably, in shadow. At the corner of Unter den Linden he almost sleep-walked into the Adlon Hotel, but decided at the last moment that an encounter with his foreign press corps colleagues was more than he could handle on this particular evening. He felt like a real drink, but decided on coffee at Schmidt's – if ever he needed a clear head it was now.

The café was almost empty, caught in the gap between its workday clientele and the evening crowd. After taking his choice of the window-seats Russell, more out of habit than desire, reached across for the newspaper that someone had left on the adjoining table. Hitler had opened an art exhibition in Munich, accompanied by the Gauleiter of Danzig and Comrade Astakhov, the Soviet chargé d'affaires. This interesting combination had watched a procession of floats, most of which were described in mind-numbing detail. Sudetenland was a silver eagle, Bohemia a pair of lions guarding the gateway to the East, as represented by a couple of Byzantine minarets. The

Führer had gone to see *The Merry Widow* that evening, but 'Miss Madeleine Verne, the solo dancer' had failed to show up.

Who could blame her?

Russell tossed the newspaper back. He didn't feel ready for re-immersion in Nazi Germany's bizarre pantomime.

At least the coffee was good. The only decent cup he'd had in America was in the Italian pavilion at the World's Fair.

Zarah, he reminded himself. The telephone in the back corridor was not being used, and he stood beside it for a few seconds before dialling, wondering what he was going to say. Not the truth, anyway. She picked up after the first ring, and sounded as if she'd been crying.

'I've seen her,' he said. 'She's fine. They've told me to come back on Wednesday, and they'll probably release her then.'

'Why? I don't understand. If they're going to release her, why not now?'

'Bureaucracy, I think. She has to receive a formal warning from some official or other. They didn't give me any details.'

'But she will be released on Wednesday?'

'That's what I was told,' he said. There was no point in her spending the next two days in a state of high anxiety. If the *Sicherheitsdienst* was playing sick games with them, she'd find out soon enough.

'Thank you, John,' she said. 'They won't let me see her, I suppose.'

'I don't think so. They won't let me see her again until then. I think it's probably better to just wait.'

'Yes, I can see that. But she's all right.'

'She's fine. A little frightened, but fine.'

'Thank you.'

'I'll ring you on Wednesday. Effi will ring you.'

'Thank you.'

He jiggled the cut-off switch and dialled Ilse's number. 'Paul's in the bath,' his ex-wife told him.

'I've seen Effi and she's all right. Can you tell him that?'

'Of course. But...'

'I think they're going to let her go on Wednesday.'

'That's good. You must be relieved. More than relieved.'

'You could say that.'

'Paul seems to have had a wonderful time.'

'He did, didn't he? I hope he doesn't find the transition too difficult. It's a bit like coming up from the ocean floor – you need to take your time.'

'Mmm. I'll watch for signs. What about this weekend? Are you...'

'He'll want to catch up with all of you, won't he? I'd like to see *him*, but maybe just a couple of hours?'

'That sounds good, but I'll ask him.'

'Thanks, Ilse.'

'I hope it all goes well.'

'Me too.'

He went back to the rest of his coffee, ordered a schnapps to go with it. He supposed he should eat, but didn't feel hungry. What would Heydrich's organization want from *him*? More to the point, would it be something in his power to give?

The *Sicherheitsdienst* – the SD, as it was popularly known – had started life as the Nazi Party's intelligence apparatus, and now served the Nazi state in the same role. It thrived on betrayals, but the only person Russell could betray was himself. No, that wasn't strictly true. There was the sailor in Kiel who had given him the Baltic fleet dispositions, not to mention the man's prostitute girlfriend. But if the SD knew anything about Kiel, he wouldn't be drinking schnapps in a café on the Unter den Linden.

So what did they want him for? As an informant, perhaps. A snitch in the expatriate community. And among the German press corps. He had a lot of friends and acquaintances who still wrote – with well-concealed disgust in most cases – for the Nazi press. Effi might be asked to report on her fellow thespians.

Or maybe they were more interested in his communist contacts. They certainly knew about his communist past, and after the business in March they probably had a highly exaggerated notion of his current involvement. They might want to use him as bait, luring comrades up to the surface.

The latter seemed more likely on reflection, but who knew what the bastards were thinking?

He paid the bill and stood out on the pavement once more. Where to go – his rooms in Hallesches Tor or Effi's flat, where he'd been spending the majority of his nights? Her flat, he decided. Check that everything was all right, make sure the Gestapo had remembered to flush.

When it came down to it, he just wanted to feel

close to her.

He walked through to Friedrichstrasse and took a westbound Stadtbahn train. There was a leaflet on the only empty seat. He picked it up, sat down, and looked at it. 'Do you want another war?' the headline asked him. The text below advised resistance.

Looking up, he noticed that several of his fellow-passengers were staring at him. Wondering, he supposed, what he was going to do with the treasonous missive now that he'd read it. He thought about crumpling the leaflet up and dropping it, but felt a sudden, unreasoning loyalty to whoever had taken the enormous risk of writing, producing and distributing it. A minute or so later, as his train drew into Lehrter Station, he placed the leaflet back on the seat where he'd found it and got off. The attractive young woman sitting opposite gave him what might have been an encouraging smile.

He collected his suitcases from the left luggage, took another train on to Zoo Station, and walked the half-kilometre to Effi's flat on Carmerstrasse. Everything looked much as he'd last seen it – if the Gestapo had conducted a search then they'd tidied up after themselves. So they hadn't conducted a search. Russell sniffed the air for a trace of Effi's perfume but all he could smell was her absence. He leaned against the jamb of the bedroom door, picturing her in the cell. He told himself that they wouldn't hurt her, that they knew the threat was enough, but a sliver of panic still tightened his chest.

He stood there, eyes closed, for a minute or

more, and then urged himself back into motion. His car should be here, he realized. He locked up and carried his cases back down. The Hanomag was sitting in the rear courtyard, looking none the worse for a month of Effi's erratic driving. It started first time.

Twenty minutes later he was easing it into his own courtyard on Neuenburger Strasse. He felt less than ready to face Frau Heidegger and the inevitable deluge of welcome home questions, but the only way to his room led past her ever-open door. Which, much to his surprise, was closed. He stood there staring at it, and suddenly realized. The third week of July – the annual holiday with her brother's family in Stettin. Her sour-faced sister would be filling in, and she had never shown the slightest interest in what was happening elsewhere in the building. Frau Heidegger was fond of claiming that the life of a *portierfrau* was a true vocation, but her sister, it seemed, had not heard the call.

He lugged the suitcases up to his fourth floor rooms, and dumped them on his bed unopened. The air seemed hot and stale, but throwing the windows wide made little difference – night was falling much faster than the temperature, and the breeze had vanished. There were two bottles of beer in the cupboard above the sink, and Russell took one to his favourite seat by the window. The beer was warm and flat, which seemed appropriate.

None of it was going to go away, he thought. Effi might be released on Wednesday, but they could always re-arrest her, and next time they might feel the need – or merely the desire – to inflict a little pain. If Effi left him – God forbid – there was always Paul. Some sort of pressure could always be applied. The only way to stop it was to leave, and that would mean leaving alone. They would never let Effi out of the country now, and Ilse would never agree to Paul going. Why should she? She loved the boy as much as he did.

If he left, they'd all be safe. The bastards would have nothing to gain. Or would they? They'd probably find jobs for him to do in Britain or the US. *Do you care what happens to your family in Germany? Then do this for us.*

He needed to talk to someone, he realized. And there was only Thomas, his former brother-in-law, his best friend. The only man in Berlin – on Earth, come to that – whom he would trust with his life.

He went back downstairs to the telephone.

Thomas sounded happy to hear from him. 'How was America?' he asked.

'Wonderful. But I've run into a few problems since I got back.'

'How long have you been back?'

'In Berlin, about six hours. I'd like a chat, Thomas. Can you find me a half hour or so tomorrow morning if I come to the works?'

'I imagine so. But wouldn't you rather have lunch?'

'I need a private chat.'

'Ah. All right. Ten-thirty? Eleven?'

'Ten-thirty. I'll be there.' Hanging up, he realized he hadn't even asked after Thomas's wife and children.

Back in his room he sat in the window, taking desultory swigs from the second bottle of beer. The roofs of the government district were visible in the distance, a barely discernible line against the night sky. He thought of Effi in her cell, hoped she was curled up in sleep, cocooned from the evil around her.

The Schade Printing Works were in Treptow, a couple of streets from the River Spree. As Russell parked the Hanomag alongside Thomas's Adler, a ship's horn sounded on the river, a long mournful sound for such a bright morning. Russell had only managed a few dream-wracked hours of unconsciousness, and the coffee he'd grabbed at Görlitzer Station had propelled his heart into an unwelcome gallop for longer than seemed safe.

The main print room was the usual cacophony of machines. Thomas's office was at the other end, and Russell exchanged nods of recognition with a couple of the men on his way through. Both looked like Jews, and probably were. Schade Printing Works employed a higher percentage of Jews than any business in Berlin, largely because Thomas insisted that he needed all his highly-skilled workforce to fulfil his many contracts with the government. The irony was not lost on his Jewish workers, much of whose work involved printing anti-Semitic tracts.

A smiling Thomas arose from his desk to shake Russell's hand. 'God, you look terrible,' he half-shouted over the din. 'What's happened?' he added, seeing the look in his friend's eyes.

Russell shut the door, which cut the noise by half. 'Effi's been arrested.'

'Why – or do I need to ask? Someone informed on her... I'm sorry, that's not helpful. Where is she?'

'Prinz Albrecht-Strasse. Can we talk outside?'

'Of course.' Thomas led him back into the printing room, through a store-room and down a few steps into the yard, where a line of tarpaulin-covered wagons stood ready for unloading in the company siding. The two men walked down past the buffers and sat side by side on a low brick wall, facing the yard and printing works. Birds sang in the weed-covered wasteland behind them; a rumble of machinery emanated from the cement works on the other side of the tracks.

'This do?'

Russell looked round. No one could get within earshot without being seen. 'They're going to let her go tomorrow – or at least I think they will. They more or less said as much. I was allowed five minutes with her yesterday – she's scared but she's okay. They haven't done anything to her, haven't even questioned her as far as I know.'

'So what...'

'It's me they're after. They'll only let her go if I agree to work for them.'

'Doing what?'

'I'll find that out tomorrow.'

'What could you do for them?'

'Ah. There's a history to this that you don't know about. You remember those articles I wrote for *Pravda?*'

'On the positive aspects of Nazi Germany?

44

How could I forget?'

'I needed the money. And the Soviets fed me a line about preparing their readers for peace which I could just about swallow. As I expected, they wanted more than my magic pen – a little espionage on the side. I refused, of course; but then I got involved with the Wiesners – remember them? Felix Wiesner was a big-time doctor until the Nazis came along – an Iron Cross, First Class, by the way – but *Kristallnacht* finally convinced him that there was no future for his family here. His son was sent to Sachsenhausen and badly beaten. Felix hired me to teach his daughters English so they'd have a head start once he got them out. But then they arrested him on a trumped-up abortion charge, sent him to Sachsenhausen, and beat him to death. His widow and daughters were left in limbo, his son was on the run from the Gestapo. Enter yours truly with a brilliant idea. The Soviets wanted me to bring a few papers out of the country, papers that would interest any of Germany's enemies. I agreed to do it if they got Wiesner's son across the border, and I offered copies to the British in exchange for exit visas for the mother and two girls. Oh, and I demanded an American passport for myself, which I've just been given. Now I won't have to leave Paul and Effi behind when Chamberlain finally stands up to Hitler.'

Thomas was momentarily lost for words. 'My God,' he murmured.

Russell gave him a wry smile. 'It seemed like a good idea at the time.' He paused as a local passenger train rattled by. 'Still does, actually.'

'It sounds like you got away with it.'

'I thought I had. The bastards don't have anything definite against me, but they've got reasons to be suspicious. They know I was in contact with the Soviets over the articles, and they know that the Soviets expect more from their foreign correspondents than journalism. Hell, everyone does these days. The Gestapo, the SD, whichever bunch of goons we're talking about – they'll all be assuming I have contacts among communist circles here in Germany. And if they want to use me as a way in, then they've hit on the perfect way of getting me to cooperate.'

'Did Effi provide them with the excuse?'

Russell told him what she'd said. 'She was reported by another actress, one that she beat to a part.'

Thomas grimaced.

'So what do I do?'

Thomas ran a hand through his spiky grey hair. 'Well, I suppose the first thing is to find out what they want. Whatever it is, you'll have to at least say that you'll go along with it. If it's more than you can stomach, then, first chance you get, you take yourself and Effi out of this godforsaken country.'

'And Paul?'

'Better an absent father than a dead one.'

'Of course. But what if they punish him for my sins?'

Thomas used the clanking of a passing freight train to think about that. 'Maybe I'm being naïve,' he said finally, 'but I don't believe they would. What could they do to a twelve year-old aryan boy? And he has his stepfather to stand up for him. Matthias is very fond of Paul – he wouldn't let anything happen to him without a real fight. Neither would I, by the way.'

'I know that. And you're probably right. I was thinking last night – this won't go away, I have to get out. But getting Effi out will take time – they won't just let her leave. Do we have that sort of time? The smart money's all on September, after the harvest, before the rains.'

'There's no way of knowing, is there? We seem to go through the same dramatic scenes every six months. Hitler stamps his foot and shouts a lot, everyone rushes around making him offers, and he graciously accepts a mere 99 per cent of what he asked for. It could happen again.'

'Not with the Poles.'

'You're probably right. I wish I could send Joachim somewhere safe.' Thomas's seventeen-year-old son was doing his compulsory year's service in the *Arbeitsdienst* public works programme, and would be shifted to auxiliary military duties if war broke out.

The two men sat in silence for a moment.

'So you're seeing the SD tomorrow,' Thomas said eventually. 'How are you going to spend the rest of today?'

'Worrying. And working, I suppose. I have a new job, by the way. Central and East European correspondent of the *San Francisco Tribune*. Salary, expenses, the works.'

'Well, that makes a welcome change. Congratulations.'

'Thanks. I met the Editor in New York – Ed

47

Cummins. An amazing old man, very pro-Roosevelt.' Russell smiled. 'He wants me to wake America up. Particularly those Americans with their roots in Germany and Germany's neighbours. The Jewish-Americans of course, but the Polish-Americans, the Hungarian-Americans, all of them. He wants them to know what's really happening in the old countries, and to get really angry about it. And not to go along with all that crap – to use his own words – about it being none of America's business.' Russell laughed. 'Of course, we weren't reckoning on the SD and Gestapo breathing down my neck. I'll just have to convince the bastards that retaining my credibility as a journalist is in their interests too. Because if I suddenly start sucking up to them in print, no one who matters will trust anything I do or say.'

'I suppose not. Are you going to be covering the day-to-day stuff?'

'Not really – they'll carry on using the agencies for that. I'm more comment than news – the big diplomatic stories and whatever else strikes me as important. The first thing Cummins wants is a piece on how the Czechs are doing under occupation. And I thought I might visit that agricultural school in Skaby that the Jews are running for would-be emigrants to Palestine. I can't believe the Nazis are still sponsoring it.'

Thomas grunted his agreement as another suburban train headed for Görlitzer Station. One carriage seemed full of over-excited young boys, most of whom were hanging out of the windows. A school trip, Russell supposed.

'Talking of Jews,' Thomas said, 'I've got a mystery of my own to solve.' He brushed a speck of dirt off his trousers. 'I had an employee by the name of Benjamin Rosenfeld. A good worker, he started here five or six years ago. A Jew, of course. About six weeks ago he came to ask if I had a job for his seventeen-year-old niece. Her family are farmers in Silesia, the only Jews in the area apparently, and she was being harassed – perhaps more, he didn't say – by the local boys. Her parents thought she'd be safer in Berlin.' Thomas's shrug encompassed both the sad absurdity of the problem and the impossibility of knowing where a Jew might be safest in such times. 'As it happened I'd just lost a young woman – her exit visa had arrived that week and she was off to Palestine – so I said yes. Rosenfeld arranged the trip, sent the ticket, and arranged to meet her at Silesian Station. That was on the last day of June. Almost three weeks ago.

'As far as I can make out, on the day she was supposed to arrive Rosenfeld left here with the intention of walking straight to the station – it's only about three kilometres away. Somewhere along the way, some thugs decided he needed beating up. Storm troopers probably, from their barracks on Köpenicke Strasse, but they weren't in uniform according to Rosenfeld. Someone took him to one of those makeshift Jewish hospitals in Friedrichshain, and he was in and out of consciousness for several days. I didn't know he'd been attacked until one of the workers told me on the following day. I wondered what had happened to the girl, but assumed she had managed to make contact with Rosenfeld's friends, and that she'd turn up for work on the Monday. But she didn't. I had no proof she'd ever left Silesia, and the fact that she hadn't turned up seemed like a good reason for doubting it. I told myself I would contact the parents when Rosenfeld had recovered sufficiently to tell me their address, but he never did. He died about a week after the attack.'

'I don't suppose the police were interested?'

'I don't think anyone even bothered telling them,' Thomas said wryly. 'I went to the funeral, and talked to as many of the mourners as I could. Most of Rosenfeld's friends knew she was coming, but none of them had seen her. Then, after the ceremony, a man I hadn't talked to came up to me with a suitcase. He told me he was Rosenfeld's landlord, and said he didn't know what to do with the man's belongings. "I was wondering if you could send them back to his family with his final wages."' Thomas grimaced. 'To be honest, I'd completely forgotten about the wages. I told him I had no address for the family, and he said he hadn't either. He was obviously eager to get rid of the stuff, so I took it, thinking I could always share out whatever was in there with his work-friends. Two days later the landlord showed up at the works with a letter which had just arrived for Rosenfeld. It was from his brother, the girl's father. He was worried that he hadn't heard from his daughter.

'There was no address of origin, only a Wartha postmark. It's a small town – a big village really – about sixty kilometres south of Breslau. About a week ago I sent a letter to the Wartha post office, asking them to forward another letter that I'd enclosed for Rosenfeld's brother, but there was no reply. So yesterday I telephoned the post office. A man who claimed to be the postmaster said he'd never got the letter and that he'd never heard of the Rosenfelds. "Jews, I suppose" – I think those were his exact words. "They've probably gone somewhere where they're wanted."

'So I went to the Kripo office in Neukolin – not, I have to admit, in a conciliatory frame of mind. It probably wouldn't have made any difference, but I certainly rubbed the duty officer up the wrong way. After I'd explained all the circumstances, he told me that the girl had probably run off with a boyfriend, and that the German police had better things to do than scour the city for sexmad Jewesses. I almost hit him.' Thomas clenched his fist reminiscently. 'And I've thought about reporting him to his superiors – there are still some decent men in the Kripo, after all – but it doesn't really seem like such a good idea. If I get on the wrong side of the authorities it won't be me that suffers, or at least not only me. It'll be the three hundred Jews who work here.' He paused for a moment. 'But I can't just forget about her. And I remembered that you did a piece – quite a few years ago now – on private investigators in Berlin.'

Russell grunted his agreement. 'It was after that movie *The Thin Man* came out. Berlin went from having one private detective to having fifty in a matter of months. Most of them only lasted a few weeks.'

51

'Can you recommend one that's still in business?'

'I don't know. If he's still in business, I mean. A man named Uwe Kuzorra. He was a Kripo detective who couldn't stomach working for the Nazis. So he quit, opened an agency in Wedding. I liked him. Knew this city inside out. But he was in his late fifties then, so he may have retired. I could find out for you.'

'If you could.' Thomas rubbed his cheeks and then clasped his hands together in front of his face. 'There were always things I hated about my country,' he said, 'but there used to be things I loved as well. Now all I feel is this endless shame. I don't know why – it's not as if I ever voted for them. But I do.'

'I'm getting to the point where all I feel is anger,' Russell said. 'And useless anger at that.'

'A fine pair we are.'

'Yes. I'll let you get back to work. I'll drive over to Wedding this afternoon, see if Kuzorra is still in business. If not, I'll try to find someone else.'

They walked back down the line of wagons and round the side of the works to the front yard. 'Give my love to Effi,' Thomas said as Russell climbed into the front seat.

'I will.' He leaned his head out of the window. 'What's the girl's name?'

'Miriam. And I almost forgot.' He took out his wallet and removed a dog-eared photograph of two men, one woman and a girl of about fifteen. 'Rosenfeld's on the left,' Thomas said. 'The others are Miriam and her parents.'

She was a pretty girl. Dark hair and eyes, olive

52

skin, a shy smile. Her figure would have filled out, but the face wouldn't have changed. Not that much, anyway.

Miriam Rosenfeld. A nice Jewish name, Russell thought, as he motored up Slessische Strasse towards the city centre. Miriam Sarah Rosenfeld, of course. It was almost a year since the regime had blessed all Jews with a self-defining second name – Sarah for females, Israel for males. Dumb as a dog in heat, as one of his mother's friends liked to say.

It was another hot summer day. The traffic seemed unusually sparse for noon, but then Berlin was hardly New York. The pavements were busy with pedestrians going about their business, but the faces showed little in the way of animation. Or was he imagining that, looking for depression to mirror his own? Berliners were aggressive talkers, but they could give the English a run for their money when it came to cold reserve.

A long stomach growl reminded him that he hadn't eaten that morning. Gerhardt's frankfurter stand, he decided, and abruptly changed direction, causing the driver behind to sound his horn. A new set of traffic lights outside the main post office held him up for what seemed an age. He found himself thumping the steering wheel in frustration, and then laughing at himself. What was the hurry?

The queue at Gerhardt's stretched out of the concourse beneath the Alexanderplatz Station and into Dircksen-Strasse. It moved quickly though, and Russell was soon ordering his bratwurst and *kartoffelsalat* from Gerhardt's brother Rolf, the sprightly septuagenarian with the drooping moustache who manned the counter.

'Haven't seen you for a while,' Rolf said, taking Russell's note and handing back some coins.

'I've been in America.'

'Lucky man,' Rolf said, passing over the food. Russell shifted down the counter to add mustard and mayonnaise, stabbed a chunk of potato with the small wooden fork and popped it in his mouth. A mouthful of steaming bratwurst followed. Paul had been right in New York. German hot dogs were better.

He walked back to the Hanomag and sat behind the wheel enjoying his meal. 'A lucky man,' he murmured to himself, and remembered Brecht's line about 'the man who laughs', who had 'simply not yet heard the terrible news.' Well, he'd heard the terrible news and he still wanted to laugh, at least once in a while. Even these clouds had a few stray fragments of silver lining hanging down. He was too old to fight, his son was too young. And Effi would be released the next day.

A drink, he decided. At the Adlon. It was time he caught up with his colleagues.

In the event, only the *Chicago Post*'s Jack Slaney was there, perched on his usual barstool. He greeted Russell with a big grin. 'Beer, whisky or both?'

'Just the beer, thanks,' Russell said, sliding onto the next stool and gazing round. 'Not too busy, is it?'

'It's like this every summer. How was the States?'

54

'Good. Very good. My son had a whale of a time.'

'Staten Island Ferry?'

'Four times. Statue of Liberty, Central Park, Grand Central Station, Macy's toy department ... not to mention the World's Fair.'

'And you're one of us now.'

'News travels fast.'

'We *are* journalists. How's next year's election looking? Any chance that Lindbergh's going to run?'

'Doesn't look like it. The way things are going in Congress it doesn't look like he needs to. Roosevelt's chances of revising the Neutrality Bill seem to be getting worse, not better. America won't be joining a European war any time soon.'

'Pity. The sooner we get into a war, the sooner I get to go home.'

'What's been happening here?'

'Not much. Lot of grumbling in the press about you British – how the guarantee to Poland has given the Poles a free hand to persecute their poor German minority. A few incidents around Danzig but nothing serious. Calm before the storm, of course.'

'Most calms are.'

'Maybe. The German universities all closed for the summer last week. Two weeks earlier than usual, so the students can help with the harvest. They're busting a gut to get it in on time this year, and why do you think that might be? If I was a betting man – and I am – I'd put money on a new batch of Polish atrocity stories in the first two weeks of August. And then Hitler will start

55

ranting again. A complete idiot could recognize the pattern by this time. I know they're an evil bunch of bastards, but what really gets me down is that they're such an insult to the intelligence.'

'Talking to you is always such a joy.'

'You love it. I'm the only man in Berlin who's more cynical than you are.'

'Maybe. I seem to be moving beyond cynicism, but God knows in what direction.'

'Despair comes highly recommended.'

Russell laughed. 'Like I said, a real pleasure, but I've got be off. I owe you one.'

'At least three actually. Where are you off to?'

'To see a man about a missing girl.'

Wedding had been a communist stronghold before the Nazi takeover, and it still seemed depressed by the outcome of the subsequent reckoning. A few faded hammers and sickles were visible on hard-to-reach surfaces, and billowing swastikas were less ubiquitous than usual. Uwe Kuzorra's office was on the east side of the Müller-Strasse, a hundred metres or so south of the S-bahn. Or it had been – his name was still among those listed by the door, but the detective himself had retired. 'End of last year,' a brisk young woman from the ground floor laundry told Russell. 'If you want his home address, I think they have it upstairs.'

Russell climbed the four flights to Kuzorra's former office, and found it empty. An elderly man with a monocle eventually answered his knock on the opposite door. A wooden table behind him was covered with clocks in various stages of dismantlement, chalk circles surrounding each separate inventory of pieces.

'Yes?'

'Sorry to interrupt, but I was told that you had Uwe Kuzorra's home address.'

'Yes. I do. Come in. Sit down. It may take me a while to find it.'

The room gave off a rich melange of odours – wood polish and metallic oil from the work-bench, soapy steam from the laundry below, the unmistakable scent of male cat. The beast in question, a huge black tom, stared blearily back at him from his patch in the sun.

The horologist was shuffling through a pile of papers – mostly unpaid bills, if the frequent mut-ters of alarm and dismay were anything to go by. 'Ah, here it is,' he said at last, waving a scrap of paper at Russell. '14 Demminer Strasse, Apart-ment 6. Do you have a pencil?'

Russell recognized the street. He had inter-viewed a dog breeder there several years earlier – some dreadful piece for an American magazine on the Germans and their pets. The breeder had claimed that *Mein Kampf* inspired him in his search for pedigree perfection.

It was only a five minute drive. The apartment building was old, but seemed well cared for. A grey-haired woman opened the door – in her early 60s, Russell guessed, but still attractive. He asked if Uwe Kuzorra lived there.

'Who are you?' she asked simply.

'I interviewed him once several years ago. I'm a journalist, but that's not why I'm here...'

'You'd better come in. My husband is in the

other room.'

Kuzorra was reclining in an armchair close to the open window, legs stretched out, eyes closed. A People's Radio was playing softly on the chest of drawers – Schubert, Russell guessed, but he was usually wrong. 'Uwe,' the woman said behind him, 'a visitor.'

Kuzorra opened his eyes. 'John Russell,' he said after a moment's thought. 'Still here, eh?'

'I'm surprised you remembered.'

'I was always good at names and faces. Are you chasing another story? Please sit down. Katrin will make us some coffee.'

'You've had your two coffees,' she said sternly.

'I can't let Herr Russell drink alone.'

She laughed. 'Oh, all right.'

'So what brings you to me? How did you find me? Surely that lunatic clock-maker has long since lost my address.'

'You underestimate him.'

'Perhaps. He *has* been mending the same dozen clocks ever since I met him. Still...'

'I need a private detective,' Russell said, 'and I thought you might be able to recommend one. It's a missing persons case – a Jewish girl. Not the sort of case that'll make anyone famous...'

'The sort of case that'll lose an investigator any police friends he still has,' Kuzorra said. 'And they're the ones you need in this job.'

'Exactly. I imagine a lot of your ex-colleagues would turn it down.'

'You're right about that. Can you give me some details?'

Russell went through what Thomas had told

him, pausing only to accept an extremely good cup of coffee from Kuzorra's wife.

'Well, let's hope she hasn't run into another George Grossman,' was the detective's initial response.

'Who?'

'Before your time, I suppose. You remember the German cannibals of the 20s? There were four of them – Fritz Haarmann, Karl Denke, Peter Kurten and George Grossman.' He almost danced through the names. 'Grossmann was the Berliner. He rented a flat near the Silesian Station, just before the war. He used to meet the trains from the East, seek out innocent-looking country girls – he preferred them plump – and ask if they needed help. He told some of them that he was looking for a housekeeper, but most of the time he just offered the girls cheap lodgings while they found their feet in the big city. Once he got them back to his flat he killed them, cut them up, and ground them into sausages for the local market. He was at it for about eight years before we caught him.'

'He hasn't been released recently?'

'He hanged himself in prison.'

'That's a relief.'

'I doubt your girl has been eaten. But the first thing to do is find out if she ever reached Berlin. I've got some friends at Silesian Station – I can ask around. What day did she arrive?'

'The last day of June, whatever that was.'

'A Friday,' Frau Kuzorra said. 'I had a doctor's appointment that day. But Uwe...'

'I know, I know. I'm retired. I also get a little

59

bored from time to time. Asking a few questions at Silesian Station is hardly going to kill me, is it? And we could do with a little extra money. That week on the coast you've been talking about.' He took her silence for acquiescence. 'My usual rates are twenty-five Reichsmarks an hour and reasonable expenses,' he told Russell.

'Fine.' Thomas could certainly afford it.

'Right then. If I go down on Friday evening there's a good chance the same crew will be working that train. Have you a picture of her?'

Russell passed it over.

'Lovely,' Kuzorra said. 'But very Jewish. Let's hope she didn't reach Berlin.' He got to his feet, wincing as he did so. 'They say old war wounds are more painful in wet weather,' he said, 'but mine always seem worst in summer. You fought in the war, didn't you?'

'In Belgium,' Russell admitted. 'The last eighteen months.'

'Well, who would have guessed we'd find a leader stupid enough to start another one?' the detective asked.

'He hasn't started one yet.'

'He will.'

Russell drove slowly back into the city along Brunner-Strasse and Rosenthaler Strasse. The area around the latter had once hosted a large Jewish population, and reminders of *Kristallnacht* were still occasionally evident – shops abandoned and boarded up, a few with crudely daubed Stars of David on their doors. He hadn't told Thomas or Kuzorra, but he already had one missing girl to

60

find in Berlin. In New York his mother had introduced him to the Hahnemann family, rich Berliners from Charlottenburg who had decided they could no longer abide life in Hitler's Germany. They had brought three of the children with them, but their oldest daughter Freya had refused to leave her Jewish boyfriend, a man named Wilhelm Isendahl, and had remained in Berlin. The Hahnemanns hadn't heard from her in months, their own letters had been returned unopened, and they couldn't help worrying that her 'firebrand' of a boyfriend had led her into trouble. Could Russell make sure she was all right, and ask her to send them a postcard? Of course he could.

Finding her might take time – there was certainly no chance of official help if a Jew was involved – but he had no reason to believe that Freya Hahnemann was in any immediate danger. And he wanted Kuzorra to concentrate on Miriam Rosenfeld, who probably was. Her face in the photograph had an air of almost catastrophic innocence.

After re-crossing the river Russell found himself heading back to the Adlan. He rang Thomas from the lobby to tell him he'd hired Kuzorra, and what the retainer was. Thomas took a note of the detective's address and promised to send off a cheque.

Slaney was gone from the bar, but several members of the British press corps had filled the gap. Russell bought a round and listened to the latest news from London, most of which seemed singularly uninteresting. One item, however, grabbed his attention. According to Dick Thornton, the British and French governments had both received virtual ultimatums from Soviet Foreign Minister Molotov. If they didn't get serious about a military alliance, then the Soviets would look elsewhere.

'They won't do a deal with Hitler, will they?' the *Chronicle* man asked.

'Why not? It would give them some time. Stalin has just killed half his generals.'

'I know, but...'

'Look at it from their point of view,' the *Sketch* man said. 'The British and French have hardly been enthusiastic about a military alliance.'

'More to the point,' Russell interjected, 'what's Stalin got to gain now? The Germans can only get at him by going through Poland, and that'll automatically bring in the British and French on his side.'

'Always assuming they honour the guarantee.'

'They will.'

'That's what the Czechs thought.'

'This is different. There's no wriggle-room this time. And no way the Poles will sign large chunks of their country away.'

'I know that and you know that, but does Hitler?'

'Hard to say.'

The discussion meandered on. Russell was interested, but had too much else on his mind to give it his undivided attention. He ought to be submitting his visa application for Prague and the Protectorate, but it felt wrong to be making travel plans while Effi was still in a Gestapo cell. And there was always the chance that a visa would be granted more quickly once he'd demonstrated his willingness to work for the SD.

But there were more sensible ways of killing time than drinking it away. When the conversation turned to cricket, he made his excuses and drove over to the French restaurant in Wilmersdorf which he and Effi visited every few weeks. It was usually half-empty these days, probably in consequence of the Nazis' remorseless trashing of everything French, but the food was still wonderful. Russell ate French bread and Normandy butter with a single glass of the most expensive wine he could find, and followed it up with a steak oozing blood, pear tart with chocolate sauce, a slice of Brie and a small black coffee.

The light was almost gone when he emerged, but it was a lovely evening, warm with a feathery breeze. He drove back up towards the Kaiser Memorial Church and found an empty table at one of the busy pavement cafés on Tauenzien-Strasse. After ordering schnapps and coffee – in theory the caffeine and alcohol would cancel each other out – he sat and eavesdropped on the conversations around him. One young couple were discussing what colour to paint their bedroom; a middle-aged couple were planning the series of trips they would make when they finally took delivery of their People's Car. Visiting his wife's family in Essen did not seem high on the husband's list of priorities. The only hint that war might be imminent came from the young man to his left, who was trying to convince his girlfriend, without actually saying so, that the time for consummating their relationship might

63

be shorter than she thought. Her replies sounded like distant echoes of those which Russell had received from prim little Mary Wright in the spring of 1917. Some things never changed.

It was dark now, the spire of the Memorial Church circled by stars. Russell drove home to Neuenburger Strasse and wearily climbed the stairs. Reaching the top, he realized that the bulb on his landing had gone again.

As he opened the door to his room – one hand turning the key, the other the knob – it seemed for a moment as if the key hadn't needed turning. He was still thinking he must have imagined that when his flick of the switch failed to produce light. A mental alarm bell started ringing, but much too late.

Two things happened almost simultaneously. A bright beam of light caught him right in the eye, and something very hard delivered a tremendous blow across his stomach. As he doubled over, a second blow in the back sent him crashing to the floor. Once, twice, feet thudded into his front and back, torchlight dancing above. A kick in the groin hurt like hell, and curled him into a foetus-like ball, arms clasped together to protect his face and head. He tried to shout out, but his lungs could only manage a rasp.

The blows had stopped, but a heavy foot planted on his stomach was pinning him down. He tried opening his eyes, but the beam of light – a torch, he assumed – was shining right in his face, and the figures above him were only flickering shadows. He felt one draw nearer, and a gloved hand dragged one arm away from his head. Something cold and metallic was rammed into his ear. The barrel of a pistol.

He could smell beer on the breath of the man who held it.

'Finish him off,' someone said.

'My pleasure,' the man holding the gun murmured.

Russell felt the flow of warm piss inside his pants as the trigger clicked on an empty chamber.

'Just kidding,' the man said. 'But next time ... well, now you know how easy it would be. We can always find you. Here or on Carmerstrasse.'

The torch shifted away from Russell's face. Blinking through the after-lights he could see it illuminating the framed poster for Effi's first major film. 'She could be on her way to Ravensbrück tomorrow,' the voice said. 'But they'd hold her in *Columbiahaus* until the next shipment. How many men do we have there?'

'Around forty,' one of his friends said.

'They'd be queuing up, wouldn't they? They'd all want to fuck a film star.' The torch was back in Russell's eyes. 'You do understand?' beer-breath said, increasing the pressure of the gun barrel.

Russell managed a rasping 'yes'.

'I think he's got the message,' the second voice said.

'You can smell it,' a third man said.

Suddenly foot and gun barrel were gone, the torch switched off. Darkness gave way to dim light as his assailants tramped out of the apartment, then fell once more as the door shut behind them.

Russell lay there, tentatively shifting his body.

65

The pain in his groin was beginning to subside, leaving more space for the one in his kidneys, but nothing seemed to be broken. He lay there in his sodden trousers, remembering the last time he had pissed himself in fear, walking towards the German lines as mates on either side of him literally lost their heads.

His eyes were adjusting now, making the most of what light there was from the city outside. He painfully worked his way across the floor to the nearest armchair, and levered himself up so his back was against one side. A warning, he thought. His visitors had been told to hurt him but leave no visible marks. To scare the shit out of him.

They'd succeeded.

He sat there for a while, then clambered laboriously to his feet. The standard lamp responded to its switch, revealing an apparently untouched room. The two extracted light bulbs had been left on the table.

Russell swapped his clothes for a dressing-gown and walked down to the bathroom he shared with three other tenants. The red patches on his body would doubtless turn blue over the next few days, but he avoided his own face in the mirror, frightened of what he might find. Back in the flat, he lowered himself onto the bed and turned out the light. Sleep came more easily than he expected, just as it had in the trenches.

He woke much earlier than he wanted to, and sat at his window for the better part of an hour listening to the city stir. His body ached in the expected places, and movement was still painful,

66

but at least there was no blood in his piss. At around a quarter to seven he ran himself a deep hot bath, and lay soaking until a fellow tenant began banging on the door.

Back in the apartment, he wondered how he should dress for his eleven o'clock appointment. A suit and tie seemed called for – the Heydrichs of this world liked a smart appearance. He chose the dark blue, took time to polish his shoes, and then spent another five minutes at the sink scraping the polish off his fingers. A look in the wardrobe mirror proved less than reassuring – the outfit was all right, but his hair was slightly over-length by SS standards, and the dark circles underneath his eyes suggested debauchery or worse. 'You don't look a day over fifty,' he mumbled at his reflection. 'Pity you're only forty-two.'

Half an hour later, as he sat outside the Café Kranzler with his first coffee of the day, an altercation broke out on the other side of the intersection. A tram-driver was leaning from his cab window and shouting at a brown-shirted team of flag-hangers, all of whom seemed blissfully unaware that their truck was blocking the rails, or that the occupants of the Café Kranzler's pavement seats were watching them with interest. One of the Brownshirts walked across to the tram, shouting as he went, whereupon the driver climbed down onto the road. His wide shoulders and impressive height – around two metres of it – clearly gave the storm trooper pause for thought. The driver, aware of the wider audience, seized his chance to show his flair for mime. These are rails, his arms seemed to say, and this thing here

– the tram – could only run on rails. Their truck was slewed right across them. Conclusion – they had to move the damn thing!

There was a spattering of applause from the Café Kranzler clientele. The storm trooper spun round, face twisted in anger, but decided with obvious reluctance against arresting everyone in sight. He turned away from the crowd and ordered his underlings to move the truck. When one of these disconsolately raised an unhung flag, he was treated to a loud burst of abuse. The truck was moved; the tram squealed through the intersection and disappeared. The breakfasters went back to their newspapers.

Russell sipped at his coffee and wondered what to do about the previous night's visit. Should he bring it up at his meeting with Hauptsturmführer Hirth? What would be the point? If the man denied SD involvement Russell had no way of proving otherwise. And if, as seemed more likely, the bastard cheerfully admitted complicity, there was no way Russell could threaten him, not when Effi's life was at stake. Better to say nothing, he told himself. Let them see that he took their warning seriously. Which he did.

A young man at the next table left a tip and walked off down the street, abandoning his copy of the *Volkischer Beobachter*. Russell skimmed through the paper in search of significant news, finding none. The leading letter, as so often in the *Beobachter*, offered a reader's heartfelt agreement with a government announcement of the previous day, which in this case amounted to a statement from some ministry or other that gluttony was a

68

form of treason. A cynic might guess that some form of food rationing was on the way.

One other story caught his eye. A German Jew and his non-Jewish girlfriend had broken the race laws by getting married, and had evaded prosecution by moving to Carlsbad in what was then Czechoslovakia. After the Munich crisis of September 1938 they had moved on to the capital Prague, intent on emigration. They had, however, still been there when Hitler invaded in March. Arrested a few days later, they had now been sentenced to two and two and a half years respectively, for the crime of 'racial disgrace.' Russell wondered whether Freya Hahnemann had married Wilhelm Isendahl, as her parents feared she had. If everything went well today – and please let it! – then tomorrow he would find the time to check out the address they had given him.

At ten-forty Russell moved the car down to Leipziger Strasse, sat fretting for another ten minutes, and then walked across to Wilhelmstrasse. Number 102 looked better than it had on his last visit. In January the garden behind the street façade had been streaked with snow, the trees lifeless, the grey building sunk beneath a grey sky. Now the birch leaves rustled in the summer breeze, and roses bloomed around a perfectly coiffured lawn. Heydrich had obviously had the mower out.

The receptionist was a buxom blonde off the assembly line, the poster bearing this week's official Party slogan – 'Let that which must die sink and rot. What has strength and light will rise and blaze' – took pride of place on the wall behind her. Russell stared at them both for a while, then decided a visit to the men's room was in order. This, needless to say, was spotless. If the SS had restricted their activities to the design and maintenance of toilets, the world would have been a cleaner and better place.

Get it out of your system, he told himself. When the moment comes, don't be a smart alec. Just listen, nod, smile.

Back in reception, a baby-faced Sturmmann was waiting to escort him to Room 47.

Hauptsturmführer Hirth, as Russell soon discovered, bore more than a passing resemblance to Stalin, at least from the neck up. He had the same cropped hair, thick moustache and cratered cheeks, but clearly spent fewer hours in the gym than some of his SS buddies. All SS men creaked when they moved – the sound of stretching leather belts – but Hirth creaked more than most. Girth would have been a better name.

He looked up, creaking as he did so, and flicked a hand towards the chair facing his desk. There was, Russell noticed warily, intelligence in the man's eyes.

'Herr Russell,' Hirth began, 'I have no time to waste, so I'll simply point out what will happen if you refuse to cooperate. One, Fraulein Koenen will spend a very long time in a concentration camp. She may survive, she may not. She will certainly lose her beauty. Her career will be over.' He paused, as if expecting Russell to protest.

Russell just nodded.

'Two,' Hirth continued, 'you yourself will be arrested and questioned over events which happened in March of this year.'

'Which events?' Russell asked. He hadn't expected this.

'On the night of March 15th, only a few hours before our troops moved in to restore order in what was then Czechoslovakia, you travelled from Prague to Berlin. The Gestapo received an anonymous tip that you were carrying illicit political materials. Your bag was searched.'

'And nothing was found.'

'Indeed. But why would anyone go to the trouble of betraying you if there was nothing to betray?'

'Mischief-making?'

'Please be serious, Herr Russell. You are a former communist. You had only just written several articles for the Soviet newspaper *Pravda*...'

'With the approval of your organization.'

'Indeed. That is hardly...'

Russell put his hands up. 'Very well. I will tell you what happened. It's very simple. I did those articles for the Soviets, and was well paid. They then asked me to do other work for them – journalistic work perhaps, but the sort that verges on espionage. I refused, and I think they contacted the Gestapo just to inconvenience me. Out of spite. That's all it was.'

'And the false-bottomed suitcase.'

'As I told the Gestapo, that was an unfortunate coincidence. Half the Jews in Germany are using them.'

Hirth smiled at him. 'Of course. And then we have the Tyler McKinley reports which appeared in the *San Francisco Examiner*. McKinley was dead by then, and there was some mystery as to how these scurrilous articles had reached the newspaper.'

'I wouldn't know.' Tyler McKinley had lived one floor down from Russell in Neuenburger Strasse. More colleague than friend, he had ended up under an S-bahn train at Zoo Station. Russell still got cold sweats remembering the risks he'd run to get the young American's articles on the secret Nazi euthanasia programme out of Germany.

'But you're now working for another San Francisco newspaper,' Hirth observed. 'Another coincidence perhaps.'

'Apparently.'

'Herr Russell, are you really telling me that you have nothing to fear from a thorough investigation of these events?'

'Not a thing,' Russell lied. Dig deep enough and they could probably have him for breakfast. 'Look,' he said, 'you don't need to dig up the past. Just tell me what you want me to do. Release Fraulein Koenen and I'll do it.'

'Good.' Hirth leant back in his chair and put his hands behind his head, a symphony in creaking leather. 'I think we understand each other. I hope so at least. And the fact that the Soviets approached you actually makes this easier. You will go back to them, say you've changed your mind, and offer to supply them with information.'

Russell hid his relief. 'What information?'

'That is not yet decided. Only that it will be false.'

'And that's all you want me to do?'

'For the moment, yes.'

'And Fraulein Koenen will be released?'

'When we are finished here I shall call Prinz Albrecht-Strasse, and she will be waiting for you. She will be able to attend the première of her latest film. It's on Friday, I believe.'

'She may not feel like dressing up.'

'She will. The Reich Propaganda Minister will be there.'

'Wonderful.' A kiss on the cheek from Joey – he only hoped Effi would refrain from kneeing the little runt in the balls. 'It may take me some time to contact the Soviets,' he said. 'I can't just ring up the Embassy.'

'Why not?'

'Because they'll know you're listening in. And watching everyone who goes in and out. They'll expect a would-be spy to be a little more circumspect. A Soviet embassy outside Germany, perhaps. Warsaw or Paris.'

'How soon could you go?'

'In a week or two. My paper wants me in Prague. Which,' he couldn't resist adding, 'is no longer a foreign capital.'

'That's too long,' Hirth said. 'Unless you're willing to wait a week or two for Fraulein Koenen's release.'

'I'm just...'

'Why not go to the Soviet Embassy for a visa? People do that all the time. And while you're there, ask for an outdoor meeting with someone. In the Tiergarten, or somewhere like that. Won't that be that circumspect enough?'

Russell agreed, somewhat reluctantly, that it might be.

'Good. Fraulein Koenen will be waiting for you

at Prinz Albrecht-Strasse. Enjoy your reunion. But let me make it clear – this is a last chance for both of you. Help us out, and we'll help you. Let us down and she'll end up in Ravensbrück. You might be more fortunate, and simply be deported, but you'll never see each other again.'

Russell listened, nodded, smiled. 'I get the picture,' he said.

Hauptsturmführer Hirth looked at him, and decided that he did. He passed across a piece of paper with a number on it. 'When you have established contact with one of the Soviet intelligence services, ring this number.'

Russell walked slowly back to the car and drove it round to the Gestapo building in Prinz Albrecht-Strasse. The kerb outside was empty, as if no one dared to park there. Why not? he thought. He was one of Heydrich's boys now.

He walked through the main doors expecting a long wait, but Effi was already sitting in the reception area. He'd half-expected to find her still wearing the oversize grey pyjamas, but she was wearing her own clothes, the deep blue dress he'd bought her a couple of Christmases ago and a pair of matching heels. Her hair was tied back with what looked like a shoelace.

She flew into his arms, and they stood there, clinging to each other. 'Oh John,' she said, and he squeezed her still tighter, revelling in the familiar softness and warmth, ignoring the pain in his abdomen.

'Let's get out of here,' she whispered.

'Gladly.'

They hurried across the pavement to the car, as

if they were escaping. Was Ritschel watching from the window, proud of his little ploy? 'Where to?' he asked Effi. 'Home?'

'Home. Yes. God, I need a bath. I must smell awful.'

'You don't.'

He started the engine, and turned to her. 'How were the last two days?' he asked.

'Better,' she said. 'Let's go.'

He moved the car off in the direction of Potsdamer Platz.

'Better once I'd seen you,' she explained. 'I knew you'd sort it out.'

'Did they question you?'

'Yesterday, though there weren't many questions. I was simply given my last chance to pledge undying allegiance to the Führer and all his moronic minions.'

'And you did.'

'Of course. I won't be making that mistake again.'

Russell glanced across at the oh-so-familiar profile. Something had changed, he thought. For ever? Or just for the time it took for the shock to fade? It crossed his mind that he didn't want Effi to change, but this thought was soon supplanted by another – that the needs of survival might well demand changes from both of them.

She returned his glance. 'You must tell me all about America.'

'It seems a long time ago.'

She smiled. 'I can imagine. But I don't want to talk about the last few days. Not yet.'

'Okay. I've got a new job.' He told her about his

meeting with the *Tribune* editor in New York, what his new brief was.

'Is that the paper Tyler McKinley worked for?'

'No, but Tyler's editor recommended me. I phoned him to find out what sort of response they'd had to Tyler's story. The answer was not much. A few angry voices, but Washington didn't want to know. The paper finally got an assurance that our Ambassador here would raise the subject with Ribbentrop, and I'm sure he did, but I don't suppose the bastard was listening.'

Neither was Effi. 'I was only in that place for five days, but I had trouble remembering what a tree looked like,' she said, gazing out at the sunlit Tiergarten. 'Can we take a walk?'

Russell pulled over, and they took the first path into the park. Most of the benches were occupied by Berliners enjoying a picnic lunch in the hot sunshine, and there was a lengthy queue at the first ice cream stall they came to. They joined it anyway.

'Has it been as hot as this for long?' she asked.

'Since I got back.'

Effi shook her head in disbelief. 'I was cold in that place. Really cold.'

Russell put an arm round her shoulder, and received a wan smile in return.

'We're giving you your life back – that's what he said. You know, I can't even remember the swine's name.'

'Ritschel?'

'That's right. He told me no one knew I'd been arrested – apart from you and Zarah, that is – that I should just carry on as if nothing had happened. The première on Friday, the new film on Monday. Oh, I haven't told you about that.'

'*More Than Brothers?* I saw the script at the flat.'

'I only agreed to do it a few hours before I was arrested.'

Having reached the front of the queue, they bought their ice creams and walked across to the lake. A pair of ducks were fighting over a floating cone a few feet from shore. The previous owner – a very young child – was watching the fight with interest while his mother berated him.

'Is it a good part?' Russell asked.

'It's a big one.'

'Tell me about it.' Talking about her films was something they'd always enjoyed.

She seemed about to refuse, then shrugged her acquiescence. 'It starts at the end of the war,' she began. 'My sister's husband gets killed in the fighting, and she's completely distraught. When she finds out that she's pregnant she gets even more hysterical, and I only just manage to dissuade her from having an abortion. So she has the baby, but he – it's a boy, of course – reminds her so much of her dead husband that she runs away. I'm left with the baby, which isn't very convenient.' She paused to take a lick of ice cream. 'I already have a baby of my own, and I'm looking after my father, who's been crippled in the war. I'm a nurse at the local hospital – it's set in Wedding by the way – working split shifts. Since my husband can't find a job, he's supposed to look after things at home, but he's not happy about looking after one baby, let alone two. He gets drunk and tells me I have to choose between him and my sister's baby. I throw him out and struggle on. Only trouble is, the boys fight all the time.' She took another lick and smiled. 'At this point the writer wants one of those through-the-years-type collages of them fighting with each other – you know what I mean? – the problem is, they always end up using children of different ages who look nothing like each other.'

In the distance a military band started up, and promptly fell silent again. They waited in vain for a resumption. 'Where was I?' Effi asked. 'Oh yes. We've reached 1932. The boys are strapping lads who still can't stand each other. Enter the hero. Several young SA men are brought into the hospital after a street-fight with the Reds. One of them's in really bad shape, and he eventually dies, but not until I've been through my whole Angel of Mercy routine. The squad leader who keeps visiting them can't help but notice how wonderful I am, and of course I can't help but notice how stern and fatherly he is. I ask him over for dinner. He gets on like a house on fire with my father and, much more importantly, takes the two boys to task for fighting all the time. After a couple of visits he has them eating out of his hand. Cue wedding bells and the boys go off to join the Hitler Youth together. It ends with another collage – the two of them hiking in the mountains together, helping an old lady across the road, collecting for Winter Relief, etc etc. My husband and I stand at our front door, new children liberally scattered around our feet, and watch the two of them go smiling off to war. The End.'

'Incredible.'

'Ridiculous, but it's a living.'

'Where's it being shot?'

'Out at the Schillerpark Studio. I don't think they'll do any location shooting.'

'How long?'

'Three weeks, I think. You don't have to work today?'

'No.'

'And you're not going anywhere in the next few days?' she asked, betraying only the slightest hint of anxiety.

'Nowhere.' Prague could wait.

'You know, I feel hungry. After I've rung Zarah and had a bath let's go and have a nice lunch.'

'What are you going to tell her?' Russell asked.

'What do you mean?'

Russell told her what he'd said to Zarah on Monday. 'It's better for everyone if she believes it was all a mistake,' he added.

'Yes, I see that,' Effi said, 'it'll feel strange, though, lying to her. But of course you're right.'

They drove back to the flat. Russell read through some of the script while Effi talked to her sister and bathed. She shut the bathroom door, which was unusual, but he knew that remarking upon the fact would be unwise. She also pulled the bedroom door to when she went to dress. 'Let's go to that bistro in Grünewald,' she said on emerging. 'Celebrate our new jobs.'

Once they were seated in the restaurant she insisted on a blow-by-blow account of his trip to America, filling any space in his narrative with questions. 'You're useless,' she said, after failing to elicit a satisfactory description of the World's Fair. 'I shall have to ask Paul. I bet he remembers everything.'

'Probably.'

'And you got the American passport?' she asked.

'I did.' This didn't seem the right moment to mention the other side of the bargain – that he was now working for American intelligence. A picture of the sunny briefing room in Manhattan crossed his mind, the gaunt-faced Murchison dragging on his umpteenth Lucky Strike of the day. Over there it had all felt a little unreal. Europe had seemed a long way away.

He still meant to tell Effi, but the events of the last few days had complicated matters.

She sensed his reticence, though not its cause. 'I know you had to promise them something,' she said quietly, meaning the Gestapo. 'And I know we have to talk about what we're going to do. Together, I mean. But I need to think. I couldn't think in that place, just couldn't. After this wretched première... Can we go somewhere at the weekend, somewhere quiet, away from Berlin?'

'Of course we can.' Introspection was not something he associated with her. Intelligence, yes, but she'd always run on instinct rather than thought.

It was late afternoon when they arrived back at the flat. 'I think I need to sleep,' she said. 'But you'll stay, won't you? Could we get into bed and just hold each other?'

Ten minutes later Russell was lying there, wide awake, relishing the scent of her newly-washed

80

hair, the feel of her body tucked into his. 'We'll work it out,' he whispered, though he had no idea how. He remembered the poster in the torchlight, the jeering threats in the darkness. 'We will,' he murmured, more to himself than to her. She managed a grunt of agreement and slid away into sleep.

A leap in the light

Thursday began well. The sun was already streaming through the curtains when they woke, and long sleepy love-making seemed to dissolve any lingering distance between them. They shared a bath, took turns drying each other, and found themselves back on the rumpled bed. A second immersion in the tub exhausted the supply of dry towels.

They drove down to the Ku'damm for breakfast and sat outside with large cups of milky coffee, watching fellow Berliners on their way to work. 'You'll need a dress suit,' Effi said. 'For the première,' she added in explanation.

'I'll hire one. And that reminds me – I've got presents for you at home.'

Her eyes lit up. 'You'll bring them over?'

'I will.'

Effi looked at her watch. 'I told Zarah I'd see her this morning.'

'Then we'd better get going,' Russell said, signalling the waiter.

During the drive out to Grünewald he told her about Miriam, and his hiring of Kuzorra on Thomas's behalf. She listened but said nothing, just stared out of the window at the shops lining the Ku'damm. When Russell realized she was crying he pulled over and took her in his arms.

'I'm sorry,' she said. 'It sounds like a story with such a sad ending.'

Outside Zarah's house she kissed him a loving goodbye, and he watched the front door close behind the two sisters before moving off. Russell had woken in the middle of the night, full of fear that Effi would leave him, that she wouldn't risk her life on his ability to satisfy the SD. Here now, in the bright light of a summer morning, the notion seemed risible, but traces of the fear still lingered.

He drove back into town, stopping for petrol at the garage halfway up Ku'damm. According to Jack Slaney, the special permits required by travellers to the Czech Protectorate were only available from the Ministry of Economics building on Wilhelmstrasse, and needed further ratification from the Gestapo. A long morning's work, Russell guessed.

The Ministry office concerned did not open for business until ten-thirty. Russell read the *Beobachter* over a second coffee at Kempinski's and arrived at the permits desk a few seconds early. The bureaucrat behind it checked his watch, raised his eyes, and asked Russell why he intended visiting the Protectorate of Bohemia and Moravia.

'I'm a journalist,' Russell said, passing over his

Ministry of Propaganda press credentials. 'I want to see how the Czechs are enjoying their liberation.'

The bureaucrat suppressed a smile. 'You're entitled to a permit of course, but I should warn you that the Gestapo are unlikely to ratify it. The border is tightly closed,' he added, with unnecessary relish. 'When do you wish to go?'

'Monday week,' Russell told him. 'The 31st.'

The man took one printed green card from the small stack on his desk, filled in the dates by hand, and signed it. 'You must take this to the Alex. Room 512.'

Russell drove across town, parked his car in the street beside the Stadtbahn station, and walked across Alexanderplatz. The bell-towered slab of a building which housed most of Berlin's Kripo detectives and several Gestapo departments was situated on the far side, the relevant entrance on Dircksen Strasse.

Room 512 was on the fifth floor. The Gestapo duty officer hardly glanced at the green card. 'Come back in a week,' he said dismissively.

Russell smiled at him. 'If there should be a problem, please contact Hauptsturmführer Ritschel at Prinz Albrecht-Strasse or Hauptsturmführer Hirth of the *Sicherheitsdienst* at 102 Wilhelmstrasse. I'm sure one of them will be able to help.'

'Ah,' the man said. 'Let me write those names down.'

Russell retraced his path to the outside world, pausing only to wash his hands at one of the green washbasins which dotted the corridors. A ritual cleansing perhaps.

The heat was still rising but a few clouds had gathered, almost apologetically, in the western sky. Resisting the temptation to eat an early lunch at Gerhardt's he drove across town, left the Hanomag in the Adlon parking lot, and walked the short distance back along Unter den Linden to No.7, where the former palace of Princess Amelia, Frederick the Great's youngest and reputedly favourite sister, now housed the Soviet Embassy.

Russell rang the bell and glanced around, half-expecting a posse of men in leather coats propping up linden trees, all reading their newspapers upside down. There were none. The door was opened by a thin-lipped Slav in a grey suit. He was holding the last few millimetres of a cigarette between thumb and forefinger.

'Visa?' Russell said in Russian.

'Come,' the man said, looking beyond him for an unlikely queue. He took Russell's press identification and passport, gestured towards the open door of a waiting room, and strode off towards the rear of the building, his shoes rapping on the marble floor.

There was an obvious couple in the waiting room, Jews by the look of them, in their mid to late thirties. Russell wished them good morning and sat down in what proved a surprisingly comfortable chair.

'You are here for a visa?' the man asked.

'Yes,' Russell said, surprised by the directness of the question. 'I'm a journalist,' he added, 'an American journalist.'

'You are not German?'

'No, but I've lived here for many years.'

Silence followed, as if the two Jews were trying to work out why anyone foreign would choose to live in Germany. They were middle-class Jews, Russell noticed. The young man's clothes showed signs of serious wear and repair, but they would have been expensive when he bought them.

'Do you know anything about the situation in Shanghai?' the woman asked him suddenly.

'Not really. A lot of German Jews have emigrated there over the last six months. I believe the Gestapo chartered several ships.'

'They did. My cousins went on one, but we have heard nothing since.'

'That doesn't mean anything,' her husband interjected. 'You know what the post is like here – imagine what's it like in an occupied country like China.' He turned to Russell. 'We are here for transit visas,' he explained.

'I still think...' his wife began, but saw no point in completing the thought out loud. 'But what are they all doing in Shanghai?' she asked her husband. 'What will we do?'

'Survive,' he said tersely.

'So you say. We could survive in Palestine.'

Her husband made a disparaging noise. 'Palestine is just a big farm. Shanghai is a city. And if we don't like it we can go on to Australia or America.'

'With what?'

'We shall earn. We always have. Until Hitler came along and said we couldn't.'

'That's all very...' She stopped as footsteps sounded in the hall.

The grey suit appeared in the doorway, a newly-lit cigarette in one hand. 'Joseph and Anna Handler? This way.'

Russell was left to examine his surroundings. The Embassy seemed remarkably silent, as if most of the staff were off on holiday. Or off on a purge. The waiting room contained framed portraits of both Lenin and Stalin, gazing severely at each other from opposite walls. He thought through what he intended to say one more time, and hoped he wasn't guilty of over-confidence. He had got away with playing both ends against the middle in March, but he knew he'd been lucky as well as clever. The penalties for failure would be even worse this time, because Effi would also have to pay them. He might be shot as a spy, might escape with deportation. She would go to Ravensbrück.

The smoker returned about fifteen minutes later, and led Russell down a corridor to an office overlooking the central courtyard. A youngish woman with short curly hair and glasses sat behind the only desk, filing her fingernails. After a minute or so she held them up to the window, examined them from every conceivable angle, and lowered them again.

'Do you speak Russian?' she asked Russell in that language.

'Only a little.'

'English?'

'I am American.'

'Yes I see.' She picked up the passport.

'I am not here for a visa,' Russell said. 'I need to see your highest-ranking intelligence officer –

NKVD or GRU, it doesn't matter.'

She just looked at him.

'I am a friend of the Soviet Union,' Russell said, exaggerating somewhat. 'I'm here to offer my services.'

'Wait there,' she said, taking his passport and press credentials and leaving the room. She was wearing bright red carpet slippers, Russell noticed.

A few seconds later the smoker took up position in the doorway. Russell's smile elicited nothing more than a faint curl of the lip. It seemed distressingly likely that the object distorting his suit pocket was a gun.

Several minutes went by before the woman returned. A single sentence of Russian to the smoker, and he gestured Russell to follow. They climbed a wide marble staircase lined with poster-size photographs of factories and dams, and walked around the balustraded gallery. The furthest door led into a spacious office, high-ceilinged with a huge glass chandelier and two tall windows overlooking the Unter den Linden. A man in a dark grey suit, round-faced and balding, stood waiting in the middle of the room.

'Mr Russell? Please take a seat. We can speak in English, yes?' He chose an armchair for himself. 'Thank you, Sasha,' he said to the smoker, who left, closing the door behind him. 'So, you offer us your services?'

'And not for the first time,' Russell said.

'No? Please tell me. I know nothing of you.'

'May I know your name?'

'Konstantin Gorodnikov. I am trade attaché here at the embassy. With other responsibilities,

87

of course.'

After sketching in his communist past, Russell told the Russian about the series of articles he had written for *Pravda* earlier that year, and the oral reports on conditions in Germany that had accompanied them. 'My initial contact was Yevgeny Shchepkin – he never told me which service he worked for – but someone took his place at our third meeting, a woman named Irma Borskaya...'

'Wait a moment,' Gorodnikov said. He walked over to his desk, took a sheet of paper from the pile beside the typewriter, and selected a pen from those in the tray. A quick search for something to rest the paper on turned up a dog-eared copy of a popular German film magazine. Fully equipped, the Russian reoccupied his chair. 'Please continue.'

Russell did so. 'Comrade Borskaya never told me exactly who she worked for, either. She asked me to bring some documents out of Germany, and I agreed to do so on condition that her people helped a friend of mine across the border into Czechoslovakia. We both kept our parts of the bargain, but then she asked me to do something else. And when I refused, she planted some incriminating papers on me and tipped off the Gestapo.

'All this happened earlier this year. The Germans were not sure that I'd actually done anything illegal, but they knew I'd been in contact with your people over the articles and they suspected that there was more. Then, while I was in America this month, they arrested my girlfriend Effi for telling a bad joke about Hitler. When I got back last Monday the SD gave me a choice – work for them or Effi would be sent to a concentration camp. When I asked what they wanted me to do, they said I was to re-establish contact with you people and offer you intelligence. The idea being, of course, that they would be giving me false intelligence to pass on. So here I am. Obviously I have no desire to help the Nazis, or I wouldn't be telling you all this.'

Gorodnikov had written copious notes throughout this exposition, only pausing to sweep an imaginary speck of dust from his trousers when Russell mentioned Borskaya's attempted betrayal. 'That is very crystal clear,' he said, once it was plain the other had finished. 'You have skill for organising information.'

'That's my job,' Russell said dryly.

'Yes, I think so. And crystal clear means little without truth. I have no way to know how true this story is, here, now, but there can be later checking – I think you know that. So, let us say your story is true.'

'It is.'

'So. First question. If our person tries to have Gestapo arrest you, I think you will be very angry with Soviets. So why you want to help us? Why not just do what Gestapo want, and then you and your lady friend will be safe?'

'As I said, I don't like them. That's the first thing. I'm not crazy about you lot either, but if I'm forced to make a choice then there's no real contest. The Soviet Union might turn into something good – miracles can happen. Nazi Germany is something else. Nothing good grows out of scum. Do you understand?'

'You are anti-Nazi. That is good, but not surprise. Many people are anti-Nazi. Many Germans.'

'True, but they're not all being asked to help the bastards.'

Gorodnikov smiled for the first time.

'And they're not all willing to work for you,' Russell went on.

'How you work for us?'

'Well, I'll be bringing you false information that you know is false. Someone should be able to work something out from that.'

'Yes, but...'

'Look, I don't want any misunderstandings here. I'm not saying that I'm willing to die for the Soviet Union. Or anyone else for that matter. I'm willing to take some risks, but not those sort of risks. I won't take any more secrets across borders for you, but I'm ready to do some courier work inside Germany. And I'll pass on all the useful information which I come across as a journalist – I have good contacts here, and in London.'

'And you'll do this because the Nazis are scum?'

'And for one other thing.'

'Ah.'

'I want an escape route for myself and my girlfriend. I want you and your people to guarantee us a way out of Germany if we need one. I don't think that's unreasonable – I mean, it must make sense for you to keep your people out of the bastards' clutches. I know you can do it, and after the trick Comrade Borskaya tried to play on me I think you owe me that much.'

'Mm.' Gorodnikov scribbled another couple of lines. 'All right, Mister Russell. I will send this information to Moscow. They will decide.'

'How long?' Russell asked, hoping the Russian would say a couple of months.

'Oh not long. One week. Two maybe. Say you come again next Friday. Yes?'

'Right,' Russell agreed without enthusiasm. The Americans, the Germans, and now the Russians. Thank God the British had given up on him.

The embassy door closed swiftly behind him, as if pleased to be rid of his presence. It wasn't personal, Russell guessed. Just that sense of care-free bonhomie which Soviet establishments exuded the world over.

He walked up to Friedrichstrasse, had another coffee at the Café Kranzler, and telephoned the number Hauptsturmführer Hirth had given him. The voice at the other end recognized Russell's name, which was hardly surprising but disconcerting nevertheless. He gave a brief run-down of his first meeting at the Soviet Embassy, and listened as the message was laboriously repeated back to him.

'That is all,' the voice said, as if expecting applause.

If only it was, Russell thought.

He walked back down Unter den Linden to the car, retrieved the Berlin street map from the glove compartment and spread it across the wheel. His next port of call, he discovered, was out beyond Friedrichshain.

His route took him past the end of the street in which the Wiesners had ended their Berlin days. There were more than a few obviously Jewish faces to be seen, but fewer stalls selling furniture and knick-knacks than there had been six months ago. Perhaps they had all been sold. Perhaps some new regulation forbade it.

He eventually reached the address he'd been given – a boarding house in a quiet cul-de-sac that had seen better days. The landlady, a thin middle-aged woman with a young woman's hairstyle, looked Russell up and down, and apparently decided that he was worthy of assistance.

The Isendahls were gone, she said. At the end of May, as far as she could remember. And yes, Freya had received letters from America. She had always given the stamps to the boy next door who collected them. Her husband had said they would send her a forwarding address, but they hadn't. And to be perfectly honest she'd been glad to see the back of them. They were always having friends round, lots of them, and no, they weren't noisy, but there was something about them...

'Were they Jews?' Russell asked innocently.

'Certainly not. That's not allowed, is it? It certainly shouldn't be.'

'Of course not,' Russell agreed. Clearly the woman had no idea that Wilhelm Isendahl was Jewish. 'What did her husband look like?' he asked.

'Oh, nice looking. Blond hair, tall, very

charming when he wants to be.'

Russell gave the woman a card with his telephone number. 'If they do send a forwarding address, could you ring me? I'll reimburse any expenses, of course.'

He drove back into the city, wondering whether he should carry on looking. The friends might be innocent, but they seemed more likely to be comrades, and he had no desire to open doors that were best left shut. He would think about it. Maybe ask Kuzorra's advice.

After lunching at Wertheim he rang Effi from the bank of booths by the Leipziger Strasse exit. There was no answer. A quick stop-over at the Adlon offered reassurance that no major news was breaking – the sundry journalists gathered at the bar were wondering how they could wheedle invitations to one of Goering's hunting extravaganzas.

Back on Leipziger Strasse he collected the last available dress suit in his size from Lehmann Dress Hire. On the last occasion he'd used this particular shop it had been trading under the name Finkelstein.

He tried Effi again when he got back to Neuenburger Strasse, but there was still no answer. He told himself not to worry – she had said she was going shopping, after all. She might still be with Zarah. And he couldn't afford to spend his days wondering what she was up to and worrying whether she was all right. That wasn't who they were.

There was still no sign of Frau Heidegger's sister, but she had stirred herself sufficiently to attach an official notice to the inside of the front door. A citywide Air Raid Protection exercise was being held on the following Wednesday, and all citizens were obliged to cooperate fully with the relevant authorities. Reading through the small print Russell discovered that a complete blackout would be in operation. Selected buildings would be 'bombed', the resulting 'victims' removed by medical teams.

Where to, Russell wondered. Imaginary hospitals? It might make a good story, though. Frau Heidegger would be in her element.

He collected Effi's presents from upstairs and drove across town to her flat. He half-expected that she'd still be out, but they arrived together, she in a cab full of her purchases. Helping her carry these up, he forgot his own pile of parcels. She looked exhausted, but barely a minute had passed when she sprung back up from the sofa and insisted on their walking down to the Ku'damm for dinner. Russell had a brief memory of himself more than twenty years earlier. On his two home leaves from the trenches he had been utterly unable to sit still.

Over dinner she described her day in fearsome detail – the morning with Zarah, lunch with a make-up artist friend who was also working on *More Than Brothers*, a shopping spree in the Ka-De-We on Tauenzien-Strasse. She'd even managed a session with her latest astrologer.

'She told me the next few weeks were a good time for grasping opportunities,' Effi told him. "Aren't they all?" I asked her. "Some more than others," she said. I paid three marks for that.'

Russell shook his head. He was never sure how seriously Effi took her astrological advisers.

Back at the flat he remembered her presents, and went to collect them from the car. She loved them all – the soft leather driving gloves from Macy's, the Billie Holiday records which he'd half-expected customs would confiscate, the French perfume she'd originally discovered on their second trip to Paris, the deep crimson dress from Bergdorf Goodman. The latter looked every bit as good on her as Russell had imagined it would.

'I'll wear it tomorrow,' she said, thanking him with a kiss.

Friday evening's première was at the Universum, the modernist cinema halfway up the Ku'damm. The stars of the film, along with their escorts, were supposed to arrive between six forty-five and seven, the stars of the Party in the following fifteen minutes. 'This is one time we can't afford to be late,' Effi told Russell the next morning. 'So please be back here by five.'

Getting a lecture from Effi on punctuality was like taking dietary advice from Goering, but he let it go. 'I'll be here. But how are we getting there? A cab?'

'No, no. The studio are sending a car. It'll be here at six-thirty.'

'Right. So what are you doing today?'

'Hairdresser and manicurist this morning. And learning this,' she added, holding up the *More Than Brothers* script. 'I was hoping you could test me on Sunday.'

'Love to.' She seemed more like her old self, he thought, as he eased the Hanomag out onto the street. Or was she just putting up a better front? He thought about the talk they had planned for the weekend, and wondered just how much it was safe to tell her.

He was intending to do some background reading that morning, but events conspired against him. A major story was breaking, according to the British colleagues who frequented the Café Kranzler, and Russell joined the rest of the foreign press corps in pursuit of the pieces. According to 'reliable sources', one Robert Hudson, Secretary of the Department of Overseas Trade in London, had buttonholed the German delegate Herman Wohkhat at – of all things – a recently-opened Whaling Conference, and made him a series of unofficial offers. According to Wohlthat, whose swift report home was now being disseminated through the Berlin rumour mill, Hudson had offered him joint rule of the former German colonies and British economic assistance in return for German disarmament. None of this was in the public sphere as yet, but it soon would be.

First things first, Russell told himself, and called an old contact in the Foreign Ministry. Was it true? he asked. Off the record, yes. Hudson had made the offers all right, but no one in Berlin had any idea what official sanction, if any, he'd had for making them. The smart money in Ribbentrop's entourage was that the man had been drunk.

Possibly, Russell thought, as he headed for the

96

central post office. He'd have put his money on Hudson being just one more defective product of the public schools, with all the confidence in the world and none of the judgement. They seemed drawn to Whitehall's flame like dim moths, and particularly to those departments dealing with the wicked outside world.

At the post office he wired a contact in London who was likely to know the score, and hurried down the Wilhelmstrasse for that morning's briefing. The spokesman, an alarmingly thin young man with a swastika-emblazoned tie, refused to answer any questions about 'The Hudson Affair', and looked increasingly annoyed by the foreign press corps' protracted refusal to take no for an answer. Finally getting his own way, he triumphantly produced a statement from the Hungarian Foreign Minister condemning the recent publication of an anti-German book in Budapest. The book in question, as one of the American journalists delighted in repeating, warned of German designs towards Hungary and claimed that Germany was bound to lose a European War. How had the German government pressured the Hungarian government into making this statement?, the journalist wanted to know.

The spokesman sighed, as if the question was beneath contempt. He had some statistics for them, he said, flourishing a piece of paper to prove it. In the previous June the United States had exported $3.4 million worth of arms to Britain in June and $2.5 million worth to France. Germany, by contrast, had received a shipment of ammunition worth $18. He raised indignant eyes to his audience, at least half of whom were rolling with laughter.

'Another day in Looneyland,' Slaney observed as they walked out.

Russell went back to the post office to see if his wire had been answered. It had – Hudson had indeed been freelancing.

And with what looked like catastrophic results, Russell told himself. The Germans might realize that no such offers were really on the table, but they might also be left with the sneaking suspicion that the British still hungered for a way out of their obligations to Poland. As for the Soviets, they'd probably take Hudson's indiscretions as confirmation of what they already suspected, that the British were much more interested in doing a deal with Nazi Germany than in doing a deal with them. 'And so to war,' he murmured to himself.

He had enough for a short commentary piece, he thought, something they could use alongside the agency reports if the story took off. He sequestered a corner table at the Adlon Bar to write it out, then headed back to the post office to wire it off. By then it was almost four o'clock. He turned the Hanomag for home.

The studio car was on time, but Effi was not. Russell treated himself and the harassed-looking driver to a small measure of the Bourbon he had brought back from America, and was gratified by the appreciative smile he received in return. 'That's good,' the young man said, just as Effi emerged looking suitably ravishing. Her dark hair fell past her face in sweeping waves, her brown eyes glowed, the clinging red dress was beautifully set off by a lace scarf in deepest violet. She had found a shade of lipstick which perfectly matched the dress.

The young driver let out an involuntary sigh of appreciation. For reasons best known to itself, Russell's mind conjured up the image of Effi in her Gestapo cell, rising from the floor in desperate monochrome. It seemed weeks ago, but it wasn't.

The Universum was at Ku'damm 153, only a few minutes away. A hundred metres short of the cinema they joined a slow-moving queue of cars waiting to unload their celebrity passengers. On the other side of the road a few hundred watchers were held behind temporary barriers by a handful of *schutzpolizei*.

The long-departed Bauhaus architect Eric Mendelssohn had designed the building, which was one of Russell's favourite Berlin landmarks. On the outside, it looked as if someone had sliced the superstructure off an ocean liner, swung the bridge round ninety degrees, and dropped the whole lot beside the Ku'damm. UNIVERSUM was spelt out in huge, solid letters along the semicircular prow; a fifty-foot poster above the doors advertised the film currently showing. This particular poster – which featured a futuristic Prussian Army galloping madly along beneath the title *Liberation* – seemed almost as *avant garde* as the cinema. Effi Koenen was one of the four names listed below the two stars.

They climbed from the car, Effi drawing appreciative murmurs from the crowd. Russell could imagine the asides: what on earth does she see in *him?*

Once inside, they were hurried to their seats. The auditorium was virtually full, but three rows in the centre had been reserved for the celebrity guests. The actors and actresses chatted among themselves, apparently oblivious to the unconcealed interest of everyone else.

The Reichsminister for Propaganda arrived about ten minutes later. His wife was expensively dressed but, in Russell's admittedly biased opinion, looked somewhat frumpy. The rest of Goebbels' retinue seemed to have been chosen on grounds of size – the seven dwarves came to mind, though they all seemed too pleased with themselves to be Grumpy. Goebbels acknowledged the rest of the audience with a cavalier wave of the hand, then sat looking round at the sweeping, modernistic lines of the auditorium. There was an almost bemused look on his face, as if he was wondering how a Jew could have designed something so gorgeous.

The film let the cinema down, of course. It was standard Third Reich hokum, with the usual tried and trusted ingredients – a misunderstood genius whose iron will saves his people, male underlings who find their true purpose by abandoning mere reason, women who reach beyond kitchen, church and children at their peril. The setting – a much-used one in recent years – was the Prussian War of Liberation against Napoleon.

Christina Bergner, sitting three seats along from

Russell, played the tragic heroine. As Countess Marianne, the wife of an imprisoned Prussian general, she goes to plead her husband's case with the French occupation commander and, somewhat predictably, falls in love with him. Effi plays her friend, her confidante and – when the Countess finally sacrifices love, life and everything else for the Fatherland – her teary exculpator. She looked rather good in eighteenth century costume, Russell thought.

She looked good in the red dress too. Goebbels seemed to hold her hand for rather too long as he greeted the cast in the huge foyer. Russell, stationed in the background with the other escorts, found himself praying that Effi would restrain herself, but he needn't have worried. She smiled prettily throughout, and only he seemed to notice how tightly she was holding herself.

'He tried to proposition me,' she hissed a few minutes later. 'With his wife a metre away,' she added angrily.

'I shouldn't take it personally,' Russell said. 'I don't think he can help himself. What did he actually say?'

'Oh, how much prettier I was in modern clothes. How he'd admired my performance in *Mother*. How he'd like to hear my thoughts on how German cinema was progressing.'

'I don't suppose he knows you've been a recent guest of the Gestapo.'

'Maybe not, but I wouldn't bet on it. I think he expects me to jump at his offer. As if he knows I could do with the protection.'

They moved outside, where some of the Party

101

luminaries were still waiting for their own transport. As they stood there, Russell noticed a woman standing a few metres away. She was fairly tall, about his height, with elaborately coiffured brown hair framing a rather stark face. Her companion, a high-ranking SS officer in uniform, was talking to one of Effi's male co-stars, and she was looking around with the air of someone who could hardly believe where she was. Their glances met for a moment, and her face was suddenly familiar. Where had he seen her before? And then he remembered – it had been at the Wiesners' flat, on the night he had gone to tell Eva that her husband was dead. This woman had answered the door. Curly hair she'd had then. What was her name? He turned to look at her again, and found she was looking straight at him. Before he could say or do anything she gave him an almost imperceptible shake of the head.

He turned away. Sarah Grostein was her name. A Jew, he'd assumed at their first meeting, though she didn't look like one. What the hell was a friend of the Wiesners', Jewish or not, doing on the arms of an SS Gruppenführer? It was an interesting question, but not, he suspected, one that he'd ever know the answer to.

Once they were home he told Effi what had happened, expecting her to share his surprise.

'I'm beginning to think that Berlin is full of people leading double lives,' was all she said.

Delightfully languorous Saturday mornings, Russell reminded himself on waking, were one of the perks freelancers received in exchange for their miserable income. Hired hacks, on the other hand, had to keep up with the news, which these days barely slowed on Sundays, let alone Saturdays. He got up, took a bath and brought a sleepy Effi a cup of coffee in bed. She was seeing Zarah for lunch – her sister was eager to hear about the première – and thought it better to save a joint outing with Paul for the following weekend. Russell headed downtown to see how the German government was dealing with the Hudson story.

It wasn't, was the short answer. In Britain the *News Chronicle* had blazed the story across its front page – 'Hudson's Howler' they called it – but there was no Propaganda Ministry press briefing scheduled until Monday morning. Hitler had, as usual, dropped everything for the Bayreuth Festival, and while the cat was away the mice were sleeping in. The German papers had nothing to say about Hudson, and were in surprisingly pacific mood. The more-than-suspicious disappearance of a German customs officer in Danzig – shots were heard minutes after he 'strayed' across the frontier – only warranted the adjective 'regrettable'. The ongoing national convention of the 'Strength Through Joy' organization was turning into 'a festival of joy and peace' according to its official convenor, the loathsome Robert Ley. Foreigners, on the other hand, were prone to unreasoning belligerence, as Ley's description of the recent Bastille Day celebrations in France – 'an atmosphere of warmongering, nervousness and hysteria' – showed only too clearly.

Russell had something to eat at the Zoo Station buffet and drove out to Grünewald to pick up

103

Paul. Ilse asked after Effi, and was obviously curious to know why she had been released. Russell told his ex-wife that it had all been a mistake, that the Gestapo had advised them against mentioning either the release or the original arrest. He thought he could trust Ilse, but he was determined not to compromise her in any way. Paul's safety – not to mention her own – might depend on it.

Over the last couple of years his son had often chosen the Funkturm for their Saturday outings, and on this particular occasion he almost insisted. Revisiting Berlin's version of the Eiffel Tower, Russell came to realize as the afternoon wore on, was an integral part of Paul's coming home. The splendid Funkturm represented a Germany the boy could be proud of, a Germany, moreover, which he could share with his English father. Standing on the viewing platform, staring out in the direction of his beloved Hertha's Gesundbrunnen stadium, was a way for Paul to hold his world together.

His son was all over the place, Russell realized. Though quick to defend his country against any slight, he was still revelling in the wonders of the very different world across the Atlantic. As Paul looked out across Berlin, Russell knew that the boy was also seeing Manhattan. 'You were right about the hot dogs,' he told him. 'I had one at Gerhardt's the other day. They are the best.'

They walked round to the other side. The Havelsee shone piercing blue in the afternoon sunshine, and Russell was just thinking how peaceful Berlin looked from 125 metres up when the swelling whine of police sirens punctured the illusion. Paul raced back to the east-facing windows to see what was happening. 'They're down here!' he shouted.

Russell was walking across to join him when a voice over the loudspeaker announced that the tower was being evacuated. 'Move to the lifts in an orderly manner,' the voice instructed. 'There is no cause for alarm.'

Russell felt a sliver of panic. 'Are there any fire engines?' he asked his son, joining him at the window.

'No, just police.' A lorry drew up as they watched, and a troop of uniformed *Ordnungspolizei* climbed out. There was no sign of smoke.

'Let's get to the lift.'

There were only three others on the viewing platform, a couple and their young daughter. The man looked worried, and grew more so when a lift took several minutes to arrive. 'It's all right,' he kept telling his wife and daughter, who seemed much less concerned than he did.

The lift dropped smoothly down to the restaurant level, fifty metres above the ground. More people were waiting here, enough to make a real squeeze for the final descent. As they poured in, Russell could see more Orpo uniforms in the restaurant itself. Several children were crying, one wailing that she hadn't finished her Coca Cola. 'It's some Jew on the roof,' a man said angrily.

They reached ground level. More vehicles had arrived – half the Berlin police force seemed to be there – and the ground around the tower was littered with leaflets. A rhythmic banging sound came from above.

'Keep moving,' an Orpo officer insisted, and Russell realized they were being shepherded towards the nearby S-bahn station. 'My car's over there,' he told the man, pointing the Hanomag out. It was the only one left in the parking lot.

'All right. But leave that where it is,' the officer added, as Russell bent to pick up a leaflet. He shifted his gun slightly to reinforce the order.

'Whatever you say,' Russell agreed, putting a protective arm around Paul's shoulder and pulling him away.

'There's someone up there,' Paul said quietly. Looking up, Russell could see the lone figure on the restaurant roof. They were too far away to see the face, but there was an impression of smart clothes, as if the man had dressed up for the occasion.

The banging suddenly stopped, and several more figures appeared on the roof. As they moved towards their quarry he simply stepped off the edge, falling soundlessly to the concrete below.

Russell cradled Paul in his arms.

'Fuck off out of here!' the Orpo officer shouted.

They walked on to the car, got in, and drove out of the parking lot. Russell headed west, crossing the S-bahn at Heerstrasse and turning south into the forest. A kilometre in he pulled the car up and turned to his son, wondering what to say.

Much to Russell's surprise, Paul pulled a crumpled leaflet from his pocket. They read it together.

The headline was 'A LIFE WORTH NOTH-

ING?'; the text beneath explained why the man had jumped. His Jewish wife had been working as a nurse at Wedding's Augusta Hospital for almost twenty years when she was forced out by the Nazis. Earlier this year she had been hit by a tram on Invalidenstrasse, taken to the same hospital, and refused treatment. In the hour it took to reach a Jewish-run clinic in Friedrichshain she had bled to death.

'Do you think it's true?' Paul asked, his voice quavering slightly.

'I can't see any reason for the man to lie,' Russell said.

'But why?' There were tears in his eyes now.

'Why are people cruel? I don't know. I like to think it's because they don't know any better.' Russell looked at his watch – he was supposed to have Paul home in a few minutes. He put a hand on his son's shoulder. 'That was a terrible thing to see. But the man did what he wanted to do. And at least he's not in pain anymore.'

'Perhaps he's with his wife again,' Paul said hesitantly, as if he was trying the idea out.

'Let's hope so.'

'Well, if there's a God I think He must treat everyone the same, don't you?'

Russell couldn't help but smile – his son never ceased to amaze him. 'I think it's time I took you back,' he said, putting the car in gear.

Ten minutes later they were turning into Paul's street. 'Will you tell Mama?' the boy asked.

'If you want me to.'

'Yes, please,' Paul said.

The moment they were inside, he rushed off up

the stairs. Russell explained what they'd seen to Ilse.

'Oh God,' she said, looking up the stairs. 'Is he all right?'

Russell shrugged. 'I don't know. It was a shock.'

'And he's always loved going to the Funkturm.' Ilse glanced upward again.

'I'd better make sure he's all right.'

Back in his car, Russell felt a wholly unreasonable anger. Why couldn't the man have jumped off some other high building – the Shellhaus or the Borsig Locomotive Works? Why did he have to spoil the one place Russell shared with his son?

Returning to Effi's flat, Russell was greeted by the rare smell of cooking. 'I thought we could stay in this evening, and you could test me on the script,' she called out from the kitchen. 'It's only macaroni and ham.' She seemed in good spirits – almost too good. He decided against telling her about his and Paul's afternoon.

The food was better than he expected, and so was the evening. Effi's mastery of the atrocious script proved near-perfect, so they set about improving it. There was a lot of unintentional comedy in the original, and the storyline seemed made for farce. Their new version featured a squad of storm troopers who mistakenly beat themselves up in an air raid rehearsal black-out, and ended with the two war-bound brothers fighting over a grenade and blowing each other up in the process. At one point Effi was laughing so much that tears were running down her cheeks.

Russell found himself wondering whether

Hitler ever gave himself up to a giggling fit.

'Where are we going for our talk tomorrow?' Effi asked as they got ready for bed.

'I don't know. How about the Harz Mountains?' Russell had begun to think that she'd abandoned the idea, and felt mixed emotions at finding she had not. He didn't know how she would react to the things he had to tell her.

'That's a long way,' she said.

'A couple of hours in the car. If we leave early we can be there by eleven.'

'All right,' she said. 'The mountains it is.'

They got up late, and Russell rang the house in Grünewald while Effi was in the bath. Paul seemed fine, according to Ilse: no nightmares, and he was out in the garden with his football. She was keeping an eye on him, though.

The drive to the mountains took almost three hours, and it was past noon when Russell and Effi reached the summer resort of Ilfeld. It was another hot day, and hikers were queuing to fill their water-bottles at the inn's outdoor tap. While Effi stood in line Russell researched their options. The most popular ascent was that of the Burgberg, which boasted a picturesque ruined castle, but already seemed crowded with groups of *Hitlerjugend* and *Bund Deutscher Mädel*. Of the other four suggested climbs, the Eichenberg seemed the least strenuous and least frequented.

They encountered two descending pairs of elderly hikers in the first ten minutes, then had the hill to themselves. The path wound upwards through the pines, offering increasingly dramatic vistas of the plain below. It was around one-thirty when they reached an ideal spot for lunch – a hillside clearing with a single picnic table over-looking the valley below. Effi unwrapped their chicken rolls, while Russell opened the bottle of Mosel and poured a couple of inches into each of the tin mugs. 'To us,' he said, clunking his mug against hers. 'To us,' she agreed.

They ate their rolls in silent harmony, staring out at the view. There was a good breeze this far up the mountain, and the heat was not oppressive.

'When they came to arrest me,' Effi said matter-of-factly, as if they were continuing a conversation already started, 'they rapped on the door really softly. I thought I'd imagined it until they did it again. But when I opened the door they just pushed me backwards into the room and closed it behind them. I thought they were going to rape me.

'But they didn't. They just told me to get some shoes on and come with them. Once I was ready they told me not to speak until we reached their car.' She grimaced. 'And now we know why. They didn't want the neighbours to know.'

She looked down at her feet and then up again. 'They told me nothing. They took me to a room in the basement where an old hag watched me change into that grey outfit, and then they took me to the cell. I had a bucket of water to wash with. No soap. I had another bucket to pee in. They emptied that twice a day. I was never questioned, never told why I was there.

'It doesn't sound bad, does it? I wasn't hurt. I didn't go hungry or thirsty. The thing was – they would come for other people at all times of the day and night. You'd hear the bootsteps, the bolts pulling back, the door swinging open, the shouts. Some people would start talking really quickly, some would sob. A few screamed. And then they'd disappear. An hour or so later the boots would be back, the door would slam. But you couldn't hear the prisoner anymore. You could just imagine whoever it was being shoved back into the cell, barely conscious. And every time the boots come back you think it's for you, and you're so, so, so relieved that it's someone else whimpering out there.

'And I thought – if I get out of here I can't forget this. And I haven't. I'm sitting here looking at this beautiful countryside and I'm thinking about those people in those cells who are dreading the sound of those boots. And that's just one building. There are all the concentration camps – more than twenty of them, someone told me.'

'I know,' Russell said. He had never seen her like this.

'We have to fight these people,' she said, turning to face him.

He felt shocked, and knew he shouldn't.

'I have to fight them,' she corrected herself. 'I don't really know how, but I can't go on living here and doing nothing.'

'You were right the first time,' Russell said, taking her hand. 'We're in this together.'

She squeezed his hand. 'So how do we start?'

With a leap in the dark, Russell thought. Or, given what they knew of the possible conse-quences, a leap in the light. 'A good question,' he said. 'There are some things I need to tell you,' he added, almost apologetically.

'I thought there must be.'

He smiled. 'First off, I'm sort of working for American intelligence.'

'Sort of?'

'They think I'm working for them, and I am, but it wasn't completely voluntary. I think I might have volunteered anyway, but they made it pretty clear that I'd only get the American passport if I agreed.'

'What ... what do they want you to do?'

'They've given me a list of people. Most in Germany, but a few in Poland. Anti-Nazi people.'

'How did they hear about them?'

'From others who emigrated. I'm supposed to check them out, make contact if it seems advisable, find out where their loyalties lie. It's all rather vague, because they don't really know what they're doing. Basically, they've just woken up to the fact that a European war is coming, and that they have no ears and eyes anywhere on the continent.'

Effi looked thoughtful. 'I'm not doubting your journalistic abilities, my darling, but is this why you were given your new job?'

'The thought did occur to me, but I don't think so.' He shrugged. 'In practical terms, it doesn't make much difference one way or the other.'

'I see what you mean. So you're going to start checking these people out.'

'Slowly. And very carefully.'

'Good. All right. So that's what the Americans wanted for the passport. What did the SD want

112

for me?'

'Not much. Yet. They may have big plans for the future, but the first thing they wanted me to do was re-enlist with the Soviets. The *Sicherheitsdienst* think they can use me as a conduit for false intelligence.'

'You've seen the Soviets already?'

'On Thursday. I told them I've been forced to work for the Germans and that the information I'll be giving them is a bunch of hooey. The ironic thing is – I was going to make contact with them anyway.'

'After last time?'

'Needs must. Effi, I'm all for fighting the good fight, but I'd really like us to survive these bastards. If the worst happens, and one or both of us ends up on the run from the Gestapo, the only people who could get us out of Germany are the comrades. They've had organized escape routes across the French and Belgian and Czech borders since the late 20s – it was them who got Albert Wiesner out. So I did a deal with myself– I'd work for the Americans, but only once I had our escape hatch arranged.'

'And the Soviets have agreed?'

'Not yet, but I think they will.'

'But what can you offer them?'

'Depends what they ask for. I could argue that I'm already doing them one service by telling them the German information is false.'

'Won't they want more than that?'

Russell shrugged. 'Who knows? It's all getting a bit surreal. Did you ever read *Alice in Wonderland*?'

'When I was a child. Zarah used to have

nightmares about the Queen of Hearts.'

'No wonder she married Jens.'

Effi laughed. 'Poor Zarah.' She held out her empty mug. 'Is there any more wine?'

He poured them both a generous measure, and they sat for a while in silence, sipping from the mugs and staring out at the landscape.

'John,' she said eventually, 'I want to help you however I can, but that's not all I want to do. You and I, well, we move in different worlds, don't we? The people I know I have to do what I can in my world. I'm going to start talking to people – carefully, of course. There are thousands of people – millions for all I know – who think the Nazis are a cruel joke. I'm going... I don't know, you'll probably think I'm an idiot, but I've asked Lili Rohde to teach me more about make-up. I've told her it's because I'm getting older, and there aren't many parts for older women and I need to think about my future, but that's not the real reason. Make-up – disguise, really – seems like something that might come in useful in lots of ways.' She looked at him warily, as if expecting ridicule.

'It could,' he agreed.

Reassured, she went on. 'And I've been thinking about something else. We don't want to keep secrets from each other, but I think we may have to keep some. I was thinking that we could talk about what we were doing without using the right names. That way...'

'I understand,' Russell said. He had expected one of two reactions from Effi – either one of her trademark rants or a rueful decision to play it safe. He had not expected a simple statement of intent, let alone a cool appraisal of risk. He had underestimated her, and fear had been the reason. This new Effi was living proof that things had changed, and he was scared. For both of them.

'I was never interested in politics,' she said, 'and I'm still not really. You have to be *for* something in politics, you have to have some idea of a different world which is better than the one you've got. I just know what I'm against. Killing children because they're handicapped in some way. Locking up anyone who publicly disagrees with them. Torturing them. And all this violence against the Jews. It's just wrong. All of it.' She turned to him, angry tears welling in her eyes. 'I'm right, aren't I?'

'I'm afraid you are.'

Rehearsals

The studio car picked Effi up at five-thirty on Monday morning, establishing the pattern for the next two weeks. Whenever she had this sort of schedule Russell spent the weekday nights at Neuenburger Strasse, but on this occasion they agreed to spend Wednesday night – and the air raid rehearsal – together. Being bombed would be so much more interesting in each other's company.

That Monday morning, Russell left the flat soon after eight and headed across town to the

Café Kranzler. The German newspapers seemed bemused by 'Hudson's Howler', unsure whether it represented a genuine offer, indignant at the very idea that the Reich could be bribed into acquiescence. As a story, Russell decided, it had run its course.

He spent most of the next two hours in one of the Adlon telephone booths, calling up a variety of German contacts in a vain trawl for fresh news. Suitably frustrated, he strode down the Wilhelmstrasse for the eleven o'clock press briefing at the Foreign Ministry. Ribbentrop's spokesman had a sneer or two prepared for the British, but, as usual, soon found himself on the defensive. An English correspondent asked about Pastor Schneider, the Rhineland clergyman who'd been in custody for twenty-seven months, and whose death from a 'heart attack' in Buchenwald concentration camp had just been announced. Had the authorities reached a decision on which law he had broken?

'An internal German matter,' the spokesman blustered. He held up his hands, as if to show they were clean.

Briefings like that could sap the will to live, Russell thought, as he drove home to Neuenburger Strasse. Frau Heidegger's door was open, the woman herself lying in wait with her deadly coffee. Russell took his usual chair and the usual trepidatory sip, and was pleasantly surprised. 'My sister washed the pot out,' the concierge told him indignantly, 'and the coffee doesn't taste the same.'

'It's a little weaker,' Russell agreed, forbearing

to add that it would still jolt a dead camel to life.

Like most Germans, Frau Heidegger had gleaned her knowledge of America from the movies, and her questions about Russell's trip were framed accordingly. She was disappointed that he hadn't seen the West, thrilled that he and Paul had visited the skyscraper made famous by King Kong. A distant cousin had once thought of emigrating to America, she told him, but the thought of giant apes running wild had put her off. The woman hadn't been very bright, Frau Heidegger admitted. But then no one from the East Prussian side of the family was.

Her own week in Stettin had been wonderful. Her brother had arranged a sailing trip, and they'd gone so far out that they could hardly see the land. Returning to Berlin was the usual tale of woe, however. It always took her two weeks to undo what her sister had done in one.

'There's one thing I should know,' she said, having reminded herself of her duties. 'Will you be here on Wednesday night for the air raid rehearsal? I'm asking because Beiersdorfer will want to write it all down.' Beiersdorfer was the block warden, in name at least. He was as frightened of Frau Heidegger as the rest of them.

'No, I'll be at Effi's,' Russell said.

'Ah, I saw her picture in the paper,' Frau Heidegger said, leaping up and riffling through the pages of that day's *Beobachter*. 'Here,' she said, passing it over. Christina Bergner was talking to Goebbels in the Universum foyer, a smiling Effi just behind them.

'It's a good picture,' he said.

'Did she talk to the Minister?'

'Just a few words. He complimented her on her acting.'

'That is good. She must have been pleased.'

'Yes, she was.' Russell took a final sip, gently pushed the cup away, and asked if any messages had been left for him.

There were two. Uwe Kuzorra had called – 'He has information for you, but he has no telephone, so you must call on him whenever it's convenient.' The second message was from a Frau Grostein. 'She said you know her. She would like you to call her on this number' – Frau Heidegger passed over a small square of paper. 'As soon as possible,' she said, 'but that was on Saturday, soon after I got back. The woman sounded ... not upset, exactly. Excited perhaps?'

Russell shrugged his ignorance. 'I hardly know her. She's a friend of a friend. I'll call her now.' He got to his feet. 'Thanks for the coffee. It's good to have you back.'

She beamed.

He walked across the ground floor hallway to the block's only telephone and dialled the number.

'Frau Grostein,' a confident voice announced.

'John Russell. I've just got your message.'

'Mr Russell. I need to talk to you, but not on the telephone. Can we meet?'

'I suppose so.'

'Today?'

'All right.'

'It's ten past twelve now. How about two o'clock in the Rosengarten? By the Viktoria statue.'

'Fine. I'll see you there.' The line clicked off,

and Russell replaced the earpiece. A mistake? he wondered. These days his life seemed like one of those downhill ski runs he and Effi had seen at the Winter Olympics in '36. The contestants had plummeted down the mountainside at ever-increasing speeds, needing split-second changes of direction just to keep within bounds. Most had ended up in exploding flurries of snow, limbs and skis splayed at seemingly impossible angles.

Russell parked close to the Wagner monument on Tiergartenstrasse and walked up through the trees to the lake. Just past the statue of Albert Lortzing – the Germans did love their composers – a bridge led him over the stream and into the colonnaded Rosengarten. He caught sight of Sarah Grostein, crouching down to smell the dark red roses that surrounded the Empress Viktoria's marble plinth.

He walked towards her, glancing around as he did so. There were a few office workers, nannies with children, a pensioner or two. No one seemed interested in her or him. No one's head was hidden behind a raised newspaper. Paranoia, he told himself sternly. It beats the axe, a second inner voice retorted.

She stood up, looked round and saw him. She offered her hand and half-whispered, 'Thank you for coming.'

He just nodded.

'I thought we could walk,' she suggested. 'Towards the goldfish pond?'

She was older than he'd thought – around his own age, probably. Still attractive, though. Tall, big for a woman, but well-proportioned. Her

119

clothes looked extremely expensive, her hair like someone had spent a lot of time on it. There was something feline about the contours of her face, something sad in the large brown eyes. 'Wherever you like,' he said.

After leaving the Rosengarten she chose one of the less-used pathways. 'Have you said anything to anyone about ... seeing me where you did?'

'I should think half of Berlin saw you.'

'You know what I mean. After meeting me at the Wiesners. It must have surprised you.'

'Seeing a Jewish woman on an SS General's arm? It certainly made me curious.'

'So did you tell anyone?'

'Only my girlfriend.'

'Will she tell anyone?'

'No. When I told her she just suggested that half the people in Berlin were living double lives. And I didn't mention your name.'

'I'm surprised you remembered it.' She fell silent as a couple walked past in the opposite direction. 'I'm not Jewish by the way,' she said once the pair had gone by. She let out a short brittle laugh. 'Now that all Jewish females have Sarah as their second name it's assumed that anyone called Sarah is Jewish, but there are thousands of non-Jewish women named Sarah. Or were. I expect most of them have changed their names by now.'

'So how...?'

'My husband was a Jew,' she said. 'Richard Grostein. A wonderful man. He died in Sachsenhausen five years ago. He was one of those Social Democrats who wouldn't shut up when the

Nazis came to power. He was an old friend of Felix Wiesner's and I was an old comrade of Eva's – that's how we met.'

'I see,' Russell said, and thought he did. 'You don't need to tell me anything more. Your secrets are safe with me. Even safer if I don't know what half of them are.'

She smiled at that. 'It's not that simple, I'm afraid.' She gave him an appraising look. 'You don't seem to hide how you feel about the Nazis,' she said. 'Of course that must be easier for a foreigner, and you may not take it any further. I have the feeling you do, though. Or maybe that you will at some time in the future. If you do, you'll probably reach that place that I've reached, where you suddenly find that your own decisions have become matters of life and death. Your own life and death.'

Russell nodded. Six months earlier, agonising over what to do with a false passport, he had experienced exactly that thought.

'I've decided to trust you,' she said. 'With my life,' she added lightly. 'I'm guessing you must be a good man because of what you did for the Wiesners, but I don't really know anything about you. Eva told me that you arranged Albert's escape with the comrades, so I'm assuming – hoping – that you're still in touch with them.'

Say no, Russell thought, but he couldn't. 'I could be,' he temporised.

'We ... I need to make contact. Our group has had no contact for four years, and we have no idea who it's safe to approach and who it isn't. We just need an address or a telephone number.'

121

Russell thought about it. She was – to repeat her own phrase – asking him to trust her with his life. He assumed she was a good person because she too had been a friend of the Wiesners, but he didn't really know anything about her either. Except that he'd seen her on an SS Gruppenführer's arm.

Her story rang true. The KPD had certainly been decimated by the Nazis in 1933. Half of its leaders had ended up in concentration camps and half had fled into exile, leaving several million rudderless members to fend for themselves. Many of those arrested had been persuaded – mostly by fear of torture – into betraying comrades still at liberty. Many had actually joined the Nazis, some from self-interest, others as a clandestine opposition. The problem was knowing which was which.

'We have valuable information,' she insisted. 'My Gruppenführer works in the Reichsführer's office.'

Russell was impressed. 'I'll see what I can do. It may take a few weeks though.'

'After four years, a few weeks won't matter.'

Russell was thinking about Effi's mutual secrets. He knew he wouldn't tell her about this meeting, and the knowledge saddened him.

Another thought occurred to him. 'Do you know a Freya and Wilhelm Isendahl? She was Freya Hahnemann until recently. She's not Jewish but he is.'

'Why are you asking?'

'Because I'm looking for her. I met her parents in New York a few weeks ago and they wanted me to check that she was all right. When I questioned the landlady at their old address I got the impression they were involved in political activity, and I don't want to put them in any danger.'

'I knew a young man of that name, back in 32-33. Not personally, but by reputation – he was one of the youth wing's rising stars. I'm surprised he's still alive. You know what we used to call our Party activists in 1933?'

'Dead men on furlough.'

'Exactly. I'll see if I can get you an address.'

'Thanks.'

'And you'd better have mine – it's safer to visit than telephone.' She gave him a number and street in one of the posher districts to the north of the park.

'Nice area,' he said.

'My husband was a rich socialist,' she said without irony. 'Family money. And he had the sense to put everything in my name before the anti-Jewish laws were brought in. I used to feel guilty about having it all, but now it just feels like part of the disguise.'

'I'll be in touch, one way or the other,' Russell said.

She leaned forward and kissed him on the cheek, scenting the air with jasmine. 'Till then.'

They set off in their separate directions. Both of them, Russell guessed, were thinking the same depressing thought – that there was one more person in the world who could, and probably would, betray them under torture. Look on the bright side, he told himself. If he was instrumental in delivering Sarah Grostein's 'valuable information' to the Soviets, they might feel like they owed him something. Yes, and pigs might soar like eagles.

The Hanomag was like an oven, encouraging the pursuit of cold beer. Several cafés in the Old City's Schloss-Platz offered large awnings for drinking under, and the sight of the square's fountain seemed cooling in itself. Russell ordered a Pilsener and reminded himself he had a living to earn. The air raid rehearsal should make a story, but was there any way of finding out where the action was going to take place? Wandering round in the blackout looking for supposedly bombed houses seemed rather hit-and-miss, not to mention potentially dangerous. The local storm troopers would probably be out shooting imaginary paratroopers, and he had no desire to be one of them.

The Propaganda Ministry might let him tag along with one of the ARP units if he asked nicely. *How Germany's war preparations contribute to peace.* Something like that.

A second beer was tempting, but he decided to get the trip to Wedding over with first. This time it was Kuzorra who opened the door. 'Schnapps?' the detective asked immediately. 'Katrin is out,' he added, as if in explanation.

'A small one,' Russell said.

'I went down to the station,' Kuzorra began once they were seated, 'and met the train your girl would have been on. I talked to three of the crew – the conductor and two of the dining car staff. They all remembered her.'

He took an appreciative sip of his schnapps,

placed the glass on a shelf beside his chair, and reached inside the jacket which was draped across the back for a small notebook. He didn't open the notebook though, just held it in his lap. 'The conductor examined her ticket soon after the train left Breslau, but he also remembered seeing her much later in the journey, between Guben and Frankfurt he thinks. A sweet little thing, he called her. A little nervous.

'And then there were the two waiters. The young one who took her order thought she was a 'looker', as he put it. Big eyes. I expect he would have told me how big her breasts were if I'd asked him. The older one – he has one of those moustaches which were old-fashioned in the Kaiser's time – he had to tell her that they couldn't serve her. Some rancid hag panicked at the thought of eating within ten metres of a Jew, and her husband insisted on their checking Miriam's identity papers. He said she looked surprised, but didn't kick up a fuss. Just went like a lamb. That was before Sagan, he thought.'

'So we still can't be certain that she reached Berlin?'

'Not completely, no. I talked to all the station staff, the left luggage people, every last one of the concessionaires – frankfurter stands, news kiosks, hair salon, the lot. I thought she must have been hungry after seven hours without food, but no one recognized her from the photograph. Several regulars were taking their week's holiday though, and they'll be back this Friday. I thought I'd go back for another try. It would be good to get an actual sighting at Silesian Station. Rule out the possibility that she got off at Frankfurt.'

'Why would she do that?' Russell asked, more rhetorically than otherwise. Kuzorra shrugged. 'She may have been more upset by the business in the dining car than she showed. Took a sudden decision to head back home.'

'She never got there.'

'No. And I know it's unlikely. All my instincts tell me that she reached Berlin.'

'And if she did...'

'It doesn't look good.' The detective reached round and replaced the notebook in his jacket pocket. 'So shall I have another go this Friday?'

'Yes, do that. Do you need any money?'

'No. I'm still earning the retainer.'

Russell got to his feet. 'I won't be around much this weekend, and I'm probably off to Prague on Monday, so leave any message at my number, and if you don't hear back straight away then just keep digging, okay?'

'Suits me. Any excuse to get out of the house,' he added, as he showed Russell out.

Clouds were gathering as he drove back into the city, and rain started falling as he crossed the Eiserne Bridge over the Spree. Effi had left her bright pink parasol in the back seat, and this protected him from the worst of the downpour as he walked from the car to the crowded portals of the Adlon.

He phoned Thomas from the lobby to deliver the latest news.

'I've never met the girl,' Thomas said, 'but for some reason she's keeping me awake at nights.'

'It's called humanity.'

126

'Ah, that.'

In the bar, his fellow correspondents assured him that 'Hudson's Howler' had died a well-deserved death, and that no new story had risen to take its place. Hitler was still in the south enjoying his opera, and all was at peace with the world. Russell headed back to Neuenburger Strasse, Sarah Grostein, Freya Isendahl and Miriam Rosenfeld competing for prominence in his thoughts.

Frau Heidegger was waiting with a message from Effi. The studio, dismayed by the possibility that its latest masterwork might be interrupted by the air raid rehearsal, had decided to put the cast and crew up at a hotel outside the city.

'Does this mean you'll be here?' Frau Heidegger wanted to know. 'Because I've already told Beiersdorfer that you won't be.'

'I'd better let him know then,' Russell said wearily. It amused him that Frau Heidegger, so scrupulous with her Herrs, Fraus and Frauleins, always refused that courtesy to the block warden. There was nothing political in it, unless contempt could be read as such.

Beiersdorfer's rooms were on the first floor, and Russell had only entered them once before, as part of a deputation formed to dissuade him from reporting a ten-year-old girl for repeating a political joke that she was too young to understand. He remembered the portraits on the wall, the Führer on one, Fat Hermann on the other. The man was too old to have served in the Luftwaffe, but he liked making model aeroplanes.

Russell was left to wait in the hall while Beiersdorfer collected his clipboard. The man then amended his finely-wrought chart with painstaking care, sighing all the while. Russell let him finish before adding that he might be out anyway, on a journalistic assignment, and was duly rewarded with a Hitlerish splutter of exasperation.

He approached his own room with an apprehension that he half-knew was unwarranted – why would Hauptsturmführer Hirth have him beaten up again? – but still felt stomach-tinglingly real. This time though, the door was definitely locked, and the light responded to his flick of the switch. There were no thugs reclining on his sofa.

He took a fresh bottle of beer to the seat by the window, and put his feet up on the sill. The rain and clouds had cleared as quickly as they'd come, leaving an unusually clear sky. The odd passing car apart, Berlin gave off a gentle hum. It was only six and a half years since the Nazis had taken over the city, but sometimes it felt as if the bastards had been there forever. Not tonight, though. He wondered whether Sarah Grostein was in bed with her unsuspecting SS General, whether Freya and her firebrand were out there dancing round the feet of the Gestapo elephant. He thought about Thomas and his missing girl, about the new look in Effi's eyes. The bastards might be in power, but this wasn't just a city of billowing swastikas and Sportspalasts and 'wild' concentration camps, and it didn't just belong to Hitler and Goebbels and their brown-shirted swamp life. Other Berlins were still alive, still clamouring for attention. The Brechts and the

Luxemburgs, the Mendelsohns and the Döblins – they might all be gone, but their ghosts still haunted Hitler's night. By the clear light of summer mornings, however, Russell felt rather less optimistic. He and his fellow foreign correspondents spent Tuesday and Wednesday trying to confirm the sundry depressing rumours circulating in the city. On the previous Saturday one German newspaper had announced that trade talks had been resumed between Germany and the Soviets. The various ministries refused to confirm or deny this, merely passing queries on to each other with a knowing nod and wink. Soviet Ambassador Astakhov, meanwhile, had invited two of Ribbentrop's officials to the All-Union Agricultural Exhibition in Moscow, which Molotov was opening on the following Tuesday. This might seem more like a punishment than a sign of deepening friendship, but the Soviets, as everyone knew, were incredibly fond of tractors.

Were Hitler and Stalin edging towards some sort of pact? On Wednesday morning the front page headline in the *Daily Express* was PACT CERTAIN, but they were talking about an alliance between Britain, France and Russia. Someone was in for a shock.

On a more definite note, the German Army manoeuvres for the coming summer were scheduled to start at the beginning of August, and to last for several weeks. These would take place throughout Sudetenland and Silesia, and in the area between Berlin and the Polish border. Or, to put it another way, right under Poland's nose. Reservists were being called up, and private

129

vehicles were likely to be commandeered.

By lunchtime on Wednesday the overall view in the Adlon bar was that war had slipped just a little bit closer. The only good news was purely personal. After several hours of squeezing himself through bureaucratic hoops Russell learned that the vehicles of foreign residents were exempt from military seizure.

He had also been successful in persuading the Propaganda Ministry to let him join one of the Air Raid Protection units during the coming 24-hour rehearsal. The exercise was due to start at 3pm, and he spent the hour after lunch driving round the city and looking at the preparations. Gangs of workmen had been out since Monday whitewashing kerbs, corners, steps and anything else likely to trip people up in the blackout. Black cloth curtaining was already edging many windows, ready for pulling across when the sirens sounded, and many a grey-overalled ARP warden was standing sentry outside his block, waiting for the chance to give orders. Beiersdorfer, as Russell discovered on dropping off the car at Neuenburger Strasse, had been unable to find a helmet small enough for his head, and had to keep tipping it backwards to see.

He walked down to Hallesches Tor and took a tram up Koniggrätzer Strasse to Potsdamer Platz. His unit was based in an old warehouse, on the street running along the eastern side of the railway station. There were a couple of ancient-looking cars in the yard, along with assorted makeshift ambulances and several of the open lorries storm troopers had favoured for their raids in the good old days. Several wardens were sitting round on packing cases flirting with the unit's nurses, all of whom seemed to have been hand-picked by the Ministry for their blonde aryan chubbiness. One warden was cutting thin slits in the black material he had just fastened to the lorry's headlights.

Russell introduced himself to the unit's commander, a weasel-faced man of around forty who seemed friendly enough. He gave Russell a press badge to pin on his shirt, complimented his choice of dark clothes, and told him to stay out of the way as much as he could. 'You can ride in the back of an ambulance when we go out, and then grab a seat wherever you can for the ride back.'

A few minutes later, at three o'clock, the exercise officially began. Nothing happened for several hours, however. Everyone sat waiting, listening to the trains come and go in the adjacent station, until someone remembered he had brought a pack of cards with him. One game of skat was inaugurated immediately, another got started when a second pack was purchased from one of the kiosks on the station concourse. Russell had lost almost a mark when the air raid warning finally sounded, three blasts of two minutes each, separated by two similar stretches of silence. 'A bit excessive,' as one of the wardens put it; 'by the time you've listened to all that, the enemy will have come and gone.'

Planes were now audible overhead, the sound of anti-aircraft fire coming from all directions. It was shortly after seven when the unit received its

131

first call-out – bombs had fallen in the Spittel-markt. One car, one ambulance and two lorries hurtled down Leipziger Strasse, Russell clinging to the rails of the rear vehicle and marvelling at the ease with which Berlin had been brought to a halt. The popular shopping street was empty of traffic and people, save for two abandoned trams and a couple of stragglers disappearing into one of the public shelters.

At the Spittelmarkt smoke was pouring out of two adjoining office buildings. A fire engine had already arrived and was pumping imaginary water in through the first floor windows. Black flags had already been placed on nearby buildings to indicate that they were in danger of collapse.

Several people were lying on the pavement in front of the offices, competing for attention with some rather histrionic wailing. Placards looped around their necks spelt out the nature of their injuries, and the nurse swiftly decided which victims were in direst need of hospital treatment. Stretcher parties transferred these unfortunates to the ambulance and one of the lorries, and both vehicles took off in the direction of St Gertraudt's Hospital. A flight of planes crossed almost over-head, but apparently dropped no bombs. Two of the firemen began arguing about how much im-aginary water they had put on the imaginary fire.

The second lorry took the walking wounded to the hospital, and Russell had the rear to himself as they headed back to the unit's base. The all-clear sounded as they crossed the Landwehr-kanal, and people were spilling out of the public shelters as they drove up Koniggrätzer Strasse.

132

The sky looked blue and empty.

'They won't call another one until it's dark,' one of the wardens guessed, as he gathered up the cards. He was right. It was soon after ten-thirty when the sirens sounded again, another ten minutes before they got the call – a major attack in the Wittenbergplatz. The whole unit crawled slowly southward down the blacked-out Potsdamer Strasse, turned right at the unlit Bülow Strasse Station and followed the dark mass of the elevated U-Bahn tracks westwards. Clinging on to his lorry Russell could see the dark shapes of planes against the stars, the flash of AA guns from the direction of the Tiergarten.

The scene in the Wittenbergplatz probably echoed that in the Spittelmarkt, but the darkness made everything more difficult and, Russell thought, more distressingly real. It was easier to imagine the burst arteries and severed limbs when the wailing victims were invisible, easier to smell the panic when pencil torches were all you had to see through the smoke and when everyone seemed to be shouting at once. Russell found himself fighting back a rising tide of trench battle memories, and grasped at the prospect of action when a warden said, 'Come with me,' and led him in through the front door of an apartment block.

The warden stopped at the first floor landing, shone his torch on Russell, and realized he'd made a mistake. 'What the hell,' he said. 'You take the east side. Knock on every door. If there's anyone in here, get them out.'

Russell did as he was told. Or almost. He thought he heard noise behind a couple of doors,

133

but didn't knock again when no one answered. The one family that did respond to his knock filed obediently down the stairs and out into the street, the adults arguing with each other, the children giggling nervously.

The ambulances were loaded and ready to go, but Russell decided he had seen enough. Effi's flat was only a ten minute walk away, hidden away in a backstreet, and as far as he could tell, the organizers of this particular exercise were going for large squares and maximum publicity. He chatted to a few evacuated residents outside the KaDeWe until the all-clear sounded, then headed up Tauenzien-Strasse to the Kaiser Memorial Church. As he crossed the eastern end of the Ku'damm he stopped in the centre and stared up the long, arrow-straight avenue. A car was moving away in the distance; barely visible in the dim blue lights, it soon became one with the shadows.

No ARP wardens came knocking at Effi's door, but the Luftwaffe's continuing antics made for a restless night. He was probably imagining it, but many of his fellow-Berliners looked distinctly bleary-eyed as they waited at tram stops on their journey to work. Not everyone had been inconvenienced, of course – Hitler had been enjoying *Tristan und Isolde* at far-off Bayreuth while the capital rehearsed. And Soviet Ambassador Astakhov, as Russell learned from Jack Slaney, had been wined and dined by Ribbentrop's East European chief, Julius Schnurre, until the early hours.

'Where?' Russell asked.

'Ewest's.'

'They must mean business then,' Russell said dryly. The restaurant on Behren-Strasse was one of Berlin's finest.

'You can bet that street didn't get bombed,' Slaney said in a similar tone.

'Anyone know what was discussed?'

Slaney shook his head. 'The trade guy Barbarin was there too, so maybe just that. They all seemed really chummy though, according to one of the waiters.'

'Another straw in the wind,' Russell murmured.

'Or on the camel's back,' Slaney suggested.

Russell headed back to Neuenburger Strasse to write up his ARP exercise article. The smooth modern typewriter he'd inherited from Tyler McKinley was at Effi's place, but he still preferred the brutal mechanics of his old one. Another consequence of living in Nazi Germany – you only felt you were getting somewhere if physical violence was involved.

The ARP exercise had spared Neuenburger Strasse, much to the dismay of both Beiersdorfer and Frau Heidegger. The former was only now removing the black-out sheets from the communal hallway, and both were eager to hear Russell's account of his attachment to one of the mobile units. Frau Heidegger seemed horrified by what she heard, and was only slightly mollified by Beiersdorfer's assurance that London, not Berlin, would be on the receiving end of such bombing raids.

Russell left them to their optimism, and went up to his rooms. He took almost three hours over the article – it was his first major piece for the *Tribune* and he wanted it to be good. After lunching at the bar under the Hallesches Tor Station he drove back into the old city and sent the story off.

Next stop was the Alex. The duty officer in Room 512 searched through a pile of refused Protectorate visa applications for Russell's, and deduced from its non-appearance that the refusal had not yet been put to paper. When Russell suggested that his application might have been accepted, the man opened a drawer to demonstrate its emptiness, only to find a single waiting permit. He examined it for several seconds, and finally passed it over.

Russell drove back across the river to the American Express office on Charlotten-Strasse. A couple of months earlier a German friend had told him that first class travellers – like army officers and government officials – were allowed to sleep through the border checks, provided they handed their documents over to the carriage attendant with a decent tip. And after his traumas at the same border in March that seemed like a really good deal, especially if the *Tribune* was paying.

As it happened, the American Express office could sell him a first class ticket and book him into a hotel, but the sleeper reservation required a trip to Anhalter Station.

By the time he got back to the Adlon bar it was gone five. Noticing Dick Normanton hard at work at a corner table, Russell bought him a whiskey. 'Anything I should know?' he asked, placing the glass down on the polished wooden surface.

'Thanks,' Normanton said wryly, and took a sip. 'Just between us,' he said. 'I don't want my fellow Brits to get wind of this.'

'My lips are sealed.'

'Have you heard of Ernest Tennant?'

'English businessman. Friend of Ribbentrop's, impossible as that seems.'

Normanton smirked. 'Not so much these days. Tennant's just been visiting Ribbentrop's castle...'

'The one he stole by putting the owner in Dachau?'

'Do you want to hear this story or not?'

Russell raised his palms in surrender.

'They arrived in Berlin together this afternoon – Ribbentrop had his two private coaches attached to the express from Munich. Tennant came straight here, and I had a chat with him in his hotel room.'

'You know him?'

'My owner does, and Tennant told him he was seeing Ribbentrop. Reading between the lines, I'd say he was hoping to emerge as a peacemaker, but ready to put some distance between himself and the Nazis if Ribbentrop refused to play ball. Which of course he did. Told Tennant that Hitler was the greatest human being since Mohammed, and then started back-tracking when he realized the implication – that the Führer was less important than a mere Arab.'

'The usual nonsense.'

'Exactly. The important part came later. On the train here Tennant got talking to Walther Hewel – know who he is?'

'Hitler's liaison with Ribbentrop, or is it the

137

other way round?'

'Both, I suppose. Anyway, his take on the current situation – and we assume Adolf's – is that Chamberlain and Co. rushed into guaranteeing Poland without really thinking it through, and that they're now desperately looking for a face-saving way out. The Germans think that Hudson's Howler was just the first of many trial balloons, that when push comes to shove the British will provide themselves with some sort of excuse not to fight.'

'Which is bad news.'

'For everybody. The Poles because they'll get squashed, the Germans and the British because they'll find themselves at war with each other without really wanting to.'

'Happy days.'

'Thanks for the drink.'

Russell played poker with several American colleagues that evening, and gave Jack Slaney a lift home in the small hours. They stopped at the all-night kiosk in Alexanderplatz for sobering coffees and early editions of the morning papers. 'What did I tell you?' Slaney asked after a few moments with the *Beobachter*. He folded the paper in half and pushed it under Russell's nose, and jabbed a finger at the editorial. Danzig, it seemed, was no longer enough. Real peace, the editor announced, would require a Polish willingness to discuss self-determination in the Corridor, in the lost provinces, in Upper Silesia. Would require Poland to lie on its back and wave its arms and legs in the air.

'They think they're pushing at an open door,'

Slaney said.

'Yes,' Russell agreed, thinking about his talk earlier with Dick Normanton. 'Question is, will it slam shut behind them?'

'You Brits will fight, but your government sure as hell doesn't want to. They should be trying to scare the Germans, not reassure them. And if Ribbentrop's wining and dining Astakhov then they should be taking Stalin out for a meal.'

'He'd probably eat them.'

Slaney laughed, and the two of them sat there drinking their coffee, staring out across the dimly-lit square.

The following morning, soon after eleven, Russell arrived for his appointment at the Soviet Embassy. The thin-lipped Sasha answered the door, and the usual receptionist ignored him while Gorodnikov was appraised of his presence. Up in the office overlooking the boulevard he found the attaché fanning himself with a sheaf of papers.

'It's like summer in Batum,' Gorodnikov said. 'Have you ever been in Batum?'

Russell had not.

'It is like this. All summer. You English call it sticky, I believe.'

'We do. So have you heard from Moscow?'

'Yes, of course,' the Russian said, sounding offended at the mere question.

'So what do they want me to tell the Germans?'

'You are to say that we accept offer, that we agree to pay you good money for any information concerning German plans that involve the Soviet

139

Union – military, economic, anything. You must say that we are most interested in German intentions towards us, that we worry about attack.'

'All right. And your side of the bargain?'

'Yes, yes. They will give you what you ask for.' Gorodnikov was shuffling through his fan for the right piece of paper. 'Someone likes you in Moscow, yes?'

'That's good to know.'

'Maybe. Maybe not. Depends who it is.'

'True.'

'Ah, here it is,' he said, extracting one sheet and putting the others down. 'Moscow agrees to help you escape from Germany. You and your lady friend. But only in real emergency. You understand? Not for holiday in the sun.'

'I understand.' And Russell did – the Soviets would get him and Effi out of Germany, but only once he'd proved his worth, and only if the Nazi authorities were actually snapping at their heels. The Soviets had nothing to gain by helping them out any sooner.

He asked for the contact number.

'We shall get to that. First, a small job you must do for us.'

Russell's heart sank a little deeper. 'What sort of small job?'

'You will go to Stettin, and see a woman there. Let me explain.' Gorodnikov leant forward, elbows on the desk and fingers interlocked. The Soviets, he told Russell, had had an agent in the Stettin docks, a man named Bernhard Neumaier. The Gestapo had arrested him on the previous Saturday, and he had died under interrogation in

Sachsenhausen on Wednesday. A couple of weeks before his arrest Neumaier had told the regular courier that his girlfriend was pregnant. He had asked the Party to look after her if anything happened to him. Her name was Erna Kliemann.

'Does she know he's dead?' Russell asked.

'We do not know.'

'Does the Gestapo know about her?'

'Our best information is that Neumaier gives nobody up. A brave man, if that is true.'

Russell hoped it was. If it wasn't, and her name *had* slipped out under torture, then the Gestapo would be waiting for someone to turn up. 'Why not send the regular courier?' he asked.

'If Neumaier tells the Gestapo anything, then this man is compromised. And *he* knows many names.'

Perfect, Russell thought. He tried another tack. 'Why risk anyone?'

'The woman needs to know that Neumaier is dead. If she go to authorities with questions – bad for her and bad for us. We not know what Neumaier tells her – maybe nothing, maybe everything. If she says nothing, then good for her and good for us. And we want to give her help.' He passed an unsealed envelope across the desk; it was stuffed with twenty-Reichsmark notes. 'We look after our people,' Gorodnikov said defiantly, as if daring Russell to deny it.

The money would help, Russell agreed. 'Why not send it?' he suggested innocently.

'Not possible to send money without explain,' Gorodnikov told him. 'She must learn how much Neumaier care for her.'

Of course, Russell thought. The money would only keep her quiet if she knew where it came from.

'And too urgent for post,' Gorodnikov added pointedly.

'When do you expect me to go?' Russell wanted to know.

'Today.'

'Oh no...'

'It will only take few hours. Two hours there, two hours back – you dine in Berlin.'

'I...'

'You want way out of Germany for you and your girlfriend. This is what Moscow expect in return.'

Russell considered. It could be a lot worse, he thought. There was nothing illegal about carrying an envelope full of cash, and if there was any sign of a watch on the woman's home he could just walk away. And the reward had to be worth it. 'All right,' he said, pocketing the envelope. 'What's her address?'

Gorodnikov had already written it out. 'You must remember and destroy before you arrive in Stettin,' he advised.

'I will. Now what about that contact number?'

Gorodnikov printed out a telephone number and passed it across. 'You ask for Martin.'

Russell looked at the number, and recognized it. It was the photographic studio in Neukolin which he often used. Miroslav Zembski, the man who owned and ran it, had to be Martin. Russell had known Zembski was a communist before the Nazi takeover, but had assumed that the fat

142

Silesian's willingness to fake him a passport earlier that year had simply been for old times' sake. Now he knew otherwise – Zembski was still on the active list. Another double life. Another reason for hope. 'I have some information for you,' he told Gorodnikov. 'A KPD cell, here in Berlin. It has had no contact with the leadership for four years, and...'

'This is a matter for the KPD.'

'One of the women has become the lover of a high-ranking SS officer. She says she has access to information that will be very useful to you.'

'Ah. This woman's name?'

'Sarah Grostein.'

'A Jew?'

'Her husband Richard was a Jew. And a prominent member of the KPD.'

Gorodnikov wrote the name down. 'I look into.' He looked up. 'If Moscow says yes, they will expect you to be woman's contact.'

'I'd rather you contacted her directly.'

'You know her. And the SD not object to you coming here. They tell you to come here!'

It made sense. 'We'll see,' he said weakly.

Sasha was summoned to show him out. As he walked down the marble stairs Russell remembered Sarah Grostein's comment about life and death decisions. Had he just taken several more?

There was an autobahn to Stettin, but Russell decided to give the Hanomag a rest. Erna Kliemann probably lived in one of the city's less salubrious districts, where cars and their occupants tended to be conspicuous. And the train

143

would be just as quick.

He arrived in Stettin soon after five. After obtaining directions for Lastadie, he walked up the west bank of the wide Oder to catch a tram across the Hansa Bridge. A five minute ride brought him to Grosse Lastadie, the dockland suburb's main street, where a helpful old woman pointed him in the direction of the junction with Schwangstrasse. No.14 was fifty metres down, a house with three storeys of living space above a small workers' restaurant and a tobacconist. The former was already closed for the day, and the proprietor of the latter was busy locking up. The entrance to the rooms above lay between them.

It was the sort of area the Nazi authorities liked to visit in strength, but Russell carefully scanned the surrounding windows, and ostentatiously examined the piece of paper he had inscribed with her address and a made-up name, before heading across the street and in through the open front doors. The smell in the stairwell, an unhappy blend of boiled cabbage and tobacco, pursued him upwards, growing stronger with each flight of creaking treads. Room 7 was right at the top, and a small piece of paper bearing a neatly-inscribed 'E. Kliemann' was pinned beside the door. There was no answer to his knock.

A second, louder knock brought no response from inside, but the door behind him opened to reveal a young boy in his school uniform. 'Erna's not back yet,' the boy announced.

'Do you know when she will be?' Russell asked.

'She goes to her sister most days. She's usually back by eight o'clock.'

It wasn't much gone six – he'd have to come back. 'Thank you,' Russell said. 'I'll try again later.'

'You are most welcome,' the boy told him.

Back on Schwangstrasse Russell noticed an open bar on the opposite side. The evening trade hadn't yet arrived, and the only two customers were sat at the back, half-hidden in a cloud of pipe-smoke. Russell ordered the only food on the menu – a sausage casserole – took a beer back to a window seat, and began his vigil.

Two hours dragged by. He was beginning to think he must have missed her when a young woman in a blue frock walked slowly by on the opposite pavement. She had straight dark hair cut to the shoulder, was small, slim and obviously pregnant. Russell watched her turn in through the open front doors.

He waited a couple of minutes, then followed her in. Responding to his knock, she pulled the door back a few inches, and placed a careworn face in the gap.

'Erna Kliemann?' Russell asked.

'Yes,' she admitted, gazing past his shoulder to check he was alone.

'I've come about Bernhard Neumaier.'

Her body seemed to sag. 'He's dead, isn't he?'

'I'm afraid he is.'

She closed her eyes, fingers tightening on the edge of the door.

'Can I come in?'

The eyes re-opened, bleak and hostile. 'What for?' she asked. 'Who are you?'

'I have something for you. From his friends.'

'Why should I believe that?'

'If I was the enemy, I wouldn't be asking.'

She gave him a searching look, then widened the aperture to let him in. Russell stepped inside. The room was right under the roof, with a sloping ceiling and a small dormer window. It was sparsely furnished, with just a bed, a single upright chair and a wide shelf for the wash bowl.

She closed the door and turned to face him. 'He died last Saturday, didn't he? I felt it.'

'I don't know when he was killed,' Russell lied. It seemed kinder to leave her believing in some special psychic connection. And who knew? – maybe some part of Neumaier *had* died on the Saturday.

'It *was* Saturday,' she reiterated, sitting down on the bed and holding her belly with one hand.

She had a pretty face beneath all the weariness and grief, Russell realized. And she couldn't be much more than eighteen.

'How did he die?' she asked.

'We think he was shot,' Russell said, taking the upright chair. There was no need for her to know that Neumaier had died under torture.

She looked at the floor for several moments, rocking gently to and fro, hands clasped against her swollen belly.

Russell asked if she'd known that Neumaier was a communist.

'Of course.' She raised her head. 'Bernhard believed in the Soviet Union. And the International.'

The recitation sounded almost defensive, but he could see that the words were important to her. Her man had died for something worthwhile, something noble. The solace of any religion,

146

Russell thought cynically.

'Bernhard told his contact that you were having his child. He asked the Party to look out for you if anything happened to him.'

A large tear rolled down one cheek. The first of a stream.

He handed her the envelope, and watched her examine its contents.

'There's hundreds of Reichsmarks here,' she whispered.

'For you and the child.'

She lowered herself to her knees and pulled a battered suitcase out from under the bed. 'It was his,' she explained, clicking it open. 'There are only his clothes and this,' she added, handing Russell a small notebook. The tears were still flowing. 'He was going to pass this on at his next *treff*.'

It was full of small, neat writing in black ink. Timetables, tonnages, names of ships. At first glance it looked like a detailed breakdown of the cross-Baltic trade in Swedish iron ore. That trade was certainly vital to the German war machine, but Russell had no way of knowing if the information in the notebook was secret or valuable.

He didn't want to know. 'This could get you arrested,' he said, holding it out to her. 'You should burn it.'

She stared at him, surprise sliding into disgust. 'He died for that,' she almost hissed.

'Then post it anonymously to the Soviet Embassy in Berlin,' Russell suggested.

She angrily shook her head. 'Bernhard said that

anything with that address was intercepted and opened. That's why he was waiting for the courier. Now you must take it.' She wiped her face with the back of her hands and glared at him.

Russell realized she wasn't going to take no for an answer. And he could always get rid of the damn notebook himself – she would never know. 'All right,' he told her, slipping it into his inside pocket. 'I'll see that the Party gets it.'

'He said it was really important,' she insisted, determined that Russell should acknowledge the same.

'Then it probably is,' he agreed, getting to his feet. 'I wish you luck,' he added, opening the door to let himself out. It sounded ludicrously inadequate, but what else was there to say? He could hear her begin to sob as he started down the stairs.

Back on Grosse Lastadie he stood at the tram stop, checking his watch and feeling somewhat exposed. It was only half-past eight on a Friday evening, and not even fully dark, but there were few people on the street and hardly any traffic. Lastadie seemed devoid of taxis, and the infrequent trams were all headed in the wrong direction. Half an hour into waiting, it was clear that walking would have been the wiser choice.

When an inbound tram finally arrived it was full of boisterous young sailors from the naval base. Russell fought his way off on the far side of the Hansa Bridge, checked his watch one last time, and gave up on the idea of catching the last train. He would have to get a hotel room. But first...

He walked out onto the bridge, intent on

148

dropping Neumaier's notebook into the Oder, and stared down at the shining black waters for what must have been more than a minute. He couldn't do it. She was right – her lover had sacrificed his life for this. Not directly perhaps, but in some essential way. Russell stood at the parapet, notebook in hand, knowing he owed the man more than this. Knowing he owed himself more than this. And cursing the knowledge.

He put it back in his pocket and started walking. His last and only other night in Stettin had been spent at the luxurious Preussenhof Hotel, and he felt in need of further cosseting. When he reached that establishment ten minutes later the bar was doing a roaring trade, and he allowed himself a couple of confidence-boosting schnapps before heading up to his room. Unfortunately, the sight of two probable Gestapo men in the lobby – both of whom watched him all the way to the lift – undid all the alcohol's good work. Russell let himself into his third floor room, double-locked the door, and frantically wondered how he could conceal the notebook from unwelcome visitors.

There was nowhere to hide it, but the en-suite toilet – a Preussenhof luxury extra – offered the option of instant disposal. Russell sat down on his and took out the notebook. After numbering all the pages Neumaier had used, he carefully tore them out, and placed the loose pile on the side of the adjacent wash-basin. If the Gestapo came to call he would flush the incriminating evidence away.

He dropped a few blank pages into the bowl to

test the efficacy of the flush. The pages disappeared. And didn't come back.

He left the toilet light on, stripped off his clothes and got into bed. Having nothing to read, he turned off the bedside lamp, closed his eyes, and tried to lull himself to sleep with happy memories. It seemed to take forever, but he was finally drifting off when a sudden noise in the corridor outside jerked him wide awake again. What was it? He could hear people whispering, and someone was trying to turn the door knob, trying to get in.

He leapt naked from the bed, rushed into the toilet, and took up position beside the open bowl, notebook pages in one hand, flush in the other. In the corridor outside a sudden bout of giggling was followed by a loud squeal of pleasure.

Russell caught a glimpse of himself in the wash basin mirror, and wished that he hadn't.

There were no more sudden alarms, but sleep worthy of the name proved elusive, and by five-thirty he was fully awake. Waiting for the early shifts to populate the street below, he debated the pros and cons of posting the pages to himself at a convenient Poste Restante. He couldn't send them to the main office in Berlin, because that was where he had used McKinley's name to pick up the envelope in February; but there were other offices, and this time there would be nothing false about his documentation. Using his own name, on the other hand, would carry its own perils. Who knew how closely Hauptsturmführer Hirth was watching him? Did alarm bells go off at the Haupt-Post when an item of mail arrived bearing his name?

He wouldn't use the mail. A two-hour train journey, a ten-minute drive to the Unter den Linden, a short and easily explainable visit to the Soviet Embassy. Nothing to it.

But where to put the loose pages? His jacket-pocket was the obvious place, but that was where he carried his identity papers and journalistic accreditation, and he had a nightmare vision of himself at an unexpected checkpoint, spilling everything out together. In his shoes, he decided. He divided the pages into two piles, folded each in half, and stuffed them in. Once the shoes were on his feet, he could hardly feel the difference. He only hoped the sweat of another hot day wouldn't render the pages illegible.

He left the room just before seven, and took a tram to the station. There was a fast train to Berlin in twenty-five minutes, a semi-fast in forty. The former took an hour less, but the latter gave him the option of getting off at Gesundbrunnen in north Berlin, which seemed a safer bet than Stettin Station, where checks on travellers were much more likely. He sat over a coffee wondering which class of ticket offered the greatest security – the perceived respectability of first, the anony-mity of third, or the no man's land of second. He opted for a first class ticket on the semi-fast and sat with another coffee, this time scanning the concourse and platform gates for men in leather coats. There were none.

His train pulled out on time, and despite the coffees he soon found his eyelids drooping with fatigue. One moment he was listening to the wheels rattling beneath him, and then someone was shouting outside his window. *'Alles aussteigen!'* 'Everyone off!'

The train was standing at a small country station – Kasekow, according to the board. Away to his left, he could see two cars and a lorry drawn up in the goods yard. A group of Brown-shirts with semi-automatic weapons were walking down the neighboring tracks.

Russell's stomach went into free-fall.

'Alles aussteigen!' the voice shouted again.

Russell stepped down onto the platform. There were about sixty people on the four-coach train, and almost all of them were men of working age. Most seemed exasperated by the likely prospect of a long delay, but some seemed buoyed by the diversion, casting delighted glances hither and thither, like visitors to a movie set. At the head of the train the elderly locomotive was audibly sighing at the interruption to its progress.

A table had been planted under the platform canopy, and two men in civilian clothes were sat behind it. Gestapo, no doubt. Another man – probably their superior – was standing with his back to the building, calmly smoking a cigarette.

'All passengers line up!' someone else shouted. 'Have your identity papers ready!'

A line formed, stretching down the platform from the table to the rear of the train. There were only four people behind Russell, an elderly couple and two cheerful young men in Wehrmacht uniforms.

Looking round, Russell realized that the whole station area was surrounded by a loose cordon of storm troopers. Several more Brownshirts were noisily working their way through the train, presumably in search of possible stowaways.

The line moved slowly forward. Edging sideways for a view of the table, Russell saw that the seated officers were doing more than simply checking papers. Pockets were being emptied, bags searched. And, as Russell watched, the man being questioned knelt down to undo his shoelaces and remove his shoes.

A cold wash of panic coursed through Russell's brain. What could he do? He cast around for hope, but there were no obvious gaps in the ring of storm troopers, and the nearest trees were two hundred metres away.

What explanation could he give? He might have been able to pass off Netsmaier's pages as his own journalistic notes, but how could he explain hiding them in his shoes?

What had he been thinking?

Could he get them out? One soldier was staring straight at him, and the man in charge also seemed to be gazing down the platform in his general direction. There was no way he could take off a pair of shoes, remove their illicit contents, and put them back on again without making it bloody obvious. He was fucked, well and truly fucked.

What would happen to Effi? How would Paul cope?

Stop it, he told himself. Don't give in to panic. Keep thinking.

Were they asking everybody to take their shoes off?

He edged out again. A man was handing his

papers, getting a smile in return from the Gestapo officers. His papers were returned with a nod of thanks, and the man turned away. He hadn't been asked to remove his shoes. Was there hope after all, or was that glint on the man's lapel a Party badge?

Two middle-aged businessmen came next. One was ordered to take off his shoes, the other was not. Was it just a matter of chance? Was there something – some magic words – Russell could say to save himself?

He never found out. There were a dozen people left in the line when a young man three or four places ahead of him calmly stepped down off the low platform, ducked under the couplings between two of the stationary carriages, and disappeared from sight.

There was a moment's shocked silence, then a cacophony of shouted orders and storm troopers running in all directions. Russell was daring to hope that incompetence would have the last word when a short burst of firing sounded beyond the train. He willed there to be more, but one fusillade had apparently been enough.

A few moments later a storm trooper appeared with what had to be the young man's papers. The man in charge ran his blue eyes over them, and gave the men at the table an affirmative nod. 'Get everyone back on the train,' one of these told an underling, who repeated the order at five times the volume. Russell walked slowly back to his compartment, struggling to hide his legs' apparent reluctance to support his body.

As the train pulled away, he saw two storm

troopers heave a bloodied corpse into the back of their lorry. While one wiped his hands in the roadside grass, his companion lit cigarettes for the both of them.

The train reached Gesundbrunnen over an hour late, and Russell decided on travelling all the way in to the terminus. He had to deliver Neumaier's pages before he picked up Paul, and there seemed little chance of a second check on the same train. But he did take the precaution of transferring the pages from his shoes to his jacket pocket.

There were no leather coats hovering by the barrier at Stettin Station. Russell collected the Hanomag, drove straight to the Soviet Embassy, and told Sasha that the crumpled, sweat-stained pages should be passed on to Gorodnikov. Back on the pavement, he looked round for the probable watcher. None was evident, but it didn't matter either way. If the Germans queried his visit he would tell them that the Soviets had asked him to collect a sealed envelope from a stranger in Stettin as proof of his loyalty.

Having secured Neumaier's legacy, he drove round Pariser Platz and into the Tiergarten. As he pulled the car to a halt in one of the less frequented byways, Russell had a sudden and sickening realization. There had never been any reason to hide Neumaier's notebook. If the Gestapo had caught him with it, he could simply have said that he was bringing it back for Hauptsturmführer Hirth. The nonsense with the hotel toilet, his near-panic on the Kasekow platform –

155

it had all been avoidable.

He had almost killed himself with his own stupidity.

Russell sat staring at the summer trees, gripping the steering wheel to keep his hands from shaking.

He arrived outside his son's Grünewald home at the appointed time, feeling less than ready to play the role of the confident father. But if he found his performance less than convincing, Paul didn't seem to notice. The boy also seemed out of sorts, but refused to admit as much. The two of them went to the Zoo, and everything seemed a bit flat, the combination of high summer heat and animal dung leaving a distressing aftertaste. Paul's favourite animal – the notorious spitting gorilla – was reputedly out of sorts, and refused to shower his visitors.

On their way home in the car Paul asked him whether America would join in a European war. Russell said he didn't know, but that most Americans seemed inclined to let Europe sort out its own problems. Paul thought for a moment and then asked another question: were the Americans afraid, or did they just not care who won?

'They're not afraid,' Russell said. 'Most politicians have no idea what a modern war's like. And in any case they won't be the ones to fight and die.'

'So they don't care who wins.'

'I think most would support England against Germany. There's a long tie between them. I mean, they both speak English.'

'Is that the only reason?'

'No. Americans believe in democracy, most of them, and the Führer's Germany, for all its achievements, is not a democracy.'

'But every plebiscite we've had, the Führer has won a huge majority.'

'True.' Russell had no desire for an argument over what constituted a real democracy.

'And if the Americans do care who wins, then why won't they fight?' Paul pressed on relentlessly. 'My troop leader calls them decadent. He says they have no sense of honour.'

'Let's hope there's no need to find out,' Russell said evasively, as he turned the car into Paul's street. 'Almost there,' he added unnecessarily.

Paul looked at him. 'Sorry, Dad,' he said.

'Nothing to be sorry for,' Russell said. 'This is a difficult time for Germany. Let's just hope we get through it in one piece.'

Paul smiled at that. 'Let's.'

Back at Effi's flat Russell found what looked, on first impression, like a pair of sixty-ish women chatting in the living room. It was Effi and her make-up friend Lili. 'We did each other,' Effi explained after introducing Lili. 'What do you think?'

Russell was impressed, and said so. Lili's work on Effi was better than vice versa, but that was only to be expected. And from more than a metre away both looked pretty damn convincing.

'I've booked a table for four at Raminski's,' Effi told him, looking at her watch. 'Are you all right?' she added, giving him a closer look.

'Fine,' he said. 'A bit tired.' He could tell her

later about Kasekow. If he told her at all.

She decided to take him at his word. 'Lili's husband should be here soon, so can you let him in while we get this stuff off?'

'Of course,' Russell said, repressing a slight surge of irritation at not having Effi to himself. Eike Rohde arrived a few minutes later, a tall man, probably just into his thirties, with cropped blond hair, pugnacious face and nervous smile. He also worked at the film studio, as a prop carpenter and scenery painter. His family was from Chemnitz, his father and brothers all miners. His wife, when she finally emerged from the bathroom, had shoulder-length blonde hair, a trim figure, and one of those faces which grew much more attractive with animation. She greeted her husband with obvious affection.

The four of them walked down to the Ku'damm. The pavements and pavement cafés were crowded, the restaurants and late-opening shops doing a thriving trade. There was a large queue for Effi's film outside the Universum, but no one recognized her as she walked past. At Raminski's they ate canapés and shared a bottle of Mosel before ordering their main courses. The discussion, as Russell expected, was mostly cinematic shop, but once the wine had worked its magic he happily listened to the familiar litany – the buffoon of a director, the cheapskates who ran the studio, the sound technicians who thought they were working in radio. Eike Rohde had news of an interesting dispute over a set, which had been referred to the Propaganda Ministry for adjudication. The director had decided

158

that a 1920s room should have 1920s books, and what better way of demonstrating this than including books banned by the Nazis ten years later? Goebbels' boys had disagreed.

As they ate, Russell became aware of the conversation at an adjoining table. Three women and one man, all in their thirties, were discussing the international situation, and their opinions seemed more than a little at odds with the prevailing orthodoxy. They seemed oblivious to this, however, and indifferent as to who might hear them. Looking round, Russell could see one man at another table pursing his lips with obvious annoyance, a couple at another sharing worried looks. He was still wondering whether he ought to do something when Effi got up, took the necessary two steps to the table concerned, and leant over to whisper something.

'What did you say?' Russell asked her later.

'I said: "It's completely up to you, but you're going to get yourselves arrested if you're not careful." They all looked at me like rabbits trapped in headlights. They had no idea anyone was listening.'

Sunday was the sort of day that Russell loved. He and Effi had a long lie-in, then walked to the Tiergarten for coffee, rolls, and a leisurely read of the papers. The weather was perfect, bright and sunny without the humidity of previous days. The terrors of the Kasekow platform seemed strangely remote.

Thomas and his wife Hanna had invited them to a late picnic lunch in their Dahlem garden, and despite Effi's best efforts they only arrived half an hour beyond the appointed time. After Russell had pulled the Hanomag up behind Matthias Gehrts' Horch in the driveway they walked round the house to the back. Matthias's and Ilse's two young girls were playing skittles with Thomas's fifteen-year-old daughter Lotte, while the males – Matthias, Thomas' son Joachim and Paul were involved in less energetic pursuits. Matthias was lounging in a deck chair, beer in hand, the two boys hunched over a book of warplanes at the long trestle table.

Paul leapt up to greet Effi. Are you really all right? his look seemed to say. I really am, her smile reassured him.

Russell shook hands with his ex-wife's husband, just as Ilse and Hanna emerged with platters of bread, cold meats and *kartoffelsalat*. Thomas followed with a steaming vat of frankfurters, which he placed on the table. Beers were fetched for the new arrivals, and everyone sat down to eat.

The next couple of hours were more than pleasant – the way life ought to be and rarely was, Russell thought. Paul looked particularly happy in his extended family – at one point Russell observed his son watching Ilse and Effi in conversation with a wonderful smile on his face. Considering their histories and all the possible resentments that might have arisen, considering how different they all were from each other, the six adults got on remarkably well.

Thomas asked if there was any news from Uwe Kuzorra, but Russell hadn't been home since Friday morning, and had no idea how the detective had fared at Silesian Station that evening.

'There should be a message waiting for me,' he told his friend. 'I'll let you know.'

Since he was leaving for Prague the following evening, Russell stayed the night at Effi's, sleepily kissing her goodbye when the studio car arrived soon after dawn. 'You are just going for the paper?' she asked before she left, as if the idea had just occurred to her.

'Yes,' he lied. Murchison had told him in New York that there would be another list of possible allies waiting for him in Prague. It would be safer for Russell to collect it there, the American had told him, than to carry it across the border.

Russell hated lying to Effi, but why give her reason to worry?

There were messages waiting for him at Neuenburger Strasse, including one from Kuzorra. Miriam Rosenfeld had indeed been seen at Silesian Station, and a man had been seen with her. Kuzorra was continuing with his enquires until Russell told him otherwise. He hoped they could meet when Russell returned from Prague.

There was a congratulatory wire from Ed Cummins, who had liked the ARP piece, and postcards from the two Wiesner girls and his agent in London, Solly Bernstein. All three had been sampling the delights of the English seaside resort, the Wiesners at Margate, Solly at Southend. Messages from outside the cage, Russell thought. But nothing from inside. Nothing from Sarah Grostein.

Realizing that three days had passed since his talk with Gorodnikov, he reluctantly called the SD contact number. After identifying himself, he reported that the Soviets had taken him on, and were happy to accept any intelligence he could offer them.

The duty officer read his words back to him, and signed off with a crisp 'Heil Hitler!'

Russell phoned Thomas with Kuzorra's news, and then drove up to Wilhelmstrasse. The two press briefings he attended that morning could and probably should have been given by chimpanzees. At the Adlon over lunch the general feeling among the foreign correspondents was that the sooner Hitler returned to Berlin the better. Nazi Germany on the prowl was scary, disgusting or both, but at least it made good copy. Nazi Germany at rest was literally too dull for words.

At eight that evening Russell's train pulled out of Anhalter Station. The last time he'd made this journey he'd been carrying a probable death sentence in a false-bottomed suitcase, and looking back he still had difficulty believing he could have taken such a risk. Today's journey, by contrast, seemed almost blissfully safe. He gazed out at the Saxon countryside for a couple of hours, stretched his limbs on the platform at Dresden, and took a nightcap in the dining car as the mountains loomed in the late evening dusk. The sleeping car attendant took his documents, thanked him profusely for the five-mark tip, and showed him to his first class bed. He lay there listening to the rattle of the wheels, enjoying the softness of the mattress. A change was as good as a rest, he thought. Even a change of cages.

The Ostrava freight

Russell's train pulled in to Masaryk Station soon after seven in the morning. Or what had been Masaryk Station – the nameboards had been removed and not, as yet, replaced with something more suitable. In all other respects, the concourse looked much the same. There were no German soldiers on display, no leather-coated myrmidons. Russell walked out through the gabled glass façade and turned left. At the far end of a shadowed Hybernska Street the famous Powder Gate basked in the morning sunlight.

He headed down Dlazdena Street towards the centre of the New Town. The side streets, he noticed, all bore bilingual signs in Czech and German, save for Jerusalem Street, which had no sign at all. The large synagogue halfway down was still standing, which seemed a good omen. He would have to visit it before he left.

Jindřišská Street was festooned with swastikas of varying sizes, the largest reserved for the central post office. Something else was different too, but he only realized what it was when a large sign told him that 'Prague is now driving on the right'. In more ways than one, he thought.

Reaching the long sloping boulevard that the Czechs, for reasons best known to themselves, called Wenceslas Square, he turned left. The Hotel *Europa* was a hundred metres up the hill, a

163

uniformed bellboy doing what looked like a tap-dance on the pavement outside.

A French friend had recommended the Alcron Hotel on the dubious grounds that the Gestapo kept a large suite of rooms there, and that, in consequence, the hotel's telephone lines were less likely to be monitored. Since Russell had no intention of using a hotel telephone for anything more than ordering breakfast he felt able to forego the delight of swapping small-talk in the lifts with the local boys in black. He had, moreover, always wanted to stay at the *Europa*, an art nouveau masterpiece from the old Habsburg Empire days. The Habsburg civil service might have been less than successful at running a modern state and economy, but few ruling classes had been more single-minded when it came to indulging themselves. And given the choice, who would turn their back on a hotel façade crowned with gilded nymphs?

The bellboy tapped his foot one last time for luck and took Russell's bag. The receptionist was half-asleep, but managed to find Russell's reservation and key. A gilded lift took him and the bellboy up three floors, and a red-carpeted corridor brought them to a lovely high-ceilinged room at the front of the hotel. Russell handed over the few small coins he'd had since March, and asked if the hotel changed money. Yes, the boy said f om the doorway, but the Thomas Cook on Na Příkopě offered a better rate. So much for loyalty.

Russell's appointment at the American legation was for ten o'clock, which gave him a couple of hours. He could walk to the Little Quarter, he thought. Through the Old Town and over the Charles Bridge. But first, breakfast. He could see from his window that most of the cafés on the Square were open for business, and sitting outside seemed preferable to the hotel restaurant, no matter how ornate the decoration.

A kiosk at the nearest intersection had a selection of Czech titles, yesterday's *Beobachter*, and a *Daily Express* from the previous Friday. He bought the latter, settled himself in the nearest café, and explored the world as seen from England over coffee and strudel. There was a society wedding in Mayfair, a thirty stone man crammed into the back of a Ford Prefect, and a spread of sepia photographs from the Indian Mutiny. The new League season was about to begin, and the paper's football correspondent was tipping Wolverhampton Wanderers to win the First Division title.

The café slowly filled around him, and the trams seemed to clank across the nearby intersection with increasing frequency. A trio of German officers walked by, slapping gloves against their thighs with alarming appropriateness, and Russell examined the faces of the Czechs they passed. Expressions of disdain, mostly. A touch of fear. No liking or love, that was certain.

He paid for his breakfast and walked down to Na Příkopě. Thomas Cook was next door to the *Deutsches Haus*, which was advertising a German Culture Week with several giant posters of aryan composers. The exchange desk was opening as Russell arrived, and the young Czech woman's demeanour switched from sullen hostility to warm friendliness the moment he showed his American passport.

'Journalist,' she murmured in English, reading it under occupation.

'Yes,' Russell agreed.

'You write about my country?'

'Yes.'

'And the Germans?'

'Yes.'

'That is good,' she said, as if the subject admitted of only one viewpoint.

The subject probably did, Russell thought, as he crossed Na Příkopě and took the nearest of the narrow streets burrowing into the Old Town. There were fewer people than he expected, and the main square was almost empty. Russell circled it slowly, reminding himself how beautiful the surrounding wall of buildings was, and trying to ignore the Culture Week posters that hung from many of the first floor windowsills. He discovered he was ten minutes too late for the hourly procession of apostles in the Town Hall clock.

The winding Karlova Street brought him to the river. Two bored-looking German soldiers stood sentry by the Bridge Tower, but the only traffic on the bridge was a single horse-drawn cart piled high with school desks. Above the far bank, the Little Quarter and its crowning castle rose to meet the blue sky.

Russell walked slowly out, examining the statues that lined both parapets. The river hardly seemed to be flowing; the whole scene seemed bathed in slow-motion tranquillity. The tram gliding across the downstream bridge seemed a different machine from the one that clanked its way around the city. Even the castle looked almost benign.

Still, looking up, Russell could understand Kafka's anxiety. The sheer size of the place was intimidating. In the days following the occupation in March one English paper had carried a picture of Hitler peering anxiously out from one of the windows, as if he was worried that someone was out there with a hunting rifle. No such luck.

Russell resumed his walk. There were another two German guards at the far end of the bridge, and more German uniforms and vehicles on Kampa Island. With twenty minutes to spare, Russell downed another coffee on Mostecka Street before continuing up the hill to the American Legation. This was housed in the former Schoenborn Palace, a four-storey building in shades of beige halfway way up the southern side of Trziste Street. A stone portico surrounded the front doors, topped by the sort of balcony the Duce favoured for ranting. The large Stars and Stripes seemed exotic in such surroundings.

Russell had barely given his name to the receptionist when a young, bespectacled man with short dark hair came almost tumbling down the stairs. 'Joseph Kenyon,' he said, shaking Russell's hand. 'I thought we might talk outside.'

'Outside' was a series of terraced gardens rising to an orchard. Beyond this, at the very top of the slope, sat an ornate pavilion. The two benches in front offered a wonderful view across the roofs and river.

Kenyon himself, as he explained on the walk up, was not so much a diplomat as a political observer, left behind with a skeleton staff now that the occupation had rendered a full embassy inappropriate. There were enough emigration requests to keep his colleagues busy, but not much new for him to observe. 'I can't say I've seen that many occupations, but I have a feeling they follow much the same pattern.'

'So how are the Germans behaving?'

'As you would expect. I can't imagine they anticipated any kind of welcome – well, maybe a few fools did – but it's been four months now, and they've made no real effort to win the Czechs over. Most of the time they seem hell-bent on antagonising them.' Kenyon recounted a story doing the rounds about a Czech from the Sudeten area in the north, which was now part of the Reich. The man's dying mother lived in the Sudeten area in the south – also part of the Reich – and he had asked permission to drive across the Protectorate to visit her. Since he couldn't produce her doctor's certificate, permission, had been refused. The man had been forced to drive all the way around the Protectorate, about three times as far. 'I don't know if the story's true,' Kenyon said, 'but it sounds like it could be, and I'm sure most Czechs would believe it.'

The American pulled a packet of Chesterfields from his shirt pocket and offered it. 'Sensible man,' he said when Russell declined, but still lit one for himself with evident pleasure. 'They've really buggered up the language business. First off, they gave the impression everything would be in German, but soon realized that wouldn't fly – I think the ordinary Czechs' refusal to understand anything a German said to them was the crucial clue. So then they started pushing for what they call linguistic parity – everything in both languages with the German version on top. And that's not working either. The Germans have announced that eighteen terms – not seventeen or nineteen, you understand – are untranslatable from German to Czech. These include Führer – which I suspect the Czechs can do without – and *Bohmen und Mahren* – which we call Bohemia and Moravia. So the Czechs are not allowed to refer to their own country in their own language. Nice, eh?

'And there's the usual cultural bias – Beethoven and Wagner are God's gift, Dvorak and Smetana not fit to tie their shoelaces, etcetera, etcetera. Plus the more serious stuff. The Gestapo have set themselves up in the old Petschek Palace on Bredauer Street, complete with special courts and guards in black. It's rumoured that the basement and top floor are both used for torture, but no one's emerged in one piece to confirm it.'

'There is resistance then?'

'Some, and it'll grow. The Czechs are still getting a kick out of booing Hitler in cinema newsreels and passing Germans their *Beobachter* face down, but they'll graduate to higher things.'

'What about the local Nazis?'

Kenyon made a dismissive gesture. 'Several groups joined together and called for whole-hearted collaboration, but not even the Germans took much notice. The Gestapo did fund one bunch of Moravian fascists. Mostly criminals, led by a Brno brothel-keeper. Turned out the only

169

thing they were good at was beating up Jews.'

'Not a talent the Gestapo dismisses.'

'No, I guess not. But maybe they like their monopoly.'

'How are the Jews doing?'

'It could be worse.' About five thousand Jews had been detained in a special camp outside Prague, and the screw was slowly being tightened on the other fifty thousand. The Jews were being pushed out of business, forced to declare their assets – 'all the stuff that happened in Germany a few years ago.' But there was no reign of terror, not yet at least. An SS Hauptsturmführer named Eichmann had been put in charge. He had arrived a few weeks earlier and set himself up in a confiscated Jewish villa in Stresovice. 'But he hasn't shown his hand yet,' Kenyon said, carefully flicking the ash from his cigarette onto the gravel path. 'Last month the Gestapo organized an exhibition at the *Deutsches Haus*, "The Jews as Humanity's Enemy" or something like that, and issued unrefusable invitations to the local schools and factories. All the usual garbage – oily Jews counting their shekels, ravishing aryan virgins, baking their Passover bread with the blood of Christian children.' Kenyon shook his head, and stubbed the cigarette out with a twist of his heel. 'Do any of them really believe it, do you think?'

'Those that aren't stupid enough are twisted enough. How are the rest of the Czechs dealing with it?'

'Better than the rest of the Germans, I'd say.' It was a mixed picture, though. The Czech administration was trying to soften the blow by drafting

170

much weaker anti-Semitic legislation than the Germans wanted. It was confiscating Jewish property, but mostly as a means of keeping it out of German hands. 'Ordinary Czechs, it's hard to tell. There are more segregation laws coming in August, and it'll be interesting to see how they react. It could be wishful thinking, but I suspect that ordinary Czechs will try and ignore them. Anti-Semitism has never been much of a force in this country, and supporting the Jews will be another way of holding a finger up to the Germans.'

'Gestures won't help the Jews.'

'Not in the long run, no. But what's happening here is good news as well as bad. The Nazis had a choice when they came in – win the Czechs over or really frighten them to death. They've fallen between two stools so far, but that wasn't an accident. The plain truth is, both options are beyond them. They've got nothing real to offer the Czechs; the only way they can win them over is to give them their country back. They can try frightening them to death, but that won't work for long – it never does. There's already passive resistance, and it'll get more active. Not tomorrow, but eventually. The Czechs know they can't drive the Germans out on their own, so they'll wait until Hitler has his hands full elsewhere. The Czechs can't wait for a European war, and who can blame them?'

No one, Russell thought, though the millions doomed to die might want a say in the matter. He now realized the reason – and wondered how he could have missed it – for Cummins's insistence

171

on his coming to Prague. His editor had realized, consciously or otherwise, that this was the template for what was to come. 'I'm seeing the German spokesman at three,' he said. 'I think I'll ask him what conquerors have to offer their conquests.'

'If you're looking for official responses, I can probably get you an interview with a member of the Czech government.'

'I am – it's what officials don't say that's usually so revealing.'

They walked back down through the gardens and in through the back door of the Legation. Kenyon's office was on the first floor, overlooking the street. He picked up the phone, tried a few words of Czech and quickly reverted to English. 'Two o'clock?' he asked Russell, who nodded. 'In the Cabinet Room. He'll be there.' He hung up. 'Karel Mares – he's the Acting Prime Minister – will give you ten minutes. Do you know where the Cabinet Room is?'

'In the Castle? I'll find it.'

Kenyon nodded. 'Now, your other business here.' He took a small folder from a desk drawer, extracted a single sheet of paper, and passed it across. There were three names, two with telephone numbers, one with an address. 'These are all supplied by a Czech exile in the States, Gregor Blazek.'

Russell copied the names and numbers into used pages of his reporter's notebook, adding letters to the former and scrambling the order of the latter to a prearranged pattern. The address he memorized. 'What was Blazek's political affiliation when he was here?' he asked.

'Social Democrat. He only left in February, so the information should be up to date. I haven't done any checking, I'm afraid. I'm not supposed to know anything, or do anything.'

'Do you know where Blazek is living now?'

'Chicago, I think,' Kenyon said, checking the file. 'Yes, Chicago. I assume you've been given some guidance as to how to approach these people.'

'Oh yes.' Russell slipped the notebook into his inside pocket and got to his feet. 'Thanks for the help,' he said, extending a hand. 'And for the analysis.'

'Remember,' Kenyon told him, 'this building is still American territory. If you should find yourself in sudden need of a bolthole,' he explained, somewhat unnecessarily.

'Thanks,' Russell said. He could just see himself toiling up the hill with the Gestapo in close pursuit.

He walked back down to the Little Quarter Square and sat at an outdoor restaurant table opposite the St Nicholas church. The plate of pancakes on the adjoining table smelled as good as they looked, so he ordered an early lunch to go with the glass of wine. The pancake-eater, a middle-aged Czech man of prodigious size, gave him a congratulatory beam. Russell took Kenyon's piece of paper out to study the names, seeking some arcane clue as to which might prove the safest one to start with. When a shadow crossed the paper he looked up to find two German officers taking the adjoining table. He put it away.

173

The pancakes were delicious, and the Germans were still waiting for the waiter when he finished. From little acorns...

He took a tram back to the New Town, alighting on Na Příkopě at the bottom of Wenceslas Square. He walked on to the post office intending to use one of the public telephones there but had second thoughts when he noticed German uniforms in a room behind the counters. Masaryk Station, he decided. Secret agents always used stations.

The booths in the corner of the concourse seemed ideal. He took the last in the line because it offered the widest angle of vision, and rummaged through his pockets for the right coins. After dropping and recovering the piece of paper, he spent several seconds deciding which of the two numbers to call, in the end plumping for the second – the name that went with it was easier to pronounce.

A woman answered.

'Oto Nemec?' he asked.

A garbled burst of incomprehensible Czech.

'Oto Nemec,' he said again. 'Is he there?' he asked, first in English and then in German.

There was a loud click as the woman hung up.

Russell did the same, not knowing whether to laugh or cry. The Americans hadn't mentioned the possibility of language difficulties, and he'd foolishly assumed that they knew the contacts spoke English or German. He had committed the cardinal sin – expecting intelligence from Intelligence.

He dialled the second number. It rang a long time, and he was about to hang up when a

174

hesitant male voice mumbled an answer.

'Pavel Bejbl?' Russell asked.

'Bejbl,' the man answered, correcting his pronunciation. 'I am Bejbl.'

'Do you speak English?' Russell asked. *'Sprechen sie deutsch?'*

'I speak German.'

'I'm an American. Gregor in Chicago gave me your name.'

'Gregor Blazek?'

'Yes.'

There was a pause. 'Have you a message for me?'

'Yes, but I need to deliver it in person. Could we meet?'

Another pause, longer this time. Russell could hear a whirring noise in the background – a fan, probably. 'Today?' Bejbl asked. He didn't sound enthusiastic.

'Around six? You pick the place,' Russell said, in an instantly regretted attempt at reassurance.

'Do you know Strelecky Island?' Bejbl asked, suddenly sounding more decisive.

'No.'

'If you're looking from the Charles Bridge, it's just upstream. The Legií Bridge goes over it – there are steps on the southern side. There are benches at the northern end of the island. I'll be there at six-thirty.'

Russell could picture the spot. 'How...' he began, but the line had gone dead. He hung up the earpiece and re-examined the piece of paper. The third potential contact – Stanislav Pružinec – lived in Vysočany. Wherever that might be.

175

Russell went back out onto the concourse and read through the platform departure boards, finding what he wanted above the entrance to Platform 2. Vysočany was the fifth stop out on the line to Hradec Králové.

A train was waiting, but so was the Acting Prime Minister. Tomorrow, he told himself. If he had the time. And sufficient inclination.

It was almost half-past twelve. He took a tram back to Wenceslas Square and walked up to the *Europa*. He felt depressed by the future that Kenyon had unrolled for him, the sheer unrelenting predictability of it all. Wars between classes might just replace one set of pigs with another, but they had some underlying point to them. Wars between nations, as far as Russell could see, had absolutely none.

The receptionist was reading Kafka's *Metamorphosis*.

'Enjoying it?' Russell asked in English as he took his key.

The man shook his head in wonderment. 'What a writer!'

'He used to work near here, didn't he?'

'You do not know?' The man scurried out from behind his desk, gesturing for Russell to follow. He crossed the road, still wildly waving an arm, and when Russell joined him in the wide central reservation pointed down towards the next intersection. 'That building on corner. He work there. See window on corner, third floor. Our greatest writer! Europe greatest writer! And he wrote about America too!'

Russell imagined Kafka hunched behind the

glass, raccoon eyes staring out. The man had been writing about Nazi Germany and Stalin's Russia before they even existed. Small wonder he got depressed. 'A great writer,' he agreed with as much enthusiasm as he could muster. 'Thank you for showing me.'

Up in his room, he took out the piece of paper and set about memorising the various names and numbers. Once he had done so he tore the sheet up and flushed the pieces down the lavatory in the adjoining bathroom. Studying his appearance in the mirror, he decided a tie would probably go down well with the Acting Prime Minister and whichever noxious flunky the Nazis had waiting for him.

One tram took him back across the river, another carried him up and round the Castle hill. The Cabinet Room took some finding, as if the Czechs had deliberately hidden it from the Germans, and Karel Mares was waiting for him, checking through a box of papers on a corner sofa. He looked bone-weary, but there was a twinkle in his eyes. Many of his answers to Russell's questions showed a well-honed appreciation of how quickly conquered peoples learn to read between the lines.

'I must point out that the banning of national songs in cafés and bars only applies to provocative songs,' he said halfway through the interview.

'But aren't all national songs a provocation to an occupier?' Russell protested.

Mares just shrugged and smiled.

Russell asked him why he had warned his people against acts of resistance.

'Our people are used to open discussions and passionate debate,' Mares said, 'but we are living in a different world now. We must get used to this new world before we ... well, before we decide what our political contribution will be.' The glint in his eyes suggested Guy Fawkes as a possible model.

Cheered by the encounter, Russell sat enjoying the view for a quarter of an hour before walking across to the Reichsprotektor's office in the Czernin Palace. After thirty minutes in the usual anteroom, stuck in front of the usual unforgiving portrait, he was taken to meet Gerhard Bimmer.

'I am permitted to speak for Reichsprotektor Neurath,' Bimmer began, as if there were others who wished to do so, but lacked the necessary authorisation. 'But I can only spare you ten minutes,' he added, somewhat untruthfully as it turned out.

Russell's use of the word 'occupation' opened the floodgates. Germany, Bimmer claimed, would rise to the challenge. The Czechs had behaved abominably to the Sudeten Germans, but the Germans would forgive them. More than that – the Germans would return good for evil, would win them over to the advantages of belonging to the Reich.

'Which advantages would those be?' Russell asked innocently.

Bimmer grunted with surprise. 'Power, of course. A seat at the table where the great issues are discussed. The Führer offers everyone the chance to help build a stronger, purer world. A hard task of course, but so rewarding.'

'You seem to be offering the Czechs a share in the burden of empire,' Russell suggested, and soon wished he hadn't. Bimmer started off in another direction, through a seemingly endless catalogue of British sins, which ended, somewhat incongruously, in a listing of every German vessel scuttled at Scapa Flow in 1918.

Russell thanked him profusely and took his leave. He had a couple of great quotes, but who would believe a high-ranking government official could be that dumb? He would have to invent something more credible. It might be bad journalism, but made-up interviews with Nazi officials were so much more enlightening – and so much easier on the journalist – than the real thing.

There were almost three hours to kill before his meeting – his *treff*, as the Soviets would call it – with Pavel Bejbl. He walked slowly down through the Little Quarter and ambled out across the Charles Bridge, enjoying the sunshine and the views. The beer garden on the far bank looked like a suitable place for getting his article in order. Two German officers were abandoning a table above the water's edge as he arrived, and the waiter wasted no time in removing their glasses. They were probably kept on a separate counter for spitting in.

He wrote steadily for an hour, conscious that he still lacked the crucial ingredient – material from ordinary Czechs. The beer garden steadily filled as the nearby workplaces emptied, and he eventually found himself sharing the table with two young women. Their English was as bad as his Czech, precluding any meaningful conversation. He listened as they chattered happily away in their incomprehensible tongue, and supposed that for them, and thousands like them, the occupation was nothing more than an occasional inconvenience. If you spent your days in an office and your evenings and weekends with your lover or family, what did it matter who ruled from the Castle?

It was another clear, warm evening. Strelecky Island was around four hundred metres away across the slow-moving Vltava, and he could see the benches under the trees on its northern end. Why had Bejbl chosen that place for their meeting? It looked a good place for a private talk, assuming the Gestapo weren't sitting in the trees. It also looked like a good place for a trap. From where he was sitting, there seemed only one way in and out. And a lip-reader with a telescope on the opposite bank...

Get a grip, Russell told himself. Lip-readers! He wouldn't even be saying anything incriminating, or at least not obviously so. The Americans had coached him thoroughly on the innocent message he brought from Gregor – how well he was doing in Chicago, the good wages and new car, but homesick of course, so any news of his old friends and comrades would be most welcome. Did so-and-so know how they were doing?

If so-and-so had no idea, then that was that. If he knew – and sounded sympathetic – then it was on to the next, slightly less innocent step. And so on.

It was a few minutes after six. He paid for his drinks and made his way down the riverbank to the Legií Bridge. The German guards at the eastern end were sweltering in their uniforms, gazes seemingly hooked on the inviting waters below. Russell crossed in front of a bell-ringing tram and walked out towards the island. As he'd feared, the steps that Bejbl had mentioned were the only way onto the island. He stopped for a moment, reminding himself he had nothing to fear. Why would anyone trap him? He had done nothing illegal, not yet anyway. In the last resort he could always reveal that he was working for the SD. Hauptsturmführer Hirth wouldn't let him down.

He trotted down the steps and turned left under the wide bridge. The island tapered to a blunt point some 150 metres ahead of him; the path that followed the water was shaded by oaks and, at the tip, a copse of white willows. Only the furthest bench was empty, the others occupied by two courting couples and a woman with a child. Russell sat down and stared back across the river at the beer garden he had just left.

Bejbl arrived ten minutes later. He was a thin, shortish man of about forty, his still-boyish face framed by floppy fair hair. He was wearing office clothes: a dark suit that had seen plenty of wear, a pale blue shirt and dark blue tie, badly-scuffed shoes worn at the heel. He sat down at the other end of the bench, pulled a half-smoked cigarette out from behind an ear, and lit it with a silver lighter. 'I am Bejbl,' he said softly in German.

'Thank you for coming.'

'What is your name?'

'John Fullagar,' Russell said, pulling his

181

mother's maiden name out of the ether. How had he forgotten to prepare a false name for himself?

'You have a message from Blazek?' Bejbl asked. He was sitting forward on the bench, elbows on knees.

'Yes.' Russell went through his spiel, ending with the request for news from home.

'We are doing fine,' Bejbl said, flicking the cigarette stub away. 'Considering the situation,' he added.

'That is bad?'

'Of course it is bad.'

'Gregor would like to help. He and his friends in America.'

Bejbl smiled, leaned back, and loosened his tie. 'How?' he asked.

'With whatever you need.'

'Ah.'

'Are you interested?' Russell asked.

'Of course, but I cannot answer for the P ... for the others.'

'Who can?'

'The man you need to see is on the Germans' wanted list, but I think I can arrange a meeting.'

'Tonight?'

'Tomorrow, I think. How can I contact you?'

'You can't,' Russell said, realizing he was registered at the *Europa* under his real name.

Bejbl took it in his stride. 'Be in the Old Town Square at ten tomorrow night.'

'All right.'

Bejbl nodded, got to his feet, and walked off towards the bridge.

Russell let his head fall back and let out a large

182

sigh. He hadn't felt any warm glow of trust surrounding them, but why should there be? For all Bejbl knew, he was a Gestapo plant. Look on the bright side, he told himself. He had made contact, apparently with the right person. What more could he ask for?

Food, for one thing – it had been a long time since the potato pancakes. He gave Bejbl another couple of minutes, then followed him back onto the bridge. A tram from the western end took him back to Na Příkopě and Lippert's, supposedly the city's finest restaurant. The food and décor were certainly excellent, but the predominance of German uniforms among the clientele added nothing to the general gaiety. Russell ordered Moravian wine as a show of solidarity, and was informed that only German wines were now being served. The pianist in the corner had taken the hint, and was sticking to Mozart and Schubert.

It was dark outside when Russell emerged. Wenceslas Square was displaying almost American levels of neon. Feeling decidedly full after four courses, Russell strode slowly up to the King's statue and back again. There were a couple of short, blonde streetwalkers in high heels outside his hotel, and he watched as two off-duty German soldiers walked past them. The girls seemed to shrink, as if they'd temporarily switched off their allure, and the men seemed to hurry their steps, perhaps frightened of where foreign temptation might lead them.

The lights were burning in Kafka's office, Russell noticed. A whirling figure appeared in the window, and for a moment he imagined the great writer pacing madly to and fro, arms hurled aloft in despair. It was only a cleaner though, brushing a large feather duster across the stacks of files.

Having forgotten to pull the curtains, Russell woke next morning with the sun full on his face. The café proprietors across the street were already drawing up their big front windows, and he decided to forego the dark hotel breakfast room for a large milky coffee in the bright morning light. After buying both Monday's *Daily Express* and Tuesday's *Volkischer Beobachter* from the nearby kiosk, he left the former out as bait for passing English-speakers and scoured the latter for Slaney's predicted escalation of hostility towards Poland. There was more trouble in Danzig, but mostly of the Poles' making. Hitler was probably still in Bayreuth.

Czechs at nearby tables were chattering away, and Russell felt more than a little frustrated that he couldn't understand a word they were saying. His English paper only snared one victim – a young Brummie who craved the latest cricket news from home. His West Midlands firm used a Czech supplier for some of their machinery, and he had been dispatched to sort out their increasingly erratic deliveries. The Czechs had told him it was all the Germans' fault, and the Germans, though polite, had been singularly unhelpful. His impression of Czech attitudes to the occupation echoed Kenyon's. 'Resignation, mostly,' was his verdict. 'They're just waiting for a war to shake things up.'

The young man went off to do some sightseeing,

and Russell was unable to find a good reason for further postponing his trip to Vysočany. He reached Masaryk Station with ten minutes to spare before the next departure, but only climbed aboard when the whistle shrilled. He was almost certain that he wasn't being followed, but the last time he'd played poker a similar level of confidence in a high straight had proved sadly misplaced.

The train – a few grubby suburban carriages pulled by a wheezing tank engine – slowly rattled its way across an industrial landscape of factories, goods yards and weed-infested carriage sidings. It seemed hotter than ever, and Russell opened a window, only to receive a shower of smuts for his pains. Vysočany Station was in a cutting, its booking office up on the bridge which carried the street above the tracks. He showed the address to the ticket collector, who gave him a long cool look before miming some rough directions.

The street outside boasted a couple of café-bars and one shop, but high factory walls hemmed them in. He turned right as directed, and right again between two industrial premises, one churning out noise, the other smoke. A couple of workmen sitting on the back of a lorry, legs hanging over the tailgate, watched him with what seemed a grim intensity. His wave of acknowledgement received a single syllable response. He had no idea what the syllable meant, but the tone was less than friendly.

An iron bridge over a small black river brought him into a residential area – streets of small houses and yards divided by cobblestone alleys. According to his piece of paper Stanislav Pru inec lived in the second. He walked down to the relevant number, and took a look around. Three women were watching from out of their respective windows. He knocked, and a fourth woman came to the door. 'Stanislav Pruzinec?' he asked, and when this produced a blank stare he showed her the name in writing. This elicited a torrent of Czech, none of which sounded welcoming.

He was turning to leave when an angry-eyed young man appeared at his shoulder. Russell tried English on him, and then German. That got a response, but not the one he was hoping for. The young man smiled grimly, and called out something over his shoulder in Czech. 'I am American,' Russell said urgently, having remembered in time that Britain's betrayal at Munich was far from forgiven. 'American,' he repeated. 'Gregor Blazek.'

This produced another torrent from the woman, but also engendered a sliver of doubt in the young man's eyes. Time to withdraw, Russell told himself. He started backing away, smiling all the time, making what seemed like placatory gestures. No one had responded to the young man's shout, and he himself seemed unwilling to go beyond scowling. Russell turned his back on them and walked away as swiftly as he could, ears alert for the sound of pursuit. Once he turned the corner he broke into a run, only slowing once he had crossed the iron bridge. The men on the lorry had vanished, and he met no one else on his walk back to the station. He sat down heavily on the only platform seat, sweating profusely.

After about fifteen minutes a trickle of prospective passengers began descending the steps, a few minutes more and another grimy locomotive puffed wearily into the station. At Masaryk Station he treated himself to a bratwurst before walking back out. He was still sweating, but so was everyone else; the street was like a steambath.

A cold beer, he thought, just as the right tram ground to a halt at the station stop. Ten minutes later he was sitting in the riverside beer garden, at the same table he'd occupied the day before. The sky was hazier, and dark clouds gathered above the Castle as he worked his way through two bottles of Pilsen. He and Paul had stood gazing at an El Greco storm in the Metropolitan Museum of Art only a few weeks earlier, and here was nature's version.

The first fork of lightning seemed to plunge into the castle, as if some resident Nazi wizard was draining power from the cosmos. A few seconds later the thunder cracked and rolled, and the sky lurched further into gloom. For several minutes Russell and the rest of the beer garden's customers watched the storm draw nearer, until a wall of rain swept across the Vltava, driving them all indoors. Already half-soaked, Russell worked his way round to the tower at the eastern end of the Charles Bridge and stood in the archway watching the storm crackle and flash its way over. As the sky lightened in the west, the thunder faded to a distant growl, and a faint rainbow glimmered above Strelecky Island. The rain slowed and stopped, and soon the sun came out, lighting the terracotta roofs and copper green spires of the Little Quarter.

He headed back towards his hotel, stopping en route at the large book shop he had noticed the previous day. It took some time – and some linguistic assistance from the proprietor – before he found a book that suited his purpose.

Back at the *Europa* he took off his wet clothes and stretched out on the bed. The trip to Vysočany had been a disaster, but he could hardly blame Blazek or the Americans for the quality of their intelligence – if they'd had an up-to-date picture of what was happening in Prague his own visit would have been unnecessary. It was just one of those things. He didn't think he'd been in any real danger, but he wouldn't want to go through those few seconds again. 'Beaten to death by Czech patriots' was not what he wanted on his tombstone.

He spent the afternoon drifting in and out of a pleasant snooze, then lay in a nicely tepid bath for another half an hour. One out of three wouldn't be bad, provided Bejbl turned up at their rendezvous later that evening.

Soon after seven he walked down to reception, where his Kafka-loving friend was just coming off-shift. 'Can you recommend a restaurant?' Russell asked. 'Preferably one without Germans.'

The man could. A small restaurant, not expensive but wonderful food, only ten minutes away. It was on his way home if Russell needed a guide...

They crossed Wenceslas Square and walked down Lepanska Street, passing the Gestapo-favoured Alcron Hotel. Russell asked the man about the occupation, and received as Kafkaesque an answer as he could have hoped for. The next war would be all about bombing from the air, the man said. The lucky cities would be those which surrendered promptly, because there'd be no point in bombing them. And Prague had shown remarkable foresight in getting itself occupied before the war even began.

He might be right, Russell thought. He was certainly right about the restaurant, a snug little family affair with six tables indoors and another four filling a small foliage-screened yard. The service was friendly, the food delicious, the Germans nowhere to be seen. His meal finished, Russell sat with a small glass of juniper-flavoured Borovička, wondering what Effi was doing that evening.

He emerged from the restaurant soon after nine. The streets were wholly in shadow, the last rays of the sun gilding the highest chimneys. The sky was still blue when he crossed Na Příkopě and entered the Old Town, but the yellow streetlights had already been switched on in the narrow streets and alleys. A Gestapo car was parked on the cobbles of the Old Town Square when he arrived, but drove off soon afterwards, its painted swastika a lurid splash in the half-light.

There were more people around than Russell expected, some sitting in the outdoor cafés, others orbiting the square like deck-circling passengers on a cruise ship. He took a seat facing the huge and wonderfully-named Church Of Our Lady Before Týn, and settled down to wait for Bejbl. A few stars were becoming visible in the rapidly darkening sky.

The ten o'clock appearance of the Town Hall clock disciples had just ended when Bejbl emerged from the alley beside the church. There was no hesitation about him. He strode out into the open, scanning the square until he caught sight of Russell, then walked straight towards him, lighting a cigarette as he did so.

'Let's go,' he said after shaking hands. 'This way.'

Bejbl led them around the front of the Town Hall and into the alley opposite. A couple of turns took them past a small church and outdoor café and into a longer, yellow-lit passage, empty of business or people. Light and sound seeped out of the upstairs windows, but there were few windows on the ground floor, only heavy-looking doors.

The words 'rat' and 'trap' sprung to mind.

Bejbl veered right into another alley, and this time there was life ahead, a car going by, the sound of someone laughing.

'Here,' Bejbl said, stopping outside a non-descript-looking double door. He glanced back up the alley and rapped softly on the wood. A few seconds later the left hand door swung open. 'In,' Bejbl said, giving Russell a helpful shove.

He found himself in a small courtyard, facing a man of considerable size. 'I am Tomas Hornak,' the man said, offering a rough hand for a brief shake. He was wearing workingman's overalls and a large cloth cap, which seemed to be losing the struggle to contain his shock of dark wiry hair. Deep-set eyes shone in a chubby face.

'I am John Fullagar,' Russell said, taking in his

surroundings. The courtyard contained several sets of iron tables and chairs, and a number of plants in large tubs. Two strings of multi-coloured lights supplied what meagre illumination there was. There were two other doors.

'Please, the seats are dry. You will drink something? A beer? Something stronger?'

'A beer would be nice,' Russell said. He chose a seat and sat down. Hornak said something to Bejbl in Czech, and the smaller man disappeared through one of the other doors, spilling café light and noise as he did so. 'I have reserved the garden for us,' Hornak said, spreading his arms to indicate that all this was theirs.

It felt like the bottom of a well, Russell thought, as he looked up through the coloured lights at the small circle of sky.

'So how is Gregor?' Hornak asked, settling his bulk onto another chair.

'Doing well, I believe. I've never actually met the man. I'm just here to pass on his messages.'

'And he wants to help his old comrades?'

'His American friends want to help,' Russell clarified. 'Your English is excellent,' he added, wondering where he'd learnt it.

'I had some good English friends,' Hornak said non-committally, just as Bejbl returned with two bottles of beer and a second glass. He put them down on the table and went back into the café.

'And why do Gregor's American friends want to help us?' Hornak asked.

'Because there's a war coming, and they want all the allies they can get.'

Hornak smiled at that. 'Well, you have come to

191

the right people.'

'I hope so. You know who I represent. Who exactly are you speaking for?'

'We are the only organized group...'

'Who is "we"?'

Hornak gave it some thought. 'The Left,' he said eventually. 'Social democrats like Bejbl. And Gregor Blazek, come to that. Communists as well. Even a few Liberals of the old school. We are all together this time.'

'How organized are you?'

'How worthy of support, you mean. You will not find anything better in Prague – we have been preparing since the betrayal at Munich.'

'Have you lost many to the Gestapo?'

'Some. Like I said, we are organized. There are several hundred of us in the city, but nobody knows more names than he has to. Sometimes we have to cut off a limb to save the tree, but another always grows.'

The classic cell structure, Russell thought. He had fallen among comrades.

'So how does the American Government mean to help us?' Hornak asked.

'What is it you need?'

'At the moment, nothing. For now we just try to annoy them. Let their tyres down, cut their telephone wires. Anything more will be suicide – we know this. But when the real war begins, well, we shall see. I think the Germans will be very successful – the Poles won't last more than a few weeks.' He laughed. 'Which will serve them right, yes, for joining all the other jackals and stealing a part of our country from us. But the Germans –

192

the more successful they are, the harder their task will become. Because each battle will cost them soldiers, and each conquered country will need a garrison, and they will get weaker, not stronger. And that is when we shall start fighting them, and when we will need help from outside – the explosives and the guns.'

'America will provide these things.'

'Yes? But how will they get these things to us? We are already surrounded by enemies.'

'Air-drops, I suppose, once radio communications have been established. I'm not here to set anything up – I'm just here to make contact, find out what you need, and how you can be reached in the future. We need a dead letter drop, an address and false name to write to. You understand the book code?'

'I think so, but tell me.'

'Both parties have the same edition of the same book,' Russell began, with the distinct impression that he was teaching Stalin's grandmother to suck eggs. 'Words are picked out by numbers. So 2278 would be either page 2, line 27, word 8 or page 22, line 7, word 8 – whichever makes more sense of the message. You understand?'

'It seems simple. Have you chosen a book?'

'*The Good Soldier Schweik*, fourth edition in Czech. That's the current edition. I bought one in the big bookshop on Na Příkopě this afternoon – they had several copies. You must buy one, and I'll send mine back to Washington.'

'All right.'

'Now all we need is a name and address.'

Hornak thought about it for a moment. 'Here

is good,' he said at last. 'The Skorepka Café. Milan Nemecek.'

Russell could see no risk in writing it down for memorising later.

'Is there anything else?' Hornak asked.

'I don't think so,' Russell said, returning the pencil stub to his shirt pocket and rising to his feet. He doubted whether anything would come of this meeting, but a possibility had been created. Which had to be worth something.

This marginal sense of achievement lasted about ten seconds. As the two men shook hands, both recognized the swelling sound of vehicles. Hornak stood there, still holding Russell's hand, as the café door burst open, revealing Bejbl's silhouette. 'Gestapo,' he hissed, and slammed it shut.

'This way,' Hornak said urgently, reaching for the third door. It opened into an unlit corridor, which led to another small courtyard, another set of double doors. Hornak opened one of these, put his head round the corner, and gestured Russell to follow him out. They were in a long, curving alley lit by yellow lamps. Hornak headed right, away from the shouts and running motors. 'Quietly,' he told Russell, settling into a brisk walk. They had only gone a few metres when two shots rang out, followed by a single shriek and more shouting. Both men jerked round, but the alley behind them was empty. As they walked on, a little quicker than before, the lighted windows above them winked out in sequence, like letters in a neon sign.

They were no more than ten metres from the end of the alley when a voice from behind them screamed, 'Halt!' Two German soldiers were jogging down the alley towards them. They were about sixty metres away, Russell reckoned. And their rifles weren't raised.

'Run,' Hornak said, taking off with an alacrity that belied his size.

Russell hesitated for a split second, and took off after him, sprinting through the narrow archway at the end of the alley. No shots followed.

Hornak was ahead of him, barrelling down a long and depressingly straight alley. Feet pounding on the cobbles, Russell's brain still had time to do the mathematics – the Germans would have around thirty metres to kill them in. Four seconds maybe. Oh God.

He strained every muscle to go faster, petrified that he might trip on an uneven cobblestone. The street seemed to end in a solid wall, or was that an archway in the corner? Hornak was still plunging onwards, his boots crashing down on the cobblestones. The urge to turn and look back was almost unbearable.

It *was* an archway. Twenty metres, ten, and a window in front of him shattered, the sound of the shot reverberating down the alley a millisecond later. As he swerved under the arch, two more bullets thudded into a wooden doorway. The bastards had missed him!

He was running past the church and café he'd noticed on his walk with Bejbl. The last few café customers had been brought to their feet by the shots, and were now standing by their tables, like sculptures of uncertainty.

Another archway brought them to an intersection. As they raced across it Russell could hear the sound of other running feet. From more than one direction.

The alley opposite was the narrowest yet, curving this way and that under the dim yellow lamps. The spires silhouetted against the starfield belonged to Our Lady Of Týn, Russell realized – they were heading towards the Old Town Square.

Another turn, another thirty metres, and they were running across it. Russell half-expected to see the Gestapo car from earlier parked mid-Square, but the only occupants were Czechs turned to stone by his and Hornak's dramatic appearance. As his feet rapped across the cobble-stones, Russell saw them drag themselves into action, moving towards the nearest exits with increasing purpose.

Hornak was heading for the left hand side of the church, and the alley from which Bejbl had emerged two hours earlier. They reached it without shouts or shots, and Russell risked a swift look back. The pursuit was nowhere to be seen – had they shaken it off in those last few alleys before the square?

Hornak was turning into another alley and slowing to a jog. He was breathing heavily, Russell realized, but there was a grim smile of satisfaction on his face.

One more alley and he slowed to a walk. Russell gratefully followed suit, feeling the stitch in his side. His own breathing was more laboured than Hornak's, and his heart was racing. He promised himself he would use the car less often when he got back to Berlin. If he got back to Berlin.

'Now we must look like innocent people,' Hornak ordered.

A succession of empty streets brought them within sight of a much larger thoroughfare. Two people walked across the opening, a man and a woman arm in arm. Ordinary life, Russell thought, but the relief was short-lived. The sound of an approaching vehicle had both men scurrying for the shelter of a shadowed doorway, and they watched as a car drove slowly past on the main road, its side-painted swastika gleaming in the yellow light.

It was cruising alone, and had vanished by the time they reached the wider street. Russell followed Hornak across, wondering, for the first time, where they were headed.

'Not far now,' the Czech replied.

A few minutes more and the familiar canopy of Masaryk Station appeared in front of them.

'I know where I am now,' Russell said. 'I can get back to the hotel from here.'

'No, please,' Hornak said. 'We must find out what happened. My office is just a short way. Please.'

Looking back, Russell found it hard to believe how meekly he bowed to the Czech's insistence. The only reasons he ever came up with were simple curiosity and good manners, neither of which, in retrospect, seemed worth risking his life for.

They turned left into the long yard adjoining the station. A couple of inlaid sidings ran the length of the yard, and a short rake of tarpaulin-covered wagons were stabled beside one of the

197

small cranes. A line of parked lorries stood between them and a row of darkened offices and storehouses.

It suddenly occurred to Russell why Hornak had insisted on his presence. 'We must find out what happened,' he had said. Someone had tipped off the Germans about their meeting. And as far as Hornak was concerned, he was a prime suspect.

His heart lurched a beat or two. Turning and running seemed ridiculous, but so did happily walking into peril.

'This is it,' Hornak said, as they reached what was almost the last door in the row. The Czech pushed it open, and invited his companion in. It was all very friendly, but Russell had the distinct impression that refusal was never an option.

Hornak shut the door behind them and closed the shutters before turning on a desk lamp. Filing cabinets filled the spaces between three desks; railway diagrams and a *Picture Post* gallery of Greta Garbo pictures adorned the walls. 'We shall wait here. It won't be long.' He walked across to the sink, ran some water into a tin kettle, and placed it on an electric ring. 'Tea will be good,' he added, as if to himself. 'We have had a shock, I think.'

Russell watched Hornak scoop tea into a pot, rinse out a couple of enamel mugs and check that there was still some sugar in its tin. 'Where did you meet your English friends?' he asked.

Hornak hesitated a few moments before answering. 'In Spain,' he said eventually.

'The International Brigade?'

'Yes. Almost two years. I came back in '38 to fight the Germans, but the British and French

198

sold us out. In Spain too, come to that.' He moved the kettle slightly on the electric hob. 'You sound more English than American,' he added, with only the slightest hint of accusation.

'My father was English. My mother's American.' The temptation was there, but Russell resisted telling his life story. This didn't seem the time to start explaining his residence in Hitler's Germany.

The kettle was boiling. Hornak poured water into the pot and stirred it with a large spoon. A stained piece of cloth provided a strainer, and after adding two huge heaps of sugar to each mug he carried one across to Russell.

'So how did you come to do this work?' Hornak asked, leaning back against a desk and carefully sipping at the scalding tea.

'I'm a journalist. We get asked to help. Times like these, it's hard to say no.'

'I am sure many do.'

'Maybe,' Russell agreed non-committally. Was Hornak complimenting him on his commitment or doubting his story? He took a sip of the sweet tea and burnt his tongue.

'And you believe the Americans are serious?' the Czech said.

'Serious, yes. But whether they know what they're doing, I'm not so sure.'

Hornak raised an eyebrow. 'Should you not be?'

Approaching footsteps saved Russell from answering. It was Bejbl. A single interrogative syllable from Hornak unleashed a torrent of Czech, none of which Russell understood. Bejbl had given him a single dismissive glance, which seemed like good news.

It was. 'We have caught the informer,' Hornak eventually told him in English. 'He was in the café and saw me arrive. He was seen using the public phone around the corner. Calling Petschek Palace.' Hornak came over and gave Russell a pat on the back, as if he was congratulating him on his acquittal. 'And the Germans are all over the New Town,' he added. 'So it's a good thing you came with me.'

Bejbl was talking again, having poured himself what was left of the tea. Hornak offered Russell a further translation. 'The informer claims the Gestapo have threatened to take his sister.'

'What about the shots?' Russell asked.

Hornak asked Bejbl, and translated the answer. 'A man was shot in the leg. He panicked and tried to run. Not one of our people,' he added dismissively. He put his empty mug down. 'We are going to see the informer now. A walk up the line, not far. I think you would be wise to come with us. Give the Germans time to pick up a few suspects.'

It seemed like a good idea, or at least the better of two bad ideas. He might get to judge how effective Hornak and his people were. 'All right,' he said.

They let themselves out into the silent yard and walked along beside the rails to the bridge beyond the station throat. Hugging the walls of the short cutting beyond they emerged into a wide expanse of tracks, carriage sidings to one side of the running lines, a large goods yard to the other. A creamy three-quarter moon had risen behind the hill ahead, edging the rails with pale light. One line of carriages was lit up, cleaners at work within, and a locomotive was at work somewhere in the goods yard, its occasional stuttering puffs interspersed with the clanking of buffers. Hornak and Bejbl walked on up the slight incline, talking softly in Czech. A brightly-lit signal box lay ahead, and as they passed it the signalman leaned out of his window to share what sounded like a joke.

A locomotive came under the bridge up ahead. It cut across their path and into the goods yard, the faces of its crew bright orange in the firebox glow. The engine seemed to be free-wheeling, not so much expelling steam as leaking it.

They walked under another bridge and round behind a line of stabled engines. A small door opened into a large brick building, where a ring of silent and enormous-looking locomotives faced each other around an indoor turntable. Another door led into a repair shop, where two more engines stood astride deep inspection pits. A final door and they were out in the open again, heading for a small building with a large chimney. Mounds of sand were piled either side of it, and a young man with a cloth cap was waiting by the entrance, a burning cigarette cupped in one hand.

The interior was larger than Russell had imagined, and surprisingly light given that the moon and a single bare bulb supplied the only illumination. There were three other men inside. Two of Hornak's men were just behind the door; the informer, an ordinary-looking man of around thirty with short dark hair, thin moustache and glasses, was standing in the sand-drying pan. He was visibly shaking, and the sight of Hornak did nothing to calm him down. Hornak's first question evoked a long but surprisingly passionless answer, as if the man had already lost hope.

Hornak turned to his four comrades with a query. Any reason to spare him? was Russell's later guess. Now he saw only the nodding heads, heard the involuntary whimper of the condemned man.

Hornak looked at his watch and said something that started with the Czech word for 'ten'. One of the others started talking, and soon they were all at it, apparently oblivious to both Russell and the informer.

About ten minutes had gone by when the sound of a train reached his ears. As it grew louder, Hornak put out his hand, and one of the others handed him an army pistol. Hornak walked onto the sand-dryer and said something to the informer. He started to protest, but suddenly the energy seemed to drain away from him, and he sunk to his knees. The train was almost on them now, rasping and roaring its way up the slope. Russell saw Hornak pull the trigger and saw the body jerk forward, but he hardly heard the shot.

He just stood there, tongue suddenly dry in his mouth, watching the dark blood seep into the sand. Outside a long line of wagons clanked by, the frenetic breath of the locomotive fading into the distance.

'Jan here will see you get back to your hotel,' Hornak shouted over the din. 'He is a student – speaks good English. And his brother is a taxi driver.' He shifted the gun to his left hand to offer his right.

Russell shook it, but his eyes betrayed him.

'We shall look after his sister,' Hornak said simply. He gave Russell one last penetrating look, and turned away.

'Come,' the young man said, and led the way outside.

The last of the wagons were rolling by, a guard with a glowing pipe standing out on his brake van's veranda.

'How far are we going?' Russell asked once the din had begun to recede.

'Only a few minutes,' Jan said. 'A bad business,' he added, as they climbed the steps towards the road.

'Same time every night,' Russell said, more to himself than his companion.

'The Ostrava freight? It always leave at one. Night-workers use it to check their clocks.'

They walked on.

'What was his name?' Russell asked after a while.

'Zámečník.'

'What will they do with the body?'

The young man gave him a surprised glance, as if this was a particularly stupid question. 'Burn it in a locomotive.'

Jan's brother Karel was due to start his shift at six, and his wife refused to wake him before five, so Russell slept for a couple of hours in one of the parlour armchairs, long enough to stiffen up without feeling noticeably rested. Karel was obviously several years older than Jan, and a good deal heavier. He seemed remarkably cheerful, though, for someone who started work at five in the morning. 'What's the story?' Jan asked. 'If we get stopped, I mean. Where did we pick you up?'

'Do you know anyone in America?' Russell asked. 'Or England?'

'A cousin in London, I think.'

'Say I brought you news from him, and stayed the night.'

'What news?'

They concocted a story between them as Karel drove the Skoda towards the city centre, but didn't need it: the streets were still mostly empty of Czechs, and the Germans had apparently tired of driving round in circles.

Russell walked through the doors of the *Europa* with some trepidation, half-expecting leather coats in the lobby. There was only a dozing receptionist though, and Russell managed to extract the room key from its hook without waking him. He used the stairs rather than the squeaky lift and let himself into his room. No one was waiting for him. The Gestapo was either ignorant of his participation in the previous night's fun and games, or they were still gathering witness statements. No one in the café had seen him, he told himself. The pursuing Germans hadn't seen his face. The chances of being recognized and reported by a Czech passer-by were infinitesimal.

That said, a swift departure from Prague still seemed the prudent course. There was a train at nine, he remembered.

He took a bath, packed, and stood by the

window watching the traffic increase. At eight o'clock he went downstairs to check out. The day receptionist was busy with a pastry and had a huge cup of coffee steaming beside her. She took Russell's crowns, stamped his bill and handed him a crumb-flaked copy.

The sky outside was an innocent shade of blue, the temperature close to perfect. He walked down Jindřišská and Dladzena Streets to Masaryk Station, and finally found a German-speaking clerk willing to change his ticket. Out on the concourse he watched prospective passengers walk to their trains with no apparent scrutiny. The usual pair of German soldiers were chatting by the entrance, but there was no sign of the Gestapo.

He boarded the train a couple of minutes before departure, and settled himself in an empty first class compartment. Two German officers swam into view, giving his heart an unwelcome jolt, but moved on to claim the adjoining compartment. They were going home on leave, Russell overheard, and pleased about it.

The train jerked into motion, and Russell sat by the window, retracing his walk from the night before. Both goods yard and locomotive depot were hives of activity, one locomotive pumping smoke as it eased forward in the shed yard. He couldn't help wondering whether it was just burning coal.

He thought about Hornak, and about the Americans. The latter had made their preference for social democrats over communists very clear, but did they really believe that there were people out there who would fight Hitler for them, and

205

then turn round and save them from Stalin? If so, they were dreaming. As far as Russell could see, the only people in Europe with a real stomach for the fight *were* the communists.

Not his problem, he told himself. Hornak and the Americans would doubtless get whatever they could from each other, and any benefit the rest of the world derived from their arrangement was up to the gods. He gazed out of the window at the Bohemian countryside until his eyelids began to droop.

He was woken by an official at the new and largely specious border between Reich and Protectorate, but not required to leave his seat. As the train wound its way round the curves of the upper Elbe he noticed the stream of overladen lorries heading into Germany. How to win friends and influence people, he thought. Stage One – invade their country. Stage Two – steal everything they owned.

The train pulled into Dresden soon after eleven-thirty, and Russell decided on impulse to break his journey. He checked his suitcase into the left luggage and took a cab to the city's Museum of Hygiene. Several years earlier a friend had told him how wonderful it was, and now it seemed like something he could bring his son to one weekend, something German which they could both admire and share.

Walking through the rooms he could see what his friend had meant. There were imaginative exhibits on anatomy, physiology and nutrition, a life-size transparent man whose organs lit up when the appropriate button was pressed. There were models demonstrating muscular movements, a room devoted to vocal organs with an explanation of how tones and timbres were produced, an apparatus for testing the lung capacity of any visitor willing to blow through a cardboard tube.

There was also, as Russell discovered on turning a corner, a new group of exhibits, put together with the same loving care and painstaking attention to detail as all the others, explaining the biological inferiority of the Jew.

He turned on his heel and sought the way out to fresher air.

Another cab carried him back to the station, where a Berlin train was waiting to leave. As it gathered speed towards the capital he sat back, eyes closed, and watched Zámečník's body pitch forward into the sand. The war has already begun, he thought. And everyone has lost.

Leafleteers

The Berlin train proved slower than advertised, spending several long interludes becalmed in the Saxon countryside. A harassed inspector explained that military transports had priority during the summer manoeuvres, and suggested that anyone with a complaint should address it to the General Staff. After that, the rumblings of discontent subsided to a mere murmur.

207

The train arrived at Anhaker Station soon after seven. The Berlin weather had turned in Russell's absence: the pavements were wet from a recent shower and a grey pall of cloud hung over the city. The taxi rank on Koniggrätzer Strasse was bare, so he walked the kilometre and a half to Neuenburger Strasse.

Frau Heidegger had company – another *portierfrau* from down the street – which was something of a relief. She welcomed him home, passed him his only message, and walked somewhat unsteadily back to the half-empty bottle of schnapps they were sharing. Standing by the only available window in the downstairs hallway, Russell struggled to decipher her scrawl. 'Frau Grostein has found your missing person,' it read. 'If you call in during the day a meeting can be arranged.' He should have asked when the message arrived, he realized, but decided not to risk a second encounter.

There was no message from Kuzorra, which disappointed him. He had hoped the sighting at Silesian Station was a breakthrough, that Kuzorra would have more news for him by this time. Maybe he had, and was just waiting for a visit.

There was nothing from the SD either, no neatly-compiled dossier of lies for him to pass on to the Soviets. They were probably having trouble sorting fiction from truth.

He walked down to the telephone, picked the earpiece and dialled Effi's number.

'Hello,' the familiar voice answered.

'It's me.'

'Hello you. Where are you?'

'At Neuenburger Strasse. I just got here.'

'How was Prague?'

'Interesting. How are things?'

'Fine, but I'm really tired, John. I was on my way to bed when the telephone rang.'

'Oh.'

'I'm sorry, but you wouldn't enjoy me this evening. I've been grumpy all day. These five o'clock starts are killing me.'

'Tomorrow, then.'

'Of course. But come as early as you can. We're shooting on Saturday as well. We're so behind. The producer's pulling out large clumps of his hair, and he can't afford to lose any.'

'Okay. I love you.'

'You too.'

Russell took the suitcase up to his rooms and dumped it on the bed. The apartment matched his mood, which didn't bode well for an evening in. It was only ten to nine – the Adlon Bar would still be busy.

The blanket of cloud was hastening the light's departure. The Hanomag started first go, and he drove it down to Belle Alliance, intent on heading up Wilhelmstrasse. Reaching the circle he changed his mind, and followed the gently snaking Landwehrkanal to Lützow-Platz before cutting north across the western end of the Tiergarten. The address Sarah Grostein had given him was an elegant three-storey building on Altonaer Strasse, between the elevated Stadtbahn and the bridge over the Spree. He parked a few doors down and walked up towards it. Light showed around the drawn curtains of two windows on the first floor, but the ground floor was dark. He dropped the lion-headed knocker against its base a couple of times, but there was no response from inside. He thought about knocking louder, but his instincts told him it was a bad idea.

He walked back to the car. Looking up as he opened the door he saw the curtains twitch open, revealing a silhouetted head and shoulders. It looked like the SS officer he had seen outside the Universum, but he couldn't be sure.

Call in during the day, the message had said. He had assumed she'd meant the day of the message, but he had been wrong.

The curtain closed again, and Russell waited a few moments before driving off. He had parked between streetlights, and didn't think he'd been seen, but he didn't want to advertise his presence by starting the engine. Let them get back to whatever it was they were doing.

In motion once more, he followed the Spree to Sommer Strasse, cut past the Brandenburg Gate into Pariser Platz, and pulled up in front of the Adlon. There were hardly any cars on Unter den Linden – in fact the traffic had been light all evening. Commandeered by the army, he supposed, and now axle-deep in Silesian mud. 'But not you' he told the Hanomag, tapping its steering-wheel.

The Adlon Bar was not exactly hopping – a party of lugubrious-looking Swedish business-men, a mixed group of SS and *Kriegsmarine* officers, a spattering of lone foreigners staring into their glasses and pining for the days when a night in Berlin spelled entertainment. And in the corner, playing rummy, Dick Normanton and

Jack Slaney.

Their steins were full, so Russell took them a couple of chasers. 'Who's winning?' he asked, just as Normanton went down with a triumphant flourish.

'The bloody English are winning,' Slaney complained, writing it down on the score sheet. 'That's two marks and forty pfennigs,' he said.

'Last of the big-time gamblers,' Russell murmured. 'Can I join in?'

'You'll need twenty pfennigs,' Normanton told him, shuffling the cards.

'So, what's new?' Russell asked. 'I only just got back from Prague,' he added in explanation.

'How are the Czechs doing?' Slaney asked.

'As well as can be expected.'

'There's more trouble in Danzig,' Normanton said, dealing out the cards. 'The Poles won't let the Danzig Germans sell their herrings and margarine in Poland until the Danzig Germans accept their new customs officers. So the Danzig Germans are muttering darkly about opening their frontier with East Prussia and selling the stuff there.'

'Are the East Prussians short of herrings and margarine?' Russell asked.

Normanton laughed. 'Who knows?'

'Who cares?' Slaney added, arranging his cards.

'So we're waiting to see who backs down?' Russell asked.

'That's about it. But I can't see Hitler going to war over herring and margarine. It's not exactly a rallying cry, is it?'

'The important stuff's happening in Moscow,' Slaney said. 'Molotov met the German Ambassador this morning, and was a damn sight more affable with him than he was with the French and British ambassadors yesterday.'

'Any hard information on what they discussed?' Russell asked.

'None. Lots of rumours though: the Germans are willing to give the Soviets a free hand in the Baltic states, they'll share Poland with the Soviets if the Poles make the mistake of starting a war. According to our man in Moscow, the German Ambassador had the nerve to tell Molotov that the anti-Comintern Pact isn't aimed at the Soviets.'

'Then who the hell is it aimed at?'

'That's what Molotov asked. The Ambassador told him there was no point in dwelling on the past. One of the Soviets leaked this to our guy because he couldn't believe his ears, and wanted a second opinion.'

'No government statement here?'

'Not a word. They're playing this close to their chests.'

'Sounds serious.'

Slaney grunted. 'The British and French don't seem to think so. Their delegation left for Moscow yesterday. Guess how they're getting there?'

'They can't have gone by train?'

'Worse. They've taken a boat, and the slowest one they could find. Some obsolete warship with a top speed of twelve knots. They should be in Moscow by the middle of the month.'

'It would be quicker to walk,' Russell observed.

'Jim Danvers came up with a good line,' Normanton said. 'He said the British and French had missed the boat by catching it.'

'Not bad at all,' Slaney agreed. 'Remind me to steal it.'

Two hours later and several marks poorer, Russell drove back through the wet and empty streets to Neuenburger Strasse. Would Hitler and Stalin really do a deal, he wondered? Both would have a mountain of words to eat, but the advantages were obvious. A free hand for Hitler, time for Stalin. Poland *kaput*.

The only message by the unhooked telephone was for Dagmar, the blonde waitress on the third floor. 'Siggi is desperate,' Frau Heidegger had written. 'He must see you tomorrow.' Dagmar was obviously not at home, and probably sleeping with Klaus. He would get an update from Frau Heidegger in the morning.

The stairs seemed endless. It was less than twenty-four hours since the sand dryer, but it seemed a lot longer. After taking off his jacket he extracted the slip of paper with Hornak's suggested contact details from his wallet. How long before they were safe to use, he wondered, now that the local Gestapo had come calling?

Friday morning was grey as Berlin stone, and the giant swastikas on Wilhelmstrasse hung limp in the humid air. In the Kranzler Café the waiters seemed more interested in arguing with each other than in serving their customers, and Russell's coffee was lukewarm. The newspapers lauded the imprisonment of a Wittenberge worker for laziness, but conspicuously failed to mention either Danzig or Soviet-German relations.

Time to earn your living, Russell told himself.

The Bristol Hotel had a convenient bank of public telephones, and while the booths lacked the luxurious fittings of those in the Adlon, they were much less frequented by his fellow journalists. He settled down on a cushioned seat to make his calls.

Over his years in Berlin, Russell had met a lot of influential people in government, arts and the media. Most leaned to the left politically, and many had lost their jobs when the Nazis came to power; some had even left the country. But a surprising number were still in the same positions, keeping their heads down and waiting for the whole shocking business to blow over.

Self-preservation was an obvious priority, and precluded open criticism, but briefings off the record were another matter. The urge to stick spokes in the Nazi wheel was surprisingly widespread.

Sometimes, though, there was no dirt to dish. After speaking to a dozen people, Russell was no nearer to knowing how likely a Nazi-Soviet agreement might be. Some of his contacts had laughed at the idea, others had thought it possible, but only one man – an economist who worked for the Trade Ministry – had anything definite to tell him. A trade agreement between the two countries was a racing certainty, the man said, but there was no guarantee that a political deal would follow.

He dropped in on the Adlon Bar to make sure no official briefings were imminent, and checked his wire service. A three word message had arrived the previous night from San Francisco:

'How about Silesia?'

'How about it?' Russell muttered to himself, but he saw his editor's point. As far as the international community was concerned, Danzig looked like a soluble problem. The Poles might not like it, but Danzig was, in the last resort, a German city. A bilateral deal that included its peaceful absorption into the Reich would not involve the Poles in giving up any of their own territory.

Upper Silesia was a different matter. Poland had been reformed in 1918 from the debris of the German, Austrian and Russian Empires, and any reversal of that process could only be seen as a national death-knell. If Hitler went for Upper Silesia – or for any of the other so-called 'lost territories' – his intent would be crystal-clear. So what was happening down there? Was the border between the two Silesias as tense as Poland's border with Danzig? It would be worth a trip to find out.

Russell went back to the Hanomag, collected the *The Good Soldier Schweik* from under the seat, and walked round the southern side of Pariser Platz to the new American Embassy. As usual, a long line of anxious-looking Jews stretched around the corner from the front entrance on Herman Goering Strasse. They were queuing, if Russell's memory served him right, for the right to enter America in 1944.

Once inside, he gave his name and asked to see someone about an American passport for his son. The receptionist gave him a quick worried look and disappeared through a door behind her desk. She returned a minute or so later with the sort of smiling young man that Russell imagined was found on Californian beaches. His blond hair was almost bleached, his tan a tribute to Berlin's summer. 'This way,' he said, beckoning Russell through the door. 'I've been expecting you. My name's Michael Brown,' he added.

They climbed to an office on the second floor. 'This was Blucher's palace,' the young man said. 'You know, the guy at Waterloo.'

'Before my time,' Russell told him.

'So, do you have anything for me?'

Russell explained what had happened in Prague, and handed over *The Good Soldier Schweik*. 'I've written the contact name and address on the flyleaf, so all you have to do is get it to the department in Washington.'

'Of course.' Brown was leafing through the book with the air of someone searching for secrets.

'Do you have any messages for me?'

Brown looked surprised. 'None.'

'So, for German consumption, you're being difficult about giving my son a passport, and you've told me to come back in a couple of weeks. All right?'

'Sure.'

Russell got to his feet. 'Nice to meet you.'

A neatly-uniformed maid answered the door on Altonaer Strasse. Was Frau Umbach expecting him?

'Frau Grostein is,' Russell said, wondering who the hell Frau Umbach was.

'Wait there,' the maid said, shutting the door in

his face.

She returned a few moments later to beckon him in. 'This way,' she said, leading him down a hallway, through a very modern-looking kitchen, and out into a small, secluded courtyard garden. Sarah Grostein was sitting at an iron table, under a pergola draped in deep red roses. She was wearing a simple blouse and slacks, smoking what smelt like a Turkish cigarette, and halfway through writing a letter. Her mass of wavy brown hair certainly looked feminine, but in all other respects she fell lamentably short of the official ideal of Nazi womanhood.

'Mr Russell,' she said, offering him a chair.

'Frau Umbach?' he asked.

She grimaced. 'I should have told you. My friend has decided I should use my maiden name. For obvious reasons.'

'I got your message.'

'Good. Freya wants to meet you. And so does Wilhelm, come to that.'

'Why?'

She smiled. 'I think he's looking for some publicity, but...'

'For what?'

'He can tell you that. Are you busy this evening, around six o'clock? That was one of the times they offered me.'

He hated giving up precious time with Effi, but she would understand. 'I'm free.'

'I'll confirm it with them this afternoon. You have a car?'

'Of a sort.'

'You can pick me up then. Say five-thirty.'

217

'Fine.' He considered telling her about Gorodnikov, but decided it would be safer to have that conversation in the car.

As she led him back to the front door, he caught a glimpse of a Kandinsky on the living room wall. 'Doesn't your friend object to the painting?' he asked.

'He likes it,' she said simply, and opened the door.

'Five-thirty,' he reiterated over his shoulder.

The Hanomag looked particularly down-at-heel in its current surroundings. The luxury models which usually lined Akonaer Strasse were nowhere to be seen, but not, Russell suspected, because they were out on military manoeuvres with the Wehrmacht. Those cars would have been hidden away for the duration at their owners' country homes.

A tap on the fuel gauge revealed that the Hanomag was running low on petrol. The big garage on Müller-Strasse was almost on his way to Kuzorra's, and had a public telephone he could use to call the studio.

The garage was open, but would only sell him five litres of petrol. There was a shortage, the manager told him, with the air of someone explaining something for the umpteenth time. The military had first claim on what there was, and everyone was running short. All over Berlin regular customers were getting ten litres, strangers five. He should go to his local garage, and not waste too much time about it – the autobahn service stations had already run dry.

Russell took his five litres and pulled over

beside the telephone to call the studio. The woman who answered seemed only half-there, but managed to repeat Russell's name and message back to him. 'That's for Effi Koenen,' he repeated. 'Oh,' she said, as if it was the first time she'd heard the name.

He drove on to Kuzorra's, wondering whether he'd even reach his local garage with this much petrol in the tank. Maybe the SD had stores set aside for their best agents. He couldn't imagine the Gestapo running dry – cruising up and down streets looking ominous was what made them happy.

Frau Kuzorra's welcome seemed chillier than before, and her husband, ensconced in his usual chair, could only manage the wryest of smiles. The man looked older, Russell thought, as he refused Frau Kuzorra's half-hearted offer of coffee.

'I won't waste your time,' Kuzorra said once Russell was seated. 'I have to give up this enquiry.'

'Why?' Russell asked simply.

'I will tell you, but I ask you not to repeat any of this. Except to Herr Schade, of course. And please ask him not to repeat it to anyone else.'

'I will.'

Kuzorra leant back in his chair. 'A few days ago I received a visit from an old colleague – a man whom I disliked intensely when we worked out of the same office. He is still on the job, a Kriminalinspektor now. He was always a brown-noser – an old term, and one that gained a double meaning when Hitler's thugs started running things on the streets.'

Frau Kuzorra muttered something under her breath.

'In my own home I will speak the truth,' Kuzorra told her. He turned back to Russell. 'I won't tell you the man's name because it's not relevant. Anyway, he came to see me last Sunday – he was waiting outside when we returned from church. He told me there had been complaints from railway staff at Silesian Station – and from some of the stall-owners – that I had been harassing them. He wanted to know why I was trying to cause trouble over some miserable Jewish girl. Her disappearance – if she really had disappeared – was police business, and I should keep out of it. I argued with him, said the police had done nothing. He just smiled and said they had done everything that needed doing, and that there was no need for a retired private detective to waste his time on such a business. I said it was my time to waste, and my living to earn. He said not anymore, that my license to operate as a private detective had been withdrawn. I tell you, the bastard was really enjoying himself. And there was more. If I carried on with the investigation I would be putting our pensions at risk. *Our* pensions, you understand. Not just my police pension, but both our pensions from the state. We could not live without them. So...' He spread his hands in a gesture of resignation. 'I am sorry.'

'So am I,' Russell said. He was wondering whether Thomas had also been leaned on. 'The last message you left for me – you said Miriam had been seen with a man.'

'I have been told to tell you I discovered nothing,' Kuzorra said, 'so please, be careful how you use what I tell you. The witness ... it wouldn't help you to know who he is. This witness thought he recognized Miriam from the picture you gave me.' He took it out of his wallet and gave it back to Russell. 'He wasn't absolutely sure, but he thought it was her. And he saw her talking to a man. A man he has seen before at Silesian Station. He's about fifty, average height, a little overweight perhaps. He has closely-cropped grey hair, a little like mine, the man said.' The detective ran a hand across his grey stubble. 'And eyebrows which are darker than his hair. He was wearing some sort of dark blue uniform – my witness thought it might be a chauffeur's.

'I spent a couple of hours at the station on the Thursday evening, but no one of that description met the train which Miriam had taken. So I went back on the Friday. More in hope than expectation, but there he was. At least, I think so. My witness doesn't work on Fridays, so I had no way of confirming that this was the man he saw with Miriam. But this man matched the description, except for the fact that he wasn't wearing a uniform. He did spend a long time on the concourse, scanning all the arriving passengers as if he was looking for someone. He didn't speak to anyone though, and there were several attractive young women whom he might have approached. After the passengers from the 9pm arrival had all gone through, he simply turned on his heel and walked out through the main entrance. He had a car – a big one – parked on

Stralauer Platz, and I managed to see the number plate as he drove off.' Kuzorra looked sheepish. 'But by the time I'd dug out a pencil I'd forgotten most of it – my memory isn't what it was, I'm afraid. I am sure the number ended in thirty-three – that's not a number I'm likely to forget.'

The year Hitler got a proper job, Russell thought. The year Kuzorra lost his. 'Why do you think your colleague came to lean on you?' he asked.

'I don't know. Just spite, perhaps. He heard about the investigation – maybe someone at Silesian Station really did complain – and he felt like making a point. Police detectives get very territorial, even the best of them, and this one's scum. Maybe he just couldn't bear the thought that someone was trying to help a Jew. Or he's been holding a grudge against me for heaven knows what reason and finally found a way of getting his own back. Who knows?

'The other possibility is more worrying, at least as far as you're concerned. Let's say that the man I followed to his car really did have something to do with the girl's disappearance. If he noticed my interest... I mean, I have no idea how he could have found out who I am, but if he had friends in high places, or he works for someone who does, then my old Kripo colleague could simply be the messenger. One who enjoyed delivering the message of course, but not the instigator.'

Russell considered this possibility, and didn't like where it took him. 'Thank you,' he said, getting to his feet. 'You've sent your bill to Schade & Co?'

'No. I...'

'Send it. You've done the work.'

'It's here,' Frau Kuzorra said, appearing beside him with a neatly-typed invoice.

'I'll pass it on to Herr Schade,' Russell told her.

Kuzorra was also on his feet, offering his hand. 'If you ever find her, I'd like to know,' he said.

'You will.'

Back in the car Russell took out the Rosenfeld family photograph and looked at Miriam. 'What kind of a mess are you in?' he asked her.

It was a little after three-thirty – time for a short stop-off at the Adlon before picking up Sarah Grostein. None of his friends were in the bar when he arrived, sparking fears that he was missing a major story, but another journalist told him that boredom had driven them upstairs for a poker session.

After some deliberation, Russell phoned Schade & Co from a booth in the lobby. Thomas was out of his office, but his secretary managed to track him down.

Russell asked him if he'd had any visits from the authorities.

'No. Why?'

'Because they resent your interference in what is clearly a police matter. And I must say, I tend to agree with them.'

Thomas was never slow on the uptake. 'I suppose you're right.'

'Well, they've certainly convinced Kuzorra.'

'I take it he's quit.'

'He has. And I think we should give up on it

too. We're not even certain the girl ever reached Berlin.'

'That's true. All right. What else can we do, anyway?'

'Good. We're agreed. Now, about that fishing trip we were going to take – we need to talk about it. Can I come over tomorrow lunchtime?'

'Yes. Good. I'll get the maps out.'

'Okay. Bye.' Russell clicked the line dead and burst out laughing.

Sarah Grostein was waiting for his knock. 'I must be back by eight,' she said as they walked to the car. She had changed since the morning, and was now wearing what Russell's English aunt called a sensible skirt. Her hair was tied back, and her face bore no signs of make-up. She was wearing low-heeled shoes, which only seemed to emphasise how tall she was.

'Where are we going?' Russell asked, starting the car.

'Didn't I tell you? Friedrichshain. The park. The café near the Konigsthor entrance – do you know it?'

'I once took Albert Wiesner there for a coffee and a fatherly chat.'

She laughed. 'Did he listen?'

'No, not really. He enjoyed his cream cake though.'

'He's in Palestine now.'

'I know. I had a letter from his sisters a few weeks ago. They're doing well.'

'Thanks to you.'

'They earned it.'

'Yes, but...' She fell silent as Russell squeezed the Hanomag between a tram and a parked car, then changed the subject. 'Was it you knocked on my door last night?' she asked.

'Yes, I'm sorry. I misunderstood your message. I hope it didn't...'

'No. I told him someone was knocking on the neighbour's door.'

'He looked out of the window.'

'Yes, he saw your car.' She took out a cigarette.

They were on Invalidenstrasse in the Friday rush-hour, and the miserly number of motorists could hardly believe their luck. Russell wondered what the Wehrmacht was doing with all the cars. There weren't that many generals to drive around.

'I have some news for you,' he said. 'I had to go to the Soviet Embassy last week on other business – journalistic stuff – and I passed your request to the relevant person. They'll check you out with Moscow, of course, and with whatever's left of the KPD leadership. Assuming that all goes okay,' he said, glancing across at her, 'they want me to be your contact here in Berlin.'

She looked surprised at this. 'I didn't realize...' she began.

He thought about explaining his involvement, and decided against. She didn't need to know.

'It sounds like a good idea,' she said at last. 'We are people who could have met and become friends in ordinary circumstances.'

He glanced at her, wondering if that was true. 'You've got my number,' he said. 'And I'll give you my girlfriend's as well. But please, only use hers in an emergency. She's not involved in this.'

They sat in silence for the rest of the journey. Every so often she flicked the ash from her cigarette out of the window, but seemed too lost in thought to actually smoke. The sun appeared behind them as they drove east on Lothringer Strasse, and by the time they reached the entrance to the Friedrichshain park the sky was rapidly turning blue. Freya and Wilhelm Isendahl were waiting by the sculptures of Hansel and Gretel at the foot of the Märchen-Brunnen waterfalls.

They looked like the ideal Nazi couple. Freya's shoulder-length blonde hair framed an open face, very blue eyes and a ready smile. Her clothes and shoes were both attractive and practical, and her skin had the freshness of innocence. Wilhelm was equally good-looking, but several years older. His neatly parted hair was a darker shade of blonde, and his eyes were green. The long nose and full mouth reminded Russell, somewhat unfortunately, of Reinhard Heydrich. Which raised all sorts of interesting questions.

Both were wearing wedding rings.

They introduced themselves, Sarah and Wilhelm exchanging nods of recognition. Walking on into the park Russell remembered his last visit with Albert Wiesner. The trees had been bare, the grass flecked with snow, and Albert had been silently daring every passer-by to call him a Jew. The café owner had risen to the challenge, and initially refused to serve them.

Russell suspected that Wilhelm Isendahl was every bit as angry, but that his defiance took a different form. Wilhelm simply assumed his right to equality, as worthy of his human status as any paid-up member of the master-race. The lack of stereotypical Jewish features helped, but the self-belief came from within. When they reached the café, which was now sporting a large 'Jews prohibited' sign, Wilhelm shared a joke with the proprietor and helped Russell carry the coffees back to their table.

Russell told Freya about his meeting with her parents.

'How are they?' she asked, without much enthusiasm. 'They were so rotten to Wilhelm,' she added, as if in explanation. 'I still find it hard to forgive them.'

Russell shrugged. 'I'll take your word for it. All they said to me was that he was a bit of a mischief-maker.'

Wilhelm grunted with apparent amusement, but Freya's eyes blazed. 'You see what I mean! A mischief-maker! What do they expect Jews like Wilhelm to do? Just let the Nazis walk all over them?'

Russell smiled. 'I understand. I'm just the messenger. They just asked me to make sure you're all right.'

'Well, you can see that I am,' she said, and Russell had to agree. She looked tired, certainly, but there was a happy sparkle in the eyes. 'Look,' she said, relenting, 'I will write to them, tell them that we are married. Do you have their address?' She looked sheepish for a moment. 'I'm afraid I threw their letters away.'

Russell wrote it out in his reporter's notebook and tore out the page. 'I'll wire them and say you'll be writing,' he said, passing it across. 'Are you still working at the University?' he asked.

'No. At Siemens,' she said. 'As a secretary in the offices. Wilhelm works there too.'

Russell raised an eyebrow.

'The government lets them hire Jews because they're short of armaments workers,' Wilhelm told him. 'And Siemens are all in favour because they can get away with paying us next to nothing. But both of them may live to regret it. We are getting organized – Jews and non-Jews together.'

'Frau Grostein said you wanted to meet me in my journalistic capacity.'

'Yes.' He pulled a much-folded piece of paper from his shirt pocket and carefully opened it up. 'Have you seen these?' he asked, passing it over.

It looked like the leaflet Russell had read on the tram. The message was different – this one concerned the recent death in a concentration camp of a prominent pastor – but the viewpoint and printing style were identical.

'Our group is responsible for these,' Wilhelm went on. 'It would be good if we could get some coverage in the foreign press. Let people know that some of us are fighting back.'

'All right, but why the foreign press?'

'Because we'll never get mentioned in the German press, and word does get back. When people come back from outside the cage they tell their friends what they've read and heard, and that gives other people hope that these pigs won't be lording it over us for a thousand years. Any news of resistance boosts everyone's morale, it really does.'

Everyone hungers after fame, Russell thought cynically, and mentally scolded himself. Who was he to judge this young man? 'I'll see what I can do,' he said. 'It'll have to be generalised, of course. I can't say I've actually been talking to the people responsible for the leaflets, or they'll want me to name names. I don't think journalistic privilege covers treason these days. But this group of yours – is it just printing leaflets?'

'It's not my group,' Wilhelm said with some asperity, 'and distribution is the dangerous part.'

'I appreciate that.'

'Good.' The young man's irritation passed as swiftly as it had risen. 'Otherwise ... well, we hold discussion meetings, and we help organize support for people with no income. And we're thinking about printing a regular news sheet...'

'Any connection with the Palestine group?'

Wilhelm looked scornful. 'You don't fight race hatred by creating a state based on race. That's what the Nazis are doing.'

'Not in the same way,' Sarah Grostein interjected.

'What's the difference?' Wilhelm wanted to know.

'I think that's an argument for another time and place,' Russell said, aware that at least one other customer was watching them. An open-air café in Hitler's Berlin hardly seemed the ideal setting for an angry argument between communists about the future of Palestine. He turned to Freya. 'If you give me your address,' he said, 'I can give it to your parents when I wire them.'

She looked at Wilhelm, who nodded.

Russell wrote it down – one of the run-down streets off Busching Platz, if he remembered correctly. 'And I'll let you know if I can get you some publicity,' he told Wilhelm. They were all on their way back to the park entrance when he had a better idea. 'You could write something yourself,' he told Wilhelm. 'About your campaign, I mean. Your motives, how you distribute the leaflets, how you keep one step ahead of the Gestapo. Say what you want to say but make it sound exciting, even if it isn't.'

'Who would print it?'

'Send it to me, along with a covering letter saying who you are and who you represent. Not your real name, of course, but something convincing. I know – you can also send me an advanced copy of your next leaflet, and tell me to look out for other copies in a few days time. On a particular tram route, say. That'll give me all the proof I need that the article and the leaflets have been written by the same people. The creeps at the Propaganda Ministry won't be very happy, but I'll just be behaving like a responsible journalist. I got sent the piece, I checked its source, and I sent it for publication. And no, I have no idea who it came from.'

Wilhelm smiled, and looked several years younger. 'I will do it.'

'Send it to me, John Russell, care of the Adlon Hotel.'

They shook hands. Russell and Sarah Grostein watched the young couple walk off arm in arm, Freya's blonde head resting on Wilhelm's shoulder. The similarities between her past and Freya's present accounted for the wistfulness in Sarah's face, but there was also something harder there, something beyond recall. Just age perhaps, or the knowledge of what could go wrong, and how you dealt with that.

In the car she lit another cigarette, took a single puff and threw it away. 'He's a brave man,' she said eventually, 'but I don't know whether he's careful enough. What did you think of him?'

'Impressive. Young. As for careful, it's hard to say. I'm not sure it matters that much. I have a horrible feeling that survival's more a matter of luck than anything else.'

'Not in the long run.'

'Because history's on our side? Even if it is, there don't seem to be any individual guarantees.'

'No,' she agreed. 'My husband would have agreed with you. Not that he ever tried to be careful.'

As they turned into Lothringer Strasse the evening sun hit Russell squarely between the eyes, temporarily blinding him. A lorry roared past only inches away, horn blasting, before the road swam back into focus. 'There're some sunglasses in there,' he said, gesturing towards the glove compartment.

'I haven't seen anything like those before,' she said, passing them over.

'I bought them in New York,' he told her. 'They're called Polaroids, which means they're reflective. They were only invented a couple of years ago.'

'Richard and I went to New York in 1929. We were on the boat home when we heard about the stock market crash.'

'Tell me about him.'

She thought about it for the better part of a minute. 'He was a lovely man,' she said eventually. 'Temperamental, argumentative, a bit too sure of himself, but always kind. A businessmen who wrote romantic poetry. A wonderful lover.'

'That's some testament.'

She looked away, and he half-suspected tears, but when she turned back towards him her face was harder. 'I expect you're wondering how I can prostitute myself with the people who killed him.'

There was no easy answer to that. 'It must be hard,' was all he said.

'Sometimes. You know the worst thing of all? He's not a bad man. He makes interesting conversation, he makes me laugh. He represents everything I hate, but I can't hate him.' She almost laughed. 'Isn't that ridiculous?'

'Not at all. I didn't hate any of the Germans on the other side of no man's land, but I was quite prepared to kill them.'

'Is that the same? I suppose it is in a way. But you weren't sleeping with the enemy.'

'No.'

She managed another half-strangled laugh. 'I suppose this is what passes for small talk in a Thousand Year Reich.'

After dropping Sarah off at her home Russell headed straight for Effi's. As he pulled the Hanomag into the yard beside her building, he noticed two men standing outside the front door. They were in civilian dress, but they didn't look like salesmen.

Both were wearing long coats and hats despite the warmth of the evening, and the shorter of the two – a slim blonde with a weasel face – sported beads of sweat on his forehead and above his upper lip. As he moved to block Russell's entrance he tried for a winning smile. He failed, but the mere attempt was reassuring.

'John Russell,' he said. It wasn't a question.

'That's me.'

'We need to talk to you. In your car, perhaps?'

There was no point in refusing. Russell led the way back to the Hanomag and opened the doors. The taller man jammed himself into the back, leaving Russell and weasel-face in the front. 'A message from Hauptsturmführer Hirth?' he asked.

The man looked disappointed that his line had been stolen. 'Instructions,' he corrected. 'You will be receiving a number of documents in the next few days. The Hauptsturmführer assumes you know what to do with them.'

'Pass them on to the Reds.'

'That is correct.' He reached for the door handle.

'Hold on a moment,' Russell said. 'How are you planning on delivering these documents? You can't come here again – the Soviets know I live here most of the time, and they could be watching the place.' He very much doubted that they were, but he wanted to keep Heydrich's goons as far away from Effi as possible. And if they got the impression he was taking his new mission seriously, it might even bolster his credibility.

Weasel-face stared out at the darkened street.

'They will also know of your other address.'

'Of course. You'll have to use the post,' Russell explained, trying not to sound like he was talking to a ten-year-old child. 'Send everything to Neuenburger Strasse,' he added.

The man nodded. 'It shall be done as you suggest,' he said, and reached for the door handle again.

Russell sat in the car watching them walk away. He expected more from Heydrich's people, and felt somewhat cheered by the utter banality of the encounter. Don't get too cocky, he told himself. Hauptsturmführer Hirth was not a fool.

He was only halfway up the stairs when Effi opened the door with a face full of questions. 'Who were they?' she asked as she almost pulled him inside. 'What did they want?'

'Nothing that important,' he told her, kissing her on the forehead. 'A couple of Heydrich's boys delivering a message. Did they come up?'

'Oh yes. They wanted to wait for you inside. I told them I had a reputation to think of, and both of them leered at me. But they went back downstairs.'

'They were well-behaved then,' he said, taking her into his arms. He could see that she'd been shaken by their appearance. 'Have you eaten?' he asked, thinking that it would be better to get her out of the flat.

'I'm not hungry. What was the message, John?'

'I thought we agreed not to tell each other certain things.'

'Yes, yes, I know we did. All right. But I've been standing by the window waiting for you to come back and wondering what they wanted with you ... whether they were going to arrest you or ask you to do something horrible. John, I don't want you doing anything that you know is wrong just to keep me safe.'

He put his hands on her shoulders. 'If it ever comes to that, I'll tell you. And we'll decide together.'

'Yes, but what choice will there be?'

'We can do what they want me to do, or we can leave. Together.'

'How could we leave? They won't let us.'

'We'll find a way.'

She looked up at him with worried eyes.

'It's going to be all right,' he said, and found, rather to his surprise, that he half-believed it.

She dropped her head on his chest and hugged him tightly.

'I haven't eaten,' he said eventually.

'No, neither have I,' she admitted, looking at her watch. 'So who needs sleep? I'm supposed to look haggard tomorrow – it's the scene where I've been sitting at the SA squad leader's bedside for nights on end. Lili will be amazed by how little make-up I need.'

They walked to the small French restaurant just off the Ku'damm. Both city and restaurant seemed quiet for a Friday night, another consequence, Russell guessed, of the military manoeuvres. As they waited for their meals in a secluded corner of the rear garden, he brought Effi up to date on the search for Miriam Rosenfeld.

'You can't blame him,' she said of Kuzorra's resignation, 'but what are you and Thomas going to do now?'

'I don't know. We've got so little to go on – nothing really, nothing definite. The one witness Kuzorra found couldn't swear it was her. And if it wasn't her, then the man he saw talking to her is irrelevant. He could have been a father meeting a daughter or an uncle meeting a niece – something perfectly innocent.'

'But the man was seen again.'

'Probably. We're not totally sure it was the same man.'

'So why did they lean on your detective?'

Russell shrugged. 'A private grudge? Someone enraged by the idea that a missing Jew needs finding? We just don't know. We still don't know for certain that she ever reached Berlin.'

'I think you do,' Effi said. 'All right, none of the things your detective discovered are a hundred per cent. But together – it's just too much. A girl who looks remarkably like Miriam meets a man who makes a habit of hanging round Silesian Station, and the moment your detective starts asking questions about the two of them he gets a visit from his old colleague. If those were the opening scenes of a movie you would know what had happened.'

Russell sighed. 'I know. I just keep hoping there's another explanation, that she never got here, or that her meeting with our mystery man was an innocent one, and she decided for some reason or other to go home. She might have found out about her uncle being beaten up and just panicked, and gone rushing back to her family. She is only seventeen, and I don't think she'd even seen a city before, let alone one this size.'

'So are you and Thomas going to look for another detective?'

'We might try, but I doubt we'll find one.'

'Then what?'

'I don't know. I'll drop in and see Thomas on my way to Paul's tomorrow. If I can find enough petrol, that is.' He explained the shortage, and the new garage policy of favouring regular customers. 'Which is fine if you have a regular garage. I don't.' He saw the look on her face, and grinned. 'I know. There are always trams. Especially for those of us who don't warrant studio cars.'

It was gone ten by the time they got home, almost eleven when Effi's breathing took on the pattern of sleep. Russell lay there, enjoying the soft warmth of her body curled into his, thinking back over his day. Two embassy appointments to discuss espionage work, an angry private detective and a rather remarkable woman, a sweet young pair of resisters and a dumb young pair of SD goons. All topped off with the love of his life lying naked beside him. Life was far from empty.

He had promised Effi that everything was going to be all right. Was it? He felt safe in Berlin, which was more than he'd felt in Prague. But was he missing something crucial? Had he taken one of those oh-so-ordinary life-and-death decisions without realizing it?

Look at the big picture, he told himself. The Germans could hardly accuse him of spying for the Soviets when it was they who had put him up to it. And vice versa. His spying for the Americans could be justified as part of his double role with the Soviets, and most of it could, at a pinch, be explained away as over-zealous journalism. And if things got out of hand there was always the emergency call to Zembski. What did he have to worry about?

Effi was long gone when he woke. After a quick breakfast at the Café Kranzler he stopped off at the Propaganda and Foreign Ministries to see if any briefings were scheduled for the day – there were none. He found out why from Slaney, who was downing his usual milky coffee in the Adlon breakfast room. 'The bastards have had their bluff called,' the American said jubilantly. 'The Nazis in Danzig issued the Poles with an ultimatum, and the Poles issued one right back. The Nazi leader blustered for a bit, the Poles held firm, and he just threw in the towel. Last thing I heard he was trying to convince the Poles that the original ultimatum was a hoax.'

'So it's all blown over.'

'Looks like it. For the moment anyway. I don't imagine Adolf will let things lie for long.'

'Have you wired it off already?'

'No point. "Small crisis in Danzig fizzles out" isn't much of a headline, is it?'

'True.' Russell got up to go. 'I'm off to find some petrol.'

'Good luck.'

As he started up the Hanomag, Russell had an idea. 'You're going home,' he told the car, directing it up Luisen-Strasse towards Invaliden-Strasse. A short drive through the maze of industrial backstreets beyond Lehrter Station brought him to the garage owned by Zembski's cousin Hunder, where he had bought the Hanomag six months earlier.

The garage yard was full of automobiles, most of them taxis. A line of lorries was parked along the far wall, under the noxious cloud of smoke provided by the adjoining locomotive depot. Hunder was doing sums in his office, small piles of bills rising from his desk and floor like ancient stones.

He greeted Russell with evident relief, and an apparently bountiful supply of petrol. Since they were friends, he would let the Englishman have a full tank at only twice the usual price.

Russell grinned and accepted – what else were expenses for? Outside, Hunder summoned one of his young apprentices to siphon fuel from the nearest taxis.

'What are they all doing here?' Russell asked.

Hunder smiled. 'In for repair, every last one of them.'

Russell got it. 'And they'll all be ready for the road the moment the manoeuvres end.'

'What a cynic you are.'

Ten minutes later he was on his way. A tap on the fuel gauge brought it springing to attention, like a fourteen-year-old in a brothel, as his old sergeant had used to say.

Berlin's other motorists seemed to be con-serving their fuel, and the trip out to Dahlem took him less than half an hour. Thomas was digging in the garden, and as grateful for the interruption as Hunder had been. He took Russell into his study, poured them both a generous glass of schnapps, and listened, with increasing anger, to his friend's account of the final meeting with Kuzorra.

'What can have happened to her?' he said when Russell was finished. 'I can understand her falling prey to some criminal, but that wouldn't explain the police threatening Kuzorra.'

'Here's his bill, by the way,' Russell said, fishing it out of his pocket and handing it over.

Thomas looked at it briefly, and put it to one side. 'What more can we do?' he asked. 'Find another detective?'

'We could try.'

'Whatever we do, we should do it discreetly. I don't want the Kripo out at the factory. Or here come to that.'

'We could give up,' Russell said. 'It would be the sensible thing to do. One girl, who may or may not be in trouble.'

'That's just it,' Thomas said. 'I've been wondering why I care so much about what happened to this girl. It's because she *is* just one girl. Not a nation or a race or a class – I've given up thinking that we could save any of those, but surely we should be able to save one person. Or at least give it a damn good try.'

His ex-brother-in-law never ceased to surprise Russell. 'All right,' he said.

'Another detective?'

Russell thought about it. 'Not yet. You still haven't heard anything from her family?'

'Not a word.'

'I'm going to Silesia for work,' Russell said, having just decided as much. His paper wanted him there, so why not take the opportunity? 'I'll go and see the family, see if they can provide any clues. There may be other relatives or friends in Berlin that we know nothing about – something as simple as that.'

Thomas doubted it, but agreed it was worth trying. Driving on to Grünewald to collect Paul, Russell tried to put Miriam Rosenfeld out of his mind. He understood – even shared – Thomas's reasons for wanting to find her, but the task itself might be beyond them.

His son opened the door of the Grünewald home in his *Jungvolk* uniform, Ilse hovering behind him. 'I've just got back,' he said. 'I need to get this glue off my hands,' he added, holding them out for inspection before shooting off upstairs.

'They've been making model planes all morning,' Ilse told Russell. 'It's one of the things he likes about the *Jungvolk*.'

'He likes a lot of it. Everything but the propaganda, really.'

'I think they're all bored by that. Paul has a whole pile of information folders in his bedroom, but I don't think he's read any of them.'

'Good.'

'They don't know what they think at that age. Paul has that badge he got at the World's Fair pinned above his bed – "I have seen the future".'

'I saw it in New York,' Paul said, rattling down the stairs. 'I got most of it off,' he added, meaning the glue.

Paul wanted to go boating on the Havelsee, an ambition shared by several thousand others. The queue for a boat was interminable, but once out on the lake their fellow-Berliners were soon left behind, mere dots in the distance, barely discernible against the wooded shorelines. Russell had hired a hat to shade himself, and when Paul insisted on rowing he sat back and watched as his *Jungvolk*-uniformed son came to grips with the oars. He was getting older, Russell thought. A trite realization perhaps, but one with some meaning. The trip to America had given the boy something, and the return to Germany hadn't taken it away.

He asked Paul about the *Jungvolk* meeting, but all the boy wanted to talk about was the World's Fair. 'Remember the Life Savers tower?' he enthused, referring to the 250-foot parachute hoist they'd both gone up in. The plunge before the chute opened had certainly taken several years off Russell's life. At the moment of release he'd been reading the quote from Lenin which topped the Soviet exhibit, and had been left with the impression that the bottom had suddenly fallen out of socialism.

'And Elektro,' Paul said, 'wasn't he fantastic?'

The Westinghouse robot had been amazing, though teaching him to smoke seemed a poor use for futuristic technology. General Motors' Futurama had been just as incredible – a gigantic scale model that took fifteen minutes to traverse in a moving armchair – but its vision of express highways policed by radio towers seemed less than heart-warming. Russell had agreed with Walter Lippman's assertion that the Fair demonstrated man's inability 'to be wise as he is intelligent, to be as good as he is great.' When Russell had showed his son the relevant article in the *Herald Tribune*, Paul had given him a withering look and said, 'I bet he didn't go up on the Life Saver.'

When Russell got back to Effi's he found her wearing the red dress he'd brought back from America. 'I feel like dancing,' she said, and after a quick snack in the Old Town they scoured the streets around Alexanderplatz for a suitable venue. Before the Nazis there had been a dozen dance halls in the area, some boasting orchestras with a real feel for the new American jazz. Six years on, the pickings were much slimmer, but they found one joint under the Stadtbahn station with a floor and a band that were just about passable. It was full when they arrived and kept getting fuller, but both were laughing with exhilaration when they left two hours later. Berlin had life in it yet.

Next morning they took their usual breakfast in the Tiergarten, and Russell announced that he was probably going to spend a few days in Silesia. 'For the paper,' he added. 'And I'm going to look up Miriam's family. I'll probably be back on Thursday.'

'I've been invited to something that evening,' Effi told him, then hesitated.

'What?' Russell prompted.

'A social gathering,' she said. 'Maybe something more. A friend has asked me to meet some people.'

'Who?'

She hesitated again. 'Christiane.'

Russell looked blank.

'My astrologer.'

'Ah.'

'She's not as wacky as you think she is.'

'That's a relief.'

She gave him the chandelier look. 'I'm going to go.'

'And I'm not invited?'

'No,' she said. 'We agreed to keep these things separate.'

'We did.'

'I can meet you afterwards. It'll be over by nine, I should think.'

Russell didn't like it, but knew he was being unreasonable.

They both sat in silence for a minute or more. It was a lovely warm morning, a breeze shifting the leaves of the trees, the ducks going about their business on the miniature lake. The smell of fresh coffee wafted out from the café behind them, the only sounds a train on the distant Stadtbahn and the rustle of morning papers.

'All this,' Effi said. 'It's hard to imagine it ending.'

Russell's first task on Monday was to check that the crisis in Danzig had really blown over. It had. The main item of news in the morning papers was a train accident in Potsdam. The crossing keeper had lifted the gates after a passenger train passed through, only for a goods train to follow. Seven had been killed, the keeper arrested.

He wired San Francisco that he was heading for Breslau and drove back to Neuenburger Strasse. There was another message for Dagmar by the telephone – 'Siggi wants an explanation!!!' in Frau Heidegger's boldest capitals. The *portierfrau* herself was nowhere to be seen, so Russell left a brief note explaining his absence and walked down to Hallesches Tor in search of a cab.

On reaching Silesian Station he found that the next express to Breslau was not for an hour. He sat drinking coffee on the concourse, wondering if Miriam had ever been there. He kept a lookout for men with grey hair and black eyebrows, but none appeared.

Silesian angels

Russell had considered driving the 450 kilometres to the Polish border – the autobahn would, after all, have carried him two-thirds of the way – but finding petrol in Silesia might prove difficult, and there was always the chance that some jumped-up uniform on manoeuvres would choose to commandeer the car. Still, as his train slipped further and further behind schedule he began to wish that he had risked it. Passages of exhilarating speed were few and far between; the train spent most of its time either advancing at a steady crawl or wearily hissing to a complete stop.

He had planned to spend the night in the border town of Beuthen, but on arrival in a rapidly-darkening Breslau he and his fellow-passengers were informed that the train's onward journey would be subject to delay. The sight of their decoupled

245

locomotive heading off into the gloom was disheartening, and enquiries at the booking office offered no compensatory encouragement. Russell decided he would rather spend the night in a hotel.

Others had already reached the same conclusion, and the taxi rank outside the station was empty. Asking after trams, he was told that the city centre was only a ten-minute walk away. 'Past the Party House,' the kiosk holder told him, pointing up the street towards a building draped with the usual giant swastikas, 'and turn right.'

Darkness had fallen, and the dimly-lit streets seemed strangely empty for nine in the evening. As he walked his spirits seemed to lift, and he realized that he usually felt safer outside Berlin. Why was that? Because he felt safer in motion? Or because he had only himself to worry about?

The first hotel he came to was the Monopol. The name was familiar, and he soon found out why – a placard attached to the wall in reception proudly announced that Hitler had stayed the night in 1932. The room in question had doubtless been preserved in all its Führer-scented glory, complete with pubic hairs trapped in amber and sheets for sniffing.

His own first floor room was small, but included a private bathroom. After testing the bed for bounce he went back down to the bar, which was almost as empty as the streets. Two men in suits dourly acknowledged his greeting and turned their attention back to their schnapps. Russell tried engaging the barman in conversation, but all attempts to elicit a quotable opinion about anything more serious than football proved fruitless. He left his beer unfinished, ordered an early wake-up call at reception, and wearily climbed the stairs to his room.

He was out of the hotel soon after seven the following morning, having reserved a room for two nights hence. It was another blue sky day, and the sun had long since risen above the thin line of mountains to the south. Russell couldn't recall a better summer, and remembered that that was what everyone had said about 1914. The 'wonderful summer before the war.'

Over coffee and rolls in the station restaurant he scanned the papers for something to follow up, and found exactly what he was looking for. Both carried virtually identical accounts of a border incident the previous day. Polish provocateurs had crossed the border some ten kilometres north-west of Beuthen and attacked a German farmer and his family in the village of Blechowka. The farmer had been badly beaten, his wife subjected to unspeakable – but unspecified – indignities. How much longer, the editors asked, could the Reich put up with such outrageous behaviour from its eastern neighbour? About a month, if Slaney was right.

Russell finished his coffee and looked up at the clock above the departure board. He had half an hour to spare – time to do a little preliminary checking. There was a man named Josef Möhl-mann on the list which Russell had memorized in New York, and he worked for the railway admin-istration here in Breslau. Half an hour should be long enough to find the building.

In the event, it took only a couple of minutes. A convenient official gave Russell the necessary information – the *Reichsbahn Direktion* building was only a short walk away, on the other side of the station. He walked through the tunnel and found it without difficulty – a five-storey stone block the size of a small football pitch. Six huge statues were perched high above the colonnaded entrance, three of which bore striking resemblances to Jesus, Cortez and Britannia. All of whom seemed somewhat unlikely subjects.

It was almost eight o'clock, and a steady stream of suited workers was pouring in through the front doors. His target might be one of them, but Russell had no time to introduce himself that morning. He would pay Möhlmann a visit when he got back from the border.

He walked back down the tunnel and up the steps to an empty Platform 3. A short train was soon shunted into the station for Russell and the handful of other passengers. Soon they were out of Breslau and chugging south-eastward towards Oppeln through fields of golden grain. Several rakes of empty tank transporters were stabled in country sidings, but the tanks themselves were nowhere to be seen.

The landscape slowly grew more hilly, and soon after noon the first pits of the Silesian coalfield loomed into view. The train stopped for several minutes in Gleiwitz, then ran on towards Beuthen and the eighteen-year-old border between Germany and Poland, stretches of forest alternating with straggling mining villages.

Before 1918 Gleiwitz, Beuthen, Königshütte and Kattowitz had been the four principal towns of German Upper Silesia, but once the new borders had been established by the Versailles peace-makers and a local plebiscite, the latter two – along with 80 per cent of the coal mines and industrial installations – had found themselves in Poland. Beuthen had been spared, but now lay in a narrow and decidedly vulnerable finger of German territory. To the north, east and south the Polish border lay less than three kilometres away.

A taxi driver in the station forecourt told Russell that the border village of Blechowka was about ten kilometres to the north-west, and proved willing to take him there in his rather ancient-looking vehicle. He made no mention of the previous day's frontier incident, and Russell decided not to tempt fate by introducing the subject, settling instead for a few general enquiries about local attitudes.

The driver, a grey-haired man in his fifties or sixties, was only too happy to list German Silesian grievances. The Poles had taken most of their coal, and they had no real need for so much – half the mines weren't even being worked anymore. And it was German men who had excavated them, and built the railways and the industries that went with them. Why should the Poles get all the benefit?

'Should we take them back?' Russell asked.

'Not if it means war,' the man said, surprising him. 'But if the Poles start one, well that's another matter!'

Russell had expected a rough ride to Blechowka,

but the roads had been recently improved, presumably by the military. The villages they passed through seemed busy and prosperous: a few children watched the taxi wheeze by, but most of the inhabitants were only visible in the distance, working in the fields. The manoeuvres were taking place thirty kilometres to the north, the driver volunteered, and the locals were hurrying to get the harvest in before they moved south.

Blechowka was on the other side of the Beuthen Forest, a straggly street of houses and farms less than a kilometre from the border. It had a couple of shops and a police station worthy of a much larger community. Russell marched into the latter and asked the duty officer about the previous day's incident.

The man asked him what he was talking about.

Russell showed him the newspaper report, and watched an emotional sequence play itself out in the man's face – from bewilderment to suspicion, anxiety to denial. 'I'll have to see about this,' he said, and disappeared through an adjoining door, newspaper in hand.

He returned with a question a couple of minutes later. 'Who are you?'

'I'm a journalist,' Russell said, getting out his accreditation from the Propaganda Ministry. 'The German people have the right to know about the threats facing them,' he added for good measure.

The man disappeared again, for longer this time. He returned with the smile of someone who had moved a problem on. 'You must talk to the authorities in Beuthen,' he told Russell, returning the newspaper. 'At the Rathaus. We cannot help you here.'

Russell didn't bother to argue. Back outside, he told the taxi driver to wait and walked up the street to the village shops. He bought himself an apple in the grocer's and asked the woman behind the counter about the previous day's excitement. She looked at him blankly.

They had made it up. Some Party hack had consulted an atlas, picked on a village near the border, and made the whole story up. Choosing a real village – one that could be checked – was more arrogant than stupid. They had simply assumed that no one would bother to check. And ninety-nine times out of a hundred they would have been right.

'We're going back,' he told the taxi driver.

The Rathaus in Beuthen was a substantial affair, the officials suitably sure of themselves. They had also had time to sort out their answers. When Russell complained about the newspaper story, one of his two interviewees asked him what more he needed to know – surely the article had facts enough to make German blood boil? When Russell pointed out that he had been to Blechowka, the other man asked him if he realized that unaccompanied foreign nationals were not allowed access to the border area.

'I didn't know that,' Russell admitted, 'and I apologise for doing so. But I still want to know why no one in Blechowka noticed this terrifying Polish intrusion.'

The first official pursed his lips in frustration. 'You can't expect local people to know every-thing that is happening in their area. I can assure you that such incidents are becoming more and more frequent. As are attacks on innocent Germans on the other side of the border. Why are you not investigating them?'

'I intend to,' Russell said with a smile. 'The border is open, I assume?'

'We have not closed it. I cannot speak for the Poles.'

His taxi driver was waiting hopefully in the square, but declined the offer of a paid jaunt into Poland. 'They might take the car,' he explained. 'And I don't have a passport,' he added crushingly.

'The station then,' Russell said, more in hope than expectation.

As it happened, there was an international train due, and it was scheduled to stop at Kattowitz. The good news ended there, however. The train was an hour late, and took almost three hours to complete the fifteen kilometre journey. Most of this time was spent at the German and Polish border posts, which glared at each other across a weed-strewn no man's land. The Germans were only interested in contraband, particularly goods smuggled out for German Jews by misguided aryans. The Poles were only interested in people, regarding every German as a potential fifth columnist. It was all very time-consuming, not to say intensely irritating. For the second day running Russell found himself arriving in a strange city with darkness falling.

A Polish railway official with a few words of English pointed out the nearest hotel, which stood almost opposite the station entrance. It had the same name as his hotel in Breslau, but Russell rather doubted whether Hitler would ever patronize this Monopol – the rooms seemed designed for a race of dwarves, or perhaps Propaganda Ministers. The bed was a carpet of springs, the wall dotted with recently slain mosquitoes, and the bathroom was fifty metres away down a barely-lit corridor. 'Welcome to Kattowitz,' Russell muttered. 'Or even Katowice,' he corrected himself.

Russell's morning interview at the old Rathaus was instructive. His interviewee, a skeletal old man with wispy grey hair and weary eyes, was Tadeusz Jedrychowski. He announced himself as Commissioner for the Silesian District, but left the nature of his responsibilities undefined. He was in civilian clothes, an open white shirt and grey suit as faded as the eyes.

His German was as good as Russell's. He responded to the first question about Polish incursions into Germany with a tired shrug. 'It's all nonsense,' he said. 'Sheer make-believe. I mean, you must ask yourself – why would we give them the excuse they are looking for?'

When Russell asked about German incursions into Poland, Jedrychowski invited him into the next room, where a huge map of the border area was festooned with pins. 'Each of these represents a violation of our border. Most have not been serious, it is true – a few hotheads with too much to drink. But some have been. Men in uniform, whether army or Hitler's private goons. And more than twenty of our people have been killed in the last six months.'

'What about the Germans who live on the Polish side of the border?'

'Some get involved, but most just want to get on with their lives.'

Russell took care with his next question. 'Those who do get involved – it would be understandable if their Polish neighbours sought to punish them.'

'It would. And it happens. But not on the scale the Germans claim. Or anything like it.' He ushered Russell back into his own office. 'We want peace, you know. We have nothing to gain from war.'

'And can it be avoided?'

Jedrychowski managed another weary smile. 'I don't think so.'

An international train was due soon after eleven, and Russell decided to catch it. A conscientious journalist would have checked out one of the pins on Jedrychowski's map, but an afternoon roaming Polish dirt-tracks and another night on a broken trampoline were far from appealing. Besides, he believed the Poles. When you looked at the overall situation, and the interests of those involved, the Polish claims made sense. Unlike those of the Germans.

The train was on time and the border rituals shorter, at least on the Polish side. As the afternoon wore on, pit wheels, slag heaps and sidings gave way to forests and fields, mining towns to market towns. Russell sat in the half-empty dining car, nursing a glass of schnapps and writing out his Silesian story for dispatch from Breslau. It was not an easy one to write, but over the years he'd grown quite adept at exposing the Nazis as shameless liars without actually saying so.

They reached Breslau soon after six, too late, Russell guessed, for catching Josef Möhlmann at work in the *Reichsbahn Direktion* building. He walked across on the off-chance, and was directed up to a room on the third floor, just in time to intercept a young parasol-wielding secretary. Yes, Herr Möhlmann was still in his office, she said, clearly keen to be on her way.

'I'm an old friend,' Russell lied helpfully.

'You know where he is then,' she said cheerfully, giving him the clue he needed with a slight flick of the head.

'Thanks,' he said, walking in the direction indicated. The first door he came to bore Möhlmann's name under the job description Deputy Director of Operations, South-East Germany. Without hesitating, he opened the door and walked in.

A man of around forty looked up from what looked like a sheaf of timetables, light flashing off his spectacles as he did so. His short brown hair was combed straight back, his face carved in the sort of angles a cubist would have admired. Elastic arm-bands held up his sleeves, red braces his trousers.

His response to Russell's precipitate entry belied the sternness of his features. 'Good evening,' he said questioningly, when most men so confronted would have spluttered something along the lines of 'Who the hell are you?'

'Good evening,' Russell replied, advancing with hand extended, his brain working overtime. He'd expected a lowly cog in the Reichsbahn's administrative machinery, not a Deputy Director of Operations. 'Your secretary told me to go straight in,' he lied. 'I have a message for you,' he said as they shook hands. 'From Franz Boyens in America.'

Möhlmann's eyes lit up. 'From Franz? He is well?'

'He's fine.'

'When did you see him?'

'A few weeks ago. In New York. Look, do you have time for a meal or a drink somewhere?'

Möhlmann looked down at his timetables, and his hand jerked slightly, as if he was checking a sudden desire to sweep them from his desk. 'Of course,' he said. 'I work too many hours in any case,' he added jokingly, taking his suit jacket from the back of his chair.

The building seemed almost empty as they walked down the wide central staircase, but Russell hadn't wanted to risk a real conversation in Möhlmann's office – there was no knowing how thick the walls were or who was on the other side.

'Where shall we go?' Möhlmann asked. 'I have a car,' he added almost apologetically.

'It's your city,' Russell said.

'The Biergartenstrasse then. It's the local name for the promenade above the Stadtgraben,' he explained. 'And not too far away.'

His car, an Opel Kapitan, was parked behind the building. They drove round the station, under the bridge carrying the westbound tracks, and up towards the city centre. Biergartenstrasse was aptly named – a series of beer gardens overlooking the waters of the ancient city moat – and doing a brisk business with after-work drinkers. 'This is the furthest garden from the loudspeakers,' Möhlmann said, pushing through a particular gate. He steered Russell to a tree-shaded table and insisted on buying the first round. 'So tell me about Franz.'

Russell did. The Americans had actually introduced him to Franz Boyens, a serious man in his thirties who yearned to do something for what he called the real Germany. He had been a signalling engineer in Breslau until 1934, when someone had informed the Gestapo of his involvement in a local strike. After six months in a concentration camp Boyens had smuggled himself into Poland on a freight train, walked all the way to the Baltic, and worked his passage to America. The New World had provided him with rewarding work and a loving wife, things that would have caused many men to forget their anger and sorrow for the old country, but Boyens' success had just made him sorrier for those he'd left behind. Men like Möhlmann, whom he'd known in the final years of the Weimar Republic.

Russell had liked Boyens. He told Möhlmann about his job with the Pennsylvania Railroad, about his expectant wife Jeannie and their house in suburban Trenton with its big garden backing onto the tracks. He told him that Boyens was active in the union, and a campaigner against the pro-Nazis who dominated the German-American

Bund. All of which was true, at least in outline.

'I'm really happy for him,' Möhlmann said. 'I didn't know him for long, but, well, it was a time when you found out who your friends were. When the Nazis were arresting anyone who'd ever said a word against them.'

'I was here,' Russell said. 'In Berlin, that is.'

Möhlmann gave him a shrewd look. 'So you know then.'

This was the moment to talk about potential American help for resisters, but Russell held back. He simply nodded, and signalled the waiter to bring them more beers. 'Have you always lived in Breslau?' he asked.

'No. I was posted here in 1920. I was called up in the last week of the war,' he added, 'and my father had a job waiting for me when I was discharged. He was a Station Manager in Hamburg, and he wanted me as far away as possible, in case anyone accused him of nepotism. And my wife liked it here.' He looked away, as if gazing out across the water, but not before Russell had seen the hint of tears in his eyes. 'She died not long ago,' Möhlmann said, as if he still had trouble believing it.

'I'm sorry.'

'It takes some getting used to.'

'Do you have any children?'

'Two daughters, both married to Party members. One in Dresden, one in Berlin.'

'Ah.'

'At least they're safe,' he said wryly.

'I've been down to the border for my newspaper,' Russell told him, 'but I had another reason for coming to Breslau.' He told Möhlmann the story of Miriam Rosenberg's probable trip to Berlin, and studied the other man's face as he did so. He wasn't disappointed.

'That's disgusting,' was Möhlmann's verdict on the Berlin Kripo's refusal to investigate.

Russell showed him his picture of the Rosenberg family.

Möhlmann studied it closely. 'You know, I think I saw this girl. A month, six weeks ago – I can't be sure. I was on my way to lunch with a friend in the station and a girl like this was sitting on the seat outside. She was with a young man. I remember thinking what an odd couple they looked – she was so dark and Jewish, and he had this tousled blond hair. Perhaps they went off together. A Silesian Romeo and Juliet.'

'I'm afraid not. She was seen on the train to Berlin. Alone.'

'Just one life,' Möhlmann murmured, unconsciously echoing Thomas. 'But that's all any of us are.' He drained the last of his beer. 'Were you ever in the SPD?' he asked Russell.

'I was in the KPD until 1929. After my son was born it seemed sensible to leave. Although that wasn't the only reason.'

'Social Democrats and Communists – we should have fought together,' Möhlmann said. 'That was the one big mistake.'

They talked for another half an hour, mostly about Germany's problematic history, but Russell's mind was already made up. Möhlmann dropped him off at the Monopol, after extracting a promise from Russell to share an evening on his

259

next visit to Breslau. A lonely man, Russell thought, as he trudged upstairs to a new room. And an angry one, with no distracting responsibilities. He would make a wonderful spy, but not for the Americans. What use would a knowledge of train operations in south-east Germany be to them? For the Soviets, on the other hand, they might be the difference between life and death.

Looking round the Monopol's breakfast room the following morning, Russell could understand why Hitler had stayed there. It was the first time he had seen it in daylight, and it was impressive in a Führerish sort of way. Huge brass chandeliers hung from the high ceiling, which was held up by enough dappled marble columns to support a small Egyptian temple. Portraits of earlier German megalomaniacs featured on all but one panelled wall, which carried a mirror large enough to encourage serious delusions of grandeur. Rolls and coffee hardly did the setting justice.

The hotel receptionist told him that the Polish Consulate was a fifteen-minute walk away, on Oderstrasse, a small street between the Ring and the river. Or at least it had been. She couldn't remember anyone mentioning it for several years.

Russell walked north up Schweidnitzer Strasse to the Ring, the market square at the city's heart. The six-hundred-year-old Rathaus which occupied the square's south-eastern corner was famous throughout Germany, and it wasn't hard to see why – the gable at the eastern end was both huge and elaborate. Walking down the swastika-draped southern side he came to the square's open space, a long cobbled rectangle flanked by classic five-storey houses in pastel shades. At the north-western corner the soaring spire of a shadowed church glinted in the morning sunshine.

The entrance to Oderstrasse was beside the church, and Russell was nearing its far end when he found a plaque announcing the Polish Consulate. A typed notice in a small glass case beside the door gave opening hours of 10am to 3pm, which left him with at least two hours to kill. Assuming the place was still in business. He looked up at the windows for any sign of life, and found none. There was still glass in them, though, which might mean something.

It was worth coming back, he decided. There had been five thousand Poles in Breslau in 1918, and it would be interesting to know what had become of them. In the meantime, another coffee.

He walked on to the Oder and across its southern channel, then stopped to watch two lightermen manoeuvre two fully-laden coal barges into the lock on the canalized section. Away to his right a cluster of spires rose out of the trees on the far bank, a picture of peace until a clanking tram drove across it.

Retracing his steps to the southern bank, Russell walked east past a row of university buildings, and finally found an open café close to the Market Hall. Music was playing from the loudspeaker on the street corner, and Russell just had time to order his coffee before a voice started droning. It was the Chief of the German Police, giving a speech on the perils of alcohol in the workplace.

The authorities' answer, needless to say, was 'sterner measures'. Like all his Nazi buddies, the Chief was not given to moderation in thought or language. 'Pitiless proceedings' would be taken against canteens where workers got drunk.

Pitiless, Russell thought, was the word that characterised the bastards best. They just loved the concept.

He gulped down his coffee and tried to leave the voice behind. It was easier imagined than done – Breslau seemed unduly blessed with loud-speakers, and only the smallest streets offered areas of relative immunity. Russell suddenly remembered that Breslau had been officially designated 'Adolf Hitler's Most Faithful City' during the previous year's Sportsfest. A future badge of shame if ever there was one.

He reached a crossroads which had been spared an outlet for the regime's rantings. Not by accident, though – the loudspeaker was there, but two lonely lengths of wire hung down beside its host pole. Someone had got fed up with listening. Russell had a mental picture of a figure creeping out under cover of darkness, wire-cutters at the ready.

A small church occupied one corner of the crossroads, and a boy was sitting outside its gate, a rough pile of books beside him. Intrigued, Russell walked across. The books were all the same – a twenty-year-old collection of Johann Scheffler's poems.

'Angelus Silesius,' the boy explained. The Silesian Angel.

Russell knew who the poet was, and he

recognized the book. Ilse had been reading it in the Moscow canteen when he first spoke to her.

'He's buried inside,' the boy said helpfully. 'The books are two marks.'

The church door creaked and groaned as Russell opened it, and even in high summer the interior felt chilly and damp. It was beautiful, though, the stained glass-filtered sunlight throwing a kaleidoscope of colour across the pews and walls.

He found Scheffler's tomb and portrait in a patch of sunlight and sat down in the nearest pew. He remembered wondering on that day in 1924 why an ardent young communist like Ilse Schade would be reading religious poetry, and he also remembered teasing her about it after they had become lovers. How could she take such nonsense seriously?

'Easily,' she'd told him, and showed him one of Scheffier's epigrammatic verses:

In heaven life is good:
No one has aught alone.
What one possesses there
All others too will own.

'See,' she said. 'He was a communist.' Russell had expressed doubts.

'It's how you read them,' she told him. 'Look at this one –

The nearest way to God
Leads through love's open door;
The path of knowledge is
Too slow for evermore.'

'Yes, but...'

'Just substitute socialism for God, and apply

the rest to our Revolution. We need love and a socialist spirit more than we need science and organization.'

It had seemed a stretch at the time, but Scheffler and she had been right, Stalin and Trotsky wrong. 'Believers,' he muttered to himself. They had all been believers then – or had aspired to be. But the world had caught up with them.

He looked up at the poet's portrait, the serene certainty in the eyes. The world had moved a lot slower in Scheffler's day – grab hold of a vision and there was a good chance you'd make it to the grave before someone else tore holes in it.

Back in the sunlight he handed over his two marks, more because the seller looked hungry than because he really wanted the book.

It was almost ten o'clock. He walked back to Oderstrasse but the Polish Consulate was still devoid of life. He banged a fist on the door rather harder than he intended, the noise echoing down the narrow street. The only answer came from behind him. 'They're gone,' a woman shouted from a first floor window. 'And good riddance!'

According to the timetable there were trains to Wartha every two hours, but only, it appeared, when the Wehrmacht was not practising in the neighbourhood. It was almost two o'clock when Russell's three-coach train trundled out past the Breslau locomotive depot and turned off the main line to Upper Silesia and Poland. Wartha was supposed to be ninety minutes away.

It was a pleasant ride, flat vistas of golden fields

as far as Strehlen, followed by gently rolling country, the fields vast, lone trees standing sentry on the ridges, the occasional red-roofed farmhouse nestling beside a copse of beeches. The telegraph poles that followed the tracks, and occasionally broke away towards a distant village, were the only evidence of modernity.

The mountains to the south slowly rose to meet them. Wartha backed onto a gap in the foothills, a widening valley to one side, the Silesian plain to the other. The station was a simple affair, a single platform with a wooden awning, a house for the stationmaster. No one was waiting to get on, and no one else got off. In the yard beyond the station building two open lorries stood unattended, and a youngish man sat, apparently waiting, on the bucket-seat of a horse-drawn cart.

Russell asked him if he knew the Rosenfeld farm.

The man looked at him coldly. 'What do you mean – do I know it?'

'Do you know where it is?' Russell asked patiently.

'Of course.'

'Will you take me there?'

The man hesitated, as if searching for an adequate response. 'I have other business,' he said eventually, and flicked his horse into motion.

Russell watched the cart disappear into its own cloud of dust, and walked back round the station building in search of staff. Knocking on a door marked 'Stationmaster', he found himself face to face with a fat, red-nosed man in a Reichsbahn uniform. Mention of the Rosenfelds elicited a doubtful sniff but no outright hostility. Their farm, it transpired, was about five kilometres away.

'Is there any way I can get a ride out there?' Russell asked.

'Not that I know of.'

'The lorries out front?'

'Their owners took the train to Glatz. They didn't have the petrol to drive there.'

Five kilometres wasn't so far. 'Can you give me directions then?'

'You do know they're Jews?'

'Yes.'

The man shrugged, shut his door behind him, and led Russell back to the front of the building. 'Straight up this road,' he said, pointing westward, where the cart's trail of dust was still hovering above the track. 'You go across two crossroads, straight towards those hills, then you'll come to a fork. The road on the left follows the slope round. There are two farms on it, and you want the second.'

It sounded straightforward enough, Russell thought, and he soon reached the first cross-roads. The outskirts of Wartha began a short distance down the road to the left, and the spire of the town church rose above the roofs a kilo-metre or so to the south. He kept going, down a rutted and well-shaded dirt track. An endless field of grain stretched away to the north, and the sound of a distant tractor carried over on the wind. When the motor cut out the silence was almost palpable, and the sudden bark of a dog seemed like a desperate attempt to fill the void.

266

It was really hot. When he reached the second crossroads Russell stood for a minute in the shade of a convenient oak, wiping his brow with his handkerchief. What was he going to tell the Rosenfelds? Everything, he supposed.

He resumed walking. In a couple of hours the sun would be behind the mountains, and as far as he could remember there had been no moon the night before. He wasn't at all sure he fancied this walk in the dark. And he hadn't even asked about trains back to Breslau.

After what seemed an age he came to the fork in the road. The track grew narrower, more rutted, but the first farm soon loomed into sight. He became aware that a woman was standing watching him. Chickens were squawking at her feet, clearly interested in the feedbag she was carrying.

'Good afternoon,' he shouted.

'Good afternoon,' she replied, more cautiously.

'The Rosenfeld farm?'

She pointed up the road and turned her back.

It took him another fifteen minutes to reach his destination. Miriam's home was on the lee side of a hill, smoke drifting up from its chimney and into the light of the sinking sun. There was a copse of trees to the right, a single cow tethered on a long rope to one of the trunks. On the left was a sturdy wooden barn, beyond that what looked like a kitchen garden.

Another woman was watching him, he realized, hidden in the shadows of the east-facing doorway. He had a sudden inexplicable hope that it might be Miriam, but of course it wasn't. This woman had streaks of grey in her hair.

267

'Frau Rosenfeld?' he asked.

'My husband will be back in a few minutes,' she told him.

'That is good,' Russell said, stopping a few metres away from her. 'I wish to talk to you both.'

'What about? Who are you?'

'My name is John Russell. My brother-in-law Thomas Schade employed your brother-in-law Benjamin.'

'Employed? Has he lost his job?'

'I'm sorry, Frau Rosenfeld, but Benjamin is dead.'

Her hands flew up to her cheeks. 'But how...' she began, only for another thought to take precedence. 'Who is looking after my daughter?'

'That is why I'm here. I'm afraid your daughter has gone missing.'

'Missing,' she echoed. She closed her eyes, and for a brief moment she seemed to visibly shrink. Then, with what seemed an almost absurd effort of will, she drew herself upright. 'I will fetch Leon,' she said. 'Please...'

'I'll wait here.'

She strode off in the direction of the kitchen garden. Russell sat himself down on the front door step, noticing the *mezuzah* on the frame as he did so. You didn't see many of those in Berlin anymore.

He felt as if he had crossed into another world. He had known a lot of Jews in his lifetime, but most had been intellectuals of one sort or another, and all had been urbanised. The Yiddish-speaking Jews of the Pale, that vast expanse of plains stretching across southern Poland and

Ukraine, were as much of a mystery to him as the Bushmen of the Kalahari.

Miriam's father came into view, half-running ahead of his wife. He looked smaller than he had in the photograph, but Russell could see the kindness in the face, even twisted as now by fear. The words came out in a rush: 'What is it that I am hearing? My brother is dead? My Miriam is missing? What does this mean?'

Russell told him. About Benjamin's murder and their worries about Miriam, about the police refusal to investigate. About the hiring of Kuzorra and the possible sighting, and the threatening of the detective.

Frau Rosenfeld mostly listened in silence, but her husband kept interrupting with hopeful questions, as if determined to find better explanations for what had happened. When Russell reached the present Leon Rosenfeld looked at the ground for the moment, then back at his guest. 'I thank you for coming,' he said. 'Now I must move the cow.'

Russell stared after him with astonishment.

'He needs to think,' Frau Rosenfeld explained. 'He will come back and announce that he is going to Berlin to look for her.'

'That...' Russell began, and hesitated. Wouldn't he scour the planet for Paul if his son went missing? He would, but that didn't make it wise for Rosenfeld to go charging off. 'I would do the same, but it would not be a good idea.'

Her look questioned his wisdom, if not his motives. 'Forgive me,' she said, 'but you are not a Jew. If she is with other Jews in Berlin, would not another Jew have a better chance of finding her?'

'I am not a Jew, but many of the men who work for my brother-in-law are. They knew Benjamin, and they have spread the word among Berlin's Jews. No one has heard from her, or of her. If your husband goes to Berlin... Let me be blunt – the police will not listen to him, and if he kicks up a fuss – which in any sane society he would and should – then they will punish him for it. The Jews in Berlin survive by keeping themselves to themselves. Your husband will be no use to Miriam – or you – if he ends up in a concentration camp. Or worse.'

'I don't know if I can stop him.'

'You must try. I will keep looking, I promise you. I will promise him.'

'I will try.' She sighed, and drew herself up again. 'Forgive me, keeping you outside all this time. Please, come in. A glass of water.'

Russell followed her into the farmhouse. It was as well-kept as the farm, and more comfortable than he had expected. The furniture was old but recovered; an even older-looking piano stood by the far wall. There was small case of books, and a game-ready chessboard on a narrow table. Vases of wildflowers flanked the menorah on the mantelpiece.

Frau Rosenfeld had just given him the glass of water when her husband returned. He walked over to his wife and put his hands on her shoulders. 'Esther, I must go to Berlin.'

She shook her head. 'I have already told Herr Russell that you would say that. He said he would do the same, but it would not be wise.' She told him why.

It was his turn to shake his head, but he said nothing more. 'Where is my brother buried?' he asked.

'In the Jewish cemetery in Friedrichshain. In Berlin.'

'That is good. He enjoyed life,' he added, mostly to himself.

Outside it was growing noticeably darker. 'I must be going,' Russell said, 'but...'

'No, no – you must eat with us,' Esther Rosenfeld interjected. 'You can stay the night in Miriam's room. Please, it will give us time to decide what to do.'

Put like that, Russell could hardly refuse. Not that he'd wanted to.

The meal was simple but tasty, a rabbit stew with large chunks of homemade bread. The conversation was sparse – Russell guessed that Leon usually did most of the talking, and on this particular evening he seemed frequently – and understandably – lost in thought.

'I saw your neighbour on my walk up here,' Russell said. 'A woman.'

'Eva,' Frau Rosenberg said tersely. 'We were friends before all this, but now they seem afraid to know us. She does, in any case. Their boy Torsten came to see us last week. Miriam told him she would write to him, but she hadn't.'

Russell put two and two together. 'Did he go to Breslau with her? Someone thought they saw her with a boy by the station.'

'He works in Breslau. He was going to see that she got the right train to Berlin. She had only been to Breslau once before.'

'I'd like to talk to him. Do you know where he works?'

'In a big store. A really modern one, Eva told me. It was designed by a famous architect. You could ask his family, of course. I think they would tell you.'

They went to bed soon after eating. 'We live by the sun,' Leon Rosenfeld said simply.

Miriam's room contained an iron bed, a wooden chest of drawers and a small table. Russell lay in bed watching the candlelight flicker on the ceiling, listening to the shuffling of the horse in the barn outside. On the other side of the inner wall a conversation was being conducted in fierce whispers. He understood Leon Rosenfeld's desperate need to go looking, but he hoped Esther would be able to dissuade him. If she didn't, the only outcome of his own visit was likely to be a third family casualty.

He leaned over to blow out the candle, and thought about losing Effi. Her mystery meeting was tonight, he remembered. He wondered what sort of people she was getting herself involved with – many of her friends and acquaintances had a somewhat tenuous grasp of political realities. Effi was sensible enough when she took time to think, but...

Who was he kidding? There were no riskless paths any more. Safety had only ever lain in keeping one's head down and one's conscience in cold storage. It was too late for that now, for him and for Effi. Hauptsturmführer Hirth had pushed them both over the edge.

272

He woke soon after six, the sun streaming through the uncurtained window and onto the wall beside him. The rest of the house was empty, the kettle only warm. After using the latrine behind the house he found Esther Rosenfeld digging up weeds in the kitchen garden.

'Good morning,' she said, straightening her back. 'Leon will take your advice,' she added without preamble. 'He wants to go, but he's also afraid to leave me unprotected. And I encouraged him in that thought, God help me.'

'It's the right decision,' Russell said.

'I hope so. Come, let me give you some breakfast.' She led the way back to the house, placed the kettle on the woodstove and cut some thick slices from yesterday's loaf. A slab of remarkably solid butter was fetched from the larder, a jar of plum jam taken down from a shelf. Tea was made in a Russian-looking samovar.

All in all, it was delicious. Life was apparently possible without coffee. At least for a short time.

'How can I contact you?' Russell asked between mouthfuls of bread. 'When my brother-in-law wrote to you, the postmaster in Wartha denied that the letter had ever arrived.'

She thought for a moment. 'I will give you the name and address of a friend,' she said. 'A *goyim*.'

She found a piece of paper and wrote it out with a slow, steady hand. 'This man is the local blacksmith. He and Leon are still friends, despite everything. Send your letter to us in envelopes addressed to him, and he will bring them to us. Leon will tell him to expect it.'

273

'Right.'

They sat in silence for a while, Russell sipping at the hot tea, Esther apparently absorbed in thought. 'Do you think our daughter is still alive?' she asked suddenly.

'I don't know. If she was dead, and the police had found her, then I think they would have informed my brother-in-law.'

'There is hope, then?'

'Yes.'

She ran a hand through her hair. 'There is a train to Breslau at around nine. We can hear it when the wind is from the east.'

'Your husband?'

'He is working in the field beyond the barn. He will want to say goodbye.' They walked out to find him. He was picking cabbages, and judging by the size of the pile had been doing so for several hours.

He wiped his hands on his trousers and shook Russell's. He looked years older than he had the evening before. 'My grandfather bought this land over sixty years ago,' he said. 'He thought they would be safer close to the mountains, and he was right. We should never have sent Miriam away.'

'There was no way you could know that your brother would be attacked,' Russell told him.

Leon was not to be comforted. 'I always said my Miriam was too good for this world,' he said. 'Like an angel.'

Walking away down the dirt-track Russell could feel Esther's eyes on his back. Should he have raised her hopes? Did he have any reason to believe that Miriam was still alive?

Smoke was rising from the neighbouring farm. He thought of stopping to ask where Torsten worked, but the thought of meeting the boy's parents was uninviting. And the clues he had would be good enough. There weren't that many big stores in Breslau, and he was surprised that even one had been designed by a famous architect.

It seemed warmer than the previous day, and he hung his jacket over one shoulder. He walked swiftly, and was approaching the last crossroads, the roofs of Wartha visible across the fields, when he heard the lorry behind him. It was bumping along the dirt-track at a fair speed, belching dust into the air, and showed no signs of slowing down to spare his lungs. A blast of the horn reinforced the message.

Russell stepped onto the verge and beyond, reaching for his handkerchief to cover his mouth. The lorry lurched by, two men in the cab, two standing behind it in the open back.

Enveloped by dust, Russell heard rather than saw the lorry grind to a halt some fifty metres down the track. He saw two shapes climb down from either side of the cab, two more jumping down to the ground. All four shapes walked towards him. As the dust cleared, he saw that the driver and his mate were both wearing brown shirts. That was the extent of their uniform, but it was enough.

'Oh, fuck,' Russell murmured to himself. 'Good morning!' he said cheerily, as if these were the folks he'd most wanted to meet on such a beautiful day.

The response was less friendly. 'Where have you come from?' the driver asked. A short balding man with wide shoulders and a barrel chest, he was a good deal older than the others – around Russell's age – and he seemed to be in charge.

There seemed no point in lying. 'I've been up to the Rosenfeld farm.'

'For the night?'

'It was too late to get back to Breslau.'

'It's against the law, staying with Jews,' one of the younger men offered. 'Why were you up there?' the driver went on, ignoring his companion. This, as Russell realized at the time, was the moment when he should have said something clever and self-exculpatory. That he was doing an article on Jews who refused to see sense and quit the Reich – something like that. But the last twenty-four hours had reduced his already limited willingness to indulge the local scum, and, in any case, the Rosenfelds deserved a bit of loyalty. 'I was telling them that their daughter is missing,' he said.

That didn't seem much of a surprise to his audience, who were presumably privy to Thomas's missing letter.

'She should have stayed here,' the same young man said with a grin. He was probably one of the gang that had intercepted Miriam on this very track, frightening the Rosenfelds into sending their daughter to Berlin.

The driver advanced a pace, close enough for Russell to smell the cabbage on his breath. 'So

276

she's missing. What the hell is that to you?'

'Just another Jew-lover,' the other Brownshirt volunteered.

'Right,' Russell said sarcastically. 'When I could be admiring an aryan like you.'

He had time to move his head a fraction, saving his nose and teeth at his cheek's expense, but the power of the blow put him on his back. He shook his head, looked up at the four silhouettes gathered above him, and felt more than a little afraid.

'There's a good tree over there,' a voice said, compounding the effect.

'I'm an American journalist,' he said, struggling to keep his voice steady. 'And I also work for the *Sicherheitsdienst* in Berlin.'

'The what?'

'It's part of the Gestapo,' Russell said, somewhat inaccurately. 'Look at my papers,' he added, 'they're in my jacket.'

The driver picked up the jacket, rifled through the pockets, and examined Russell's journalistic accreditation. 'This says nothing about the Gestapo or the ... *Sicher*-whatever-it-was.'

Russell decided it was time to get to his feet. 'You can ring their HQ at 102 Wilhelmstrasse,' he said, as he rose. 'Hauptsturmführer Hirth. He'll tell you.'

'Why would a Gestapo agent be visiting Jews?'

'Why do you think? Their daughter may be mixed up with enemies of the Reich...'

'Miriam Rosenfeld?!?'

'You know a lot about the Jewish opposition groups, do you?' Russell asked scathingly, risking

277

another assault. 'It's very unlikely,' he admitted in a kinder tone. 'But we have to be vigilant.'

The driver still looked unconvinced. 'Get up on the lorry,' he said. 'You are coming with us.'

Those five words had never sounded sweeter. Wherever they were going, it had to be an improvement on a dirt track between open fields, with a 'good tree' close by. The police station or the local Party House?

It was the latter. They turned right at the crossroads and drove into Wartha, along a surprisingly deserted street lined with neat, well-kept houses. The Party House was just beyond the town square, a two-storey building with the usual oversized flag. There were two main rooms on the ground floor, the common room at the front for drinking, the office at the back for keeping tabs on the citizenry.

The local leader, a bespectacled man of around thirty-five with closely-cropped black hair, was in the latter. He was wearing full SA uniform, with every belt, buckle and button polished to perfection. Like most small-time Nazis of Russell's acquaintance, he looked like a puffed-up shopkeeper. Err on the side of flattery, Russell told himself, and for God's sake don't talk down to him.

The driver told his story. He and his friends had received a tip-off that an outsider was staying with the Jews, and they had stopped him before he could reach the station. 'He admitted it,' he added, passing over Russell's papers. 'He says he's a journalist and that he works for the Gestapo,' he added grudgingly.

'The *Sicherheitsdienst*,' Russell corrected him. 'The SD,' he added helpfully.

The man was examining his papers. 'I know what the *Sicherheitsdienst* is,' he said curtly, without looking up.

'May I know your name, Sturmbannführer?' Russell asked politely.

'Lempfert. Wilhelm Lempfert.'

'The headquarters of the *Sicherheitsdienst* is at 102 Wilhelmstrasse, Sturmbannführer Lempfert. Hauptsturmführer Hirth will vouch for me.'

'Not Gruppenführer Heydrich in person?' Lempfert asked sarcastically.

'I have never had the honour of meeting the Gruppenführer.'

Lempfert gazed at Russell for a few moments, as if wondering whether his sarcasm was being returned. 'I will check your story,' he said. 'Take him through,' he told the driver.

Russell was hustled into the common room, and his others captors looked up expectantly, still hopeful of a lynching. The driver shoved him towards an upright chair by the near wall and joined his companions in the circle of beaten-up armchairs by the window.

Minutes went by, rather more of them than Russell was hoping for. What would Lempfert do if Hirth wasn't there? And what would Hirth say when he heard about the Rosenfelds? The false papers for the Soviets should be waiting for him at Neuenburger Strasse by now. Surely Hirth wouldn't let a little race hatred cost him a good agent?

Almost an hour had gone by when

Sturmbannführer Lempfert emerged from the office. 'The Hauptsturmführer wishes to speak to you,' he said shortly, gesturing Russell into his office. Much to the latter's surprise, the door closed behind him. Hirth must have asked for a private conversation.

The Hauptsturmführer was displeased. 'What is this about? Who are these Jews?'

Russell explained about their daughter's disappearance. 'This is a journalistic matter,' he added, not wishing to involve Thomas.

'Can't you find anything more useful to write about?'

'If I stopped criticising the regime the Soviets would smell a rat.'

Hirth grunted his disapproval. 'So why did you mention this department?'

'Because I feared for my life, and I assumed you would want to save it.'

A lengthy silence followed. 'A big assumption,' Hirth said dryly. 'As it happens, you will find something waiting for you when you reach home. Something in need of your urgent attention. You *are* coming back to Berlin today?'

'I am.'

'Very well. Put the Sturmbannführer back on.'

Russell fetched Lempfert, and watched as he listened to Hirth. 'It will be as you suggest,' Lempfert said finally. 'Thank you for your time, Hauptsturmführer.' He replaced the telephone and looked up. 'You are free to go, Herr Russell. But next time, perhaps you would do us the courtesy of informing us of your plans in advance. It is we who are responsible for enforcing

280

the race laws.'

'Of course. I apologise for not doing so.' He offered his hand across the desk. 'Thank you again.'

Out front, his original captors watched him leave with new expressions on their faces. A simple enemy had turned into something of a mystery – a foreigner who worked for the famous Heydrich, and who made enormous sacrifices for Reich and Führer, like sleeping in a Jewish bed. Russell went across to the driver and offered his hand. The man seemed somewhat surprised, but accepted it.

'Can we drive you to the station?' he asked.

'Thank you, but no,' Russell said, keen to put the Wartha SA behind him. 'I need the exercise.'

It was a refusal he regretted ten minutes later, when the smoke rising above the station told him he had just missed his train. The next one, as he soon discovered, was not for another two hours. He spent them in the shade of the platform awning, sitting on the only bench and staring out across the sun-drenched grain. Hundreds of birds chattered in the copse of beeches beyond the empty siding, and every now and then a party of them would fly off towards the red-roofed farm in the far distance. It was an idyllic scene.

Russell remembered reading Wilde's *The Picture of Dorian Grey* in the trenches, and idly wondered whether the Silesian countryside had made a similar pact with the devil. He imagined a landscape painting in Sturmbannführer Lempfert's attic, fields of rotting crops under a red sky, an SA lynch party driving away from a

281

burning farm.

It wasn't until he was settled in his compartment seat, and the train was pulling out of Wartha, that his hands began to shake. He sat there watching them, remembering the same reaction over twenty years before, some hours after a much-dreaded assault across no man's land had been cancelled.

His train reached Breslau just before three, saving him the choice between interviewing Torsten and catching the same service that Miriam had caught. The next Berlin train was not until nearly six, which gave him plenty of time to find the department store where the boy worked and collect his suitcase from the hotel.

He tried to telephone Effi from the Monopol but there was no answer. The receptionist took one long look at his battered cheek but said nothing. She told him the only modern-looking store in Breslau was the Petersdorff, and agreed to keep his suitcase behind her desk while he visited it. Following her directions, Russell walked up Schweidnitzer Strasse and turned right opposite the Rathaus. The Petersdorff store was on a corner one block down, a futuristic oasis in a sea of German tradition. The windows of the main frontage stretched the length of the building, and were rolled around in a semi-circle at one corner, like a six storey-lighthouse. The overall impression was of six trams piled on top of each other, speeding into the future. It looked like it had been left behind by aliens.

In a way it had. It reminded Russell of the

Universum, and he was not surprised to find that Erich Mendelssohn had designed it. He was, however, surprised to find that fact still acknowledged on a plaque by the main entrance – Mendelssohn's name had long since disappeared from the Universum.

Inside he asked for the manager's office, and was directed to a suite of rooms on the second floor. The manager was a youngish man with a Pomeranian accent and an obvious desire to please. He confirmed that Torsten Resch worked there, and obligingly agreed to Russell's request for a short private chat without asking for details of the 'family matter' in question. Torsten arrived a few minutes later, a gangly youth with a shock of fair hair. He looked suitably bewildered.

The manager left them to it.

'What is this about?' the boy asked. 'Has something happened at home?'

'Nothing. I'm here about Miriam Rosenfeld.'

The boy's features seemed to soften. 'You have a message for me?'

'She has disappeared,' Russell said bluntly.

'What?'

'She travelled to Berlin, but no one has seen her since she arrived.'

'But that was weeks ago. And her uncle was supposed to meet her.'

'He was beaten up on his way to the station. He died a few days later. You saw her onto the train, right?'

'Yes, we had lunch together. She said I could write to her, but she hasn't sent me her address...'

'She didn't say anything about what she intended to do in Berlin?'

'I told you. She was going to meet her uncle. He had arranged a job for her.'

'She didn't know anyone else there?'

'No, I'm sure she didn't. How could she?'

He seemed genuinely distressed. 'All right,' Russell said. 'Thank you for talking to me.'

Torsten got up slowly. 'If you...' he began. 'If you find out what has happened, will you let me know? I like Miriam,' he said simply. 'I know she's Jewish, but...' He shrugged away his inability to change that fact. 'I've always liked her,' he added, as if it was a shameful secret he had to share.

'I'll let you know,' Russell promised.

The Berlin train left on time, and much to Russell's relief suffered only a few minor delays. It pulled into Silesian Station a few minutes short of midnight, and he stopped at the first public telephone to call Effi. She answered immediately, sounding excited. 'What's happened?' he asked.

'I'll tell you when you get here.'

A Stadtbahn train arrived within minutes. It was full of citizens ignoring the government's ongoing anti-alcohol campaign, one of whom held the train up for five minutes at Friedrichstrasse by jumping in and out of the door like a demented rabbit. The train eventually reached Zoo Station, where an even rowdier Friday night crowd was waiting to get on. Russell alighted with some relief, and walked down the steps to street level. In the space in front of the station, two uniformed cops were asking a boy of about four where his mother was. He looked around as if searching for her, then screamed a simple 'I don't know!' at his questioners.

Russell walked under the Hardenberg Strasse bridge and crossed the road. Three minutes later he was approaching the flat. There were no suspiciously loitering cars, no leather coats clogging up the entrance.

Effi was in her dressing-gown. Her excitement turned to horror when she saw his face.

'It's much worse than it looks,' he said.

'But how...'

'One of the local lads in Wartha didn't like my attitude. Don't worry about it.'

They hugged and kissed until Russell reached for the cord.

'No, no, no,' she said. 'First we must talk.'

He grinned. 'Okay. How did your meeting go?'

'Oh that.' She dismissed it with a wave of a hand. 'I went to the station to meet you,' she said. 'I thought you'd be on Miriam's train, and...'

'I missed it.'

'I know. But I saw *him*. The man with the dark eyebrows. *And* he tried to pick up a young girl.'

The wave of the past

'Tell me,' Russell said, somewhat unnecessarily.

'He was just the way your detective described him. A dark blue uniform with a peaked cap, and when he took it off I saw his grey hair. And the eyebrows, much darker, black I think. A slight beer belly, but not really overweight. He just stood there watching the bottom of the staircase. You know the smoker's kiosk? He was standing right next to it.'

She paced to and fro. 'I watched him, but not all the time. You know they say that people have a sixth sense that they're being watched, and I didn't want him to notice me. And of course I was also watching for you, so I had to take my eyes off him every now and then. Anyway the train arrived and the people started coming down the steps – quite a few of them, but not really a crowd – you could see each person. And he was looking at this one girl. She looked about twenty, and she was quite smartly dressed. Dark hair and one of those little felt hats that were fashionable about three years ago. She put her suitcase down and she was digging around in her bag for something. A little book – an address book perhaps. And he walked towards her, a big smile on his face. He said something to her, and she looked relieved. He went to pick up her suitcase, but at that moment she caught sight of someone she knew over his

286

shoulder – a young man in a Wehrmacht uniform. She said something to Eyebrows and he smiled back at her, but the moment her back was turned his face seemed to curdle. He was really angry. He walked back to his place by the kiosk and watched the last few people come down the stairs, but he didn't approach anyone else.

'There were other single women, but they all looked like they knew where they were going.'

She paused for breath. 'When everyone had come through he lit a cigarette and walked out through the main entrance. I followed him – don't worry, I kept a good distance and there were lots of people around and he never looked back. His car was parked at the end of the cab rank, and there were cops around – you'd have thought they'd have had a word with him...'

'It says something that he still has use of a car,' Russell added.

'I suppose it does. It was a Mercedes Cabriolet, by the way – my father used to have one.'

'Did you get the number?'

'I memorized it as I walked past,' she said. 'I ran for the cab at the head of the line, almost knocking over a pair of old ladies in the process, and jumped in the back. I asked the driver for a pencil, but he didn't have one, and then I realized I'd forgotten the number. I looked round just as he drove past us and what do you think I said?'

'Follow that cab?'

'More or less.'

'The cabbie was a Bavarian, so I had to say it twice, but we caught him up at the Michael Kirche-Strasse lights.' Effi lifted the hem of her dressing-gown halfway up her right thigh to reveal a red scrawl. 'I wrote the number down with my lipstick.'

'That must have made the cabbie's evening,' Russell said, noticing the two threes which ended the registration number.

'He was watching the lights. I told him to hang back a bit in case Eyebrows noticed he was being followed, and we sort of played hide and seek behind a Wehrmacht lorry all the way to Alexanderplatz. We all followed the Stadtbahn for a couple of blocks and then he turned up towards Schönhauser Platz and stopped outside that line of shops at the bottom of Dragoner-Strasse. We stopped about fifty metres short of him but the traffic had thinned right out, and when he came out of the shop with his bag of groceries he looked right at us. He got back in his car and moved off, and I told myself I had his number and it would be better if he didn't know he'd been followed. I told the cabbie to let him go, and was still wondering whether I'd done the right thing when he turned off the street about two hundred metres further up. We gave him a couple of minutes and drove slowly by. His car was parked beside an apartment block – one of those old three-storey ones at the top of the street. There was no sign of him.

'I was just about to tell the cabbie to take me home when I thought – oh my God, what if Eyebrows got the taxi number and tracks down the driver and asks him where he took me. So I got him to drop me at Friedrichstrasse Station, and took the Stadtbahn home. And there I was, basking in my untrackability when two young soldiers came up and loudly asked me for my autograph. The whole carriage watched me get off at Zoo Station.'

Russell smiled, but Effi's story had left him feeling more than a little anxious. He wondered why. She might have been a byword for recklessness in the past, but in this instance she seemed to have acted with commendable caution. Was he under-estimating her again?

'Well?' she asked.

'You did brilliantly,' he said.

'I thought so.'

'I could do with a drink,' Russell said.

She poured them both one.

'The girl he approached,' Russell asked. 'Did she look Jewish?'

'She was dark, and she looked sort of lost – haunted even – at first. But you don't see many Jews smiling the way she did when her soldier boy appeared. Not in public anyway.'

'But she looked distressed enough to be Jewish before that,' Russell said dryly.

'Yes.' Effi sat down beside him on the sofa. 'Do you think it's possible he's holding Miriam prisoner in his apartment?'

'If so, he doesn't seem satisfied with just her,' Russell said. Unless, he thought, the man was abducting girls to rape and kill them. Or eat them, like Kuzorra's famous cannibal, whose name he'd already forgotten.

'So what are we going to do?' Effi asked, putting her head on his shoulder.

'I'm damned if I know,' Russell said. 'There's

289

no point in going to the police – it might even be dangerous. We have to find out more about Eye-brows, I suppose. Watch his apartment, see where he goes. Talk to his neighbours, if we can do it without giving ourselves away. Hope he leads us to Miriam.' He found himself yawning and looked at his watch – it was almost two o'clock. 'We can draw up a plan of action over coffee in the park.'

'That sounds good.'

'It does. How did your meeting go, by the way?'

'Don't ask. I don't think I've ever met so many brilliant people in one room, and every last one of them with a death wish. They cracked jokes about all the Nazi leaders, and were practically praying for someone to kill Hitler. They're organising discussion groups on the possibilities of sabotage. The possibility that one of them might be a Gestapo informer doesn't seem to have occurred to them. I think they'll talk themselves into their graves. I came out of there feeling quite frightened, because by law I should have reported every last one of them to the Gestapo. I decided my defence would be that I hadn't taken them seriously, which at least had the virtue of being probable. I certainly won't be going back.'

'And what about Madame Voodoo?'

'She seemed a bit surprised too. I think she'll be sticking to the stars from now on.'

He wasn't at all sure why, but he had rarely found Effi more desirable. He slipped the dressing gown off her thigh, revealing the lipstick number. 'I hope you've copied that down,' he said, 'because it's likely to get smudged.'

Next morning the sky over the Tiergarten was a disappointing grey, and they had the café almost to themselves. Russell divided the newspaper between them, but it only took Effi a few moments to throw her pages down in disgust. 'It's that day again,' she said, pointing out a headline.

It was Hitler's mother's birthday, and thousands of German women would be receiving their Honour Crosses from local Party leaders for providing the Reich with extra children.

'If only she'd come back and give him a slap round the head,' Effi muttered.

Russell laughed.

'So what are we going to do about Miriam?' she asked.

Russell folded his paper. 'All right. Let's assume Eyebrows kidnapped her. Why would he do that?'

'For sex?'

'Perhaps. For himself or for others?'

'You mean like a white slaver or something like that?'

Russell grimaced. 'I'm not sure white slavers exist. The fictional ones usually sell their victims to Arabs, and they always want blondes.'

'The whole world seems to,' Effi said wryly.

'I don't,' Russell told her.

'That's sweet. But look, if he took her for himself he'd have to keep her somewhere, and I can't imagine him keeping her in his flat. The walls are thin in those buildings. I suppose he could be keeping her drugged, but not for weeks on end, surely. He must have another place. Maybe somewhere out in the country.'

'Maybe. Let's take it one step at a time. Eliminate the apartment first.'

'How are we going to do that?'

'I don't know. Start with the *portierfrau*, I suppose. We can drive over there tomorrow morning.'

'Yes, let's do that.'

'You haven't told me how the filming went,' Russell said, deliberately changing the subject.

'Oh, the usual mess. They think it's finished, but that's only because they haven't looked at the rushes yet. I expect I'll find out on Monday or Tuesday that they've decided to re-shoot a few scenes. The last one in particular. It's supposed to be uplifting, but half the crew were laughing behind their hands. You never know, of course.' She looked at her watch, and got to her feet. 'I've got to go. My parents are expecting me for lunch, and they seem to eat it earlier each time I see them.'

They took cabs from the Zoo Station rank, hers heading out towards the family home in Wilmersdorf, his to Neuenburger Strasse. The Hanomag was where he had left it, Frau Heidegger hovering in her apartment doorway.

She made sympathetic noises about Russell's bruised face, and seemed satisfied with his story of walking into an open car door. 'I have a parcel for you,' she said. 'And there's some coffee in the pot.'

Some of it had been there for several days, Russell guessed, after taking the first bitter sip. The parcel turned out to be a large envelope. It was sealed with red wax, suggesting either a nine-teenth century eccentric or something more atavistic, like Himmler's gang. At least they hadn't scrawled 'Return to Heydrich' on the back.

'Something official?' Frau Heidegger asked, with all the casualness of an SS attack dog.

'It'll be my new accreditation from the Propaganda Ministry,' Russell said, placing the envelope to one side. 'They had to re-issue it now that I've become an American citizen,' he added glibly. 'How have you been?'

Frau Heidegger was as well as could be expected, given the state of her knees. The doctor had told her to keep bending them, and now they were more painful than ever. Her brother was still frightening her with visions of Berlin under air attack, and one of her skat partners had heard that food rationing would be introduced the moment war broke out with England. She claimed that Dagmar's romantic entanglements were wearing her out, but she seemed to be enjoying them almost as much as Dagmar. Siggi had taken things a little too far the other evening, serenading her from the courtyard like some crazed Hanoverian Romeo – 'I'm afraid he stood on the roof of your car, Herr Russell' – but it had worked. Dagmar had eventually taken him inside, probably for a good talking to.

After one last sip of coffee, Russell looked at his watch and made his excuses. Up in his flat he spread the envelope's contents out on his table. There were three carbon copies of official documents, each on headed Air Ministry notepaper, and a covering note, signed by 'a comrade', which purported to explain the sources. The same 'comrade' also announced his willingness to answer questions.

Russell skimmed through the documents. The first listed up-to-date production figures – current and projected – for the Stuka dive-bomber. The second contained the minutes of a meeting held to discuss a new American bombsight. The third detailed the experimental fixing of supplementary fuel-tanks to the Luftwaffe's longest-range bomber. This, the document's author explained, would extend the effective round-trip range of these bombers by approximately five hundred miles.

It was like one of those old parlour games where you had to guess which one of several stories was false. The last one, Russell decided. It was the only one of the three from which the Soviets could draw conclusions that were both vital and wrong. Everyone knew that Stalin was moving his industrial base eastwards, and here was something to help him decide how far he needed to move it. Russell reached for his atlas and checked the distances. If what the document said was true, then only catastrophic setbacks on the ground would render Soviet cities east of Gorki vulnerable to attack. Conclusion: the five hundred mile figure was a lie, designed to discourage the Soviets from moving their industries still further east.

A nice idea, Russell thought. And nicer still that the Soviets would know that the information was fake, and take the appropriate steps. He grabbed a dusty sheet of paper from his typewriter, thought for a second, and scrawled 'first instalment' across it. He put this in the envelope with everything else, and sat for a moment, staring at his flat.

It was beginning to look like a place that nobody lived in. Which was just about right. Waiting for sleep the previous night he had again found himself thinking about asking Effi to marry him. The trouble was, one good reason for doing so was to give her the possibility of American citizenship, which might make practical sense but certainly muddied the emotional waters. Russell wanted there to be only one reason for their marriage – the fact that they loved each other. 'Some hope,' he murmured to himself.

It was almost twelve-thirty. After inspecting the Hanomag's roof for damage he drove over to Grünewald. Paul was sitting on the wall at the end of the drive, still in his *Jungvolk* uniform. The boy's mouth dropped open when he saw his father's face.

Russell managed to convince him that the damage was superficial, but detected a hint of scepticism when it came to the supposed accident. 'Where are we going?' he asked, hoping to avert any questions.

'We haven't been to the Aquarium for a long time.'

They spent a couple of hours peering into illuminated tanks of varying sizes. The shoals of exotically coloured minnows glistened, the sharks gazed out of seemingly dead eyes, the anaconda refused, as usual, to unwind. After the porpoises had cheered them up they sat outside with their

295

ice creams and watched barges chug by on the Landwehrkanal.

On their way home Paul announced that there was no *Jungvolk* meeting in three weeks' time – could they go camping that weekend?

'Leave Saturday morning and come back Sunday? I don't see why not. Has your mother agreed?'

'Not yet, but she will. I thought about asking Effi to come as well, but she doesn't seem the camping sort, really.'

'No. Just the two of us will be better, I think.'

'I think so.'

'Where do you want to go? Camping, I mean?' Russell felt absurdly pleased that his son wanted to go camping with him.

'The Harz Mountains?'

'The Harz Mountains it is.'

The sun finally broke through as they reached the house in Grünewald. Paul insisted on asking his mother about the camping while Russell was there, and Ilse agreed readily enough. He casually told her about his visit to Scheffler's tomb in Breslau, and, rather to his surprise, saw a softness in her eyes which he hadn't seen for years. Her husband Matthias asked Russell in for a drink but he declined, claiming, truly enough, that he was late for work.

Half an hour later he was parked outside the American Embassy. He sat in the front seat for a while, examining the wide boulevard through windscreen and mirrors, but no one seemed to be loitering with intent to spy. And what if they were? he asked himself. The Germans had all but ordered him to knock on the enemy's door.

He took the SD's envelope from the passenger seat, got out, and walked swiftly down the pavement to the Soviet Embassy. The letter-box was small, as if the Soviets were fearful of receiving too much information, and he had to force the envelope through.

A few minutes later he was joining Slaney in the Adlon Bar.

'I see you stirred up some trouble in Silesia,' was the American's first comment, his gaze fixed on Russell's bruise.

'I couldn't find any trouble,' Russell replied. He told Slaney about his search for alleged victims of Blechowka.

'There's been another imaginary incident, then,' the American said. 'It's in there,' he said, indicating the *Beobachter* which Russell had been carrying round with him all day. 'Hand it over.' He leafed through the pages, found what he wanted, and passed it back. 'Top right.'

The article was heavy on indignation, light on facts. The Polish police in Katowice – or Kattowitz as the *Beobachter* insisted on calling it – had 'frightfully mistreated eighteen members of the German minority, beating them with rubber truncheons and twisting their limbs.' The officers had been acting on 'direct orders from Warsaw' and 'indirect orders from England.'

Russell laughed. 'I can just see it,' he said. 'Chamberlain and Halifax plotting in the Cabinet Room. "Why don't we get the Polish police in Kattowitz to twist the limbs of a few Germans?" God, I don't suppose either of them

297

has even heard of Kattowitz.'

'It's the "eighteen" I like,' Slaney said. 'You can just imagine them trying to decide what number of victims the story can bear before it becomes completely unbelievable.'

'So there's no real news?'

'Nothing to get excited about.'

'Has Chamberlain's team reached Moscow yet?'

'Yesterday. Their ship docked in Leningrad just before midnight on Wednesday. The galley staff were all Indian, so the diplomats had nine days of curries for lunch and dinner – I dread to think what the atmosphere was like. Anyway, they had a day's sightseeing on Thursday, took the overnight Red Arrow, and presumably spent most of Friday recovering. The talks were supposed to start today.'

'No word yet?'

'No. And there won't be anything positive. You know what'll happen next. The Brits and French will ask the Russians to join them in guaranteeing Poland, and the Russkis will say, "Fine, but how we can get at the Germans if the Poles won't let our troops into their country?" The Brits and French will try to pretend there isn't a problem, but everyone knows the Poles would never agree to a single Russian soldier on their blessed soil, let alone the Red Army. So the whole thing's dead in the water.'

'Probably,' Russell said. He realized he was still clinging, like most Europeans, to the hope that enough opposition would force Hitler to back off.

'The real point,' Slaney continued relentlessly, 'is that Stalin's got absolutely nothing to gain from signing up. If Hitler attacks Poland, and the British and French honour their guarantee, then Stalin can join the fun whenever he wants to, or just sit back and let the Western powers tear each other to pieces. And if the Limeys and Frogs leave the Poles in the lurch, then Stalin can thank his lucky stars he didn't sign up, because he would have found he was fighting Hitler all on his own.'

'How come you're so wise, Daddy?'

'Beer must be good for the brain.'

Russell grinned at him. 'Fancy getting some food? I haven't eaten since breakfast.'

'No thanks. I had a late lunch.'

Russell stopped off at the reception desk on his way to the restaurant. Like most of Berlin's foreign correspondents he used the Adlon as a second business address, and there were two items waiting for him – a wire from Cummins and a plain envelope with his name on it.

He opened the latter after ordering his meal. It contained everything he had suggested to Wilhelm Isendahl – the group's latest leaflet, a covering letter, and a typed article of around a thousand words. 'Father of Liars!' the leaflet proclaimed, and proved its point with a string of extracts from Hitler's speeches. The article looked, at first glance, like a serious exposé of Nazi economic policies, but an Adlon restaurant heaving with Nazi uniforms didn't seem the place to read it.

He turned to Cummins' wire, which was short and depressingly to the point: POGROM BRATI-

SLAVA AUGUST 11 STOP FIRST OUTSIDE GERMANY STOP SUGGEST INVESTIGATION SOONEST CUMMINS.

'I'll be back in a minute,' he told the waiter, who had just arrived with his wine. Making sure to take Isendahl's envelope with him, he walked back across to the bar. 'What do you know about a pogrom in Bratislava?' he asked Slaney.

'Nothing. Has there been one?'

'Apparently there was one yesterday.' He showed Slaney the wire.

'I'm glad my paper has a Central Europe correspondent,' he said. 'Bratislava's not my idea of a good time.'

It wasn't Russell's either, but he saw Cummins' point. A pogrom in Slovakia was like a secondary outbreak of plague, a sign that the disease was spreading, and couldn't be contained. Back in the restaurant he sipped at the glass of Mosel, wondering how the hell he was supposed to get there. The quickest way by train was via Prague, and that would take at least twelve hours. Worse still, he realized, his permit for the Protectorate had run out, and the chances of getting another before Monday morning were zero. He would have to go round the Protectorate in a bloody great circle – down to Nuremberg and Munich and then across to Vienna – and that would take at least a day. The blood would be dry by the time he got there.

He rushed his meal in the hope that Thomas Cook would still be open, but the frontage on Unter den Linden was firmly shut up. He drove on down to Anhalter Station, where trains left for the South; there was one to Leipzig at ten o'clock, with only a two hour wait for the connection to Nuremberg. He would be there by six-thirty, in Munich by eleven. The trains to Vienna were slow on Sundays, but he should arrive before nightfall.

Russell decided to think about it, and ordered a coffee at one of the concourse cafés. The arrivals board caught his eye, a litany of long delays and cancellations. The Wehrmacht manoeuvres were still wreaking havoc with the schedules.

He could fly, he suddenly realized. At least to Vienna, if not Bratislava. He drained his coffee and set out for Tempelhof in the gathering dusk. There would be no more flights that day, but someone might still be around.

The Lufthansa information desk was closing as he arrived, but the young man behind it seemed in no hurry to get home. There were no flights to Bratislava, he told Russell, and none to Vienna on Sundays. There were, however, flights on every other morning, and they left at nine. The price seemed astronomical, but with any luck the *Tribune* would pay it. If they didn't, too bad. An extra day with Effi was worth it.

He asked how long the flight took, and was told two and a half hours. This was progress, he thought. Getting from one atrocity to another had never been easier.

'So what do we do,' Effi asked, 'just knock on his door and ask if he's holding any girls prisoner?'

They were sitting in the Hanomag, about fifty metres down from the apartment block on Dragoner-Strasse. The street had a Sunday quiet-

301

ness about it, just a few smartly-dressed couples walking towards the spire in the distance, presumably intent on attending a late morning service.

'We wait,' Russell said. He was still recovering from Effi's performance at the wheel on the drive over.

'For how long?'

He smiled at her.

'Patience is not one of my strong suits,' she admitted.

'I'd never have guessed.'

'I...' she began, just as the nose of the Mercedes peered out from between the buildings.

'Look at me,' Russell said, as it turned towards them. 'As if we're talking.'

The Mercedes drove past on the other side of the road, and its driver cast a cursory glance in their direction. There was nothing suspicious or interrogative in the look, but Russell was left with a fleeting impression of cold purpose.

'Shouldn't we be following him?' Effi said, hand on the ignition key.

'No. He'd see us. And now we know he's out, we can go and question the *portierfrau*. Or I can,' he corrected himself.

'Why you? I can charm people.'

'I know you can. And if she's a movie fan – which, in my experience, ninety-nine per cent *of portierfrauen* are – she'll recognize you, and our anonymity will be shot to shreds.'

'Oh, all right. But what are you going to say?'

'I don't know yet.'

He crossed the street to the front entrance. The front door responded to his push, and a sign above the stairway to the basement told him where to find the *portierfrau*. He walked down the narrow stairs and knocked on a door with attractive stained glass windows. A woman of about sixty pulled it open, a small schnauzer dancing happily at her feet. Beethoven was playing in the background, and the passage behind her was full of expensive-looking *objets d'art*.

She shooed the dog back in and pulled the door shut behind her.

'Good morning,' Russell said with a smile. 'I'm sorry to disturb you on a Sunday morning, but the local garage have told me that one of the tenants here owns a Mercedes Cabriolet, and that he might consider selling it. I'm wondering if you can tell me which apartment he occupies.'

'That would be Herr Drehsen in Number 5. But I'm afraid he's just gone out. I heard the automobile leave not ten minutes ago.'

Russell looked suitably distressed. 'That is a pity. I'm interested in buying a Cabriolet for my mother to use,' he explained, 'and I was hoping to ask the owner – Herr Drehsen, you say? – if he really was interested in selling it. I don't suppose that any other members of his family are likely to be at home?'

'His family? Herr Drehsen lives alone.'

'Excuse me for asking, but do you know him well?'

'Not well, no. I do his cleaning for him once a week, but Herr Drehsen is one of those men who keeps himself to himself.' She seemed somewhat relieved by the thought.

'He hasn't mentioned the idea of selling his car

to you?'

'He has not.'

'Well, thank you very much, Frau...'

'Frau Jenigebn.'

'Thank you. I may return on another day, but I have others cars to look at this afternoon, and it's possible that one of those may meet my needs.'

'Can I pass your name on to Herr Drehsen?'

'Of course. Bloch. Martin Bloch.'

Russell walked back up the stairs and across the street.

'Well?' Effi demanded.

'His name's Drehsen. The *portierfrau* cleans for him, so he can't be keeping any girls in his apartment. And I'd be surprised if he brings any women here. She's the sort who would disapprove, and she gave no hint of it. And his car's usually parked outside her back window.'

'What did you tell her?'

'That I thought his Mercedes might be for sale. It was the best I could think of.'

'Clever.'

'That's me. So, this is where he comes when he fails to pick a girl up. We need to know where he goes when he succeeds.'

'We need to see him pick one up.'

'We do. Presumably he'll try again on Friday.'

'We don't know he only goes on Fridays,' Effi protested.

'All three sightings,' Russell reminded her.

She sighed. 'It seems a long time to wait if Miriam's still in danger.'

'If she's still in danger. It's been six weeks now.'

'But this might be the week that matters.'

Russell looked at her. 'What else can we do? If we start following him everywhere he's bound to spot us, and when the right time comes we need him not to recognize this car. We know there's no point in involving the police. And I'm off to Bratislava tomorrow for God knows how many days.'

'You'll be back by Friday though?'

'I hope so.'

He left Effi half-asleep in bed the following morning, and drove across town to leave the Hanomag at Siggi's mercy in the Neuenburger Strasse courtyard. A tram from Hallesches Tor got him to Tempelhof Field, where he posted Isendahl's envelope to himself at the Potsdam *poste restante*. He had several ideas for getting article and leaflet out of the country, but carrying them across the border between Vienna and Bratislava was not one of them.

The aeroplane looked similar to the one which had carried him, Zarah and the children to London earlier that year, but Paul was not around to confirm the name and number, or to volunteer a raft of technical specifications. There seemed more seats than before, and the air hostess, busy dispensing twists of cotton wool to his fellow-passengers, was noticeably prettier.

The aeroplane took off on time, rising over Wilmersdorf and Grünewald before veering round to the south. The pilot straightened her out at about two thousand metres, and the parched Saxon fields spread out beneath them. The sky was clear in all directions, and as they passed over Dresden the peaks of the Erzgebirge were clearly visible up ahead. Around half-past ten Prague appeared to their right, nestling in the silver bend of the Vltava. It looked serene and peaceful, as most places did from a kilometre up. Another hour and Vienna was visible across the wider ribbon of the Danube. As their plane taxied to a halt, the clock on the single storey aerodrome building read exactly eleven-thirty.

Once inside, Russell asked for the quickest way of reaching Bratislava.

'You mean Pressburg?' the young German at the desk responded.

'I mean the town that used to be called Pressburg,' Russell agreed. Until 1918 most of Slovakia had been ruled from Vienna.

There were several options, the young man told him curtly. He could take the *gratis* automobile into Vienna and take a train back out again. He could try his luck at the local station, which was much closer to Pressburg. He could take a boat down the Danube, though that would take around seven hours. He could look for an autobus outside.

Following up the final suggestion, Russell walked into an argument between a cab driver and a rather ancient German. Their dispute, he quickly discovered, was over the fare to Pressburg – the old gentleman insisting that it was only half of what the cabbie was demanding. 'I'll pay the other half if you'll take me too,' Russell offered.

Both seemed angry for a moment, as if he'd deliberately spoiled their fun, but his suggestion was accepted.

The capital of the newly independent Slovakia was about sixty-five kilometres away, and the drive took about ninety minutes. The border formalities consumed around thirty of those, the Slovaks keen to demonstrate their new independence. Every item in Russell's suitcase was meticulously examined, leaving him highly relieved that he had left Isendahl's leaflet and article behind.

During the final leg of the journey he asked both driver and fellow-passenger about Friday night's pogrom, but neither had much to say. The old German had been visiting relatives in Berlin for several weeks and the driver – a Slovak – pleaded a lack of fluency in any language but his own. Russell hoped his reticence had something to do with shame.

Bratislava looked down on the Danube from the end of a range of hills. Dropped off in the square at the centre of the Old Town, Russell consulted the street map in his vintage Baedeker. German cartographers were still including synagogues in 1929, and a cluster of them signified the Jewish quarter.

It was only a few blocks away, and easy to recognize from the debris littering the pavements. A whole line of shop fronts had been staved in, and while some were covered with hastily-nailed planks, others still gaped open, their shelves bearing nothing but shards of glass. There was a normal flow of people on the narrow street, but there seemed less noise than there should be, as if someone had turned the city's volume down.

The first synagogue he came to was daubed

with swastikas and other insults, but the entrance was guarded by a posse of Slovak policemen. Russell showed his press card to the likely leader, but the man just shook his head. Pleas in German and English were met with a brief but noticeably hostile burst of Slovak.

Russell gave up for the moment. A café-bar down the street offered food, drink and the possibility of conversation. He was not an expert on central European cuisines, but the menu seemed like a mixture of Hungarian and Jewish, and most of the clientele looked the latter. One young man was staring at him from a nearby table. His face and angry expression reminded Russell of Albert Wiesner.

'I'm a journalist,' he said in German. 'An American journalist.'

The boy looked surprised. 'Can you prove it?' he asked in perfect German, looking around him as he did so.

'Yes,' Russell said simply, taking out his passport and journalistic accreditation.

The young man came over to examine them.

'Have a seat,' Russell offered. 'Can I get you a drink?'

'Whatever you're drinking. I'm Mel,' the youth added, offering his hand.

Russell took it and called for another Pilsen. 'Tell me what happened on Friday night,' he said.

Mel took another precautionary look around the bar. 'It was actually Saturday morning,' he began. 'About a hundred of them came roaring down from Masarykplatz. They were mostly Germans, but there were some Slovaks. You can see what they did.'

'What set them off?'

'Nobody knows for sure, but most people think it was organized by the *Freiwillige Schutzkorps* – the local storm troopers.'

'Was anyone killed?'

'No. A miracle really. A lot of people were hurt, though. Some were punched or battered with staves when they tried to defend their shops, and a lot of people were cut by flying glass.'

'Did the police come?'

'Oh yes. Four hours after they were called. Their station's up on Stefanikstrasse – a five minute walk away.'

The story – and the bitterness – seemed all too familiar.

'The worst thing for most people – not me, because I'm not religious – but the bastards destroyed a lot of important stuff in the synagogues. Stuff that was hundreds of years old.'

'The local police wouldn't let me in,' Russell told him.

'You want to see it? There's a back door.'

'Show me.'

'When we've finished our beers.'

A few minutes and several alleys later, they reached the small yard at the rear of the synagogue. The door opened to Mel's push, and they found themselves in a small storeroom. Another door brought them through to the main chamber, and a scene of devastation. Pools of water lay across the stone floor, and still-sopping carpets had been thrown across seats to dry out.

'They turned on the water hydrants,' Mel whispered.

Hangings had been ripped from the walls, and replaced with more red daubs.

'Who are you and what do you want?' a voice asked.

'He's an American journalist, Uncle Ignaz,' Mel shouted. 'He's come to see what the scum did.'

'Has he? Then bring him over here.'

Uncle Ignaz was leaning over a desk that contained several scrolls of scripture. All were torn and some were stained.

'They defecated on the Torah scrolls,' he said. 'They squatted over them and they forced their shit out with their hatred.'

'Did they steal the ornaments?' Russell asked, remembering *Kristallnacht*.

'Oh yes. They took everything that glittered. But these are what matters,' the man almost cried, looking down at the scrolls.

Back on the street, Russell thanked his young guide and headed for the town centre. A lone policeman gave him directions to the *Freiwillige Schutzkorps* headquarters, which were down near the port. Two Slovaks gave him further help en route, both with expressions of surprise at his choice of destination. Reaching the flag-bedecked warehouse-turned-barracks, he was told that the local leader was in Vienna for a conference. One of his deputies, a young dark-haired German with blue eyes, was happy to explain the recent outrage.

Friday's violence, he claimed, had been provoked by an attack on two of his men. A gang of Jews had fallen upon them in the ghetto and beaten them very badly.

Could Russell speak to these men?

The young German regretted that that would not be possible.

Russell went in search of a hotel. The Central, an elegant old pile at the bottom of Stefanik-strasse, seemed both adequate and eager for his custom. The German officers all stayed at the Savoy-Carlton, the manager remarked after seeing his passport, and the German presence had discouraged other foreigners from visiting the new country.

Russell asked whether any other foreign journalists had come to investigate Friday's events.

'Only one stayed here,' the manager said. 'And only for one night,' he added, handing Russell his key.

His room overlooked the street, with a chair and table placed by the window. He spent the next hour writing up his story, and hoped that Cummins would think it worth the expense. He could have written most of it in Berlin, but his description of the flooded synagogue and soiled scrolls had added an extra dimension. Where were the boys from Pathé News when you needed them?

He reached the post office a few minutes before closing, and persuaded the clerk he had time to wire the story off. That done, he walked down to the Danube in search of a restaurant with a river view. As he waited for his food he read through that morning's *Beobachter*, which he had earlier abandoned in favour of the *Times*. Only one story caught his eye. A 'renowned German economist', interviewed by the paper, claimed that recent border changes had resulted in the Poles having too much coal. 'The nation which needs coal most is entitled to it,' the Professor noted, leaving little room for doubt as to which nation that was.

It was an interesting argument, Russell thought. He imagined Africa laying claim to East Prussia's farmlands on similar grounds – surely they needed the grain more than the Germans did.

He should have been collecting stories like this, he told himself. There had been enough of them over the years, and once Hitler and his thugs were confined to history no one would believe the *Alice in Wonderland* aspects of the world they had spawned.

If they ever were confined to history. He had always assumed that they would be – 'when?' and 'how?' were the questions which mattered. But were he and the old Marxist inside him kidding themselves? Perhaps a rolling programme of conquests could keep economic logic at bay, like a locomotive consuming the carriages it pulled.

So much insanity, and here he was, eating a lovely meal, enjoying a beautiful view. As night descended a crescent moon slowly rose above the distant Hungarian plain, flooding the Danube with pale light and sparkling in the wake of the passing barges.

So much peace, until a convoy of lorries, their headlights blazing, rumbled up to the bridge on the German side of the river. There they stopped, and soon small fires were burning by the riverbank, groups of men gathered around them. War was coming, but not tonight.

He was woken next morning by a smiling young bell-boy with wire in hand. His story had reached San Francisco, and here was the grateful reply – REPORT FROM WARSAW SOONEST. He groaned, and the bell-boy looked as sympathetic as anyone could with a palm outstretched. Russell gave him the only coin he could find, got dressed, and went in search of a newspaper.

The local German paper offered some explanation for Cummins' request. Late on Monday the German authorities had closed the Silesian frontier in the Beuthen area and cut off all local telephone communications. This, the newspaper said, was in response to the 'terrible events in Kattowitz'.

That was it. No mention of a Polish response, or of wider implications. It could be another storm in a teacup; it could be the first shots of a second Great War. Warsaw did seem a good place to find out.

But how to get there? According to the hotel manager, the only passenger flights from Bratislava's tiny aerodrome went to Prague, so it had to be the train, at least to begin with. He walked up Stefanikstrasse to the station, intent on taking the train into Vienna, but a bad-tempered booking clerk told him he might have to wait all day. 'Address your complaints to your own government,' the man added disgustedly, mistaking him for a German.

Russell put him right, and asked if there were through trains to Poland.

'Who knows? If you take the Poprad train to Zilina Junction you may be able to reach Teschen. Or even Nowytarg. The Germans are running their military trains as if this was their own country. And they tell us nothing.'

A mystery tour through the Slovakian backwoods had limited appeal, but what choice did he have? He bought a through ticket to Krakow, and went in search of the Poprad train. It was waiting on the far platform, and rapidly filling up. In the yard beyond a troop train was waiting for a locomotive, soldiers sitting in the boxcar doorways, swinging their legs like bored children.

The time for departure arrived, and a collective whoop of surprise greeted the jerk into motion. The first forty kilometres raced by, but beyond Trvana the stops grew longer and more frequent. Time after time their train was held in a refuge siding for military trains to pass, those heading north with troops and equipment, those heading south to pick up more.

Russell had neglected to bring any food, and was fortunate in his fellow-passengers, a Slovak family of five who shared their lunch of bread and cold sausage with him. None spoke a word of English or German, but their simple pleasure in sharing lifted his heart. Another large family filled the compartment next door, but not with joy. They were Jews abandoning Bratislava, fleeing to the supposed safety of relatives in Poland. The words 'frying-pan' and 'fire' came to mind.

314

The train reached Zilina Junction at five in the evening. The footplate crew uncoupled their locomotive but left it where it was, offering hope that someone might reconnect it. Russell walked down to the end of the platform and took in the view. Zilina Junction seemed to be a Slovakian Crewe, a station more important than the community it served. Hills rose on all sides of the small red-roofed town, yellow fields rising to pale green meadows, and these to dark green forests.

An hour or so later a station official arrived with the news that their train was going no further. Questioned about alternatives, he managed to sound vaguely optimistic. Services to the north and east were scheduled, he said, and he had no definite word of cancellations. A train might appear at anytime, and passengers who wished to spend the night in the station hotel would be roused if one did.

As he finished speaking the sounds of an engine could be heard, and everyone turned to see the smoke pumping skyward above the trees, but it was a troop train, and it hardly slowed as it passed the station. Several soldiers waved to those watching from the platform, but only one child waved back. Russell heard the deep rumble as the train crossed the river, and stood there watching the tell-tale trail of smoke as it burrowed into the distant hills. The locomotive had been Slovakian, but the boxcars and troops had been German.

By the time he arrived at the station hotel all the beds had been let several times over. There were other hostels in the town, but it seemed wiser to stay within sight and sound of the trains. A bowl of stew and two Pilsens later he walked back across to the station, only to find that every square metre of the waiting room had already been colonised. It was still warm, so he stretched out on a bench in the open and watched the darkening sky reveal its stars.

Around ten another troop train steamed in from the south, but this one took the line heading east towards Poprad. If the Germans were sending troops to every border crossing between Slovakia and Poland, Russell realized, the chances of civilians getting across seemed depressingly remote. He had a horrible feeling his next journey would be back to Bratislava.

He tried to sleep, but only managed the occasional doze before the hard awkwardness of the bench woke him up again. A marked drop in the temperature compounded his discomfort – he hadn't been this cold since his last night stroll on the deck of the *Europa*. Only four weeks had passed since then, but it felt like months. He lay there wondering if he could have managed things better, but no obvious alternatives suggested themselves.

At Russell's umpteenth time of waking a thin ribbon of light was silhouetting the eastern hills, and a few minutes later the first sounds of activity were audible in the hotel across the road. He went in search of a hot drink, and found the early kitchen staff seated round a happily boiling samovar. His American status gained him a warm welcome, a large mug of tea and as much bread and jam as he could eat.

One grey-haired old Slovak had a smattering of German, and his summary of local opinion was short and to the point. The Germans were even worse than the Czechs, and the Slovaks just wished they would all bugger off. If he was thirty years younger, he would get the hell out of Europe as soon as he could, and head for New Zealand. He didn't know much about the place, but it had hills and sheep, and it was a wonderfully long way from anywhere else.

The sound of an arriving train penetrated the hotel kitchen. It was the Orava valley train, sent on from Kralovany with some stranded south-bound passengers. The Zilina Junction night shift – a pair of middle-aged Slovaks with cheery smiles and not much else – seemed bemused by the train's appearance off its usual route and were unprepared to forecast its future movements. The locomotive driver, on the other hand, was quite sure where he was going, and that was back where he had come from. And yes, he told Russell, the Orava valley route into Poland was open. Or at least it had been on the previous afternoon.

The tank locomotive ran round its train, took on water, and backed onto the other end of the three wooden coaches. Russell decided he might just as well be stranded high in the mountains as where he was, particularly when the chances of returning to Bratislava seemed so remote. And there was always the chance the border would still be open.

He took his seat and watched as others arrived from the station hotel. The Jewish family from

317

Bratislava brought up the rear, laden with belongings and sleeping infants.

The little train set off at a sedate pace, and only changed speed thereafter when a particularly steep gradient slowed it still further. The sun slid down the valley sides, and was sparkling on the river when they reached Kralovany soon after eight. German troops milled around boxcars in the nearby sidings and a line of vehicles in the station yard, causing Russell to fear further delays, but their train only stopped for a few minutes before setting out on its usual run to Szuchahora.

The Orava valley was more dramatic, slopes soaring on either side of the tracks as they climbed towards Poland. The border, much to Russell's relief, was open. He and his fellow travellers walked past an untended hut on the Slovak side and along a pair of rusted tracks towards a small modern building on the Polish side. Inside, a couple of young soldiers with antique-looking rifles looked on as a single customs officer meticulously examined and stamped each arrival's passport. His entry granted, Russell stood outside the waiting Polish train and admired the view of the Tatra Mountains, rising like a wall into the southern sky.

The train left with admirable promptness, and rattled down through the pines to the junction at Nowytarg. A connection arrived from Zakopane half an hour later, and spent the next three hours, twisting and turning its way out of the foothills, reaching Krakow's Plaszow Station soon after two. Russell had spent the final hour of this journey dreaming of a slap-up lunch in Krakow's Rynek Główny, but the imminent departure of the day's last Luxtorpeda express to Warsaw changed his mind. He bought some Polish currency at the station *bureau de change* and climbed aboard. Advancing to the restaurant car, he was relieved to find a long and mouth-watering menu.

After his last few trains, this one seemed to fly along, as if its wheels were barely touching the rails. One hour to Kielce, another to Radom, and they were sweeping down onto the plain of the Vistula. As the wide sluggish river appeared on their right, a long line of barges struggling downstream, the locomotive whistled a welcome to the outskirts of the Polish capital. Ten minutes later it was hissing to a halt in Central Station.

Russell had not been to Warsaw since 1924, and then only for a night. He and Ilse had been travelling from Moscow to Berlin, and, in the manner of those times, had spent the night on a comrade's floor. He did, however, remember a recent conversation with a German journalist just back from the city: there were two good hotels, the Europejski, which prided itself on being the most expensive in Europe, and the Bristol, which was cheaper and better.

The Bristol was full to the brim. Russell walked on to the Europejski, reasoning that his enforced frugality at Zilina Junction more than made up for a touch of extravagance in Warsaw.

There were rooms available. He looked at three of them, realized they weren't going to get any better, and took the third, a vast space under a distant ceiling with windows overlooking the inner courtyard. The bath was stained an attractive green, the toilet a complementary brown. Flies had drawn intricate patterns on the huge gold-framed mirror with their own waste. The furniture and fittings had been at their peak a century earlier, but at least the bed was softer than the bench at Zilina Junction. Too soft, in fact – as Russell stretched out, the mattress curled around him like a frankfurter roll. He lay there for several moments, laughing like a lunatic.

In the bathroom the water coughed, spat and coughed again, before finally running hot. Working on the assumption that the miracle might not repeat itself, Russell shaved, washed his hair and took a long and very pleasant bath. By the time he emerged the light outside was fading, and ominous noises from the courtyard below suggested an orchestra in the process of tuning up.

The Europejski's restaurant had a higher reputation than its rooms. He walked downstairs and found a table in the open courtyard, just as the band swung into a better-than-expected version of Louis Armstrong's 'Potato Head Blues'. Not the sort of the music you could hear in Germany any more, and sitting there in the warm Warsaw evening, working his way through a very acceptable bottle of French wine, he realized how much he had missed it these past few years. His fellow-diners, most of whom looked like rich Poles, seemed to take it all for granted – there was nothing in their faces or behaviour to suggest that a war might be imminent. Every now and then another couple would wend their way between the tables to the small dance floor in front of the orchestra, and glide around the floor in each other's arms, as if life was just a happy procession of songs.

After dinner Russell went, rather reluctantly, in search of his fellow journalists. In the Bristol bar he found a clutch of Brits earnestly debating the coming football season with one bemused American, and pulled the latter aside. Connie Goldstein was an Irish Jew from New York City who had spent most of the 1930s tracking the rise of anti-Semitism in central and eastern Europe. He was a good journalist and even better writer, but the big agencies he freelanced for were always begging him to write about something else for a change.

Russell had known him quite well during Hitler's early years in power, but the American's reporting of the Nuremberg Laws had got him expelled from Germany, and they hadn't met again until the previous month, when Goldstein had joined the *Europa* at Southampton on its voyage to New York.

'You're back, then,' Russell said, as they waited to be served at the bar.

'For the last time, I expect,' Goldstein said. 'The proverbial's about to hit the fan.'

'Why Warsaw?'

'I don't know, really. It feels almost voyeuristic, like watching a bull in its pen before it goes out to die.'

'Nice.'

Goldstein grimaced. 'You think that's strange. I've been in Lublin the last few days, visiting some long-lost relatives. They live in a large block of flats in the Jewish quarter, and I made a list of everyone in the block. I took down their names and ages. Eighty-seven people, all of them Jews.'

'Why?'

'I wanted a record, just in case.'

'In case of what?' Russell asked, though he knew what Goldstein feared.

'In case they disappear.'

Russell looked at Goldstein, wondering if the man was letting his hatred warp his judgement.

'It's not just the Nazis, you know,' Goldstein said. 'Hungary, Romania, Slovakia, Ukraine, Lithuania, here in Poland ... if the Nazis start murdering Jews they'll have plenty of helpers.'

'No doubt about that.'

'And think about Poland. The Nazis inherited about half a million German Jews, and six years later they've still got 200,000. If there's a war with Poland they'll win it, and then they'll have three million more Jews to deal with. Where will they send them? Where *could* they send them?'

The logic was compelling, as logic often was. If Goldstein was right, they were heading into something like hell, and Russell felt more than a little reluctant to accept the inevitability of such a denouement. He clutched for a straw. 'I don't suppose the Germans have re-opened the Beuthen frontier?'

'No, and the Poles have shut down the entire Silesian frontier in retaliation.'

'Wonderful.'

'Gestures have their place. And it's surprising how much both of them seem to enjoy their mutual stupidities. You've heard about the latest postal row?'

'No.' Russell explained that he'd been out of touch for forty-eight hours. 'Ah, well, that idiot Frick has ruled that Polish addresses on letters originating in Germany have to be spelt in the German way, or they won't be allowed out. The Poles have retaliated by saying that all letters with such spelling will simply be returned to the sender. So no one will get any mail from Germany.'

'When's the next press briefing?'

'They're at ten every morning at the Foreign Office press department. It's on the other side of the Square. But don't expect to learn anything new.'

'I don't suppose there's any good news from Moscow?'

'Only bad. The talks with the British and French have been adjourned, and they won't be resumed until the Poles agree to the presence of Soviet troops. Which no one believes they will. Everyone's expecting some hapless British or French diplomat to arrive here in the next day or so, and be told as much by the government. Meantime, rumour has it that the Germans are pushing really hard for a non-aggression pact, and receiving more than a little encouragement. Ribbentrop's just waiting for an invitation to Moscow.' Goldstein looked at his watch. 'I'm headed that way myself, and I ought to be getting to the station.'

'You think a deal's that imminent?'

'Who knows? But the crucial decisions are

being taken there, not here.'

Russell watched him walk away, and experienced a momentary feeling of panic. He had gotten used to war being a few weeks away, not a few days. Across the room, the laughter of his fellow journalists seemed almost ghoulish.

Abandoning his drink, he strode the short distance to Pidsulski Square in search of ... what? People who hadn't yet heard the bad news, or showed no sign that they had? They were there all right – the prostitutes lingering by the ornate lampposts, the droshky drivers dozing on their seats behind shuffling horses. A couple walked across in front of him, the young man full of enthusiasm for something, the girl sharing it with her smile.

Lambs to the slaughter.

Russell trudged back to the Europejski and took the lift up to his floor. The band in the courtyard below was playing loud enough to keep Europe awake, and the small dance floor was a scrum of swaying bodies. He undressed and lay on the bed, enjoying the cool breeze and the joyous blaring of the horn section. Sleep seemed unlikely but he woke a few hours later, sweat streaming off his body. He had dreamt that the walls were closing in, but it was only the mattress.

Over breakfast the next morning Russell needed a few moments to work out which day it was: Thursday, which gave him less than thirty-six hours to get back to Berlin for his appointment at Silesian Station.

In Pidsulski Square the droshky drivers were

standing around smoking, the prostitutes nowhere to be seen. The Foreign Ministry press briefing was well attended, and as uninformative as Goldstein had predicted. A silver-haired Pole wearing spats and a wingtip collar obligingly invited questions about his country's willingness to allow Soviet troops on her soil, then suavely refused to answer them. The only point of substance was provided by another official, who gravely announced that the foreign press corps would shortly be issued with gasmasks.

Russell was still digesting this piece of news when an incongruous sight met his eyes. As he descended the steps outside, a troop of Polish cavalry clip-clopped into the square, pennants fluttering from their lances, scabbards and helmets glinting in the morning sunshine. And all courtesy of H.G. Wells' time machine, Russell mused, as the troop trotted off towards the old royal palace. 'The wave of the past' a familiar voice said behind him, precisely echoing his thought.

It was Yevgeny Shchepkin, the man who had knocked on his Danzig hotel room door in the opening hour of 1939 and lit the fuse of his reluctant espionage career. Shchepkin was wearing a light cotton suit, open shirt and what seemed rather smart-looking shoes for a Soviet agent. His face looked gaunter, but the grey hair was more luxuriant, perhaps in compensation. Russell smiled at the Russian. 'I thought I'd seen the last of you.'

Shchepkin smirked, as if mere survival was a major accomplishment.

In his case it probably was, Russell thought.

'A walk in the park?' the Russian suggested, indicating the entrance to the Saxon Gardens at the side of the palace.

'Why not?'

They strolled in silence to the gateway, as if conversation in the open was forbidden. 'I don't suppose this is a chance encounter,' Russell said as they passed through.

'Well, yes and no. Our being in Warsaw at the same time is a matter of chance. But a meeting had already been decided on, and once one of our people at the Europejski had reported your arrival...'

'It must be fate,' Russell said wryly. 'So why do we need a meeting?'

'Ah, Moscow has decided that using the legation in Berlin smacks of amateurism, and they want to convince the Germans that they're taking your deliveries really seriously. So you and I will be meeting outside Germany on a regular basis – your new job offers ample justification for such trips.'

It did, but such an arrangement would involve Russell in carrying supposedly secret information across the German border. Hauptsturm-führer Hirth would be party to the arrangement, of course, but the border authorities would not be. Did that really matter? Or was he still sweating over the experience in March, when his last Soviet contact had planted incriminating material in his suitcase? 'Whatever happened to Comrade Borskaya?' he wondered out loud.

Shchepkin made a face. 'Ah, Irma. She was

very keen. Her plot against you was all her own.'

'She *was* very keen?'

'I'm afraid so.'

'What happened?'

Shchepkin shrugged. 'She was found guilty of working for a foreign power. And I assume executed.'

Russell pictured her exasperated expression, and remembered her telling him he would have the satisfaction of supporting world socialism in the struggle against fascism. He wondered what she'd been thinking when they led her down the last corridor in the bowels of the Lyubyanka. That someone had made a mistake?

'You seem to have gotten yourself into something of a bind,' Shchepkin observed, as they passed a series of baroque statues symbolizing the human virtues. 'Blackmailed into working for the Gestapo, and turning to us for assistance.'

'Turning to you with a mutually beneficial suggestion,' Russell corrected him. 'And if Borskaya hadn't tried to betray me, the Nazis would never have known there was anything to blackmail me for.'

'True. How did you talk yourself out of that, by the way? Comrade Borskaya assumed it was dumb luck.'

It had been in part, but Russell was reluctant to admit as much. He told the Russian the whole story, up to and including the donation of his Soviet fee to a German official as a wedding present. 'I'm probably the only man who ever bribed his way *in* to Nazi Germany.'

'Not a pleasant epitaph,' Shchepkin muttered.

They stopped in the shade of an old water tower, the first one in Warsaw according to the accompanying plaque. It had been built by Marconi in 1850, when the city had still belonged to the Russia of the Tsars.

'The questions for your fake German spy are waiting in Moscow,' Shchepkin said casually, as if all Russell needed to do was nip round and collect them.

'Moscow? You don't expect me to spend days travelling there and back for a couple of pages? If the post's good enough for Heydrich, why isn't it good enough for Beria?'

Shchepkin grinned at that, but persevered. 'They also want to talk to you.'

'About what?'

'That's for them to tell you. But look, as a journalist you should be there in any case. That is where the decisions are being taken,' he went on, unconsciously repeating Connie Goldstein's line.

'A deal's coming? In the next few days?'

'Nothing is 100 per cent certain, you understand, but if you travel to Moscow I think I can guarantee you a – what do you call it in English? A scoop – that's the word. A scoop,' he repeated, enjoying the sound of it.

'He's really going to do it – sign a pact with the devil?'

Shchepkin sighed. 'It will buy us time. Though I agree it will be hard to explain.'

'Ah, go on. If you can get away with calling collectivization and five million dead an advance towards socialism, then a pact with the devil should be a piece of cake.'

Shchepkin stopped and looked at him, a strange look on his face. 'You know, I never realized before just how angry you are.'

'Aren't *you*? When we met in 1924 ... is this where you hoped we would be fifteen years later?'

'No, of course not. But this is where we are. A dream that hasn't come true is not necessarily dead. And there are many comrades still willing to die for ours.'

'Yes, but...'

'You remember Fritz Lohr, the sailor you met in Kiel?'

'I never knew his name.'

'He died without telling them yours. He jumped out of a third-floor window at the Gestapo headquarters in Hamburg.'

Russell was shocked. At the sudden intrusion of death, at the horrible realization that his own life had been hanging by a torturer's thread, and he hadn't even known it. 'When?' he asked.

'In May, I think. Perhaps early June.'

Russell could see the man's face, his utter belief in what he was fighting for. And his companion, the prostitute Geli, with her dark-ringed eyes and cynical smile. What had happened to her?

'And this woman in Berlin,' Shchepkin continued relentlessly. 'Sarah Grostein. She seems willing to risk her life for the cause.'

'She is,' Russell agreed. Almost too willing.

'What is she like?'

'Clever. Determined. Resourceful. And she feels she has nothing to lose. An ideal agent.'

'And you like her,' Shchepkin said.

It was not a question, but Russell answered it anyway. 'Yes, I do.'

They had reached the side of a small lake. A tall fountain was spraying water into the air, crafting rainbows.

'Let me speak as a friend,' Shchepkin said. 'I understand why you find it hard to trust us, but hear me anyway. When we talked in Danzig and Krakow I asked if you planned to take sides in the coming war. Do you remember your answer?'

Russell did. 'I said not if I could help it.'

'Exactly. But you have changed in the last eight months, and maybe your answer has too.'

Russell smiled at him, and gestured him to a nearby seat. 'Perhaps it has,' he admitted. 'There's a man in Breslau,' he continued after they had both sat down. 'His name is Josef Möhlmann, and he's the Reichsbahn Deputy-Director of Operations for South-eastern Germany. I don't know his home address, but it shouldn't be difficult to find out. He was an SPD member, and he thinks it was a mistake to fight the communists rather than the Nazis. He's recently lost his wife, he's lonely, and he drinks too much. I think he's in a position to give you advance warning of any invasion, and I think he will if you approach him in the right way.'

Shchepkin was staring intently at him, his lower lip glistening slightly. 'How did you meet this man?'

'By accident,' Russell lied. This didn't seem the moment to explain his connections to American intelligence. 'I could be wrong about him, but I don't think so.'

Shchepkin massaged his chin with the fingers of his left hand. 'Perhaps you could approach him?'

'No, it needs to be a fellow German. One who'll convince him that betrayal is the only way to save their country.'

Shchepkin thought about this. 'You are right,' he said at last. He turned to face Russell. 'So can I persuade you to visit Moscow?'

Russell held his gaze. 'Let me ask you something. As a friend. Can you guarantee my safety? That I won't be arrested and shipped off to Siberia for thwarting Comrade Borskaya's little plot?'

'Of course. For one thing, you are a well-known journalist. For another, you are useful to us, and have just proved as much. Why would anyone wish to send you to Siberia?'

It fell somewhat short of a guarantee, but it made sense, Of a sort. And Moscow did seem like the place for an East European correspondent to be at this moment in history. Russell sighed at the thought of another endless train journey. 'All right,' he said. 'Since you asked so nicely.'

Shchepkin delved into his inside pocket and brought out some papers.

'Your ticket and your visa. The train leaves at two.'

As it rumbled across the Vistula Bridge, Russell stretched out in his first class compartment and went back over the conversation, wondering at the skill with which Shchepkin had manipulated

331

him. The sort-of-apology for Borskaya's betrayal – regrettable, of course, but these things happened, and one could hardly criticise over-enthusiasm, particularly when the person responsible had just been shot. The touch of flattery – encouraging him to relate his own resourcefulness at the Czech border. And the tugs at his conscience provided by the dead Fritz Lohr and the living Sarah Grostein, made more compelling by what sounded – and perhaps even was – a genuine plea for help. There had even been an appeal to his journalistic greed – the 'scoop' in Moscow dangled in front of him like a big fresh carrot.

And, Russell realized, there had been no hint of a threat. Which somehow felt much more threatening. Shchepkin was a master, no doubt about it.

The train made good time across the plains and low hills of eastern Poland. Here too the fields were bursting with grain, but there were no signs of urgency in the harvesting, no gangs of students or soldiers helping the farmers. Reckoning the food would be better on this side of the border, Russell ate an early dinner, and was just sipping the last of his coffee when the train emerged from a stretch of forest and eased past a huge sign bearing the slogan 'Workers of the World Unite'. Behind it a wide swathe of cleared land stretched towards a barbed wire barrier lined with watchtowers. Beyond that, the Soviet border authorities at Niegoreoje were waiting to check each visitor's credentials.

Russell's passport and visa were given the most

cursory of glances, almost, he joked to himself, as if they were expecting him. A first class sleeper compartment was waiting for him in the Soviet train, complete with beautifully starched sheets and a bar of Parisian soap – the sort of accoutrements that any member of the Romanov family would have taken for granted. Russell hoped there was no one he knew on the train.

Darkness fell as his fellow-passengers queued to enter the workers' state, and it was almost nine by the time the train got underway. This was usual, his coach attendant assured him – they would only be the usual two hours late reaching Moscow. Russell considered a drink in the restaurant car, but decided his body was in more need of sleep.

The bed was surprisingly comfortable, but anxieties over Effi kept him awake. Once he had realized he wouldn't be back by Friday, he'd been afraid she would try something on her own. Another attempt at following Eyebrows perhaps, or something more dangerous which he hadn't even thought of. Before leaving Warsaw he had tried to wire her, but all communications with Berlin had been cut, and he'd been forced to send a message via his London agent Solly Bernstein. The man had never taken a holiday as long as Russell knew him, but there was always a first time. 'Please, Effi,' he murmured. 'Be sensible.'

It was almost ten in the morning when the train rolled into Moscow's Byelorusskaya Station, and Russell emerged into the stifling heat of the Soviet capital. He was looking forward to a first ride on

Moscow's famous new Metro, but a uniformed NKVD driver was waiting for him at the platform entrance, eyes shifting to and fro between the arriving passengers and the photograph he held in one hand.

'Citizen Russell?' he asked politely, using the non-Party form of address.

'Yes.'

'Come with me please,' he said, with the precision of someone who'd learnt the phrase in the last hour or so.

The sleek black car that was waiting outside looked custom-made for American gangsters, with its thick glass windows and wide running boards. His chauffeur opened the back door, but Russell mimed his wish to sit up front. He hadn't been in Moscow since 1924 and he wanted a good view of what Stalin had done with it. 'Which hotel are we going to?' he asked, but got no answer.

He tried again five minutes later, when it became obvious that they were driving out of the city rather than into it, and eventually teased out a reply.

'Festival Aviation,' the man told him, taking both hands of the wheel to mime an aeroplane in flight. 'Tushino,' he added definitively.

Russell was more interested in a bath than an aerial pageant, but explaining this to his companion proved impossible. Not, he suspected, that it would make any difference if he could. If the NKVD had decided he needed to watch aeroplanes, then that was what he'd be doing.

They drove for about twenty minutes through

Moscow's north-western suburbs. The architecture was uninspiring, the streets almost empty of people, and the only other vehicles on the road seemed to be lorries. Part of the drabness, Russell realized, was the complete absence of advertising hoardings. But only part. The Party had obviously legislated for only two colours of paint in the latest five year-plan.

After passing a line of giant hangars, they stopped at gates in a high wire fence and the driver showed his documentation to the waiting guards. A dim roar in the distance swelled with astonishing speed, and well over a hundred bombers appeared in the windscreen, flying across their line of sight in close formation, no more than four hundred metres from the ground.

His companion made an enthusiastic noise, and gestured towards the disappearing bombers with obvious admiration.

It was just like home, Russell thought.

The aerodrome building was flanked with what looked like temporary grandstands. The driver drew up behind the one on the right, said 'Come with me please,' again, and led Russell around to the front. 'Foreign press,' his guide said, pointing to a particular section of seats. Not that Russell needed the help. His fellow hacks were easy to pick out – less conservatively dressed, less interested in the proceedings, and smoking cigarettes which didn't jettison all their tobacco if held in anything other than a horizontal plane.

There were also seats to spare, which couldn't be said of the other sections. Russell noticed a couple of familiar faces – a German journalist

335

whom he had loathed for years, and an American whom he remembered meeting somewhere in the Rhineland, in the days that followed Hitler's reoccupation. He raised a hand to the latter, and received a wry smile in reply.

The bombers had gone wherever bombers went to, and a succession of fighter pilots were now showing their skills, twisting and turning and inverting their speeding planes at alarming proximity to the ground. Binoculars had been provided for the journalists, and Russell pointed his at the terrace of the aerodrome building. As he adjusted the focus Stalin swam into view, dressed in a lightweight suit, smiling broadly at the acrobatics on display. Molotov, by contrast, looked like he'd just swallowed something particularly nasty. That, or he'd just found out that Ribbentrop was on his way.

It was scary, Russell thought, how much damage a few deranged bastards could do.

The demonstration of potency went on. An autogyro was wheeled out in front of them, lifted off by its rotors, and driven out of sight by its engine. A fleet of gliders hove silently into view and landed in almost perfect harmony across the wide field. And that, as Russell saw from his programme, concluded the morning session. 'Luncheon gratis' came next.

As he left the grandstand in search of the promised repast, a thin man in a very shiny suit fell into step beside him. 'You will attend a meeting tomorrow morning,' the man said in near-perfect English. 'That is August 19,' he added for good measure. 'You will be collected from your hotel at 10am.'

'Okay,' Russell agreed. 'Do you know which hotel I'm staying at?'

'Metropole,' the man said with a surprised look. 'Yes?'

'If you say so.'

'The press bus will take you,' the man said, just to be sure. 'And this is for your expenses,' he added, handing Russell an envelope. An address in Russian had been crossed out, most of a stamp torn off.

The man disappeared as abruptly as he had materialised. Russell ripped open the envelope, transferred the small wad of brand new notes to his back pocket, and walked on to the VIP refreshment tent. He was half-hoping to find Stalin at the front of the queue, but the great leader was obviously lunching in private. Russell found his American acquaintance hovering by the buffet of cold meats, either spoilt for choice or wondering where the least potential damage lay. They shared recent histories and reasons for being in Moscow, and agreed that things looked ominous.

So did the weather. As the first event of the afternoon – the bombing of a dummy factory on the far side of the aerodrome – got started, dark clouds were looming above the low hills to the west, tiny forks of lightning fizzing inside them. As the thunder of exploding bombs rolled across the airfield, nature's thunder offered a distant counterpoint, like an enemy drawing near.

There was time for two small airships to sail languorously past before the first drops of rain fell, but the sky grew darker by the second, and a steady downpour was in progress when the final act began – the mass dropping of airborne troops from a fleet of transport planes. The parachutes opened like a frenetic garden of flowers, and floated down like so many windblown petals. The troops rolled as they fell and bounced back up, except for one left clutching his ankle and writhing in pain. His comrades ignored him, racing to their designated rendezvous points, a series of flags planted in oil drums, glowing red in the stygian gloom.

The press bus deposited Russell and most of the other foreign journalists outside the Metropole soon after five. His third floor room had a spartan no-nonsense feel to it, but was comfortable enough, and the view across Sverdlov Square was impressive. A huge portrait of Stalin adorned the Bolshoi Theatre, causing Russell to ponder the possibility that the General Secretary had been taking dancing lessons. It seemed unlikely.

The storm had passed, leaving a slightly fresher feel. Russell stood by the open window, wondering about next morning's rendezvous with the NKVD.

Everything seemed relatively straightforward – he had nothing to hide, or at least not very much. They would ask him about Sarah Grostein and Josef Möhlmann, and he would tell them all he knew. They would hand him their fake responses to the SD's fake questions, along with any additional briefing they considered necessary. If they wanted him to do anything else – shoot Goebbels, perhaps – he would politely decline. What could they do? As far he could judge the NKVD needed him as much, if not more, than he needed them.

Everything would be fine.

He needed to check in with the press liaison people, and find out when and where the briefings were being held. A fellow hack would know, and a fellow hack was more than likely to be propping up the bar. He headed downstairs.

A solitary English journalist was drinking tea in the bar. He looked about sixteen, and claimed to be a freelance, but the upper-crust accent made Russell suspect, perhaps unfairly, that the young man was spending pater's money on a Thirties version of the Grand Tour. He had the information Russell required, and passed it on with a sneer, as if keen to show how little official briefings mattered to a real journalist.

Outside the sky had cleared, and a fiery dusk hung over the eastern end of Marx Prospekt. Russell walked up the slope into Red Square, remembering the excitement of doing so fifteen years before. The square looked much the same, the huge expanse of cobbles, the sombre majesty of the surrounding walls and buildings. Some public spaces, like Times Square or Piccadilly Circus, evoked a frantic joy in modern life; others, like Pariser Platz or Trafalgar Square, seemed merely pompous. None evoked raw power like this place did. Whether draped in snow or bathed in a sultry evening haze, Red Square almost hummed with power, as if the stones were straining to hold it in.

He had felt this in 1924, and been reassured – all this power at the service of the revolution! But now it felt different, both empty and sinister, and the illuminated red stars above the Kremlin walls seemed like baubles, worn only to flatter and deceive.

Later in that same visit, he and Ilse had walked around the square after making ever-so-silent love in the crowded dormitory. It had been two in the morning, but a politburo meeting must have been imminent, because cars carrying Trotsky and Zinoviev swept across the cobbles and in through the Kremlin's Spassky Gate as they watched, and a few minutes later Nikolai Bukharin had hurried across the square on foot, looking, as ever, like an absent-minded young professor. Stalin had presumably already been inside, trying on the dead Lenin's shoes for size. He was probably in there now, finalising his price for letting Hitler off the leash. Slaney had been right. The British, the French, the Poles ... they had given Stalin no choice. And boy, would they pay for their mistake. They and everyone else.

Saturday proved interesting. Emerging from the Metropole a few minutes early, Russell found his driver sitting in his shirtsleeves on the gangster car's running board, thoughtfully smoking a cigarette. The sun was already high in the sky, the heat shimmering off the pavements.

Russell was expecting a first visit to the NKVD's Lyubyanka headquarters on Dzerzhinsky Street, and was somewhat cheered when the driver headed off in the opposite direction.

340

Five minutes later he pulled up outside an innocent-looking office building on a road Russell didn't recognize. They climbed the stairs to the third floor, where two men in different uniforms were waiting in the large and surprisingly modern Room 303. Both were younger than Russell, but not by much. Both had short fair hair and typical Slavic faces, hawkish eyes over high cheekbones and small mouths. They introduced themselves as Comrades Moskalenko and Nazarov, the first representing the Party, the latter the Army.

So both the NKVD and the GRU wanted a piece of him. It was nice to be wanted.

Dual questioners apart, the meeting went much as he'd expected. Moskalenko handed him a list of the questions they wanted the SD's fake informer to answer. They were in German, but encoded. A book code, he explained, passing over the book. Russell faked a suitable look of bemusement, and had the principle explained to him. The Soviet choice was an old German translation of *War and Peace*, which had the advantage of not being banned in Germany, but would add considerably to the weight of Russell's suitcase.

The GRU man took up the baton, asking Russell a series of questions about Möhlmann, almost none of which he could answer. Asked again how he'd met the man, he made up a chance encounter in a beer garden. Nazarov seemed less interested in Sarah Grostein, and Russell could understand why. She might provide access to higher decision-makers, but there was something shockingly urgent about trains heading your way full of troops and military vehicles.

And that was it. No new tasks were announced, promised or threatened. He would function as the cut-out between Sarah – now to be known as 'the violinist' – and Shchepkin; he would continue to transmit false information between the knowing Soviets and the unknowing Germans. There were only two bombs strapped around his life.

One last question, he said. If their government signed a non-aggression pact with the Nazis, how would that affect him?

Not at all, they said. No pact had been announced; and even if one should be, the Party had no illusions as to its permanence. Was Russell suggesting that they would betray comrades to the Nazis?

Of course not, Russell answered, recalling the list of German comrades – real or imaginary – which Borskaya had planted on him. It had taken more than one individual's 'keenness' to produce that. Still, he couldn't see any point in them betraying him again. He left the building feeling less than satisfied, but relieved that it hadn't been worse.

His driver took him on to the late morning press briefing, which proved an utter waste of time, but gave him the opportunity of joining his fellow journalists for lunch. The general opinion was that the trade agreement would be signed that afternoon, and the non-aggression pact in a week or so.

At the American Embassy he was given ten minutes with the press attaché, who cheerfully told him that the Soviets had been warned –

make a deal with the devil and he'll stab you in the back. At the devil's embassy they had nothing to say, but the smiles and smirks suggested bad news for Poland. He went back to the hotel, thought about decoding the NKVD's questions for the fake agent in Berlin, and decided he wasn't that curious.

He wrote a brief, doom-laden piece on the upcoming deal, and spent the next two hours traversing the bureaucratic hoops required to wire it. Another lonely dinner, another stroll in Red Square, and he returned to find a woman in his bed.

A naked one, as became apparent when she pulled back the sheet.

A present from the chaps in Room 303, he thought. And beautiful too.

He stood there stupidly for what was probably only a couple of seconds, caught between bodily desire and every other conscious impulse, of which loyalty to Effi and suspicion of spooks bearing gifts loomed largest.

She smiled at him and moved slightly, causing the bedsprings to squeak.

'No,' he said, turning his eyes in search of her clothes, and finding them neatly folded on the chair. He picked them up and passed them to her. 'Thank you, but no.'

Her smile turned into a shrug.

Two minutes later she was gone. Russell gazed out at the empty square, reliving the movement of her body in his mind's eye. 'You would have hated yourself in the morning,' he muttered to himself.

343

Sunday morning's press briefing was as short as the name implied. The Soviet spokesman announced the signing of an economic treaty with Germany on the previous evening, but refused to divulge any details or take questions on whether the economic agreement was the forerunner of a political pact. The assembled foreign press corps grumbled its way back out to the heat.

Russell decided that now was a good time to explore the new Metro. Descending into the depths at the Comintern station, he rode out to the far end of the original line, inspecting the stations as he went. On the way back he alighted at a couple, and spent the time between trains exploring the *avant garde* architecture. It was very impressive.

He emerged at Pushinskaya Station, and sought out a shaded bench in the square. A few people were out for a Sunday morning stroll, but the city seemed quiet, lost in its summer torpor. Stalin's revolution, Russell thought, was like the dog that didn't bark in the Sherlock Holmes story. What mattered was what wasn't there – there were no church bells on a Sunday morning, no advertising on trams and hoardings, no conspicuous wealth. All of which could be construed as signs of success, at the least as proof of survival. But something else was also missing, something that could only mean failure. There was no popular enthusiasm.

Where had it all gone? In 1924 this city had overflowed with young idealists from around the world, all drawn to the workers' state by its international sponsorship of justice and equality. Fifteen years on, and it was full of homegrown cynics. Somewhere along the way the hopes of something better had become the dread of something worse.

News of the forthcoming Pact seeped out over the next forty-eight hours, like blood from a heavily-bandaged wound. Monday morning's *Pravda* was full of praise for the already-announced economic agreement, and hinted at a future extension into the political realm. The Soviet spokesman at the morning's briefing refused to confirm any such intentions, but his tone said otherwise; and as the day progressed the foreign press corps slowly gathered in the Metropole Bar, rather in the manner of steamboat passengers waiting for the order to abandon ship. Mid-evening, one intrepid hack bearded a gloomy-looking member of the British negotiating team in a hotel toilet, and was told that a member of the Russian team had confirmed an imminent visit from Ribbentrop. In the early hours of the morning a short-wave listener at the American Embassy heard German radio make the official announcement, and quickly tipped off one of the American journalists. The Metropole Bar greeted the news with a cynical cheer, but the silence thereafter was more telling. The journalists began drifting off to their rooms, most of them looking every bit as depressed as Russell felt.

The official Soviet news agency Tass removed any lingering doubts on the following morning: Foreign Minister Ribbentrop would be arriving 'in the next few days' to sign a non-aggression pact. Russell and a fellow American journalist ran two members of the British negotiating team to ground in their hotel lift, and were blithely informed that the Anglo-French negotiations with the Soviets were still ongoing. Wishful thinking or blind idiocy, the two journalists asked each other in the foyer, before realizing it didn't matter.

So why stay in Moscow? Russell asked himself. It was bad enough sharing the same continent with Ribbentrop, let alone the same city. All the agencies would carry the official details of the signing – he'd be better off in Warsaw, seeing how the Poles reacted. Nearer to Berlin and home as well.

He wrote and sent off his story, and took the Metro up to Byelorusskaya Station to reserve a sleeper on the afternoon train. Back at the Metropole he noticed Connie Goldstein in a secluded corner of the bar.

'You made it,' Goldstein said.

'I've been here since Friday. And now I'm heading back to Warsaw. The phrase "all over but the shouting" seems applicable.'

'Yes, I suppose it is.' Goldstein capped his pen, closed the notebook he'd been writing in, and smiled up at him. 'Have you got an hour or so? I'd like to show you something.'

'Sure. What is it?'

'Wait and see.'

Goldstein led him outside and hailed one of the waiting 'taxis'. 'Khodynka airfield,' he told the NKVD driver in Russian.

Russell half-expected an argument – the taxis were usually reluctant to take foreign journalists beyond the invisible boundaries of the government district – but the driver made no objection. As they sped up an eerily empty Gorky Street, Goldstein chattered happily about returning to the States, and a new grandchild born earlier that year.

The trip to Khodynka only took twenty minutes, and Russell was astonished by what greeted them: the buildings of the small airfield, along with all available poles and stretches of fencing, were hung or emblazoned with swastikas. Either the Nazi flag had figured in the last five year-plan or every seamstress in Moscow had been up all night stitching the damn things together.

'He's arriving tomorrow,' Goldstein said.

Russell didn't reply. He was dumbstruck by the sea of swastikas. Playing for time was one thing – communists the world over had come to accept the Bolsheviks' insistence that some degree of *realpolitik* was necessary to the survival of the workers' state. But this went way beyond any judicious trimming of sails. This felt more like self-abasement, more like gratuitous over-compensation. Like Judas turning up at the crucifixion and insisting on having his picture taken. Ribbentrop's ego would probably explode.

'This is where Nicholas II's coronation was held in 1884,' Goldstein observed. 'They didn't make enough souvenir mugs, and fourteen hundred people were trampled to death in the stampede.'

'Wonderful,' Russell muttered. 'Just wonderful.'

347

The journey back to Warsaw was slower than the journey out. The train clanked to halt after halt, occasionally at a barely-lit platform, most times in the middle of a seemingly endless plain. When dawn broke they were still on the Soviet side of the border, and the only breakfast came courtesy of a few enterprising peasant women, who approached the train at one of its interminable stops with scraps of bread and a few raw carrots. It was almost ten in the morning when their train rolled out of the Soviet Union through the gap in the barbed wire, and almost noon before their Polish train left the border station. It was faster than its Russian equivalent, but not by much, and the sun was low on the western horizon by the time it reached Warsaw.

Russell made sure that trains were still running into Germany, checked into a cheap hotel opposite the station, and took a taxi to the Europejski. Finding no fellow-journalists, he moved on to the Bristol, where several foreign correspondents were lined up at the bar. There had been no official announcement of a pact, he was told, but Ribbentrop had arrived in Moscow that morning, and everyone knew that an agreement was about to be signed.

There was one Pole in the party, an English-speaking journalist with one of the local dailies. He had obviously been drinking for a while, which both explained his belligerent attitude and facilitated its expression. 'The sooner the better,' he said, thumping his palm on the polished bar. 'While we still have allies,' he added pointedly, marching an accusative gaze down the row of English faces.

Out on the street Russell saw other Polish faces brimming with a similar bravado, the facial equivalent of the cavalry he had seen in Pidsulski Square. But there were also eyes dulled by resignation, or seemingly stunned that the moment had finally arrived. The Poles he spoke to in English had only one question – would England and France live up to their obligations? Yes, Russell told them, though part of him hoped the answer was no. If sacrificing Poland would keep his son out of a European war, he'd do it in a heartbeat. The trouble was, it wouldn't.

His hotel was quieter than expected, his bed more comfortable, but he still slept badly, hovering most of the night between waking and dreaming, fragments of his own war flickering harmlessly out of reach, like a silent movie through a curtain of gauze. He woke with the smell of the trenches in his nostrils and the old familiar feeling that this was the day he would die.

As he walked up Nowy Świat towards Pidsulski Square he scanned the faces of passers-by, and thought he saw something approaching relief. The Pact had been announced, he guessed, both in Moscow and here on the radio. The die was cast.

The Foreign Office Press Department spokesman confirmed as much. He added little of a specific nature, but resolutely refused to accept that Polish intransigence was in any way to blame for the country's new vulnerability. Germany and

Russia had always been Poland's enemies, he insisted, and always would be. Poland would fight them both if she had to, hopefully in the company of her Western allies.

Back on the square, Russell felt a sudden over-whelming need to be home, and had to dissuade himself from taking an immediate cab to hotel and station. There was a train mid-afternoon, he told himself – time to write and wire off his piece. There was no need to hurry.

He wrote his impressions of Warsaw on the brink, and walked down to the Post Office. There was no wire traffic out through Germany, but the elderly clerk was aggressively confident of the route via Copenhagen. He and his fellow Poles were not surrounded, he seemed to be saying. The rest of the world was still within reach.

Russell checked out of his hotel, bought his ticket and lunched in the station restaurant. The concourse seemed unusually busy, with lots of children chasing each other around piles of luggage, but there was no hint of panic, despite the headlines announcing the Pact in the lunch-time editions. There was a photograph of Rib-bentrop arriving at Khodynka, beaming for the Soviet cameras.

Russell's train failed to leave on time, raising fears that it might be cancelled, but the French *wagons-lit* eventually jerked into motion. He wondered how many more trips they would be taking across Europe, and where they would be stranded when the frontiers slammed shut.

Jewish ballast

After Russell's train had stood for more than ten minutes in Berlin's Alexanderplatz Station, a voice over the loudspeakers announced that it would proceed no further. Those passengers travelling to a stop in western Berlin were invited to take the next train from the neighbouring Stadtbahn platform, and Russell seized the opportunity to call Effi from a public telephone.

'I knew it was you,' she said.

'I'll see you in about half an hour.'

'Wonderful.'

He replaced the receiver, surprised at the enormity of his relief. Someone in his subconscious had been more worried than he cared to admit.

He climbed up to the Stadtbahn platform, and stood watching for the lights of a westbound train. It was almost eleven, but the air was still warm and humid, with no hint of a breeze. The sky through the canopy opening was black and starless.

The train was almost empty, and Russell picked up an abandoned evening newspaper from one of the seats. 'German Farmhouses in Flames' the headline screamed, above the all-too-familiar litany of grievances real, imagined and invented. He looked at the names of the villages and wondered whether their inhabitants knew of their new-found status as victims of the 'Polish arch-madness'.

'It looks serious this time,' a man sitting opposite said, with a nod in the direction of the newspaper.

'Yes,' Russell agreed.

'But at least the Führer is back in Berlin,' the man added hopefully.

Whoopee, Russell thought to himself.

The streets between Zoo Station and Effi's flat were empty, her porch mercifully devoid of loitering SD agents. She met him at the door with the sort of sweet, soft embrace that made going away worthwhile, and pulled him into the living room. 'Thank God you're back,' she said.

'Well...'

'Because it has to be tomorrow.'

Russell sunk into the sofa. 'What does?'

'Eyebrows, of course. There's going to be a war, isn't there?'

'Well...'

'So this could be our last chance. Things will change once the war begins.'

'True. But he may not come tomorrow.'

'He did last Friday.'

'What have...'

'I went to see. I didn't do anything. I got your message from Solly Bernstein, but I just had to see. Don't worry, I was in disguise. I'm getting really good at the make-up. All he'd have seen was a fifty year-old spinster, but he didn't even look at me.'

'He didn't pick anyone up?'

'I don't know. I only stayed a few minutes because I was afraid I might do something stupid if he did. I should have stayed.'

'I'm glad you didn't.'

'I'm glad you're glad, but you do agree – tomorrow could be our last chance?'

'Yes, of course, but he may not pick anyone up tomorrow.'

'Oh yes he will. Me.'

'No, absolutely not. I knew you'd think of this eventually, but it won't work. Believe me, I've thought about it too. But follow it through. If you offer yourself as bait, and let him drive you off in his car, what happens then? I can follow, but if I get too close he'll spot me, and if I don't I might lose you. And if we're incredibly lucky, and neither of those things happens, we're still left with a problem when we get wherever it is we're going. I could probably deal with Eyebrows – assuming he doesn't pull a gun, that is – but the chances are there'll be others. I can't see any way of making it work.'

She smiled at him. 'I can.'

Next morning he took the NKVD papers from his suitcase, kissed a half-awake Effi goodbye, and walked down to Zoo Station. He'd half-expected a thorough search at the Polish border, and the need for another emergency phone call to Hauptsturmführer Hirth, but his suitcase hadn't even been opened. The border authorities had been far too busy strip-searching a large family of Poles returning to their German home.

He called the SD number from the station, and rather to his surprise was put straight through to the Hauptsturmführer. When Russell suggested a lunchtime *treff* in the Tiergarten, an exasperated

Hirth told him to leave the papers in reception at 102 Wilhelmstrasse and hung up. Russell replaced the receiver, wondering what had happened. Had the Nazi-Soviet Pact rendered his supposed intelligence irrelevant, or had Hirth and Co. drawn the conclusion that caution was no longer necessary? Did he care? Chances were he would find out eventually, and probably wish he hadn't.

The garden in front of the SD building was full of roses in bloom, all much too fragrant for their owners. Russell presented his Russian envelope to the usual blonde receptionist, feeling more like a postman than an agent. She put it to one side, and went back to her reading as if he'd already gone.

Out on Wilhelmstrasse he became aware of activity on the roofs – soldiers, for the most part. A coup? he asked himself, without any real conviction. War, more likely. Thin gun barrels were also silhouetted against the blue sky – for all the much-trumpeted prowess of the Luftwaffe the regime obviously shared Frau Heidegger's fear of air attacks. The street was full of people hurrying to and fro, almost feverishly it seemed, and the Wertheim at the intersection with Leipziger Strasse was unusually crowded, the faces of emerging women full of grim satisfaction at a job accomplished. The German *hausfrau* was stocking up.

He walked on up the long canyon of grey blocks, past Goering's Air Ministry, the Reichsbahn building, Hitler's appalling new Chancellery. According to the man on the train he should be in there now, making the world a safer place for Germans. Of course, if the rumours of a nocturnal lifestyle were true, he was probably still in bed. Russell wondered what his dreams were like, whether his sleeping face was younger, more innocent. The stuff you never found in history books. The important stuff.

The Adlon Bar presented a stark contrast to the bustle outside. Slaney was sitting at his usual table, picking pastry crumbs off his tie, but the only other visible journalists were two of Mussolini's pet scribes.

'They're gone,' Slaney announced in response to Russell's bemused look. 'The Brits and French, that is. They all took trains to Denmark last night.' He lifted a large ring of keys from the table and let it drop. 'I've been left seven cars to look after.'

'Just the journalists?' Russell asked.

'Everyone but the diplomats.'

Russell sat down. 'It's coming that quickly?'

Slaney shrugged. 'Tomorrow, it looks like.'

'Christ.' It was possible, he realized, to both expect an event and be surprised when it actually happened.

'The only question is whether Hitler will waste any time trying to buy off you Brits and the French. But I don't think it'll make any difference, one way or the other. He needs a war. It's the only way he can get the last one out of his system.'

Russell said nothing. He needed to talk to Paul, he realized. The schools were still out – he might be at home.

Ilse answered. 'He's out playing football with Franz and a few other friends,' she told him. 'You could try later.'

'No, I'll be seeing him tomorrow. Ilse,' he began, not sure what to say, 'Ilse, things are not looking good. Does Paul have any real idea of what's coming, what it's going to be like?'

There was a brief silence at the other end. 'Who knows?' she said eventually. 'He says all the right things. But do any of us know, really? Matthias says the people who went through the last war will all make the mistake of expecting the same, and those that didn't won't have a clue.'

It always galled him to admit it, but Matthias was probably right. He said so.

'Why don't you ask Paul tomorrow?' Ilse suggested.

'I will. We may be at war by then.'

He hung up, took his leave of Slaney, and took a tram south to Hallesches Tor. The Hanomag was still in the courtyard, its roof devoid of obvious footmarks, and an anxious Frau Heidegger was at her usual post. She greeted him with a big smile, which made him feel good – he hadn't expected that she would hold his British ancestry against him, but you never knew.

She was, however, keen to learn the prospective enemy's intentions. 'It all seemed so clear yesterday,' she said, reaching for the dreaded coffee pot. 'Everyone thought the Pact would sort everything out. The English and the French would realize that they couldn't help the Poles, and the Poles would have to come to their senses and there'd be no need for a war. But nothing seems to have changed,' she lamented. 'The English and French won't give up their guarantee. I don't suppose they can now. It was so stupid of them to give one in the first place...'

Russell took a sip of coffee and wished he hadn't.

'When it comes down to it,' Frau Heidegger went on, 'does it really matter who owns Danzig or the Corridor? It's been twenty years and this is the first we've heard about Germans being killed in the Corridor. If they are then I suppose we have to do something about it, but it doesn't seem worth another war. Let's hope another conference can sort it out. By the way, don't forget there's another air raid rehearsal next Wednesday – Beiersdorfer will want to know if you'll be here.'

It was a timely visit from another *portierfrau* that set Russell free. He picked up a few clothes from his apartment – his entire wardrobe was moving across town, piece by piece – and headed back to the city centre in the Hanomag.

He and Slaney had only just finished lunch when two pieces of news filtered through to the waiting journalists in the Adlon Bar – the British Ambassador Sir Nevile Henderson had gone to see the Führer and, rather more significantly, all telephone and telegraphic contacts between Germany and the outside world had been cut. As one wag put it, if Henderson and Hitler emerged naked onto the Wilhelmstrasse and danced a waltz together, there was no way of telling the world.

Russell hung around, keen to know how the meeting turned out, but the Embassy refused to release a statement, let alone answer questions, and the pointlessness of remaining became increasingly obvious. That and the danger of drinking too much ahead of their appointment with Eyebrows.

He arrived home to a transformed Effi – he had to look at her twice to make sure it was her. She had, as she'd implied, become a veritable mistress of disguise. The basics had not been changed – she was still a slim, dark-haired, reasonably young and attractive woman – but everything else had been subtly shifted. Her hair seemed thicker, her eyes darker, her nose slightly larger. She looked more like a stereotypical Jewess, he thought, which was presumably the intention.

She was dressed differently too. Neatly, but austerely. Everything about her wardrobe was slightly old-fashioned, as if the world had ended in 1933. As indeed it had, in so many ways, for Germany's Jews.

And when she got up and walked around there was an awkward defensiveness in the way she moved that bore no relation to Effi's natural grace. It was uncanny. He had seen every film she had made, but never before had he realized just how good she was.

'And now for you,' she said.

They arrived at Silesian Station an hour ahead of the train's scheduled arrival time. There was no sign of Drehsen's Mercedes in its usual spot, and no sign of the man himself on the concourse. Effi took the suitcase and hurried up the steps to the platform, leaving Russell to check that the train was running and on time. It was.

He bought a newspaper and took up position

opposite the taxi rank, leaning up against the stone wall of the station. The human traffic slowly thinned as the rush hour drew to a close, the majority of faces more drawn and anxious than a Friday evening usually warranted. Most Berliners, he guessed, were going home to turn on their radios, hoping not to hear martial music and warnings of an 'important announcement'.

Fifty minutes went by with no sign of the Mercedes. Time was running out. Russell walked back into the concourse and there the man was, standing in the middle of the open space, facing the steps to the platform. Where the hell had he parked his car?

Russell hurried back out. It wasn't on the station forecourt, so where? He strode briskly down the side of the station to Koppen-Strasse, which ran under the elevated tracks at the western end. Nothing. He hesitated, looked at his watch. He only had five minutes.

A train rumbled across in the right direction, steam bellowing into the early evening sky. Too early for the Breslau train, he told himself. Another headed the same way as he walked under the bridges, this one with the reassuring hum of a Stadtbahn electric. Turning the corner he saw a short line of cars parked alongside the far side of the station. The last was a Mercedes Cabriolet, but it carried the wrong number.

Russell started running. The station side seemed to stretch forever, and he had a painful stitch in his side by the time he reached its end. Turning into Frucht-Strasse, which ran eastwards under the tracks, he saw the car. It was parked on the far corner, in – as Russell ruefully realized – the very next place that Drehsen would have tried if his usual spot had been occupied.

He was out of time, and a train was steaming into the station above him, thundering over the bridge. As he reached the car a couple of girls, prostitutes probably, walked across the end of the street, the click of their heels amplified by the iron ceiling. He stopped for a second, as if searching his pockets for cigarettes, and caught sight of a man with a moustache and slicked-back hair in the black window of a defunct shop. It was himself.

The girls gone, he took another look round, crouched down, and stabbed the driver's side front tyre with the awl Effi had purchased that morning. There was a commendably violent hiss, and the tyre began deflating. From his other pocket he drew a small package of newspaper, gingerly removed the sharp piece of bottle glass it contained, and placed it just behind the wounded tyre. The temptation to disable the spare tyre as well, and make absolutely sure, was almost overwhelming, but he knew that would look too suspicious.

He ran down the southern side of the station, paused outside the entrance to regain his breath, and slipped back into the covered concourse through the stream of exiting passengers. Drehsen was standing in the same spot, his eyes now fixed on Effi. She was standing beside her suitcase some thirty metres away, a few paces from the bottom of the steps, anxiously scanning the concourse for her imaginary welcomer. She looked both lost and slightly angry, as if she was about to burst into tears.

Drehsen moved towards her almost apologetically, a hawk turning into a friendly owl. As she caught sight of him a hint of hope crossed Effi's face.

He let her speak first, and knowing what she intended to say, Russell had no trouble reading her lips: 'Have you come from my uncle?'

Drehsen smiled like an uncle's friend would, said a few words, and reached, almost tentatively for the suitcase. She hesitated for a second, then smiled gratefully back. He gestured towards the exit.

Russell followed them out. As they headed down the side of the station towards Frucht-Strasse he crossed the busy road beyond the taxi rank and headed along the opposite pavement, looking for any sort of concealed vantage point. He found one of the ubiquitous *Der Stürmer* display cabinets standing almost opposite Frucht-Strasse, and stood there pretending to enjoy the usual cartoons about Jewish bakers draining the blood from Christian children to make their *matzoh*.

Drehsen and Effi had reached the Mercedes, which she seemed to be admiring. He had opened the back door but Effi, as they had agreed, was insisting on sitting up front. Drehsen shrugged, put the suitcase on the back seat, and opened the front door for her. She got in.

He walked round to the driver's side and was reaching for the door handle when he saw the flat tyre. He got down on his haunches, picked up and examined the piece of glass, and dropped it again. He squatted there for a moment, presumably considering his options. Would he go for the spare?

He opened the driver's door and leaned in, talking to Effi. Was he suggesting a taxi? If not, then she would be. The exchange seemed to last a long time, but eventually he straightened his back, closed the door and went to retrieve the suitcase from the back seat. Effi got back out, and Russell found himself sighing with relief.

She and Drehsen walked back towards the taxi rank in the station forecourt, Russell keeping pace on the opposite pavement. The queue for taxis had evaporated and three were waiting in line. The driver of the leading cab took the suitcase from Drehsen and opened the rear door for Effi. Drehsen said something to him and got in on the other side.

Russell was around thirty metres ahead, close to the western throat of the forecourt. As the taxi pulled out he rushed diagonally across the road towards it, waving frantically. The driver slammed on his brakes, swerved to the right and ground to a halt inches from the kerb.

Effi erupted from the taxi. 'Uncle Fritz!' she cried happily.

'Magda,' he said. 'I'm so sorry. I was held up.'

She explained the situation to the driver, and apologised profusely for losing him his spot at the head of the line. Drehsen climbed slowly out of the back, seemingly unsure what to do, and exchanged glances with Russell. Making up his mind, he touched his cap to Effi and walked back into the station without another word.

It was what they had expected – after all, what else could he do? – but the coolness with which he did it was breathtaking.

Russell took the suitcase and they began walking the short distance to Breslauer Strasse, where he had left the Hanomag. Putting an arm round Effi's shoulder, he realized she was shaking. He stopped, put the suitcase down and enfolded her in a hug. She took a huge deep breath.

'All right?' he asked after a while.

'Yes,' she said. 'What a creepy man. And so convincing...'

'Did it work?' Russell interrupted her.

'Oh yes, it did. He told the cabbie Eisenacher Strasse and my heart sank, but the cabbie – God bless him – asked what number. It's 403. We were lucky really. If it hadn't been such a long street he'd never have asked.'

'You did wonderfully.'

'You too.' She reached up to kiss him. 'But the sooner we can dispense with the moustache, the better.'

'First things first,' he said, picking up the suitcase. 'We can take a look at 403 Eisenacher Strasse while Drehsen's getting his tyre changed.'

'He wanted me to wait while he changed it. And he didn't like the idea of a taxi. I had to get quite hysterical before he agreed.'

Eisenacher Strasse ran north to south across Schöneberg for almost two kilo-metres. Number 403 was a third of the way down, one of a row of detached three-storey houses immediately above Barbarossaplatz. It was impossible to tell which house it was – the sun had set and all were silhouetted against a deep red sky. On the other side of the road, bathed in reddish light, were a typing college and a small bookbinding factory. This part of Schöneberg had seen better days, but it still represented a considerable step up from Neukölln or Wedding. There were no tram-tracks, and not much traffic, but several modest-looking cars were parked in the spaces between the detached houses.

There was no way of stopping without drawing attention to themselves. Russell drove on to Barbarossa Platz, took the third exit, and pulled the car to a halt. 'Let's take a walk,' he said.

Three right turns brought them back onto Eisenacher Strasse, some two hundred metres above the row of houses. There were several other pedestrians on the pavement, and they fell in some twenty metres behind a uniformed young man and his girlfriend. The pair walked ever so slowly, as if intent on stretching out their time together.

The college and factory were in darkness but most of the houses had one or two lighted windows, some curtained, some not. 403 was the third from the end. Every window was curtained, and all showed lines of light. In the parking space alongside, two vehicles were drawn up, and there were two uniformed men talking in the front seats of the one nearer to the road. As they walked past one looked up, caught Russell's eye, and seemed to move them on with an almost involuntary twitch of the head.

'How,' Effi asked, when they'd walked another few paces, 'are we going to find out what's inside?'

'God knows.'

'One more look,' Effi suggested, as they reached the Hanomag.

'Why not? It's dark enough.'

Their persistence was rewarded. As the Hanomag drew level with the house the front door swung inwards, spilling yellow light down the steps to the street, and framing two uniformed men. There was a glimpse of shiny boots descending, a muffled shout of farewell. Effi twisted round in her seat to catch them under the streetlight and identify the black uniforms. 'SS,' she said, turning the consonants into a hiss.

'What a surprise,' Russell murmured. 'And emerging, unless I'm very much mistaken, from a brothel.'

'Oh no.'

'It could be a lot worse. If it is a brothel, then there's a good chance that Miriam is still alive.'

Russell woke early on Saturday morning, shut the door on the still-sleeping Effi, and waited heart in mouth as her People's Radio warmed up. When the strains of one of Beethoven's lighter sonatas emerged, he clicked off the set with a sigh of relief. No war had begun.

He went down to the Adlon to find out why.

According to the small coterie of American journalists already gathered in the bar, the answer was far from obvious. There were rumours that Mussolini had abandoned his buddy, rumours that Hitler had offered to guarantee the British Empire in return for a free hand in eastern Europe. If the latter rumours were true the Führer had already had his answer – the previous afternoon the Brits and Poles had finally formalized the British guarantee as a pact of mutual assistance.

All in all, it looked as though Hitler had pulled back from the brink. The British Ambassador had travelled to London, presumably with something new to communicate, and the telephone and telegraph connections with the outside word had been restored in the early hours of the morning. Berlin's foreign press corps could again tell the world that they hadn't a clue what was going on.

There were no Foreign Office briefings to help them out, no press releases to interpret. Russell telephoned several contacts, all of whom proved less than communicative. His colleagues had much the same experience – German officials, it seemed, were loth to confirm or deny the dates of their own birthdays. Russell wrote out his version of what was happening and wired it off, aware that it would be overtaken by events long before it reached the newspaper bins around San Francisco's Union Square.

He had lunch with Slaney – who, for the first time since Russell had met him, seemed subdued by the weight of events – and headed out to Grünewald for his Saturday afternoon with Paul. The boy was waiting by the gate, dressed, for once, in normal clothes.

'No *Jungvolk* meeting?' Russell asked as his son

got into the car.

'Yes, there was, but it ended early. I had time to change.'

He'd had time before, and hadn't changed, but Russell decided not to probe. 'What shall we do?'

'Can we just go for a drive? Out of the city, I mean. Take a walk in the woods or something.'

'All right.' Russell thought for a moment. 'How about the Brauhausberg?' he asked. They could take the Avus Speedway most of the way, and take one of the southbound exits before Potsdam.

'That would be good,' Paul agreed, though without a great deal of enthusiasm. 'If America comes into the war, will you be arrested?' he asked abruptly.

Russell waited at a crossroads while a line of troop lorries drove past. 'No, I'd just have to leave Germany. Like the British and French journalists have done.'

'They've left already?' Paul blurted out, obviously surprised.

'On Thursday, most of them. The rest yesterday. But they may be back. And in any case, there's no chance of America coming into the war. You really don't need to worry about me.'

'Joachim's already gone,' Paul said.

'When?'

'A few days ago.'

'Where?'

'They won't tell the families that,' Paul said, sounding surprised at his father's stupidity.

'No, no, of course not.' He wondered how Thomas and Hanna were coping with their son's call-up. He should have phoned them.

They were on the Speedway now, and Russell was surprised by the volume of traffic. Cars full of families heading out for a day in the sunshine, anywhere beyond the reach of their radios and the city's loudspeakers. If they didn't get the dreadful news until evening, then that was one more day of peace they'd grabbed from their government.

'Do you think England will really go to war for Danzig?' Paul wanted to know.

'I think they'll stand by Poland.'

'But why? Danzig is German. And it's not England's fight.'

'Maybe not. But the English can't break their word again. And it's not about Danzig. Not really.' He expected Paul to ask what it really was about, but he didn't. He already knew.

'We've been doing a project on the victory in Spain,' Paul said, 'and how important the Luftwaffe was. They'll bomb London, won't they?'

'I expect so.'

'And the English air force will bomb us.'

'Yes.'

Paul was silent for more than a minute, looking out of the window and, Russell guessed, picturing a sky full of English bombers. 'It will be terrible, won't it?' Paul said eventually, as if he'd suddenly realized what a war could do.

Russell didn't know whether to be glad or sad.

'You never talk about your war,' Paul said almost accusingly. 'I used to think it was because you fought for England and you didn't want to

368

upset people here, but it's not that, is it?'

'No, it's not.' He wondered what he should say, what he *could* say to a twelve-year-old boy and have him understand it. The truth, he supposed. 'It's because, in a war, you see what damage people can do to each other.' He paused for breath, like a man about to walk through fire. 'Exploding bodies,' he said deliberately, 'limbs torn off, more blood than you can imagine. The look in a man's eyes when he knows he's about to die. The smell of rotting human flesh. People without a scratch whose minds will never be the same again. The constant fear that it'll happen to you. The terrible knowledge that you'd rather it happened to anyone else.' He breathed in again. 'These are not things you want to remember, let alone share.' He glanced sideways to check Paul's reaction, and saw, for the first time, pity in his son's eyes.

What have I done? Russell asked himself, but over the next couple of hours, as the two of them walked and talked their way along the wooded paths of the Brauhausberg, Paul seemed more his usual self, as if some sort of burden had been lifted. Or perhaps it was just the sunshine though the leaves, the birdsong and the leaping squirrels, the mere insistence of life. There was no way the boy could have any real notion of the enormity of what was coming, and perhaps that was a blessing. Sometimes knowledge set you free, as one old comrade used to say, but sometimes it locked you up.

During the hours with his son Russell hardly

spared a thought for Miriam Rosenfeld or 403 Eisenacher Strasse. Effi, he discovered on reaching home, had not been so fortunate. She had set aside the afternoon for evaluating a film script – an ensemble piece about soldier's wives in Berlin during the Great War – but had found the necessary concentration hard to come by. 'I can't stop thinking about her,' she said angrily. 'It's driving me crazy. I'm sure there are people being beaten to death in the concentration camps all the time, but they don't haunt me. Maybe they should, but they don't. Nor do all the children starving in Africa. But I can't stop thinking about one girl in a Schöneberg brothel. I can't get her out of my mind.'

Russell poured the two of them a drink.

'And you know what else I realized,' she continued. 'They're Jews. The girls will all be Jews. Jews for the SS to fuck.'

'Maybe.'

'No, definitely. Don't you see? Blonde is good. Blonde is worthy. Blonde is about pure love and motherhood and child-breeding. There's no place for pleasure in any of that, no sensuality. It's all about duty. Dark, on the other hand, is bad and dirty and unworthy. Dark is all about pleasure. I see the way most of these creeps look at me, as if I must be able to give them something they can't get at home. And Jewish girls are the darkest of the dark, the ultimate forbidden fruit. Who would the SS want more?'

'You're probably right,' Russell said, 'but what can we do?'

'We have to get Miriam out. And the others.'

'But how? We can't storm the place. We can't knock on the door and tell them we don't approve. We can't go to the police.'

'How about going over their heads?' Effi suggested. 'Write to Himmler. I could probably get a meeting with Goebbels after the way he drooled all over me at the Universum.'

Russell shook his head. 'I think they'd decide it was easier to shut us up than shut the brothel down.'

'All right. You told me you know the people who produce the anti-Nazi leaflets. Could we persuade them to publicise the place? Let the whole of Berlin know what their aryan knights are up to. Shame the bastards.'

Russell grunted. 'They have no shame.'

'They must want to protect their reputation,' Effi protested.

'Maybe. But if the girls are Jews then they'll have broken the law by having sex with non-Jews.'

'Not by choice!'

'Of course not, but what Nazi court would find them innocent? They might convict a couple of SS officers for form's sake, but their punishment would be a slap on the wrist. The girls would go to Ravensbrück. It sounds a terrible thing to say, but they'd be better off staying where they are.'

'Oh John.'

'I know, but... Look, I'll tell Thomas the whole story tomorrow. Maybe he'll have an idea.'

They went out to eat on the Ku'damm, then drove across town to the dance hall they'd found a few weeks earlier, but it wasn't the same. Effi

371

insisted on their driving down Eisenacher Strasse one more time, but there was nothing new to see. 'What can we do?' she murmured to herself several times, putting different emphases on the four words, but neither she nor he could think of an answer. It was after one in the morning when Russell had the first glimmering of an idea. One good enough to wake her.

Effi was excited by his plan in the dead of night, but more subdued than usual when morning came. It seemed to Russell that there were two new Effis he had to get used to: the one who seemed to take their new situation far too lightly, as if it were a game with no real consequences, and the one sitting beside him now in the sunlit Tiergarten, who took it all far more seriously than he had ever imagined. Both Effis, he realized, had been there all the time, but the latter in particular still needed getting used to.

It was, he admitted, hard to sustain an acute sense of peril when housemaids wheeled their prams through hopping squirrels, and hard to take the world seriously when the front page of the *Beobachter* was almost all headline: 'Whole of Poland in War Fever! 1,500,000 men mobilized! Uninterrupted troop transport towards the frontier! Chaos in Upper Silesia!' Skimming through the editorial Russell noted an escalation of demands – not just Danzig and the Corridor but all the territories that Germany had lost in 1918.

Around eleven o'clock Effi set off for Wilmersdorf and a long-arranged family lunch. Russell had also intended to go, but work and the matter of Miriam's rescue seemed a lot more pressing. He arrived at the Adlon Bar to find it buzzing with an unconfirmed rumour that some German units had actually advanced into Poland on the previous Friday morning. An invasion had apparently been scheduled, and news of its cancellation had not reached the units in question. More significantly, as the journalists discovered at an Economics Ministry press briefing that morning, food rationing was starting the following day. The cards had been sent out a couple of weeks earlier, but Russell suspected that their activation would still come as a salutary shock to most Germans.

Frau Heidegger hadn't heard the news when he reached Neuenburger Strasse, and he wasn't about to spoil her morning. He did accept her offer of coffee with more inner enthusiasm than usual, because he was keen to confirm that her set of apartment keys was still hanging in its usual place by the door. She only had one item of mail for him – a formal letter from the US Embassy advising all Americans whose presence was not absolutely necessary to leave Germany. He wasn't expecting anything from the SD or NKVD, and he assumed Sarah Grostein would make contact when she had something for him.

On the way up to his room he knocked on Beiersdorfer's door, and told the block warden he didn't yet know whether he'd be home for the ARP exercise on Thursday. He would let him know on Tuesday. Beiersdorfer sighed, and reminded Russell that the weekly Party meeting

373

was on Tuesday evenings, causing him to be out between seven and nine.

He had phoned Thomas from the Adlon and been invited to lunch. The family mood, as expected, was coloured by Joachim's absence – Thomas looked drained, his wife Hanna seemed withdrawn, and their fifteen-year-old daughter Lotte was trying rather too hard to cheer them up. They ate in the sunny garden, but it felt all too different from the last such gathering, on the eve of Russell's trip to Prague. The first member of their extended family was gone. How many others would follow?

Afterwards, in the cool of Thomas's study, he told his friend about 403 Eisenacher Strasse and his plan for freeing its inmates.

Thomas was shocked, and surprised that he was. 'Are you sure you've got it right?' he asked.

'One missing girl. A man who approached her and others at Silesian Station. People who can use the police to prevent any investigation. A house with every window lit and SS officers coming down the steps. The same house our man was taking Effi to. Can you think of another explanation that fits?'

'No.'

'And if by any chance we have got it wrong, and the place is full of SS manicurists and etiquette tutors, we'll just leave them on the pavement.'

Thomas looked lost. 'I didn't mean...' he began.

'You were right,' Russell told him. 'About saving one life.'

Thomas grunted. 'How can I help?'

'I need a small van and a lorry. With full tanks, and without Schade Printing Works emblazoned all over them.'

'That shouldn't be a problem. But what...'

'Don't ask. If it ever comes back to you, just say I asked for the loan of the vehicles.'

'I feel I should be doing more.'

'You're doing enough already. I sometimes think you're providing the Jews of Berlin with half their income.'

After arranging to pick up the two vehicles on the following evening Russell drove north into Fried-richshain. The streets around Büsching Platz looked even more run-down than he remembered, and Büsching-Strasse was no exception. He drove slowly past the address Freya Isendahl had given him, looking out for any sign that the block was being watched, but the only humans in sight were two young children playing Heaven and Earth on the opposite pavement. He parked the car fifty metres further down, hoping that the mere presence of motorised transport would not be enough to provoke curiosity.

The Isendahls, he discovered, shared a fourth floor flat with another couple. They were comrades, according to Wilhelm, but Russell was still pleased they were out. Wilhelm and Freya's room was large, low-ceilinged, with distant views of Friedrichshain park. Russell glanced around, and was relieved by the lack of seditious leaflets on display. The room was certainly crowded, but there was nothing to suggest it was anything other than the first home of a young couple struggling to make ends meet.

Wilhelm offered him the single battered arm-chair, removing the copy of Rilke's *Duino Elegies* which was perched on one arm. Freya put a saucepan of water on the electric ring to make tea.

'Has my article been printed?' Wilhelm asked, taking one of the two upright chairs. Even in blue overalls he managed to look vaguely aristocratic.

Russell admitted that it hadn't, that he was still looking for a safe way to get it out of Germany. He asked about the situation on the Siemens shopfloor, which kept Wilhelm talking until the tea was made.

'I need your help with something else,' Russell said once Freya was seated. He told them the story of his search for Miriam Rosenfeld, from her original disappearance to her probable imprisonment in the house on Eisenacher Strasse. They both listened intently, Wilhelm's face growing grimmer as Freya's eyes brimmed with unshed tears.

Russell explained his plan for getting the girls out, realizing as he did so that this was one of Sarah Grostein's life and death moments, when you opened yourself up to the possibility of betrayal. 'It's very simple,' he said in summary. 'On the day of the exercise – that's next Wednesday, the 30th – we turn up disguised as an ARP patrol, declare that the building has been hit by a bomb, and order everyone out. Even the SS have to obey ARP instructions, so we shouldn't have any trouble. We just separate the men from the girls, say we'll be back for the men, and drive away with the girls.'

'What do you want us to do?' Wilhelm asked.

'I need at least three more people to make it realistic. Can you drive?'

'Of course.'

'Then I'd like you to drive the ambulance.'

'Where are you going to get one of those?'

'I've been promised a vehicle, which I'll pick up tomorrow.'

'Do they use ordinary vans as ambulances? I've never seen...'

'They do. I was attached to a squad during the last rehearsal. They just paint the usual cross on them. And I'll be getting you some paint. Do you have anywhere we can keep the van? Out of sight, I mean.'

'I can find somewhere.'

'Good. And if you can get hold of any stretchers, that would be a bonus. The more details we get right the more convincing we'll be.'

'What will I do?' Freya asked.

Russell hesitated, expecting Wilhelm to oppose her participation, but he looked every bit as interested in her prospective role as she did.

'You could be a second nurse,' he suggested, hoping that Effi could get hold of two uniforms. It would be good to have two women, if only to inspire trust in the rescued girls. But another two men were needed, if only to intimidate the uncooperative.

'I can get them,' Wilhelm said. 'I know half a dozen who'd be more than willing to join us.'

'Jews?'

'Yes.'

'Then choose the ones who look least Jewish,' Russell said bluntly. 'We may have to order the SS around,' he added in explanation, 'and we can't afford the slightest doubt that we're who we say we are.'

'Understood,' Wilhelm said, ignoring the outraged expression on his non-Jewish wife's face. He asked Russell how much he knew about ARP procedures, seemed relieved by the answer, and agreed to bring two volunteers to a meeting in Friedrichshain park the following evening.

Russell drove back across the city feeling more confident than he'd expected – Wilhelm Isendahl was an impressive young man. He felt a little guilty at luring Freya into danger – this was hardly what her parents had had in mind when they asked him to make contact with their daughter. But she was no longer a child, and they were a long way away. He felt a surge of wholly unreasonable anger towards them, safe in their Brooklyn brownstone on the other side of an ocean.

He arrived home to find Effi taping black paper across the windows ahead of Monday's trial black-out. 'It seemed like a bad week to get arrested,' she explained.

The next few days were busy. Doing his job, and keeping abreast of all the rumours circulating Berlin's corridors of power and influence, left precious few hours for organizing what seemed, in his less optimistic moments, like a particularly bizarre method of committing suicide.

On Monday afternoon he drove up to Hunder's

378

garage in Wedding, bought a full tank of petrol for the Hanomag and hired a parking space for Thomas's van. Hunder raised one oil-streaked eyebrow at the latter request, but didn't ask any questions. Russell found himself wondering whether Hunder was a secret comrade like his cousin Zembski, and hoping, if he was, that it wouldn't prove relevant.

He drove back across the city to Neukölln, beating the rush hour but leaving himself an hour to wait before the Schade Printing Works emptied out. Thomas showed him the vehicles and handed over the keys, refraining from expressing the anxieties all too obvious in his eyes. Russell drove the lorry north to Hunder's, slowly getting used to its size and controls. After leaving it in the designated spot he walked to Lehrter Station for the convoluted train journey back. It would have been easier to get Wilhelm to collect the van, but Russell didn't want anyone else knowing of Thomas's part in the operation.

It was almost seven by the time he got back to the printing works, but it only took him fifteen minutes to reach the large hospital on Palisaden-Strasse in the van. He parked across from the emergency department entrance and drew a rough copy of the ambulance cross in his note-book. It was one of those symbols that everyone recognized, Effi had said, but that everyone found hard to replicate from memory.

The Friedrichshain park was only a few minutes away. He left the van close to the gates and walked up to the agreed rendezvous point. Wilhelm was waiting with two young men, whom he introduced as Max and Erich. Neither looked particularly Jewish, and both had an undoubted physical presence. The four of them sat on a bench discussing meeting times, clothes and – something that Russell realized with a shock he had barely considered – what they would do with the rescued women. 'We can find Jewish families who will take them in for a few days,' Wilhelm announced. 'And after that we can see about getting them back to wherever they came from.'

When they had finished and the new recruits had headed off towards a different gate, Russell handed Wilhelm the key of the van. 'There are cans of red and white paint in the back,' he said, handing over the sketch he had drawn. Wilhelm looked amused, but placed it in his pocket. Russell watched him drive off in the direction of the Central Stockyards, where an unnamed relation had promised him use of a garage.

It was getting dark by the time he reached the West End, and the blacked-out Ku'damm looked like a vast railway tunnel. This time he found Effi stitching together pieces of cloth. 'I could only get one uniform,' she said. 'I couldn't think of a good reason for needing two' she added in explanation.

'What reason did you give for the one?'

'That my boyfriend likes playing doctors and nurses.'

Russell's first visit on Tuesday was to the American Embassy. The official letter recommending departure from Germany seemed an ideal excuse in the event that one should prove necessary, and he felt it wise to explain his lack of progress in contacting the men on Washington's list. This was no time to lose his American passport.

A harassed-looking Michael Brown listened to his excuses – that reporting the international crisis was both dictating his whereabouts and taking up all of his time – and blithely told him not to worry. 'Probably better to get this present business out of the way,' he said, presumably alluding to Poland. 'Wait for things to settle down again.'

Russell wholeheartedly agreed.

Dropping in at the Adlon, he found what remained of the foreign press corps twiddling its collective thumbs. The 'present business' showed no signs of resolution, but none of escalation either. The diplomatic channels between England, France, Poland and Germany were doubtless buzzing with activity, but none of the relevant governments were giving anything away. Rumour had it that the Germans had insisted on a Polish plenipotentiary coming to Berlin, and that England and France had pressed the Poles to send one. The Poles, mindful that a Czech President answering a similar summons had almost been bullied into a heart attack, were not racing to comply.

All of which was thoroughly irritating for the journalists. 'No-shows,' as one of the Americans pithily exclaimed, were 'no-news'.

Russell hung around until mid-afternoon, then went to meet Wilhelm Isendahl in the Alexanderplatz Station buffet. The young man was already there, gazing round at his fellow customers with a superior smile. As a closet Jew in a *judenfrei* establishment he could be forgiven, Russell thought.

They brought each other up to date with their respective preparations. Everything was going smoothly, which seemed far too good to be true. Wilhelm went off with Effi's paper-wrapped needlework clasped under one arm and Russell sat with a second cup of coffee, running another mental dress rehearsal in search of potential flaws. He found none, and wondered why that didn't seem more reassuring.

Driving south to Hallesches Tor he ate an early supper at his usual bar, listening to the U-bahn trains clattering their way in and out of the station above. At around eight he drew up in the Neuenburger Strasse courtyard and cut the engine. The sound of several women, all seemingly talking and laughing at once, filled the silence. Frau Heidegger's weekly skat night with her fellow-*portierfrauen* was well underway.

Her doors were open as usual. He walked through, causing all four women to look up. Frau Heidegger's smile of welcome was not echoed by her skat partners, who offered expressions ranging from irritation to outright hostility. He had, he guessed, committed two major sins – he had interrupted their game and been born English.

'Don't get up,' he reassured a struggling Frau Heidegger. 'I just wanted to leave a message for Beiersdorfer – I won't be here on Wednesday.'

'I'll tell him, Herr Russell.'

'Please, go on with your game,' Russell told the assembled company with a wide smile. He watched for a moment, waited until they were concentrating on their cards, and slowly backed away. As he passed through Frau Heidegger's open front door he slipped the ring of keys off its hook.

He walked up to his own apartment, found an old sweater to wrap Beiersdorfer's ARP helmet in, and came back down to the first floor landing. He stood outside the door for a few seconds, hearing nothing within. Should he knock to make absolutely sure the man was out? No, he decided – it was better to take a slight risk than make a telling noise. The keys were neatly labelled with their apartment numbers and there was no sound of anyone on the stairs. He let himself in.

The apartment was in utter darkness – Beiersdorfer had rigged up blackout curtains that Dracula would have found comforting. Russell found the light switch and began looking for the man's helmet and arm-band. He tried the bedroom first, seduced by the idea of Beiersdorfer trying them on at his dressing table mirror, but eventually found them in a less fanciful place, in the box seat by the front door.

He had just removed the items when footsteps sounded on the stairs. He reached for the light, then realized that turning it off would look more suspicious than leaving it on. It sounded like two people, which probably meant Dagmar and Siggi, or Dagmar and whoever the other one was. Her familiar giggle came from almost outside the door, confirming his guess. The sound of feet receded upwards.

Russell wrapped the helmet in the sweater and

stood there, ear pressed against the wood, until he heard the reassuring click of Dagmar's latch. He re-locked the door, took his booty out to the car, and went back in to return the keys. A sudden peal of laughter from inside Frau Heidegger's flat made him jump, but the skat players were far too absorbed in their entertainment to notice his hand reach across the necessary inches and replace the borrowed ring on its hook.

Back in the car, giving his heart time to slow down, he realized he should have risked taking the keys without advertising his presence to Frau Heidegger. Because what would Beiersdorfer do when he found his stuff was missing?

Russell groaned as he realized he had made a second mistake. By locking the door when he left he'd as much as signalled that it was an inside job. He should have broken the lock somehow. Beiersdorfer would go straight to Frau Heidegger, the only other source of a key. Would she put two and two together? Perhaps. And if she did, would she say anything? She did loathe the man.

Should he go back in? Or would that be a third mistake? He decided it might. With any luck, Beiersdorfer wouldn't realize his stuff was missing until the ARP exercise started, and then he'd too busy to make trouble for the rest of the evening and night. And by mid-morning his precious things would be at the bottom of a canal. He could huff and puff all he wanted.

Russell headed back to the Adlon for his final felony of the night. Leaving the Hanomag on Unter den Linden, he slipped around the side of the hotel and into the dimly-lit parking lot at its rear. The cars left in Slaney's care were lined up along the far wall, each bearing Embassy stickers in the corners of their windscreens. Crouched out of sight behind them, Russell carefully unscrewed four of the number plates.

Wednesday passed slowly, for both Russell and the Führer. The latter was supposedly waiting for a Polish plenipotentiary to bully, but the cynics at the Adlon had him hoping that none would show up. 'The war's a done deal,' Slaney said. 'The bastard's just waiting for a decent excuse.'

Russell had more immediate worries. Who and what were they going to find in the house on Eisenacher Strasse, always assuming that they got there without being stopped and arrested for impersonating an ARP unit? Would the uniforms and vehicles be convincing? Would the latter be reliable? Would someone make a mistake, say the wrong thing, panic? Would he? By mid-afternoon, when the sirens announced the beginning of the exercise, his mental list of things that might go wrong would have covered several sheets of paper.

How, he asked himself, had he involved Effi in something so dangerous?

She seemed oblivious to the possibility of failure, and was happily applying the first touches of her make-up when he set off, soon after four, for Hunder's garage in Wedding. He was half expecting to get caught in an imaginary air-raid, and have to spend time in a shelter, but his luck held. He had contrived to leave the Schade Printing Works lorry in a distant corner of Hunder's yard, and now parked the Hanomag in front, masking the lorry from anyone watching in the garage office. Suitably screened, he removed the lorry's number plates and screwed on those he had taken from the Adlon parking lot. If anyone compared them they would be in for a surprise, but it didn't seem likely.

He fixed slitted pieces of black cloth to the lorry's headlights, drove it out of its corner, and put the Hanomag in its place. Hunder had promised to leave the gates unpadlocked that night, but Russell thought it worth double-checking. 'Yes, yes,' the garage-owner confirmed, looking up briefly from what looked like accounts.

Russell drove the lorry back towards the Ku'damm, leaving it outside one of the old Jewish workshops near the Savigny Platz Stadtbahn station. The business had been 'aryanised' in 1938, and there was a fair chance that passersby would assume the lorry was there on official business. As he walked the few hundred metres to Effi's flat the sirens began to sound. Just like last time, he thought – a first imaginary raid at around six. With any luck the second would also follow the previous pattern, and begin a couple of hours after dark.

He and Effi ignored the call to the nearby shelter, and judging by the lack of activity in their rapidly darkening street so did most of their neighbours. Effi, in any case, would have surprised a few of them. She had put on ten years while Russell was out, her eyes and mouth slightly lined, her tightly-bound hair suffused with grey. She was also, as she showed on standing, noticeably plumper. 'Padding,' she explained, pressing

386

down on the nurse's uniform. She ordered Russell onto the dressing table stool.

It took her half an hour to recreate 'Uncle Fritz', this time with a slightly more military moustache. Examining himself in the mirror, complete with overalls, armband and helmet, Russell had to admit he looked different. 'I would recognize you,' Effi said, standing beside him, 'and Paul probably would. But no one else. Especially in the dark.'

The all-clear sounded just before seven-thirty. It was virtually dark now, and with the black-out regulations strictly in force it was hard to make out the buildings on the other side of the street. Earlier that day Russell had checked the weather and moon for the coming night – a clear sky was expected, with a quarter-moon rising soon after midnight. By that time, he hoped, everyone concerned would be safe in bed.

The two of them drank some warmed-up soup, and watched the clock tick slowly by. Eight-thirty – the Isendahls and their two friends should be setting out from Friedrichshain. Eight forty-five, and it was time for them to leave. Effi put a summer coat over the nurse's uniform, and Russell packed his helmet and armband in an old carpet bag. They walked downstairs and out into the night.

It really was dark, much darker, Russell thought, than during the previous exercise, and by the time they found the lorry he was beginning to wonder if they would ever find anything else. But the white-painted kerbs and the slitted beams of light did make a difference, and once they reached the Ku'damm it became clear that visibility was better on the bigger streets. All those cracks of lights added up, Russell guessed. He could think of no other reason.

It took them about ten minutes to reach their destination, a stretch of road by the Landwehr-kanal, close to the Lichtenstein Bridge which connected the Zoo and the Tiergarten. Russell drove slowly past the vehicle that was already parked there, and made out the cross on its side.

He u-turned the lorry at the intersection with Rauch-Strasse and pulled up behind the fake ambulance. As he climbed down there was a loud screech from inside the Zoo.

'The animals don't like the darkness,' Wilhelm said, materialising out of it. He had managed to get himself an armband, and so, Russell dis-covered, had Max and Erich. And in this light Freya's uniform looked very convincing. After introducing Effi to the others as Magda, Russell said as much.

'We fooled one policeman already,' Wilhelm said. 'He came past about ten minutes ago, and wanted to know what we were doing here. I told him we were waiting for our commander, that he'd brought his son on the first callout and was dropping him off at home between air raids. He believed me, thank God. I didn't want to shoot him.'

'You have a gun?'

'Of course.'

Russell didn't know what to say. He could hardly blame the man, but... 'Only in the last resort,' he insisted.

'Of course.'

Russell handed him the two spare number plates and a screwdriver, and held the torch as Wilhelm swapped them with the ones on the van. Once that was done, he addressed the assembled company, feeling like a gang-leader in a bad Hollywood film. 'All right. So we know what we're doing. We set off when the next raid begins, or at eleven if it still hasn't started. Max and Erich will come with me, Magda will travel in the ambulance with Wilhelm and Freya. No second names – the less we know about each other the better.'

They had less time to wait than Russell expected. Shortly before ten o'clock the roar of aeroplane engines brought forth the sirens, and these in their turn triggered a cacophony of screams, mewls and roars from the occupants of the neighbouring Zoo. Seconds later the flash of anti-aircraft fire from a nearby roof caused even more consternation, and Russell was convinced he heard the trumpeting of an elephant. As another volley of skybound blanks threw spasms of light across the road and canal they moved off in convoy, the lorry leading the way.

It was little more than a kilometre to the top end of Eisenacher Strasse, but the lack of lighting restricted their pace to a near crawl, and Russell had to circle Lützow-Platz twice before he found the right exit. Once on Eisenacher Strasse it was a matter of judging distance, and trying to recognize familiar landmarks. Russell was beginning to worry that he had come too far when he spotted the sawtooth roof of the bookbinding factory.

He pulled up alongside the row of houses

opposite and climbed down, just as a flight of planes flew noisily over. In the silence that followed faint voices and music were audible, and as his eyes grew more accustomed to the darkness he saw cracks of light where windows must be. The slitted beam of his torch revealed the number of the building in front of him. It was 403.

There was no noise from within, which seemed like good news. He walked round the corner of the building and found an empty space where the cars had stood. That *was* good news.

The others had gathered on the pavement, and the combined light of their muted torches created a pocket of half-light. A collective halo, Russell thought. How fitting.

He walked up the steps to the front door and used the brass door-knocker, loud enough, or so he hoped, to bring a reaction without rousing the curiosity of the whole street.

No one answered.

He banged again, louder this time. Beside him, Effi looked anxious.

This time there was a response. Footsteps inside, the click of a bolt being drawn back, a spillage of light as the door edged open.

Russell shoved his way through, causing a cry of consternation from within. Effi and Wilhelm followed. 'Air Raid Protection,' Russell barked at the man who was struggling back to his feet. 'This house has been bombed. I want everybody out. Now.'

'That's not possible,' the man said, but there was a welcome lack of certainty in his tone. Thin, balding and bespectacled, he was wearing a bizarre mixture of clothes, a civilian shirt and tie with police trousers and boots. 'You do know that this is SS property?' he almost pleaded.

'I don't care whose it is,' Russell told him. 'Targets are chosen at random, and it's a criminal offence to obstruct an Air Raid Protection unit in the course of its duties. Now, what is your name?

It was Sternkopf.

'Well, Herr Sternkopf, how many people are there in this house?'

'Four. Five including me.'

'How many women?'

'Four.'

Russell breathed an inner sigh of relief. 'Get the other lads,' he told Wilhelm. They had decided beforehand that the two of them would deal with any outside interference while Max and Erich searched the house.

'I must telephone Standartenführer Gründel,' Sternkopf was saying.

Russell rounded on him. 'Herr Sternkopf, this is a serious exercise. If British bombers do attack Berlin there'll be no time to make telephone calls. Now please, this way.'

Sternkopf hesitated, but only for a second, as Russell escorted him outside. Max and Erich, who passed them on the steps, had already laid out the half-dozen stretchers which Wilhelm had borrowed from one of the few remaining Jewish clinics in Friedrichshain.

'Lie down on one of these,' Russell ordered. Sternkopf did so, and Freya hung a home-made placard around his neck that bore the words 'severe head injury'. She then squeezed some of the fake blood that Effi had borrowed from the studio onto the side of his head. 'It has to be realistic,' Russell told him sternly. 'Please moan as if you are in real pain.'

The front door opened again, spilling light across the pavement, and Russell saw Sternkopf staring at him, as if keen to remember what he looked like. 'Let's get him in the ambulance,' he told Wilhelm. 'It'll make it harder for him to remember our faces,' he added in a whisper.

They lifted him in, reminded him to moan, and shut the ambulance door. On the pavement, two young women were being told to lie down on stretchers. As far as Russell could make out in the gloom, both were young, dark and quite probably Jewish, but neither matched his picture of Miriam Rosenfeld. Both were wide-eyed with fright, and Effi was kneeling beside them, asking their names and quietly explaining that they were involved in an ARP exercise. She and Freya had insisted that telling the girls what was really happening would be more likely to panic than reassure them.

The street remained empty, the darkness occasionally breached by the distant flash of anti-aircraft batteries. Wilhelm's friends reappeared with another dark-haired girl. This one looked about fifteen. She clung to Erich with one hand, and held the neckline of her nightdress up against her throat with the other. 'This is Rachel,' Max said. 'We can't find anyone else.'

'The man said four,' Russell reminded him. He was damned if he was going to come this far and not find Miriam.

'Let me ask Ursel and Inge,' Effi said, and hurried across to the two girls on their stretchers. She returned a few moments later. Miriam's room was on the second floor, at the back.

'I'll go,' Russell told Wilhelm, and headed up the steps.

Inside, the doors were all hanging open. There was a big bed in Miriam's room, but no sign of the girl herself. Russell was looking under the bed when he heard the faintest of whimpers.

She was cowering in a cupboard, knees pulled up against her chin. 'Miriam,' he said, touching her shoulder as gently as he could, and she jerked back as if he'd given her an electric shock. 'Miriam, I'm here to take you away from this place. I've come from your mother and father. From Wartha. They're worried about you.'

She lifted her head and examined his face with a small child's eyes.

'Come,' Russell said gently. 'We must go.'

She wouldn't allow him to help her out of the cupboard, pushing his hand away with a sharp intake of breath. She extricated herself and stood looking at him, dressed in a long white night-gown which accentuated her black hair and olive skin.

He took a robe, and handed it to her. 'You'll need this outside.'

She put it on, and looked at him again, as if awaiting another instruction.

'Let's go downstairs,' he said, and, after only a slight hesitation, she accepted his invitation to walk down ahead of him. Outside she shied away from Wilhelm's helpful arm, but meekly laid

393

down on one of the remaining stretchers.

'It's Miriam, isn't it?' Effi said, squatting down beside her.

The girl just looked up at her.

'Let's get Sternkopf out of the ambulance,' Russell said, but the sudden sound of an approaching vehicle stopped him in his tracks. Two thin headlights were coming towards them. 'Keep going,' he murmured, but the vehicle was slowing down. As it inched past the ambulance and turned into 403's parking space Russell caught an unwelcome glimpse of silver runes on a black collar.

The car door slammed, and a bright torchbeam leapt out of the darkness, illuminating the pavement in front of the house. 'What is this?' a voice asked.

Russell turned his weaker beam on the intruder. 'This is an ARP exercise and your torch should be masked,' he said sharply, noticing, with a sinking heart, the uniform of a Waffen SS Standartenführer, the holstered gun. He turned to the others. 'Let's get the wounded in the ambulance.'

'Not that one,' the Standartenführer said. He was shining his torch at the fifteen-year-old. 'Rachel and I have a date.'

'You must postpone it,' Russell insisted. 'We can't leave her behind.'

'You can and you will,' the Standartenführer told him, his tone hardening. 'This time tomorrow I shall be with my unit, and I have no intention of letting an imaginary air raid spoil a very real pleasure.'

Several options flicked across Russell's mind, none of them good. Should he, could he, leave Rachel behind to save the others?

A decision proved unnecessary. There was a sudden shift in the darkness behind the Standartenführer, a glint of metal. The man's head jerked forward and his legs gave way, pitching him onto the pavement. Wilhelm had hit him with what looked like an ancient Luger.

'I couldn't see any alternative,' he said almost apologetically, and gave the prone body an exploratory kick in the ribs. 'He'll be out for a while.'

'Let's put him on a stretcher,' Russell heard a voice say. His own.

'No need for fake blood,' Wilhelm said cheerfully, as they carried him across.

He was right – the back of the man's skull was bleeding most convincingly. 'Sternkopf next,' Russell decided. As they carried the caretaker back to the pavement he gave no sign of having overheard the confrontation, but he did recognize the body on the stretcher.

'Standartenführer Geisler,' Sternkopf muttered to himself. 'Another serious head wound,' he added, reading the placard which someone had already put round the unconscious SS officer's neck.

'The Standartenführer is taking the exercise seriously,' Russell told Sternkopf reprovingly.

The rescued girls were sitting in the back of the ambulance, each wearing a placard describing a slight injury. Freya and Effi got in with them, leaving Wilhelm alone in the front. Erich and

Max were waiting for Russell in the lorry cab.

'We'll be back in twenty minutes,' Russell told Sternkopf, and clambered up into the cab.

'Why can't you take us on the lorry?' the man complained.

'Health regulations,' Russell said glibly, and started the engine. Since they were supposedly headed for a hospital, they had included one in their itinerary. If they were stopped before they reached the Elisabeth on Lützow-Strasse, they had their explanation ready. If they were stopped between the hospital and the Landwehrkanal, they would claim they'd got lost in the dark.

No one stopped them. Fifteen minutes after leaving the house on Eisenacher Strasse the two vehicles pulled up alongside the wall separating Schöneberger Ufer from the dark waters of the Landwehrkanal. As Effi swapped vehicles with Max and Erich, Russell handed Beiersdorfer's helmet over to Wilhelm. 'See you tomorrow,' he said.

The ambulance drove off, leaving Russell and Effi alone. 'Miriam didn't say a word,' she said, her voice sounding harsh in the darkness.

Russell drove north through the deserted Tiergarten and across the Moltke Bridge. Beyond the blue-lit Lehrter Station the streets seemed darker still, and he was past the entrance to Hunder's garage before he realized it. He backed up and drove in through the open gates.

Ten minutes later the lorry was back in its corner, complete with its original number-plates. Russell and Effi sat in the front seats of the Hanomag, helping each other remove their make-up by torchlight. 'We're back,' Effi said when they were finally done, and leaned over to kiss him. 'We did it,' she added, sounding almost surprised. 'We really did.'

'We're not home yet,' Russell reminded her.

As they headed south the sirens began sounding the all-clear, but it seemed as if Berlin had already written the night off and gone to sleep. Russell stopped the car halfway across the Moltke Bridge, checked that nothing was coming, and dropped the two Adlon number plates, the false moustache and Beiersdorfer's armband into the Spree. He hoped Wilhelm was being equally thorough.

It felt good to reach home, but the feeling was short-lived. As they came in through Effi's front door the telephone began to ring. They looked at each other, wondering who it could be. 'Did you give Wilhelm this number?' Effi asked.

'No.'

Effi picked up, listened, and said 'Yes, he is.'

'Someone named Sarah,' she told Russell.

He took the receiver. 'Sarah?'

There was a gulping noise at the other end. 'I have to see you,' she said.

'Okay, but...'

'And it has to be now.'

'Ah. All right. I'll walk over.'

'No, no. You must bring the car. Park it round the back. There's an alley runs up from the river end. I'll be waiting.'

Russell replaced the receiver and told Effi he had to go out again.

'What's happened?'

'Trouble,' he told her. 'She didn't explain.'

'You have to go?' It wasn't really a question.

'It's not far,' he said, as if that helped.

'Would it be useful if I came?'

'Probably. But this is one for me to sort out.'

She clung to him for a moment, then pushed him away. 'Hurry back.'

It was noticeably brighter outside – the recently-risen moon was bathing roofs and sky with pale light. The still-warm Hanomag sprang to life, and Russell sat behind the wheel rubbing his eyes and wondering which route would be safest. He then remembered that the all-clear had been sounded, and that he was driving his own blacked-out vehicle. Until he reached Akonaer Strasse he had nothing to worry about.

The streets were not as empty as they had been earlier, but he encountered only a dozen or so vehicles during the ten minute-drive. The cobbled alley that ran behind the houses on Altonaer Strasse was as dark as anything he'd encountered that evening, and he had to proceed at walking pace to avoid scraping the walls. He was about two hundred metres along when a light ahead flickered on and off.

Another hundred metres and his slitted headlights picked her out, a ghostly figure in a long white nightgown. 'This way,' she whispered, opening a back door and almost shoving him in. In the dimly lit kitchen he got his first good look at her, and his heart sank. She looked on the edge of hysteria, and her nightgown was splattered with what had to be blood.

'I've killed him,' she said, as if confirming the fact to herself.

Oh Christ, Russell thought. Several chains of consequence jostled for consideration in his mind, including the one featuring her arrest, her torture, and his name being taken down by an eager Gestapo scribe. 'What happened?' he asked, much more calmly than he felt.

She looked at him blankly for a moment, then snapped back into the present. 'He's upstairs,' she said. 'I'll show you.'

She raced up the carpeted stairs, Russell following at a suitably reluctant pace. Her Gruppenführer was lying on his back by the empty hearth in the front bedroom, one arm at his side, the other twisted beneath him. His uniform tunic was unbuttoned, the jackbooted legs splayed out. A dark corona of blood surrounded the head, and his face had been battered beyond recognition.

'It was an accident,' she said.

Russell looked at her with disbelief.

'Not the face,' she admitted. 'But he fell. Honestly. He... I'd been reading some of Richard's poems, and I forgot to hide them away. He found them, and started reading one out loud, like it was all a huge joke... I tried to take the book away from him and he fell back across the arm of the chair and cracked his head on the edge of the fireplace. And then... I don't know, I just went out of my mind. I knew he was dead but I could still hear him laughing and I started hitting him with the poker and I couldn't stop.'

Russell ran fingers through his hair. Even if it had been an accident – and there was, he noticed, blood on the tiled surround of the fireplace – there was no way they could pass it off as one now. Even without her Jew-tainted past, she would be facing a murder trial and execution. With it, the process would be that much quicker. What could she do? He stood there staring at the body and its red mess of a face, trying to get his mind in gear.

'Who knows he's here?' Russell asked.

'The maid let him in. The neighbours on that side' – she gestured towards one wall – 'have left for the country, but the couple on the other side may have heard us arguing. I doubt it though – they're both quite deaf, and they sleep at the back.'

She could tell any investigators that the man had left, Russell thought. As long as the body wasn't found, no one could prove she was lying. Ah, but who was he kidding? This was Nazi Germany – they'd investigate her past, and once they knew who they were dealing with they'd get a confession. She might have money, but there was no way someone with her past could brazen it out. She had to disappear.

He asked when the maid would be back.

'At eight o'clock.'

'What will she do if no one answers the door?'

'She has a key.'

Russell exhaled noisily. 'Okay. First things first. We need to wrap him up and get rid of the blood.'

'A blanket?'

She looked better, he thought. The shock was wearing off. 'A thin one if possible,' he answered.

'He's going to be heavy enough as it is.'

They got to work. Russell rolled the body into a brown blanket, tying the ends with some twine until the whole ensemble resembled a giant Christmas cracker. Sarah mopped up the blood and got to work on the stain, scrubbing and scrubbing until it made no difference. The patch no longer attracted attention, but anyone who knew what they were looking for would find it.

Russell was already wondering where to take the body. It was a pity there was no locomotive depot nearby, no glowing firebox to cremate it in. 403 Eisenacher Strasse came to mind, but only for a moment – the Standartenführer might still be unconscious but Sternkopf would have smelled a rat hours ago. And the moon would be up, making it much easier for the police to see what was going on. The shorter the distance he had to drive with a dead body in the car the better.

Which ruled out a trip to the country, and a clandestine burial in the woods. It had to be the Spree or the Landwehrkanal, he told himself. The simple option. The canal, he decided – the river bridges were too exposed. The spot where they had said goodbye to the ambulance earlier that evening.

'Time you got dressed,' he told her. 'And you can't come back here, so pack yourself a suitcase – nothing too big. Just a few changes of clothes and whatever else you want to keep.'

She didn't argue. As she began gathering things together Russell slid the wrapped body down the stairs and into the kitchen. Slipping out through the back door he found the sky had lightened, but the alley was still cloaked in darkness. There were no signs of life in any of the neighbouring houses.

He opened the passenger's side door, tipped the seat forward, and went back for the body, dragging it as quietly as he could across the stone, ears alert for the sound of any curious onlooker opening a window. He propped the legs up in the opening, walked around, pushed the driver's seat forward, and laboriously levered the whole bundle into the back seat. By the time he'd finished his breathing seemed loud enough to wake half the neighbourhood.

Back indoors, he stood in the hall thinking about the maid. 'You should leave a letter on this table,' he told Sarah when she came downstairs. 'Tell her you've gone away for a while and leave her a couple of weeks' wages. With any luck she'll just take it and go.'

Sarah did as he suggested, taking the required Reichsmarks from a healthy-looking bundle. 'I was afraid this day would come,' she said, leaving Russell to wonder whether her expectation had included these particular circumstances. She took a last wistful look around, and turned off the light.

Russell squeezed her suitcase into the boot and got in behind the wheel. 'Can we get out this way?' he asked.

'No. But there's a space at the end for turning.'

He started the engine, which sounded deafening. He told himself it didn't matter if people saw and heard them. As long as no one stopped them...

He drove slowly forward, the dark wall of the Stadtbahn viaduct looming to meet them, and turned the car in the circular space beneath it. The drive back down the pitch-black alley felt like an epic voyage, and Russell's shirt was slick with sweat when they reached the street beside the Spree. Everything seemed quiet, and dropping the body off the nearest bridge seemed, for a few moments, a more tempting prospect than driving round Berlin with a high-ranking corpse in the back seat. He told himself to be sensible. The quarter-moon had risen above the buildings to the west, greatly increasing visibility. And while a body dumped in the Spree would float and be found within hours, it might take days to arrange Sarah's escape from Berlin. Stick to the plan, he told himself. Schöneberger Ufer would be dark and deserted. They could take their time, do it right.

Assuming they reached it. As he drove back down Altonaer Strasse Russell had enough butterflies in his stomach to start a collection. He half expected to find police cars drawn up outside Sarah's front door, but the street was mercifully empty. Crossing Hansa-Platz, they headed into the Tiergarten, and as they arced round the Grosserstern circle a car went by in the opposite direction. Russell found he was approaching each bend as if the enemy was hidden around it, and almost gasping with relief at finding another stretch of empty road.

Sarah Grostein sat silent beside him, hands clasped together in her lap. What she was feeling he could hardly imagine – a few moments' loss of control had cost her everything but her life, and that still needed saving. He remembered her saying she liked the man, and tried to square that admission with the obliterated face. Maybe liking him had been the last straw.

Russell realized he didn't even know the man's name. He asked what it was.

'Rainer,' she said. 'Rainer Hochgesang.'

They reached the canal above Lützow-Platz and drove along the southern bank towards Schöneberger Ufer. A car pulled out in their slipstream and stayed behind them for several blocks, before vanishing down a side street. Heart thumping, Russell checked the mirror several times to convince himself it was gone.

Finally they were there. Schöneberger Ufer was certainly deserted, though less dark than it had been a few hours earlier. He asked Sarah to stay where she was and walked across to the wall. The moon had turned from yellow to cream, and the waters of the Landwehrkanal were glistening with a beauty they hardly deserved. The usual red light was shining atop the distant Funkturm, which seemed like a sensible breach of black-out regulations. He wondered if they'd turn it off in a real air raid, and sacrifice the tower for an English bomber.

All was silence and stillness. The street on the far side of the canal was lined with old workshops, most of which now served as offices. On this side the overgrown site of a ruined synagogue lay between two warehouses. They should all be empty, give or take the odd night-watchman.

There was no point in waiting. Russell gestured

Sarah to get out, pushed her seat forward, and pulled the blanket-bound body out onto the pavement. He dragged it quickly across to the wall and left it there. 'We need to weigh him down,' he said. 'You untie the strings while I find something.'

He hurried across the road and into the site of the burnt-out synagogue, searching for ballast. The remains of a fallen wall were scattered along one side. Somewhat appropriate, Russell thought, sending a dead Nazi to the bottom of the Landwehrkanal with Jewish bricks. He could almost hear the celestial applause.

He piled six bricks in his arms and staggered back across the road, ears straining for the sounds of an approaching car. Sarah had undone the strings, and they rammed three bricks into each end of the roll.

'Okay,' Russell muttered once they'd re-bound the ends. He began lifting one end up towards the chest-high parapet. The canal was just as deep at the sides, and there was less chance of the Gruppenführer catching on a propeller.

Sarah helped him lever the body onto the parapet, and held it in balance while he made sure he had it round the ankles. As they pushed it over, the strain on his arms was almost too much, but he managed to hang on, and to lower it down for another foot or so, until the hidden head was only a metre or so from the water.

He let go. There was a louder splash than he expected, but no lights appeared in the surrounding buildings. He stared down at the surface of the water, half-expecting the body to flop back up, but there was only a flurry of bubbles.

A small indeterminate sound escaped from Sarah's lips.

'Are you all right?' he asked.

'No,' she said. 'But yes.'

Russell took another look round. If someone out there was watching them, he or she would have telephoned the police. 'Let's get out of here,' he said.

They reached Neuenburger Strasse in less than ten minutes. He took her up to his apartment and showed her where everything was. 'I'll bring you some food tomorrow,' he told her, 'and I'll contact our people about getting you out. The tenant below has been called up, so you don't have to worry about moving around, but the bathroom's one floor down... If you do run into anyone just say you're an old friend from ... where do you know well?'

'I grew up in Hamburg.'

'Then say you're an old friend from Hamburg, just visiting for a few days. Nothing else.'

She looked utterly lost, and he felt guilty leaving her, but Effi would be worried sick. He could telephone her from downstairs, but...

'I'll be all right,' she said, and tried to look as if she would.

He took the offered release. Twenty minutes later he was letting himself into Effi's apartment, feeling like he'd lived several lifetimes in a few hours. She let out a cry of relief and burrowed into his arms.

Russell's sleep was full of dreams, most of them

anxious. He woke in the strange darkness of the blacked-out room and lay there on his back, compulsively listing all the things that could still go wrong. The Standartenführer might have recognized someone – Wilhelm or one of his friends. Sternkopf could be down at Prinz Albrecht-Strasse, leafing through photographs of the state's enemies. Wilhelm and the others could have been stopped on the way back to Friedrichshain and taken to the cellars for interrogation. Sarah Grostein's maid might have found the bloodstain, or the body might have jettisoned its Semitic ballast and floated to the surface, making sense of what someone had seen in the middle of the night. In fact two separate police units could be out on the porch right now, arguing over which had precedence.

'Jesus,' Russell murmured. He might as well turn himself in and be done with it.

Effi stirred beside him. 'We're still here,' she said sleepily.

Russell found himself smiling. 'We are, aren't we?'

Over coffee they discussed the day ahead. During his drive home six hours earlier, Russell had decided to tell Effi about Sarah Grostein. The latter could hardly be compromised any more than she already was, and calling on the comrades to get her out was a decision he thought Effi should share. No one had told him that his and Effi's exit voucher was a one-time offer, but he couldn't help thinking that Moscow was unlikely to sanction unlimited escapes. If Sarah went, their chances of a similar exit were probably reduced.

Effi, of course, saw no dilemma. 'If they get her, they'll torture her,' she told Russell.

'Probably.'

'And yours will be one of the names she has to give,' Effi added, reinforcing her instinctive generosity with that cold calculation which still surprised him.

They went their separate ways, she to a meeting at the studio offices, he to the Adlon. After calling Thomas on the hotel phone with news of Miriam's rescue, he walked across to the bar. Work was low on the list of his priorities, but abandoning it completely would be foolishly suspicious. As it was, there was nothing new to report. No prominent Pole had arrived, and none was expected. One of the correspondents had been out walking the streets and riding the trams. Berliners, he said, were unanimous twice over. All of them expected the war that none of them wanted.

Russell dedicated the rest of the day to his own survival. He withdrew a large sum of cash from his bank, used his ration card to buy groceries at the Wertheim food hall, and drove down to Neuenburger Strasse with them. Frau Heidegger intercepted him, and the usual cup of undrinkable coffee was accompanied by a litany of complaints. Her knees were bad, the rations inadequate, and, to top it all, Beiersdorfer had threatened her with the police. 'The fool says someone stole his helmet,' she said, 'and as I'm the only other person with a key it must have been me. What an idiot! I mean, what would I want with his stupid helmet?'

Russell made his escape, grateful that Sarah's presence had so far gone unnoticed. She seemed unnaturally listless when he arrived, but made a visible effort to perk up as he explained what he intended doing. She had only made one trip to the bathroom, she said, and that in the middle of the night. He promised to drop in again on the following day.

From Neuenburger Strasse he drove east towards Neukölln. He had considered following instructions and calling Zembski on the telephone, but why risk a Gestapo listener? Privacy was easier to ensure in person. The photographic studio on Berlinerstrasse was open but empty – the river of parents bringing sons in uniform for a farewell portrait had presumably dried up, now that the boys in question were all leaning over the Polish frontier. The fat Silesian emerged from his small office and smiled when he saw who it was. 'Herr Russell. Long time, no see.'

'It's good to see you too,' Russell said, offering his hand.

'Do you need your picture taken again?' Zembski asked. Russell had last visited the studio to pick up a fake passport which the photographer had created for him.

'I was given your telephone number by mutual friends,' he said softly. 'They said to ask for Martin.'

Zembski looked surprised, but only for a second. 'You need to get out?' he asked, glancing over Russell's shoulder as if fearing to find the Gestapo in close pursuit.

'Not me. A woman. Tell them it's "The

Violinist". They'll know who she is. Tell them she has to get out now – there's a body involved. And tell them she's bringing them some useful information,' he added, hoping it was true.

The door opened behind them – a middle-aged couple. 'I'll only be a moment,' the Silesian told them, and turned back to Russell. 'Your photographs should be ready tomorrow,' he said. 'If you call in the afternoon, I'll let you know.'

Russell left the studio and walked down Berliner Strasse in search of lunch. Most of his fellow-Berliners were wearing resigned expressions that morning, but then they usually did. He ordered a bowl of potato soup and sausages at the first bar he came to, washed it down with a beer, and stepped reluctantly back into the summer sunshine. He spent a few minutes in the Hanomag working out logistics, and then headed north towards the Schade Printing Works. Leaving the car in a street nearby, he took one tram to Alexanderplatz and another out to Friedrichshain, arriving at the park almost half an hour early for his meeting with Wilhelm Isendahl. He sat on the agreed bench and reflected that while Wilhelm had performed brilliantly the previous evening, nothing would persuade him to work with the man again. Wilhelm was too damn sure of himself already, and each dart he planted in the neck of the Nazi bull would make him more so. He would come to feel invincible, and then the bull would get him.

Watching the young man walk up the path towards him, Russell hoped he was wrong. Wilhelm was his usual calm, efficient self. The van

410

was parked opposite the gate, he said, complete with original number plates – the others were in the Spree. The four young women were staying with two different families. It had seemed better to keep them in pairs, so each girl had someone who understood what they'd been through. The one Russell had brought out – Miriam – had still not spoken, and spent most of her time staring into space. Ursel, Inge and Rachel were in better shape, though all seemed prone to sudden fits of weeping. Russell had been right – their captors had told the girls that if any of them tried to escape they would all be sent to concentration camps for having sexual relations with aryans.

'There's some money in the *Beobachter*,' Russell said, indicating the newspaper beside him, 'for the families who are looking after them.' It had been Effi's idea. He almost gave her the credit for it, but remembered in time that Wilhelm didn't know her name.

They agreed to meet in a week's time. Russell walked out to the gate, and stood for a while scanning the road for possible watchers. Satisfied, he strode towards the vehicle, anxiously searching for the telltale signs of a painted-out cross on the side of the vehicle. There were none.

He drove the van back across town to the Schade Printing Works. Thomas was in his office, looking as tired as Russell felt. He came out from behind his desk and embraced his friend, a glint of tears in his eyes. Once outside in the yard Russell gave him a blow-by-blow account of the rescue. Finding Miriam in her cupboard had Thomas closing his eyes in anguished disbelief, the appearance of the Standartenführer had him opening them wide with alarm. 'But wouldn't he recognize you again?'

'I don't think so. He only saw us by torchlight, and we *were* disguised.'

'God, I hope you're right.'

'You're not the only one.'

'Where are the girls?'

'With families in Friedrichshain. Miriam's in a bad way. She hasn't said a word since we found her. I don't think she'll be going anywhere for quite a while.'

'We should tell her parents that she's alive, at least.'

'I will. I'll write to them at the address they gave me.' Russell looked at his watch. 'I have to pick up your lorry in Wedding. I should be back in an hour or so.'

'Where's your car?'

'Around the corner.'

'Then why don't you drive us both up there and I'll bring the lorry back?'

'Sold.'

Half an hour later they parted outside Hunder's gates. Russell followed the lorry as far as Lehrter Station, where he stopped off in search of coffee and a newspaper. The main buffet had none of the former, thanks to a storeroom robbery that afternoon – someone was stocking up for a future black market. The newspaper was full of quirky, inconsequential tidbits, as if the editor was clearing the decks for something altogether more serious.

He drove home by way of Altonaer Strasse.

Sarah Grostein's house was bathed in the last rays of the evening sun, a picture of urban serenity. If any of Gruppenführer Hochgesang's friends had come looking for him, they'd had the good manners not to break the door down. And if the body had flopped to the surface of the Landwehrkanal, the police were probably still trying to identify it.

Effi looked up anxiously as he came through her door, but relaxed when she saw it was him. 'Is everything all right?' she asked.

'So far.'

They went out to eat, returning in time to hear a special news broadcast.

New proposals had been presented to the Polish Government, the official voice claimed. These were then outlined – Danzig's incorporation into the Reich, a plebiscite to decide the future of the Polish Corridor, extraterritorial roads and railways for the nation that lost that vote. But – and here the voice seemed torn between disbelief and righteous indignation – the German Government had received no reply to these eminently reasonable proposals. The Führer, it seemed, had 'waited two days in vain for the arrival of a Polish negotiator.'

'As if he had anything better to do,' Effi said contemptuously.

When they turned on the radio next morning, they discovered that Germany was now at war. The Polish Army had supposedly attacked a radio station in German Silesia, and the Führer had responded with characteristic restraint,

413

invading Poland from north, west and south. He would be explaining his actions to the assembled Reichstag later that morning.

Three hours later, Russell and his fellow American journalists gathered on the pavement outside the Adlon to watch the motorcade go by. September 1st was another bright sunny day, but only a handful of Berliners had ventured forth to cheer their leader.

'Where's Gavrilo Princip when you need him?' was Slaney's comment.

The loudspeakers were soon crackling, the familiar voice echoing down the wide streets of the old city. The Czechs had turned into Poles, but the plot remained the same. Whoever they were, their behaviour – even their very existence – was intolerable. He had ordered the German armed forces across the border, and had himself donned 'the uniform of a soldier' until victory was assured.

There were chants of *Sieg Heil*, but the Reichstag deputies were out of practice – there was none of the rhythmic baying that Sportspalast audiences excelled at. It would be an hour or more before copies of the speech were distributed, so most of the journalists headed indoors in search of a drink. Russell called Zembski on one of the public telephones, and was told that his film wasn't ready – he should try again tomorrow.

He drove down to Neuenburger Strasse, where Frau Heidegger was keen to discuss the coming hostilities. It took him twenty minutes to extricate himself, and another ten to help Siggi carry a new mattress up to Dagmar's apartment. He found Sarah reading one of Paul's John Kling detective novels, and told her that German forces were heading into Poland.

'Have the British and French declared war?' she asked.

'Not yet.' He told her that he'd made contact with the comrades, and was waiting for instructions.

He took the long way home, stopping off at the Potsdam and Stettin stations to see what trains were running. There were no international services leaving from the former, but the latter was packed with foreigners trying to get places on the trains still running into Denmark. Domestic services seemed to be running more or less as usual.

He bought several papers at Stettin Station and skimmed through them, expecting the worst. But there were no photographs of missing Gruppenführers, no reports of floating corpses in the Landwehrkanal.

He was about to return home when the sirens sounded. The people on the station concourse looked at each other, wondering if it was exercise, and then shrugged and headed for one of the station shelters. Russell went with them, moved more by journalistic curiosity than any real fear of Polish bombers over Berlin. He found himself in a well-lit underground store-room, surrounded by a hundred or so Germans of varying ages and classes. Those who spoke did so in whispers, and only, it seemed, to people they already knew. Most read papers or books, but some just sat there. There was little sign of anger or resentment, but faint surprise featured on many of the faces, as if each was silently asking, 'How did it come to this?'

Saturday September 2nd dawned without a British or French declaration of war. Notes had arrived the previous evening demanding the suspension of German operations in Poland, but opinions were divided in the Adlon Bar as to whether the attendant threats to 'fulfil obligations' constituted a real ultimatum. Mussolini was rumoured to be organising another Munich-style conference which, the cynics claimed, would provide London and Paris with all the excuses they needed to leave another ally in the lurch. Russell's instinct told him that the British and French were just taking their time, but experience warned him that it rarely paid to over-estimate the honour of governments.

Later that morning, he telephoned Zembski.

'Yes, your pictures are ready,' the Silesian told him.

'That's good,' Russell said looking at his watch. 'I'll be there in half an hour.'

The city's traffic was already thinning with the restriction on civilian petrol purchase, and the drive took only twenty-five minutes. Zembski was with a customer, a woman dissatisfied with her daughter's photographic portrait. The Silesian was insisting on the accuracy of his portrayal, and Russell came to his assistance, leaning over the woman's shoulder and remarking what a lovely daughter she had. She gave him a suspicious look, but grudgingly paid up. The door pinged shut behind her.

Zembski lowered his voice, more out of habit than need. 'Your friend must travel to Bitburg – it's a small town in the west. She should check into the Hohenzollern Hotel, or one of the others if that's full. There's no time to arrange new papers, so she'll have to register in her real name. It's a risk, but I think the authorities are going to be busy with other matters for a while.'

'Thank God for war,' Russell said dryly.

'Indeed,' Zembski agreed. 'She must wait to be contacted. It may take several days, perhaps even longer. It's impossible to say.' He reached under the counter and came up with an envelope. 'Your photographs of the Havelsee,' he explained.

'Are they any good?' Russell asked.

'Of course. I took them myself.'

Russell decided he had enough time to visit Ncuenburger Strasse with the good news, but reckoned without Frau Heidegger. She waylaid him on his way in, and took him to task for 'that woman in your apartment'. It was against regulations, she told him, and 'that idiot Beiersdorfer' was already causing her enough trouble. If he found out, there'd be no stopping him.

Russell promised his friend would be gone by the next day. 'She's just lost her husband,' he added, knowing that a fellow-widow was guaranteed to enlist Frau Heidegger's sympathy. 'She needed a few days of solitude in a place that holds no memories. She's going back to Hamburg in the morning.' He was halfway up the stairs before he realized he hadn't been offered coffee.

Sarah was boiling water for tea on Russell's electric ring. She took the news calmly, and together

417

they searched Russell's atlas for Bitburg. It was close to the border with Luxemburg, which made sense. A night trek through the hills and she'd be on a train to Brussels or Antwerp, long a centre of Comintern activities.

'I'll check the trains and pick you up tomorrow morning,' Russell told her.

'I'll be here,' she said wryly.

He drove across town to Grünewald, arriving only ten minutes late to pick up Paul. His son was in his *Jungvolk* uniform, but seemed as subdued as the rest of Berlin by the outbreak of war. Strangely for a mostly German boy, he seemed more angered than relieved by Britain's hesitation in honouring the guarantee to Poland. 'Of course,' he added a few minutes later, 'if they do declare war on us, then next year's match at Wembley will have to be cancelled.'

At Paul's request they went to the fairground at the southern end of Potsdamer Strasse. Russell was afraid they would find it closed, but his son's optimism proved justified. It was not only open, but twice as crowded as usual. A good proportion of Berlin's children seemed to be screaming away their unconscious anxieties on the various rides.

Driving back from Grünewald after dropping off his son, Russell found himself wondering how many of those children had seen their fathers for the last time. Paul, at least, was lucky in that respect – neither of his would be sent to war.

He bought a paper when he reached Potsdamer Station, but no corpses had been discovered, no war declared. As for the trains, nothing was certain, but a journey to Bitburg was still theoretically possible. Trains were scheduled to depart for Cologne at nine and eleven on Sunday mornings, and both had connections to Trier and Bitburg. And yes, the clerk replied to Russell's query, both stopped at Potsdam. At twenty-two minutes past the hour.

Russell stopped off at Hunder's garage on the way home, and paid the usual inflated price for a full tank of petrol. Back at the flat, Effi was waiting in the red dress. 'It seems like a good night to go dancing,' she said.

They ate on the Ku'damm and headed east. The dancehall under Alexanderplatz Station was packed with people drinking too much, dancing too vigorously, laughing too loud. Berlin's adults were also saying farewell to peace, and the popping corks of their *sekt* bottles sounded like an ironic echo of the war unfolding in Poland.

Russell and Effi danced themselves to near exhaustion, then drove up to the Kreuzberg. The moon was yet to rise, the sky bursting with stars, and they sat on a wooden bench for a long time, looking out across the war-darkened city.

Russell arrived at Neuenburger Strasse soon after seven the following morning. He expected to find Sarah asleep, but she was emerging from the bathroom as he came up the stairs. Fifteen minutes later they were motoring south towards the Avus Speedway.

He had thought it better for her to join the train at Potsdam, and so avoid any possible checks at the main Berlin termini. He was probably over-reacting – nothing had appeared in the papers to suggest a search was underway – but it was a nice day for a drive, all blue sky and late summer sunshine.

Their destination reminded him of Wilhelm's leaflet and article. He told Sarah about them, and his difficulty in getting them out of Germany. Would she be willing to take them across the border?

'Yes, but how...'

'I'll send them to you at the Hohenzollern Hotel. The post office will be shut today, and I wouldn't want you taking them on the train – there'll probably be spot-searches, particularly as you get near the border. But once you leave Bitburg...'

'It'll be just one more charge against me if I'm caught,' she said dryly.

'Something like that.'

'Of course I will,' she said.

'I'll send them off tomorrow. And if they get there after you've left, too bad.'

They reached Potsdam with almost an hour to spare. Sarah bought her ticket and they shared a mostly silent breakfast in the cavernous station buffet. The man in the ticket office had assured them the train was running, but it was still with some relief that Russell saw it round the long curve and ease in to the platform. It was less packed than some he had seen over the last few days, but still uncomfortably crowded.

Sarah Grostein didn't seem to mind. She climbed aboard with her small suitcase, turned briefly to mouth the words 'thank you', and disappeared into the throng. Russell watched the train pull out, frantic belches of steam giving way to a steady pumping. It wasn't over, he told himself – it wouldn't be over until she was out of the Gestapo's reach. But he had got her out of Berlin, which had to be safer for both of them. Slowly but surely, he thought, the artefacts and people that linked him and Effi to their various crimes and misdemeanours were disappearing. Perhaps they really were going to get away with it.

The two men were waiting for him at Neuenburger Strasse. He had a fleeting glimpse of Frau Heidegger's frightened face in the doorway as they bundled him into the back of the government Mercedes, a surprised look from the returning Beiersdorfer as they drove out of the courtyard. 'Where are we going?' Russell asked as calmly as he could, and wondered whether his abductors could hear the tremor in his voice.

'102 Wilhelmstrasse,' the man beside him said.

The SD? That had to be better news than the Gestapo, unless, of course, Hauptsturmführer Hirth had come to know of his treachery. Russell wondered if the Soviets had betrayed him to the Germans, had added him to the list of gifts they were offering Hitler as part of their wretched Pact. He almost hoped they had, because Effi had played no part in his dealings with them.

Had she been arrested as well? He could see her back in that cell, so frightened and pale... Stop it, he told himself. Keep calm. Whatever they had, it was unlikely to be conclusive. Whatever the Soviets had said, he could always claim that he'd been stringing them along. You can do this, he told himself. A schoolmaster had once told him he could talk his way out of anything.

The car drew up outside SD headquarters, and the two men escorted him through the gardens and in through the main doors. They seemed almost friendly now, or maybe he was mistaking condescension for kindness. The blonde receptionist gave him a winning smile, but she would have blown Jesus a kiss on his way up Calvary.

The two men took him up to Hauptsturmführer Hirth's door, knocked, and ushered him in. The Hauptsturmführer's face showed irritation and disdain in equal measures, but that was probably how he got up in the morning. 'Please sit down,' he said, with unexpected courtesy.

Russell began daring to hope.

'There has been...' the Hauptsturmführer began, only to be interrupted by a voice on the loudspeakers outside. He got up and closed the window. 'Do you know what that is?' he asked rhetorically. 'The English have declared war on the Reich. Their Prime Minister made the announcement an hour ago.'

'Ah,' Russell said. It seemed the safest thing to say.

'We've been expecting this for several days, of course. And that's why you're here. You, Herr Russell, have become a victim of your own success. Of the breadth of your connections, shall we say? Your links with the Soviets have proved most rewarding, and for that the Reich thanks you, but the Pact has reduced our need for

422

intelligence from that direction. Your connections with your own country now seem more relevant, and the Abwehr has asked for your services.' He paused, and actually offered Russell a thin smile. 'You know what the Abwehr is?'

'Military Intelligence.'

'Precisely. Well, the SD may want you back at some time in the future, but for now the Abwehr's need is greater. They have your details, and will no doubt be contacting you in the near future.'

Hauptsturmführer Hirth got to his feet, and Russell did likewise. 'Heil Hitler!' the Hauptsturmführer said, and Russell managed a nod of recognition in response. He walked down the stairs and out past the chubby blonde secretary, repressing the urge to laugh out loud. As he crossed the rose-scented garden he made himself a promise – he would prove as faithful to the Abwehr as he had to Hauptsturmführer Hirth.

Ruins

In the last week of September Russell took the early morning train from Silesian Station to Breslau. The fighting in Poland seemed almost over, the British and French were managing little more than rude gestures across the western frontier, and the Reichsbahn was running almost normally. As he travelled up the autumnal Oder valley, it seemed to Russell that for a nation at war, Germany seemed strangely at peace.

There had been no news of Sarah Grostein, which was probably good news. She might have been killed crossing the border, or she might have made good her escape – he would obviously have preferred the latter, but either would have rendered him safe. It was the third possibility – her capture and continuing interrogation – which sometimes sent a chill up his spine. He was learning to live with that and other uncertainties, but it wasn't easy.

Her lover's body was still feeding whatever fish there were in the oily Landwehrkanal. Russell had found no official mention of his disappearance – a bureaucratic oversight perhaps, or just one of those loopholes that a war tended to open. If someone missed him now, they would probably search in vain.

Three of the young women rescued from 403 Eisenacher Strasse were on the mend, or at least gave that impression. Ursel, Inge and Rachel ate, talked and slept like ordinary people, and even laughed on occasion. If they still seemed prone to flinching in close proximity to men, then no one was very surprised. During the previous week all three had visited the Aliyah offices on Meinek-strasse to enquire about emigration to Palestine.

Miriam, though, was still mute. A week or so after the rescue she had been seized by a violent fit, and others had followed. It looked like epilepsy, but the local Jewish doctors had ruled that out. What it actually was, they couldn't say. Russell had hoped to be taking her home by this time, but there was no way he could expose her to a journey like this, particularly when their reception in Wartha was so uncertain. Her parents had never replied to his letter.

His train reached Breslau in mid-afternoon, too late for a return trip to Wartha. He booked in once more at the Monopol, and then walked over to the Petersdorff store, intent on keeping his promise to Torsten Resch. The manager told him that the boy had been called up a couple of weeks earlier, and was probably in Poland.

Russell thought about contacting Josef Möhlmann, but decided it would be a mistake. He had often wondered whether Shchepkin – or someone like him – had honey-tongued the Reichsbahn man into working for the Soviet Union. Probably not, he guessed. There hadn't been time before the signing of the Pact, and Stalin's gloating opportunism wouldn't have appealed to a man like Möhlmann.

Russell hadn't heard from the Soviets himself, which, while not surprising, was still something of a relief. He had expected to hear from the Abwehr by this time, but they hadn't made contact either. Too busy mopping up in Poland, Russell guessed. He could cope with the wait.

He dined alone in one of the Ring's restaurants, and walked back to the hotel to ring Effi. Sounding both tired and wide awake, she treated him to a long and funny account of her day on set. He carried her voice up to bed with him, and quickly fell asleep.

The sky was overcast on the following morning, and a long hospital train rumbled through the station as he waited for the Glatz local. He imagined Thomas's son Joachim laid out on a pallet in one of the rattling boxcars, and wondered how Thomas and all the other parents – German and Polish – were getting through each day.

His own train finally departed, steaming south under a steadily-darkening sky. There was no transport for hire in Wartha's station yard, and again he set out on foot. The countryside seemed emptier than before, and as he turned up the dirt lane which led to the Rosenfeld farm a thin rain began to fall, blurring the line of the distant mountains.

There was smoke drifting up from the chimney of the neighbouring Resch farm, but no other sign of life. He walked on, rehearsing what he meant to say about Miriam, and was nearing the final bend in the lane when he realized that the field on his left was a sea of rotting crops. And that no column of smoke was rising above the screen of trees.

He quickened his pace, hoping against hope.

The stone walls and chimney were still standing, but that was all. The glass was gone from the windows, and a few blackened stumps were all that remained of the roof. The barn beyond had been burnt to the ground.

He walked to the open doorway and looked in. Scorched tiles lay half-buried in a slough of cinders and ashes. Everything was black.

It had happened a while ago, several weeks by the look of it.

There were no bodies in the house. He walked across to where the barn had stood and examined the blackened ground. He circled the ruins, and found no signs of digging in the overgrown kitchen garden or the copse of trees. He suddenly remembered the horse and cow – stolen, no doubt. But where were Leon and Esther Rosenfeld?

Perhaps they had been arrested. Dragged away to some unknown destination while the local thugs looted and burnt their home.

Or perhaps their blacksmith friend had warned them, and they had headed up into the mountains that Leon's grandfather had provided for such an eventuality. Russell stood in the lightly falling rain, gazing at the faint line of crests which marked the old border with Czechoslovakia. There were Nazis on both sides now.

Wherever they were, they wouldn't be back.

Ruins and more ruins, he thought. Of a farm and a family. Of the country he had known and once loved.

The publishers hope that this book has given you enjoyable reading. Large Print Books are especially designed to be as easy to see and hold as possible. If you wish a complete list of our books please ask at your local library or write directly to:

Magna Large Print Books
Magna House, Long Preston,
Skipton, North Yorkshire.
BD23 4ND

This Large Print Book for the partially sighted, who cannot read normal print, is published under the auspices of

THE ULVERSCROFT FOUNDATION